MYSTERY TOUR

MYSTERY TOUR

A CRIME WRITERS' ASSOCIATION ANTHOLOGY

Edited by

MARTIN EDWARDS

ORENDA
BOOKS

Orenda Books
16 Carson Road
West Dulwich
London SE21 8HU
www.orendabooks.co.uk

This collection first published by Orenda Books in 2017

HB ISBN 978-1-910633-91-5
PB ISBN 978-1-910633-92-2
eISBN 978-1-910633-95-3

Typeset in Garamond by MacGuru Ltd
Printed and bound by CPI Group (UK) Ltd, Croydon CR0 4YY

SALES & DISTRIBUTION

In the UK and elsewhere in Europe:
Turnaround Publisher Services
Unit 3, Olympia Trading Estate
Coburg Road, Wood Green
London N22 6TZ
www.turnaround-uk.com

In the USA and Canada:
Trafalgar Square Publishing
Independent Publishers Group
814 North Franklin Street
Chicago, IL 60610
USA
www.ipgbook.com

In Australia and New Zealand:
Affirm Press
28 Thistlethwaite Street
South Melbourne VIC 3205
Australia
www.affirmpress.com.au

For details of other territories, please contact *info@orendabooks.co.uk*

Contents

Dedicated to the CWA Committee, in appreciation of
their commitment to the cause of crime writing.

Introduction

Welcome to *Mystery Tour*, an anthology of new stories by members of the Crime Writers' Association. Contributors were invited to write stories reflecting the unifying theme of travel and intriguing destinations, and they have interpreted the brief in fascinating and diverse ways.

Diversity and quality are also hallmarks of the list of contributors. Two stories come from recipients of the CWA Diamond Dagger, while the others are the work of a pleasing mix of bestsellers, relative newcomers, fast-rising stars, and stalwarts of the genre. Contributions from overseas members emphasise the book's international flavour.

The crime genre embraces so many different types of writing that it offers something of interest to almost any reading taste. The CWA plays a central role in promoting crime writing in general and the work of its members in particular. Producing anthologies of stories (as well as occasional non-fiction collections, such as *Truly Criminal*, which appeared a couple of years ago) is just one of many aspects of the CWA's activities. It's an important aspect, though, because it has helped to keep the crime short story alive in the UK, offering a valuable outlet when many others have long since vanished.

When the very first CWA collection of stories appeared back in 1956, the editorial committee did not hide their gloom about the future prospects of short crime fiction. By publishing an anthology almost every year over the past six decades, as well as by inaugurating the prestigious CWA Short Story Dagger more than thirty years ago, the CWA has made sure that those anxieties proved unfounded. Past winners of the CWA Short Story Dagger include Jeffrey Deaver, John Connolly, Ian Rankin, Denise Mina, Stella Duffy, Reginald Hill – and also Peter Lovesey, who has written a brand-new story for *Mystery Tour*.

Today, even more so than when the CWA was founded sixty-four years ago, the publishing industry is in a state of flux. For all its massive global popularity, crime writing, both fact and fiction, is as susceptible to the winds of change as any other branch of the creative arts. This means that the need for an effective professional organisation for crime writers has never been greater. The CWA has risen to the challenge, pursuing an ever-increasing range of activities on behalf of its members. And this has borne fruit. Membership numbers have, at the time of writing, reached an all-time high.

So have revenues, but because the CWA is a non-profit organisation, income from publications like *Mystery Tour*, as well as from subscription fees, sponsorships and other activities, is invested in expanding the range of benefits for members, including promotional opportunities via social media and other platforms. The recent appointment of both a CWA Libraries' Champion and a CWA Booksellers' Champion are innovations that reflect a strong commitment to supporting libraries and library readers, as well as booksellers and book-buyers.

All this activity has many knock-on benefits for the reading public. These include the opportunity to subscribe to free publications, including the monthly Crime Readers' Association newsletter. Meanwhile, the establishment this year of the British Crime Writing Archives at Gladstone's Library near Chester means that crime fans and researchers from all over the world now have the chance to explore the genre's rich heritage in unique and attractive surroundings. In the archives they'll find, among much else, correspondence revealing that the title of one of the CWA's earliest anthologies was dreamed up by Raymond Chandler, who urged his friend Michael Gilbert to call it *Some Like Them Dead*.

The appearance of *Mystery Tour* therefore forms part of a much bigger picture. It's a collection that offers a showcase for some splendid writers and for an organisation whose achievements even the ambitious John Creasey couldn't have foreseen when he founded the CWA back in 1953. My thanks go to all the contributors, the CWA Board, and everyone who has offered help and support in bringing this book into existence. I hope that crime readers, whatever branch of the genre they prefer, will find plenty to keep them entertained as they embark on this particular mystery tour.

Martin Edwards

The Queen of Mystery

Ann Cleeves

At Malice Domestic they call me the Queen of Mystery. Of course I'm flattered by the description but I'd never use it about myself. Malice is a crime convention for true lovers of the traditional mystery novel, a celebration of the gentle art of killing. And I do kill my characters very kindly, without torture or the gratuitous description of pain. But we aren't brash or flash at Malice. Self-promotion is frowned upon. Unfortunately, some of the newer writers don't observe the conventions. I've seen t-shirts printed with jacket covers, giveaway candy, the blatant canvassing for awards. I'm Stella Monkhouse and I'm above that sort of thing.

I feel at home at Malice. It's *my* convention. When I walk in through the hotel lobby I sense the flutter of the fans as they point me out to each other. I always dress my best to arrive. There are writers here too of course, and I wave to them as if we're tremendous friends, but really this is a performance for the common reader and the wannabe writer. I need those people's admiration, and their envy, more than the shared gossip over dreadful wine with fellow authors.

It helps that I was born British. Malice Domestic is always held in Bethesda, Maryland, but it celebrates the English detective tradition. Most of the regular attendees are ladies of a certain age, and the weekend always ends with afternoon tea. I came to the US when I was young to work as a secretary for a publisher in New York City; perhaps I had ambitions to write even then – certainly I hoped to make a name for myself. My husband was a senior editor with the company and much older than I; we never had children. I thought then that was a good thing because it allowed me to focus on my work. Now I wonder what it might be like to leave behind more of myself than a pile of stories.

People sometimes mistake me for my series character. Molly Gregory is the gentle owner of a coffee shop in rural Massachusetts. She quilts, has a cat called Sherlock and solves murders in her spare time. I'm nothing like Molly, though I smile when readers ask me to send their love to Sherlock. One has a certain responsibility not to disappoint one's audience. But I've always adored living in the city and I wouldn't know one end of a knitting needle from another.

Publishers and other writers consider me ruthless, overly ambitious. They call me a monster behind my back though they turn on the charm when I arrive. I'm the star. The multi-Agatha-award-winner. So why shouldn't I upstage them a little when we appear together on a panel? I'm a professional and this is a competitive business. Besides, I'm more entertaining than they are, and it's me the readers have come to see.

There's no line to check in, and the receptionist recognises me. 'So glad to have you with us again, Ms Monkhouse.' This year I'm not guest of honour and I have to pay for my own room. That rankles a little, but someone else has to have a chance to shine, and next year they'll all be talking about me again. This year it's little Emily Furlow. She sets her books in Cornwall, though she'd never stepped foot outside Idaho when she started writing. She sent me her first book to blurb, but I couldn't bring myself to comment. On my way to the elevator I see her surrounded by a group of readers, but I don't join them. I give a regal wave as befits the Queen of Mystery and move on.

In my room I unpack and hang up the dress I'll wear for the awards dinner. I've been nominated again for an Agatha so I need to look my best. It's expected. The winner is chosen by readers over the weekend, and I'm confident that their loyalty will see me through. The sight of Emily with her entourage has unnerved me a little though. It's essential that I end my career on top. Second best has never been good enough for Stella Monkhouse, and it certainly won't do for this weekend. For a moment I feel something like self-pity. Or old age. Emily is at least thirty years younger than I am. In that moment I suspect that my recent books lack the wit and pace of the earlier titles and that she's a better writer than I am. I ban the thought immediately and prepare to meet my fans.

There is nowhere for me to sit to do my make-up. The only mirror is the long one just inside the door, where the light is appalling. My husband called the make-up my war paint, and today I need it more than I've ever done. Clive and I were never passionate, but for a while we suited each other. Squinting in the gloom to fix my mascara I wish that he were here with me.

I sweep into the lobby just as everyone is gathering for the opening reception. There's a pay bar and I'm tempted to buy myself a large glass of wine, but today I need a clear head. I target members of the committee, hitting them with my special smile and the force of my personality. I need to dazzle them. These are the influential women who plan the convention and whose superb organisation keeps it going year after year. Like a politician I can make them feel special. I remember the names of their husbands and who has a son or daughter looking for an internship in the business. Many of them do. I don't actually *promise* that my publisher will provide their offspring with work experience, but they're left with the impression that it's a real possibility. I haven't put this much effort into working a convention since I was a young writer struggling to make a name for myself with my first book.

When I feel at the top of my game, glittering, I head for Emily Furlow. She's sitting on the floor next to a group of women who sit on the bright-red cubes of plastic that pass as seats. There's a glass of juice on the floor next to her – Emily, of course, never drinks alcohol. It occurs to me that I could slip an overdose of my medication into it and lose the competition forever, but I know that Emily dead will be much more popular than Emily alive. Dead, *she* would certainly upstage *me*.

There's a stir as I approach. 'Stella,' she says. 'How lovely!' She's on her feet in one movement, and we kiss on both cheeks. She's shorter than me, and I have to stoop. 'I adored your latest book.'

I smile and murmur that she's very kind, then I turn my attention to the readers. The voters. There are a couple of women from Texas who come to Malice every year, and I ask after their grandchildren. That's always a winner. We're called into the reception, and the group walks along with me leaving Emily behind.

That night I struggle to sleep. The following evening will be the awards ceremony and I want to look my best. I think about Clive again. Before his death I thought I might enjoy living on my own with no distractions, but suddenly I realise I'm missing him dreadfully. I think of a possible parallel universe, one where I live like most of the attendees – a life cluttered with children and responsibilities, the demands of friendship. For a moment it has its attractions, but I know I couldn't stand it.

I wake to a beautiful Maryland late-spring day and decide that I'll go out to my favourite French café for breakfast. I can walk that far, despite the arthritis in my spine, and the fresh air will be good for me. In the far corner of the café Emily Furlow is sitting quite alone, her nose in a book. My book. For a brief second I'm tempted to join her. I wonder what she really makes of it, whether she thinks it's up to my usual standard, but the moment passes and I find a corner of my own and pretend I haven't noticed her. Because I'm in a strange mood. If she were kind to me I might be prompted to some sort of confession, and that isn't part of the plan at all. Not yet.

The awards dinner is just as it always is. The women have dressed in their finery and some of the men are wearing tuxes. Tradition is respected at Malice. The toast mistress is Catriona, another of my rivals – a Scottish woman based in California. She's witty and keeps things tight and fun, so we come very quickly to the announcement of the prizes. When the moment arrives, I wonder if I've lost the passion to win. Perhaps I could drift into retirement after all, take up knitting and quilting like my heroine. Bring a dog into my life. Perhaps it would be better if Emily took over my mantle. I hate to admit it, but she is a fine writer.

I pour myself a glass of wine; the other people at my table turn out not to be great drinkers. Catriona is opening the envelope. I fidget in my purse – after all, this mustn't seem to matter too much – so I'm not looking at the stage when the announcement is made.

It's me. I've beaten the record for the longest reign as Agatha champion. The glad-handing, the enquiries about grandchildren, the promises of internships that will never be kept, have all paid off. The people at my table rise to their feet and begin cheering. I grab my wine and walk a little unsteadily to the stage. There Catriona kisses me on both cheeks, though I sense her disappointment. She admires Emily's work. I sip the drink and take the microphone. The custom is that speeches are kept very short, but this is an unusual occasion. As soon as I start speaking they will listen to me.

'This is my last time at Malice, and I thank you all for making it so special. There will be no more Molly Gregory and no more Sherlock.'

There are horrified boos and cries of 'Shame!' I pause. I've always had a sense of dramatic timing.

'By tomorrow morning there will be no more Stella Monkhouse.'

There's a sudden silence, a few embarrassed giggles, because they think I'm making a tasteless joke.

'In my fiction I take research seriously. I know about poison, the prescription meds that can kill.' I lift my glass in a mock toast. 'In here there's more than enough to finish me off.' I'd taken the pills from my purse while Catriona was speaking and I drink the remainder of the wine with a very unladylike gulp.

Ironically, I've never felt more alive. Not even when I was holding the pillow over poor Clive's mouth to kill him. He asked me to do it – after the stroke he knew he was holding me back – but he never expected me to agree. When I can't sleep I'm haunted by his pleading eyes, begging me to let him live. However, this isn't a time for regrets. This is what I've always wanted: to be the centre of attention, to shock and thrill with my words. And I know that when I'm dead my books will shoot to the top of the bestseller lists, for a while at least. Articles will be written about me. The obituaries will tell the world that I died as a champion. I couldn't have borne to be a woman who once *was* the Queen of Mystery, who slid into obscurity as her writing lost its power. Now, I'll reign for ever.

Return to the Lake

Anna Mazzola

The evening air was sharp with the tang of salt, algae, barbecue smoke, and the lake shifted silver in the fading light. Two small boys were wading in the shallows, shouting, trying to collect something in empty jam jars, and Alice, standing on the cracked front steps of the house, almost wanted to warn them. But that was absurd, of course. It happened years ago. She drew on her cigarette and stared at the water stretching before her, edged with tall fir trees, which moved in the breeze.

'You don't have to come,' her mother had told her back in England. 'But I thought it might be nice: the family together again. A chance for Michael to get to know everyone properly before the big day.'

'Yes, of course.' For they had barely met him. Michael was her new world, her better world; she had done what she could to keep them apart, but she could not do so forever.

She stared, still, at the lake. Here and there, she glimpsed dark, undistinguishable shapes beneath the surface, rippling the water, changing its flow. She had not been able to ask why her mother had chosen to return here after all this time. Perhaps it was a kind of memorial, or a way of letting go.

Alice heard footsteps behind her, felt Michael's arm around her waist. She leaned into him, smelling sweet sweat and suntan lotion. He didn't speak, and for that she was grateful. There was nothing she could say about it now. There never really was.

The lake was a favourite haunt of picnickers – mostly French, but with a smattering of Germans, Austrians, Italians, Brits. Some came just for a day trip; others camped on a hill by the lake, as she and Clara had done that night. The apartments her parents rented were in a large, shambling house overlooking the water. In the years since they had last visited the place had been allowed to decay: paint flaked from the front door and the windows were coated with a film of dirt.

'You're a strong man, Michael. See if you can carry this.' Her father was struggling towards them with a large suitcase, his breathing heavy. He was sixty-two now, his hair thinner over his scalp, his stomach straining at his belt, but he was still proud; still protective.

'You'd best treat this one right,' he'd told Michael the first time they'd met – joking, but not joking. 'She's still our little girl.'

A little girl. At twenty-eight.

'I'd best go and help Mum,' Alice said, not looking at him. She took a last pull on her cigarette and threw it to the ground, crushing the end beneath her shoe.

She found her mother in the stone-flagged kitchen, unloading crates of food and wine. 'How many people are you feeding here, Mum?'

Her mother smiled, the lines carving deeper into her face – the face Alice knew, but worn by time.

'Got to make sure my children are properly looked after, haven't I?'

As her mother unpacked, Alice's eyes were drawn to her thin arms, papery skin wrinkled over bone.

'Can I help?'

'No, no. I'm fine, love. You show the children around the house. They'll like that.' What she meant was that she would rather not deal with them, her grandchildren. They were too loud. Too vibrant. Too much.

'All right. If you're sure.'

From the door, she looked again at her mother, a small figure in a faded print dress. Every time she saw her, she noticed how life had crushed her a little further. Her mother had felt responsible, of course, for Clara had been on holiday with them. And they had lost her.

Alice's nieces were six and four – all elbows, arguments and delight. They were already running about between rooms, sizing everything up, working out what was theirs, while Alice's brother and his wife, travel-worn and weary, carried their luggage in from the car.

'There's a funny smell,' Ada said, wrinkling her little nose. And there was: the scent of must and dust, and things unwashed.

'It's just how old houses smell,' Alice explained. 'Especially houses by lakes.'

She showed the children the large, chequer-tiled bathroom, their blue-papered room, the bunk bed in which she herself had slept all those years ago. As they squabbled about whose bunk was whose, Alice remembered the excitement of introducing Clara to the place that summer, pointing out where they kept the fishing nets and the wetsuits, the towels and torches. She remembered them brushing their teeth together in the bathroom, huddling down beneath the blankets in the blue bedroom, Clara in the top bunk, because Alice had let her choose.

'How about we never go back?' Clara had said as they lay in their bunks that first night. Alice had laughed, thinking it was a joke. But maybe it had been a real question.

Thank God for Michael, tolerating the defects of others – her own lack of words, her father's excess. He had become more brazen over the years: more wisecracks, more 'cockney charm', almost a caricature of his former self. Perhaps she should have found it amusing, but it was false, cloying. He was making up for something by being someone he was not. She left them in the back garden and went to help her mother prepare the dinner. Through the kitchen window, she could see her father gesticulating, embellishing some story, while Michael quietly sipped his beer. From upstairs came the occasional slam of a door or the shriek of a child being unwillingly bathed.

'Here,' her mother said, handing her a bowl, 'you make the salad.'

They worked then, without speaking, the radio on.

Just before eight o'clock, Alice ran up to their room to change into a silk shirt and cut-off jeans, to pop little silver studs into her ears. She had caught the sun, she noticed. She looked healthy, even pretty. She would never be beautiful, though. She would never be Clara.

They sat at the table outside to eat, amid the whine of mosquitoes and the scent of citronella candles. They talked of nothings: their journeys, the weather, Michael's job, Charlie's new school. Her mother served quiche, a casserole, cheeses, crusty bread. Her father poured everyone too much wine.

'Is it all booked, then? The venue, the caterers?'

Michael looked at Alice. 'Yes, I think so, we're keeping it pretty simple.'

Simple and small. A plain white dress. Her brown hair straight and unadorned. Alice wished they could run away – avoid all the fuss and formalities – but it wouldn't be fair. Their only daughter, their little girl.

'Already preparing my speech,' her father said, and winked at her.

She smiled. She could imagine it, and her insides curled.

Robert's wife, Caroline, came down sometime later, glared at Robert and drank a glass of white wine almost in one. Did she know, Alice wondered, as she watched her drinking – did she know what happened here? Robert was more open than she was, less of a closed book, but this was different. Alice suspected that Robert, like her, rarely discussed it. Perhaps he never talked of it at all.

'A toast to the chef,' her father said, raising his beer. 'Santé!'

Then came the clink of glasses, the polite laughter, her mother shaking her head.

And all at once Alice could not bear it – that they were here in this very place where Clara had slid from time, and yet her name had not even been spoken.

She picked up her glass again and her father smiled. 'To Clara too. Never forgotten.'

A silence, her father's smile froze, and then Michael raised his bottle, met her gaze. 'To Clara.'

The others followed then. 'Yes. Clara.'

Her father's eyes were on the tablecloth, her mother's cheeks were flushed. Caroline did not seem surprised, only uncomfortable. She knew, then. And yet she had brought her children here.

Coughs, the scraping of cutlery. Robert talked in an overly bright voice about their plans for tomorrow: boats, shops, things to buy. He always wanted to make things right; make them all get on. Alice, however, was not really listening, but remembering. Thinking of Clara sitting across from her at this table for lunch, her freckles already darkened by two days in the sun.

What's the point of having a tent and not using it, though? Go on, Alice. Ask your mum.

She realised then that her mother was staring at her, her expression sharp. After a moment, her mother smiled, but it was too late, Alice had seen it. It was the same look everyone had always given her: watchful. Uncertain. Cold.

She rose early the following morning, slipped from the bed, in which Michael still slept, gathered a towel and pulled on her swimming costume. She could hear voices from the kitchen – the high whining of a child; Caroline's hushed tone. In her bare feet, Alice stole down the stairs and crept out of the house through the front door. Outside, the air was crisp with the remnants of the night chill, the light translucent, the sky a bleached blue. Green-winged dragonflies hovered over the lake, and a breeze ruffled the surface as she took her first steps into the cool water, feeling the velvet silt between her toes. Before she could lose her nerve, she submerged herself entirely in the lake, her arms pulling her forward into the water, her legs barely breaking the surface. There was only the sound of the wind on the water, the rustle of reeds, the call of a bird: bubbling, sad.

She closed her eyes and felt the water caressing her body, the movement of her limbs. Then she stopped kicking and allowed herself to float, the water covering her chin, cloaking her shoulders. And all at once Clara was there, her long hair trailing, the sunlight shining on her narrow shoulders, forming a halo of light about her head.

'They didn't want me to come, you know.'

'Why?'

A shrug. 'You know what my mum's like.'

Clara's mother: tight lips, suspicious eyes. Never wanting Clara to play at hers. Alice wasn't good enough for her, presumably. Too lumpen and awkward, lacking Clara's spark. She lived in a terraced house on a mediocre street. Was that it? Or was it something else?

'What did your stepdad say?'

'Who cares what he thinks? He's a prick.' Clara closed her eyes, held her nose and disappeared beneath the surface in a spray of water, leaving Alice to wonder in what particular way she'd failed.

Clara was different that summer, harder perhaps, more closed. Maybe it was just to do with being fifteen. They'd known each other since junior school; since they were gap-toothed eight-year-olds in matching check dresses and boater hats. But it was only in senior school that they'd become friends – when Clara, now tall and graceful, had sought Alice out. She was never sure why Clara had wanted her friendship, why someone so special would have wanted anything to do with her. But maybe it was Alice's very ordinariness that made her attractive – her dull and stable home life, the lack of drama and disaster. Clara's mother was already on her second marriage and third house – a tall modern building, all glass, chrome and no mess. To Alice, Clara always seemed desperately exciting and superior. This was why, by and large, she let her have what she wanted: stickers, hairbands, the window seat. It was why, that summer, she had agreed to ask her parents about the tent.

Alice's mother had been against it. There were two perfectly good beds for them to sleep in, she said. And they'd be bitten to death by mosquitoes – they were rife that year. Alice's father, though, had laughed. 'They'll only be a few minutes from the house. I was off for days by myself at their age. Stop making excuses, Bev.'

So she had. And they had gone.

Alice remembered the exhilaration, packing their rucksacks, stocking up on apples and crisps from the kitchen. A flask of tea from Mum. A flask of rum from her father. 'Just to keep off the cold, eh? Don't tell your mother.'

He and Robert came with them to help them pitch the tent in the small camping site that looked onto the lake. Her father was in his element amid the guy ropes and tent poles, finding them a shady spot by the trees. Robert, meanwhile, was sullen and unhelpful, whining about being left out again. He'd been sulky all holiday, with no friend of his own. Thirteen years old, pimple-skinned and lanky, insatiably in love with Clara, of course.

'Couldn't I stay with you? Until you go to bed?'

'No,' they both said at once, and Alice had added: 'Sorry, Bobs. Girls only.'

But in fact, that was a lie.

They'd seen them earlier in the week, as they sat on the pontoon, watching the dark, moving shapes of small fish darting below. Three boys, two girls, laughing, talking, taking it in turns to steer a small blue boat.

'Ahoy there!' one of the boys shouted.

'Ahoy!' Clara returned, raising her arm.

'Are you English?' He was tall with dark hair and grey eyes, narrowed into slits against the sun.

'Yes,' Clara said. 'From London. Watch – you'll fall!'

But he had not fallen. He had climbed out of the boat, sat beside them on the creaking wooden boards and taken out a packet of cigarettes, nonchalant, easy. His name was Max, he told them. He was seventeen.

'Where are you staying?'

He pointed to a hill just beyond the lake. 'We're camping just over there.'

'On your own?'

'Of course on our own. What, you think we came with our mums and dads?'

He lit a cigarette, offered them the pack.

It didn't take Clara and Alice long that evening to find them. They were sitting on deckchairs outside their tent, smoking cigarettes, drinking small bottles of French beer.

'Hello,' Max said, pushing his sunglasses up onto the top of his head. 'Fancy seeing you here.'

Alice felt her sunburned skin grow hotter, but of course it wasn't her he was really talking to.

Clara approached the group, ponytail swinging, and took the deckchair one of the boys pushed forward. She turned back to Alice: 'Come on, then.'

'Yes, come join us,' another of the boys said. 'We don't bite.' He bared his teeth, and the others laughed.

Alice hesitated then walked closer, standing awkwardly at the edge of the group.

'How come you're camping, then?'

'Just fancied it.'

'Really? I'd give anything for a proper bed.' That was one of the girls, her lips glossy as blood, her hair coiled up on her head like a snake.

'Where's that rum, Alice?' Clara's voice was hard, strange, and all at once it came to Alice that Clara didn't even like her, was embarrassed about her. Had come on this holiday only to escape her own family, whom she disliked even more.

Without answering, Alice turned and walked slowly back to their tent by the trees to fetch her father's flask. When she returned, the others had moved their chairs into more of a circle, Clara closer to Max, their arms almost touching. Alice sat at the entrance to one of the tents, conscious of her pale legs, her too-thick calves and unmanicured nails. Outside the tent opposite, a plastic toy windmill turned in the breeze.

They passed round the rum, and Alice took a few sips, ignoring the burn in the back of her throat. The boys all looked at Clara, of course, Clara with her dark eyes and nut-brown hair, and Alice shrank into herself, her dejection deepening. She wished herself anywhere but there. More beers were brought out, and the stars grew brighter, the dusk darkening into an ink-blue night. They talked about the usual things – what class they were in, what college, what subject, how long they were staying here, what things they had planned. Clara's laughter was high and false, and Alice felt her skin crawl with rising resentment, with the realisation that she had been used, once again.

At around midnight, the girl with the red lips said she was too tired, she was going to bed, and everyone decided to turn in for the night.

Had that been it? Had there been something else, something that could provide her with a clue, or a reason? An odd look, a strange remark? Alice had gone over it again and again, thinking she could piece together every moment of that evening, but there must have been a fragment missing: a shard or scrap of information that she had missed or forgotten.

She remembered them brushing their teeth together and spitting the froth into tin cups.

'I think he liked you – the short one.'

'No, Clara. They all liked you. They always do.'

They had changed into their night things without speaking, and Alice had climbed into her sleeping bag, inhaling the peculiar smell of must and polyester. She heard Clara moving about beside her, then lying still, her breathing soft.

'It isn't as good as you think.'

'What?

'Being the pretty one.'

The words were like a sharp slap, leaving her ears ringing: the acknowledgment that Alice was not special, was not pretty – was not, in fact, anything at all.

'Yes, poor you.' Her throat was tight. 'The pretty one.'

'You don't understand what it's like, Alice. It's not like I always want the attention.'

Alice turned away from her, her eyes burning. 'And what do you think it's like for me?'

'Oh, forget it, then.'

'I will.'

Clara turned onto her side too, and Alice could feel the hostility emanating from her, her shoulders tense. Alice lay in the dark, her anger subsiding into sadness, but she could not bring herself to say anything. It was too late. She could hear the wind on the water, the rustling of the trees and – from somewhere across the lake – laughter. She nestled down inside her sleeping bag and listened to Clara's breath: even, slow, slower. If she could sleep, she could not be that angry. By tomorrow, maybe it would be OK.

Alice woke early in the morning to the patter of light rain on the outside of the tent and to the smell of canvas. Clara was gone.

Her mother's panic was immediate. Her father's took longer to set in. Clara must have wandered off around the lake, he reasoned. Maybe she couldn't sleep. Perhaps she'd had a bad dream. Girls did silly things at that age.

'But why on earth would she go walking before six o'clock in the morning, Paul? Clara's a sensible girl.'

Sensible. Was she? Alice thought of Clara, ponytail swinging; the false laughter. She thought of the argument, their final words. But she didn't say anything, even later. She could not bear the thought that she might be to blame.

They asked other families first, couples camping with young children who were up early, eating breakfast; older people in camper vans or caravans. At around eight o'clock, the girl from the previous night emerged from her tent, the red lipstick gone. She regarded Alice strangely while her mother asked questions, as though she thought the whole thing a hoax or a terrible joke. She woke Max and the others then, and they emerged from their tents, groggy, grumpy, hair disarranged. They squinted at Alice, shook their heads. No, they hadn't heard anything at all.

The plastic windmill still turned in the breeze, but the tent opposite had gone, leaving a patch of flattened grass.

They went then to people in holiday houses, people who might have seen something from a window, heard a shout or a scream in the night. Alice remembered her mother's voice growing shriller, her father quieter, more angry. She remembered Robert crying, all of his thirteen-year-old bravado gone. Mostly she remembered the panic spiralling within her like a sickness and the looks of those other people: part pity, part curiosity, part suspicion. It was the way people always looked at her, even many years later.

By the time the police came, her mother had grown silent and afraid. And that was far, far worse.

On the second day, they began to trawl the lake: teams of masked men in black-and-blue wetsuits, emerging from the surface like strange water beasts. Clara's mother and stepfather had arrived by that stage – tearful, hostile, pale. They wouldn't stay in the same house as Alice's parents. They would barely even talk to them. This seemed grossly unfair to Alice. It had, after all, been Clara's idea to camp, Clara's insistence that had led to them being in the tent that night, alone.

'Please don't worry about it, Alice,' her mother said. 'They're upset. People do funny things when they're upset.'

But Alice had heard what Clara's mother said to her parents: 'I should have trusted my instincts. I should have said no. I should never have let her come here with you.'

Two days after that, Alice flew home with Robert and their mother to make the start of term. Her father remained behind to 'keep a watch on things'. He had become strained and argumentative by this stage, insisting that the boys in the other tent must have had something to do with it, even though the police had discounted them early on. 'I don't like the look of them, Bev. I don't like their manner. If you ask me, they've got something to hide.'

Back in England, the teachers had been gentle with Alice. The children less so.

'How could you not have heard her leave?' one of the girls asked her. 'Were you drunk, or something?'

'No. No, I wasn't.' And she hadn't been. Had she?

As Alice lay next to Michael, watching the curtains in the open window drift like ghosts, her memories of it all seemed remote and false. She had gone over what happened so many times since then, relived it for so many people – the French police, the British police, the coroner, the teachers, the parents – that she no longer fully remembered the real events. They had been trodden into the dust, mingled with other footprints, lost.

What stayed with her was the guilt. Even here, now, she could not entirely shift the fear that she was to blame. The belief that, somehow, she should have stopped Clara before she stepped out of the tent and into empty space.

The next day broke bright and fine, the sky a watercolour blue. From downstairs came the sound of water running, Charlie shrieking, Ada laughing. Alice was glad Robert's children were there, carefree and oblivious. They gave the adults something to fuss over, something to focus on that was not the spectre of the girl who had vanished years before.

They spent that morning and those that followed boating or swimming in the lake, taking Ada and Charlie to the wooden playground, shaded beneath the trees. In the afternoons, they would read or snooze in the sunshine; in the evenings, play cards or watch TV. Only once more had Clara been mentioned, and this time, strangely, it was by Robert.

Alice was sitting in the garden, a book in her lap, when he took a seat next to her and gripped its arms. 'I think she's at peace, Alice.'

She closed her book and turned to her brother, glad that her sunglasses obscured her eyes. She had never believed Clara to be at peace. She remained in Alice's mind, uneasy beneath the surface, waiting to be heard.

'Why do you think that, then?'

'I don't know. I just get that feeling, being back in this place. I think she's still here, but she's OK. You know?'

Still here. Alice looked at Robert, his long, earnest face, his large, pale eyes. Little Bobs, who had cried for Clara, who still wanted it all to be all right. She turned away. If Clara was still here, it was surely as fragments or as the echo of a scream. Sometimes Alice imagined draining the entire lake, just to know once and for all – finding a cluster of bones, fragments of cloth. It would be better that way; it would allow her to release Clara from the prison of her mind. Because, how could you grieve if you have no bones? If you had nothing to bury at all?

But she would allow Robert to think Clara was at peace. There was no harm in it. She almost envied him his delusion.

By the last day of the holiday, Alice was desperate to be gone. She never liked other people being too close, and here they were inescapable – their sounds, their smells, their opinions, brushing up against her like the wings of the moths that flew in at dusk. Again, she swam early in the lake, the outlines of the trees reflecting black on the surface of the water. It was cold this morning, but she forced herself to remain in the lake, her limbs white phantoms beneath the surface. It was her goodbye to Clara. Her apology. This was the last time she would visit this place.

When Alice returned to the house, a towel wrapped around her, her bare feet leaving watery prints, she found her mother in the kitchen, her hands around a mug of tea.

'You're up early, Mum.'

She nodded. 'Let me make you a cuppa. The kettle's just boiled.'

Alice pulled her towel tighter, not wanting to stay talking, but not wishing to offend her mother, who stood at the work surface, putting a tea bag into a cup.

'Does it bring things back, being here?' Her mother did not look up.

Alice felt her body tense. She had not expected the question. 'I suppose so. Maybe. It's not been as bad as I thought it would.'

At first Alice had thought that coming back would be impossible – too close, too painful. But she knew now that Clara had never really left her. She was always there, just out of reach. Alice was always straining to hear her voice, to catch a glimpse of her. Occasionally, she would see her out of the corner of her eye, and her heart would speed up and her skin prickle with sweat before she realised that, of course, it was not Clara at all, but some dull, dark-haired woman going about her day – a life Clara should have been living.

Her mother was watching her now, her blue eyes flecked with red. 'It doesn't make you remember anything new, love?'

Alice looked at her mother's drawn, tired face and felt a wave of irritation – that she had spoiled her swim, her moment of peace; that she was demanding she speak again of the events she had re-remembered beyond recognition.

'What do you mean, Mum?'

'I just wondered.' She poured the water into the cup. 'It doesn't matter, really.'

Alice stared at her mother. Was that why she had brought them back, then? To see if it might prompt Alice to remember something, or to speak out about something she'd long concealed?

'I didn't see anything, Mum.' Her voice was flat and dull. 'I didn't hear anything. I can't remember something I didn't see, no matter how much you might want me to tidy things up for everybody.'

Her mother was pouring the milk. 'I've just always wondered if perhaps you did see something that night but thought it best not to say.' She spoke gently, as though to a child.

'What?'

No answer.

'You don't seriously think that I've known all these years what happened to Clara, but kept quiet about it?'

Her mother's lips were a thin line.

'Really? After what her parents have suffered? After what we've all been through? After every look, every snide comment I've endured over the years – people who think I must have known, must have heard, must have done something? You can't think that.' Her heart beat jerkily, too fast.

Her mother didn't answer. She still stood at the work surface, her hands to her mouth, her fingers tugging at her lips – an odd, painful gesture.

As Alice watched, she felt her anger drain away, leaving her cold, shivering, on the flagstone floor. 'Mum, what is it?'

Quietly, her mother began to cry – an odd, choking sound, a sound that made the air leave Alice's lungs and her heart squeeze tight, like a fist.

She left the kitchen, left the house, returned to the lake, which was glass-still, dark in the shadows of the trees. She stood at the edge, her arms wrapped around herself, and thought. She thought of her mother, cowed and diminished. She thought of Robert: delusional, hopeful.

She thought of her father. Her father insisting that they camp near the trees. Her father handing them a flask full of rum.

Something in the water disturbed the surface, bubbles rose, then disappeared.

All these years her mother had been waiting for Alice to grow up. To work it out. To tell. Because she couldn't.

Alice walked back into the lake, aware only vaguely of the coldness of the water. She walked until she was submerged up to her shoulders, then closed her eyes, held her nose and disappeared beneath the surface to where it was dark and cool and safe.

You'll Be Dead by Dawn

C.L. Taylor

The man is lying face down on the soft Thai sand. I keep expecting him to roar to life, to jump to his feet and come at me, swinging, but he doesn't move a muscle. There's a bloody gash at the base of his skull, a sandy crimson halo around his head.

'You killed your friend,' I say.

'He's not my friend.' The man standing beside me has a belly so large it's balanced, beach-ball-like, above the waistband of his neon-green swimming shorts. At his feet is a large, jagged rock smeared with blood.

'He'd have killed me too if he'd got the chance.' He pulls a sheet of paper out of the pocket of his shorts, crumples it into a ball and throws it at the body. It bounces off the dead man's back and lands in the sand. 'Sick bastard.'

I close my hand over the sheet of paper in my own pocket. I don't need to re-read it to check what it says.

You'll be dead by dawn.

Beachball Belly was the first one to find his note. He was lying on the beach with a grey-haired man, a green beer bottle raised to his lips, a pile of unopened bottles peeping out of the top of a cool box beside him, the crystal-clear sea licking at his toes when I sprinted towards them across the sand, sopping wet and screaming.

'The boat's come untied from the jetty. We're stranded!'

Beachball took another slug of his beer and grinned. 'Very funny, girly.'

'It has. Look!' I pointed out to sea where our white motorboat was happily bobbing about on the turquoise water well over a mile away.

Beachball rooted around in his bag and pulled out a pair of metal-rimmed spectacles and swapped his sunglasses for them.

'Shit.'

He set off along the sand, jogging towards the jetty on the other side of the island. Grey-hair and I exchanged a look then set off after him.

Beachball was doubled over and panting when we reached the jetty. He pointed at the post our boat had been tethered to, then into the distance, and shook his head.

'I could swim out to it,' I offered. 'I was a county swimmer when I was at school.'

'You?' He snorted derisively. 'You couldn't swim from one side of the bath to the other.'

I said nothing. Instead I watched as he yanked his t-shirt over his head and, still gasping, waded into the sea, assuring us that he was a strong swimmer and he'd reach the boat in no time. Ten minutes later the old grey-haired guy – the one that's lying dead at our feet now – had to wade in after him and drag him back.

'Bloody asthma,' Beachball gasped as we half carried, half dragged him back across the island to where he'd left his bag.

He spotted the note as he lay on the sand, squirting his Ventolin inhaler into his mouth and gulping in air like a beached puffer fish. The note was sticking out of the pocket of his rucksack, quivering in the light sea breeze.

You'll be dead by dawn.

'Is this your idea of a joke?' He crumpled it in his fist and threw it at Grey-hair's head. 'Not so funny now we're all stranded here for the night, is it? Or was that all part of your plan? Pop off into the jungle for a piss, untie the boat and then see how much you could freak me out?' He shook his head. 'I know you like a practical joke but…'

I opened my bag and glanced inside, then patted the pockets of my shorts and gasped so loudly Beachball and Grey-hair immediately stopped talking and stared at me.

'I've got one too.' My hand shook as I held out an identical piece of paper, torn from a lined notebook, the words scratched onto the page with a blue biro. 'I just found it in my pocket. How the … what…'

'Mate!' Beachball stared incredulously at the page fluttering in my hand. 'Winding me up is one thing, but you don't even know this woman. That's not cool.'

'Oh, sod off!' Grey-hair picked up a handful of sand and threw it at Beachball. It rained down on him, sticking to his wet body like cake sprinkling on fresh icing. 'This is a sick stunt, even for you. Where did you put my note then, eh?'

He reached into his pockets, then frowned as he pulled them inside out, revealing only the white lining. 'In here?' He tipped his black rucksack onto the sand. A bottle of suntan lotion, a packet of cigarettes and half an apple tumbled out, but no note. The colour rose in his cheeks as he swore under his breath and began rooting through the bag's pockets. I took a small step back, one eye on the jungle to my right, and tightened my grip on my own bag. If either of them made any kind of move to attack me it was my only escape route. They were both bigger and stronger than me, but I was at least twenty years younger and lighter by a good ten stone. It was always going to be risky, tagging along on a boat trip with two total strangers – men at that – but there was no point to my trip if I didn't.

'There, look!' Grey-hair's voice was jubilant as he scooped from the sand a crime novel with a black cover and vivid orange lettering, and flicked through the pages. He paused near the middle, plucked a piece of paper from the heart of the book and waved it victoriously in Beachball's face. 'There you go – "*You'll be dead by dawn*". If I'm playing a sick joke, why would I write a note to myself?'

Beachball looked from him to me and back again. I took another small step backwards. Unlike some of the islands off Phuket where paths have been worn into the vegetation by thousands of tourists' feet, there's no obvious route into the jungle here. I'd have to plough through it and find somewhere to hide if either man decided to attack me.

'Because if you didn't you'd definitely look guilty!' Beachball scooped up a handful of sand and chucked it back at Grey-hair, but there was a grin on his face and amusement in his voice.

'I told you. I didn't write the bloody note. That's not the sort of thing I find very funn—'

'Whatever.' Beachball reached for a beer. 'What we need to do is work out how the hell we're going to get off this sodding island, not get into a debate about your crap sense of humour.'

'So what happened, then?' Beachball nods at Grey-hair's body. The top of his bald head is crimson from the hot sun, the knuckles of his right hand raw and bleeding. He flicks the sheen of sweat from his brow onto the sand. 'He told me he was going to find somewhere to have a shit. Next thing I know you're screaming like a banshee.'

I press one hand to my vest, covering the rip in the neckline that is exposing my bikini top.

'He attacked me.' I look Beachball straight in the eye, but there's a quiver in my voice. 'I came back to the jetty because I was suspicious that the boat didn't just sail off on its own and I was right. Look.' I duck down under the jetty, pull out a piece of rope and run my fingers over the short, stubby cords at one end. 'It was cut. Deliberately. I was examining it when your friend discovered me and attacked me. I think he was planning on killing us both.'

Beachball glances down at the dead man. 'Why would he do that?'

'I don't know. He's your friend.'

'I told you. He's not my *friend*.' His lip curls as he says the last word.

'But you're on holiday with him.'

'That doesn't make us friends. There were supposed to be three of us on this trip, but one of the guys dropped out at the last minute.'

'So how do you know him?'

He shifts from one foot to the other and rubs his hands over his red, sweaty face, momentarily hiding his eyes from me. 'We know each other from an internet forum.'

'What kind of internet forum?'

Beachball peers through his fingers, suspicion and fear flickering across his face for a split second, then the emotion is gone, replaced by a cold smile. 'Let's just say we share an interest.'

'What kind of interest?'

'My, aren't we a nosy little girl? How about you answer some questions for a change?'

I glance out to sea. The boat has drifted further away in the last hour or so – it's still bobbing about, alone, on the clear, blue water. There are no other boats that I can see. With its dense jungle and tiny stretch of beach this is one of the least popular islands off Phuket. Most of the tourists will be at the festival in the town – drawn by the noise, the booze and the dancing. We could be alone here for hours yet.

'OK.' I look back warily at Beachball. Just because Grey-hair is dead doesn't mean I'm out of danger. 'What do you want to know?'

He looks me up and down again. 'Why would a young girl like you earwig on two total strangers in a bar and then ask if you could share their boat to a deserted island? It's weird. Where are your friends?'

I want to tell him that *he's* the weird one, coming on holiday with someone he barely knows and then killing him without a moment's hesitation. Instead I say, 'My friends are back in England. None of them could afford to come travelling with me.'

'So you're a rich girl, are you?' He openly sneers. 'A Trustifarian living off Mummy and Daddy?'

'Actually I'm an orphan. My mum died of cancer last year, I was only seventeen. And my … my…' I swallow, my throat suddenly dry, '…my stepdad passed away recently. He left me some money.'

'Oh.' The expression on Beachball's face changes, but it's not one of pity. Is he planning on stealing from me? Worse? He hasn't shown the slightest regret for braining Grey-hair while I was grappling with him. What's to stop him killing me next? He rubs a hand over his lips and looks at me thoughtfully. 'Why us? Why ask to share our boat?'

I look him straight in this eye. 'I overheard you talking, and when you said you were coming here it seemed like an opportunity too good to miss. I'm not in Phuket for the beaches or the bars. I'm looking for dangerous species.'

'Of what?'

'Now who's the nosy one?'

We stare at each other, neither of us saying a thing, and I brace myself, all the muscles in my body tensing as I prepare to run but, instead of lunging towards me, Beachball throws back his head and roars with laughter.

'Touché!'

His laughter turns to a wheeze, and he reaches into his bag and pulls out his inhaler. He puffs on it twice then looks up at me. 'Two more questions for you, clever girl. One: what are we going to do with the body? And two: how the fuck do we get off this island?'

Sweat rolls off my eyebrows and drips into my eyes, and I pass a hand over my face for what must be the third time in as many minutes. Beachball is doubled over in front of me, puffing on his inhaler as if his life depends on it. We're standing in near darkness in the middle of the jungle, a canopy of leaves blocking out the sun, an army of cicadas chirping frantically. Grey-hair is lying dead at our feet. We striped the sand with his blood as we hauled him from the beach to the jungle, pausing every couple of seconds to catch our breath and wipe the sweat from our eyes. It must have taken us hours, and we're both scratched and bleeding. The vegetation was thicker than I thought.

'Now what?' Beachball looks up at me, still bent over, his hands on his knees. 'We can't bury him – we don't have a spade.'

'I know.'

He frowns. 'So we just leave him here?'

I nod.

'But they'll find him. Sooner or later someone will find him here.'

'I know that. His body will serve as a warning.'

'For what?' Beachball straightens up, but it's an effort, and he presses one hand to his chest as he shakes his inhaler with the other.

'A warning to paedophiles.'

'What?' His cheeks pale and he stares at me open-mouthed.

I crouch down, pick up my bag and slide my hand inside, keeping my eyes on Beachball the whole time.

'He was a paedophile?' he says, his eyes darting to his left, his right, to the trail we created that's directly behind me. 'Fuck. That's awful. How do you know?'

'Same way I know you're a paedophile – from the forum where you discuss your shared *interests*.' I spit out the last word.

'You've made a mistake, girly.' Beachball shakes his head. 'You've got me confused with someone else. We're into trains, me and him, not kids; that's sick.'

'And that's why you came to Thailand, is it?' I smile. 'In search of trains?' I'm breathing quickly now, in and out through my nose, but not because I'm scared. My fingers graze the rough lining of the bag and then touch the object I've been searching for. I close my hand around it.

You'd think it would be hard to crack an online paedophile ring, wouldn't you? Not if your stepfather suddenly died and left you everything, including his computer. Not if he was logged into the forum when he breathed his last breath. Not if the last thing he'd typed was: 'Yeah. I'm up for a trip to Thailand. We could have a lot of fun.'

'That's right, girly. We came to Thailand for the trains.' Beachball's gaze drops to the ground. His own bag is lying on the forest floor, an equal distance between him and me. I saw what was in Grey-hair's bag when he tipped the contents onto the sand in search of his note, but Beachball didn't do that. There could be anything in his rucksack, anything at all.

'Any particular kind of train you were hoping to see in Thailand?' I ask as I slowly, slowly slip my hand from the bag. 'A steam train perhaps, or a TGV. Maybe a—'

'What the fuck?' Beachball looks from Grey-hair, who's still face down on his stomach, to the thick streak of blood that stretches from his feet to the path we created from the beach. 'I hit him on the back of the head. That blood can't have come from…'

I jump back as he throws himself at Grey-hair's body and, grunting with the effort, flips him over onto his back.

Beachball takes a step back, one arm outstretched, pointing at the gaping wound in Grey-hair's stomach. He stands there, staring, point-ing, saying nothing for what seems like an age, then, ever so slowly, ever so deliberately, he turns and points at me.

'You.'

I smile. It's a genuine smile. A proud one. 'Yes.'

'You did that.'

'Yes. Yes I did. Poor thing. He only wanted to know if I had some loo roll.'

His gaze flicks towards his bag, now less than half a metre from him. 'You fucking bit—'

He doesn't get to finish his sentence. I cut it out of him, twisting the knife in his guts until his knees buckle and he tumbles backwards. He lands on top of Grey-hair and slumps onto him, their heads nestled together like sleepy lovers entwined.

I'm slightly out of breath when I get to Phuket airport. It took me longer to swim out to the boat than I'd anticipated, then I had to drop the knife into the sea, speed back to the shore and pick up my laptop and belongings from the hut I'd rented on the shoreline.

I wasn't lying when I told Beachball that I was a county swimming champion. I took up swimming after Mum died and it was just me and my stepdad left in the huge, sprawling house she'd inherited from my grandparents. I trained every Monday, Tuesday, Friday and Saturday – a weights session followed by three miles in the pool. Training made me fast and strong. It also meant that, four times a week, I'd be miles away from home – and safe – when he would peel himself out of bed, stumble into my bedroom for a bit of 'fun' then log on to the computer in the dining room. I try not to think about the other three days a week.

'Got anything nice planned in Kuala Lumpur?' the check-in desk stewardess asks as I hand over my passport and ticket.

I killed my stepdad instead of serving up Sunday lunch. One minute I was standing beside the dining-room table, a carving knife in my hand and a steaming turkey in front of me, and the next I'd driven the knife between his shoulder blades. He was sitting at the computer desk in the corner of the room at the time. I don't know why I did it. Maybe it was the sound of his fingers tap-tap-tapping on the keys, the squeak of his chair's wheels on the dirty tiles, or his groans of pleasure as he looked at image after image after image; whatever it was, something inside me snapped. I stabbed him again and again and again, feeling a delicious rush of satisfaction each time the blade crunched against bone. So much for going to the police. Now I had to run from them instead.

I spent four hours on the forum, notebook in hand, and then half an hour inputting my stepdad's credit-card details into a travel website. I knew exactly where I would go.

'I'm sorry?' I look up at the check-in stewardess as she slides my boarding card and passport back across the counter. 'You just asked me something?'

She smiles widely, her overly made-up face the picture of professional interest. 'I asked whether you had something nice planned in Kuala Lumpur?'

'Yes. I'm going in search of … one second.' I reach into my bag and pull out my notebook. I flip through the pages, pausing momentarily on a blank, lined page to chastise myself for pressing too hard with my biro. *You'll be dead by dawn* is imprinted on the page. 'Oh yes, I'm going in search of BlueBottle78 and MyTurnNow.'

'I'm sorry?' She inclines her head to one side and frowns. 'What was that? I didn't catch—'

'Don't worry, I will.'

She's still frowning as I turn and walk towards the departure lounge.

The Last Supper

Carol Anne Davis

We're sitting on Brighton Pier, where visitors last year munched their way through thirty-two thousand ice creams and twenty-four thousand doughnuts. I fear that Valerie ate most of them. Don't get me wrong – I'm not one of those husbands who object to the natural thickening of a middle-aged woman's waistline, but we're not talking about two or three stone.

We visit several British seaside towns every June, shortly after our winter sun holiday. We recently returned from the Canary Islands, where each day she worked her way through pork ribs, butter-drenched corn on the cob and twice-fried chips. For myself, I was happy with a vegetable consommé followed by some grilled grouper. I find that eating lightly makes it easier to think.

I suspect that Valerie is trying hard not to think. She's been increasingly remote since our fifth attempt at IVF failed, and I fear that she blames me, although tests have shown that my sperm are long-distance swimmers. She was forty when we married and first went to the clinic; I was thirty, so perhaps she thought my youth would compensate for her age.

'I think I'll treat myself to the fish and chips,' she says now.

I glance at my watch and find it's just after eleven, a mere two hours since she had a full English breakfast.

'Just a mineral water for me.'

She heaves herself up from the cafeteria chair and walks, legs awkwardly apart, to the self-service counter. A group of teenage boys look up from their mobiles to stare at her then glance in my direction. I hope that they'll think that I'm her employee or her neighbour – anything but her spouse.

My mobile vibrates against my thigh, and I realise that it's the first thrill I've had in months. I could take a lover, of course, but Valerie holds the purse strings and would cut me off without a euro. And, now that I'm thirty-eight, there's not much modelling work out there. Oh, I make the occasional appearance in *Country Man* catalogue, decked out in an oilskin coat with my arm around a springer spaniel. And last year mine was the stock photo used in a newspaper article about – ironically – the male pill. But work offers are few and far between now that I'm too old for the youth market and too young for the retirement catalogues.

'They didn't have any balsamic vinegar,' Valerie says on her return, before cutting into what looks like whale in batter. The chips are piled so high that several have fallen off the plate, while the mushy peas are a laboratory-enhanced shade of green. She washes them down with a bucket of cola as I make my second attempt at solving yesterday's cryptic crossword. I notice that my mineral water is conspicuous by its absence but I don't complain.

In the honeymoon phase I had no complaints. We worked hard and played hard and made love on a daily basis. I didn't have a particular desire for children but was sympathetic when Valerie wanted them. But the initial fertility treatment made her cramp and bloat, and become exceptionally irritable, and the later, more intensive, medication gave her headaches and made her feel faint. She began to overdose on chocolate every day in the hope of regaining her vigour, and, when that failed, added red wine and dark beer. A couple needs similar energy levels if they are to go walking and dancing together, so our social life became increasingly small. Oh, we still travelled frequently but increasingly saw the world from a cruise liner or a hired limousine.

The month after our trip to the British seaside we go to Malta and take up residence in the hotel's finest suite. However, driving rain greets us when we open the curtains each morning. I want to go and see the barracks and the catacombs, both described to me during childhood by my grandfather. I'd also like to wander around the museums and art galleries, but Valerie, who hates the cold, refuses to hire a car for us, so we sit in the restaurant, and I watch her devour goat's cheese and ricotta pastries, followed by sugared almonds and candied fruits with cream.

The cream smears at the side of her mouth, drawing my unwilling attention to her hamster-like cheeks as she wolfs down the cakes the way a pelican swallows a duckling. I feel slightly unwell at the prospect of ever having to kiss her again.

It's hard to believe that she was once a successful model; then again, her father owned several mail order clothing businesses, so she grew up in front of the camera. At first, she featured in the baby-clothing catalogues, then in those aimed at the youth market. By the time I met her she was in her late thirties and modelling for the fifty-plus set. She still looked great, but manufacturers always choose younger models for their clothing lines; hell, even the pensioner market has models that haven't yet experienced their first perimenopausal sweat.

At forty-five, Valerie could start having hot flushes soon and become even more tired and jaded. It doesn't bear thinking about. I can't envisage spending the next few decades following her around like a lapdog, but I also loathe the thought of getting a divorce and living in a bedsit. It seems hopeless, unless…

I'm sure that every out-of-love spouse has considered murder at some point, even if only briefly during a shrieking, fist-clenching argument. They invariably make up and the thought is forgotten, or at least pushed into the background until the next angry dispute. But what if they don't make up? What if his sense of feeling trapped and controlled grows by the second? What if it seems the only sensible way out?

I continue to visualise my happy single life as she munches her way through Morocco and Tunisia (she favours the baklava and glass after glass of heavily sweetened tea) before returning to Britain for a tour of a chocolate factory where we learn that a certain wafer is sold in the UK every two seconds. I wonder if Valerie is bulk-buying most of them and force back a mirthless little laugh. We are encouraged to taste the confectionery as we make our way through the building, and afterwards she takes home a giant bag of truffles and an Easter egg that would make even the world's biggest laying bird sweat and scream.

That night, I barely sleep, partly due to the fact that overdosing on confectionery has made Valerie flatulent, and partly because she has recently begun to wake up every few minutes with a grunt due to sleep apnoea.

In the morning, I go out to clear my nose and to buy a newspaper. Returning I curl up for a read in the lounge. The main feature is about a private investigator who doubled as a hit man; the article mentioned several other PIs who have also committed murders for cash. Apparently, many were disgraced former coppers who were struggling to make a living as investigators and chose to go over to the very dark side.

I am too astute to research the subject online so go through the local telephone directory and copy down a few names. I phone each of them from a new, pay-as-you-go mobile, make introductory appointments and pretend that I am thinking of buying a substantial local property and need to know if the neighbours are nice, quiet types. Naturally, I give each investigator the name of a different house, as the last thing I want is for them to bump into each other as they go through the owner's trash.

I use most of my savings to pay all four men's fees, but rationalise that you often need to spend money to make money, and that, if everything goes to plan, I'll be inheriting all of Valerie's wealth…

The next few weeks are very interesting indeed, as each of the investigators bring me details of the people I've asked about, everything from their qualifications to their debts and their sexual lifestyles. (Apparently spanking and threesomes are big in the suburbs.) I thank them, only to arrange another meeting shortly afterwards and explain that I've heard that I was about to be outbid. 'It's a guy I used to work with and he's really shafted me. I could kill the bastard,' I say.

Three of the men make sympathetic noises, but the fourth – Barry, whom I'm guessing was born and bred in Birmingham – says, 'Sounds

like he's made a few enemies. Maybe he'll meet with a little accident.'
He says it in a pseudo-jokey voice, but his gaze is unblinking and it is
obvious that he is sizing me up.

'What if there was someone else who deserved a short, sharp shock?'
I ask, then take a hasty sip from the blended whisky that Barry has
poured for me. The tumbler is the type you buy at a car boot sale, as
are the soft furnishings. He is operating out of a room in his flat, and
anyone can see that his main meal of the day is a liquid lunch.

'I was a karate instructor for a few years,' he says in a matter-of-fact
tone.

'Yeah? I wasn't thinking of anything too athletic. Actually, all you
should need is a handful of cake…'

We spend the next couple of weeks sorting everything out, and eventually the plan seems foolproof. Valerie and I are to spend a few days in
Polperro, indulging in her newly acquired love of Cornish pasties. One
afternoon I'll order room service. Earlier, I'll have put sedatives in her
cola to slow her responses down. While we're eating, Barry will knock
on the door and say that he's forgotten to give us our complimentary
wine and chocolates – the rich are particularly partial to anything that
is free. He'll set down the tray and grab hold of Valerie, putting her in
a headlock while I block her windpipe by stuffing it with a large piece
of scone. It will be fitting in a way – her last supper: she will die doing
what she loves. If the scone doesn't quite work its magic, we will suf-
focate her with the pillow and stuff more cake down her throat immediately afterwards. Men and women die every day from choking on
meals at home and in restaurants. In fact, it's the fourth leading cause
of accidental death.

As the death day draws closer, I try to be especially kind to Valerie.
It's customary to tell the larger lady that she has beautiful eyes, but it's
hard to see hers due to the pouches of fat, so I settle for complimenting
her on her new perfume. I even hold her in my arms (well, most of her)
when she finds out that her latest fertility treatment has failed. We sing

along to the car radio as I drive us to Cornwall, and I force myself to eat a chicken nugget from her family-sized box – it must have been aimed at the Manson family – when we stop at a service station for a snack.

And at first it goes so well that my confidence trumps my nervousness. We settle into our hotel suite and I go for a long, hot bubble bath, while she drinks her lightly medicated sparkling brew. On my return, I phone down to the kitchen and ask for a cream tea for two to be delivered. She is dozing on the bed when the waitress arrives with it. Five minutes later, Barry raps on our door, dressed in a black ensemble that vaguely resembles that of the serving staff, though they don't share his aroma of mingled whisky and fags.

I let him in, take the wine and mutter, 'She's all yours,' only to find the doorway suddenly blocked with several exceptionally well-nourished members of the local constabulary. I look over at Valerie, only to find that she is no longer sleeping.

'Barry has told me everything,' she says.

Needless to say, the bastard has taped our meetings for the delectation of the boys in blue and I am found guilty of conspiracy to murder and sentenced to a lengthy staycation at an English jail.

During my first year behind bars I earn an NVQ in drama and spend time in the prison workshop doing a woodworking course. (I make a storage box and a jumbo-sized jigsaw as I'm not allowed to make a smoker's pipe or a wine rack.)

I dumb down a lot and started reading an American magazine devoted to sightings of Elvis and kidnappings by extraterrestrials. One week they have a two-page spread on extreme eating competitions, and, to my amazement, they include a few words about Valerie and the cash prizes that she's won.

Shortly afterwards, one of the younger guys gets hold of a mobile phone (you don't want to know where they store these things), and I get to see my ex-wife in jaw-aching action. I can see that it is the perfect job for her as she gets to travel, as always, but now she can eat without guilt. Extreme eating has given her a purpose, a new part-time career, a fan base. She's always had a competitive side to her nature and now she is top dog – well, top hot-dog eater – in her chosen field.

I bear her no ill will, and my ire only comes to the fore when I click on a photo montage and see one of Barry in the background. He is lifting a glass of whisky towards the camera (I bet he's upgraded to a single malt) and is named as her tour manager. In other words, he's taken on the pleasures of my role as kept man and world traveller without the pain of the sex.

He's ruined my life and now I shall ruin his. It shouldn't be difficult. After all, his itinerary is online and my fellow prisoners are being released into the wilderness every day. Several of them would beat a man to death just for the fun of it, but I'm willing to throw in the little money I have left, plus the handcrafted storage box and jigsaw, of course. I'll toast his demise in the prison canteen with some bread and water, and neither will ever have tasted so good.

The White Goddess

Cath Staincliffe

The waves cast her onto the rocks, skinning her knees, shins, elbows. Her thirst was raging, her eyes were cloudy with exhaustion. There were buildings clustered half a mile or so along the coast but when she tried to stand her muscles shrieked and shivered. All she wore was a bikini.

Get up. Get up now!

On trembling legs, her tongue dry as the pumice sold in the mini-markets, she staggered on. No path. Thorns bristled all around, ripping fresh wounds in her legs. Dust billowed from the sere land, coating the blood that streaked in rivulets to her bare feet. Blood the same colour as the poppies sprayed among the scrub. Flies came to feed. Grasshoppers sprang away as she walked.

What was the Greek for husband? For help? For coastguard? For please find him, find my love? She would cry but there were no tears, everything parched. Sharp stones jabbed at the pads of her feet, making her grimace. The gesture caused her lips to crack anew.

Perfection. Lazy days under the brilliant sun. The rickety footbridge from the jetty to the tiny taverna. An aroma of garlic and prawns and wild oregano making her mouth water. Her skin tight with salt and heat. Her hunger for him ever present, ravenous.

Eyes narrowed against the rippling haze, she saw with a punch to her heart that the settlement was unfinished. A ghost resort. Raw breeze-block walls and steel rods. Hotels and apartments just shells, staring at her with blind malice as the wind blew sand and cement powder into her face.

She nearly gave up then. Why keep going when she had lost him?

The thought tore at her insides. She wanted to howl, to throw herself down and beat the ground.

Walk. Keep walking.

Counting steps, she followed the rough track, cut to create access to someone's dream development. Losing count and starting again and again until she reached a tarmac road. There she stood, hesitant, dizzy. Which way? The heat burned her shoulders and her scalp.

They loved the island. Honeymooned here. Returned often. Cistus, broom, vetch and daisies flowering in the dirt. The air perfumed by thyme and sage and eucalyptus. Waiters and shopkeepers greeted them with broad smiles. Tourists were money. And with the country ravaged by austerity, they were the lifeblood of the islands. It was his idea to hire the boat. Named Leucothea, *for the goddess who rescued Odysseus from the deep.*

Roaring and the blurt of a horn. The refuse truck swept past, trailing a miasma that had her bent double, vomiting into the ditch. Thin yellow bile splashed over the plastic pipes and lumps of concrete, rusting cans, rubbish bags and broken palm fronds. Then voices. Two old Greek men, wizened walnut faces. A small van. Incomprehensible questions. She pointed to her wedding ring, her finger swollen sickly white around it. Then at the sea. Implored them with shaking palms outstretched. Tried to speak – *My husband, please save him* – but the back of her skull was melting, her knees buckled, and she fell.

Kisses. The salt on his lips, small crystals dried on his chest. The scent of him, briny among the sweet coconut of sunscreen.

Cold white hospital bed, a metallic smell, a drip in her arm, throat full of glass. Dehydrated, punch-drunk with sunstroke. And shock. The soundtrack of the town was too close. The shriek of scooters, the frenzied barking of a dog, car horns, the chatter of sparrows, snatches of mindless bouzouki music and blaring rap, the bass so heavy it thumped through her stomach. Had she told them he was missing? They must find him. She pressed the buzzer.

Walking back to the boat, the earth giving up its scents to the night. Sweet jasmine and fennel, and a whiff of trash from the bins on the road that were alive with cats. Lulled to sleep by the rocking of the ocean, the slap and suck of the waves. She'd never imagined that the trouble with the business would follow them here.

She described it all. The water that rose so quickly, capsizing the boat. How, when she surfaced, she could not see him. They showed her charts. Talked of time and tides. He wasn't wearing a life vest? Her face flushed. We'd been ... making love. Drifting. The land a smudge on the horizon. The sea all theirs.

Is there any sign? He was the stronger swimmer, after all. There had to be hope. She asked every time the police came, but there was no word.

Butterflies bobbed and house martins dipped over the restaurant pool on the day they collected the Leucothea. *The sea beyond was clear turquoise. The air busy with the hiss of spume and the sizzle of cicadas. Squeezing his hand, she met his gaze, saw her smile reflected in his.*

She wept when they abandoned the search, when they told her gently that his body might never be recovered. The consulate had arranged clothing and essentials, temporary accommodation, her passage home.

The night before the sinking they stopped in a sheltered bay, accessible only by water. Shared bread and olives, wine so cold it hurt her teeth. She kissed his neck, his mouth, his belly. He touched her. She came watching the stars glitter above, the moon casting its silver beam across the oil-dark sea. She never wanted to leave.

They sought her out in the departure lounge. Took her aside. We've found your husband.

Her heart burst, the room swam. Thank you, she said when she could speak. I'll wait, fly back with his ... with him.

Cold eyes and the ghost of a smile. He has told us everything.

Drowsy after lunch, reaching for him. The wings of his shoulder blades flinched at her touch. Revulsion in his eyes as he turned. His voice catching: 'I can't do this. I thought I could. I've tried ... but ... I love her. I still love her. I'm sorry. I'm so sorry.'

She was silent. Stunned, as if he'd hit her. He had promised. They had agreed. He'd said the bitch had gone, left to work elsewhere.

Rage funnelled through her like wildfire. Rushing up her spine, into her neck, exploding in her head.

'Need a pee.' He stood silhouetted against the sky.

One shove was all it took.

She scuppered the boat within sight of shore, cruising past the ragged limestone cliffs of the west and on to where the plains began, in striking distance of land. But she had misjudged the demands of the swim, not allowing for the fierce currents that robbed her of progress. The undertow that sucked her back time and again and had her praying for salvation.

Fishermen found him, clinging to a spit of rock miles from anywhere. The policeman drew handcuffs from his pocket. Truly a miracle.

Gooseflesh puckered the honeyed tan of her arms as she held out her wrists. Through the plate-glass windows, beyond the runway, the sea shimmered cobalt, calm and still.

High Flyer

Chris Simms

He sat stiffly in the chair, head angled to the side, face turned in annoyance from the computer screen. 'Come here, Pakpao!'

A couple of seconds passed before he heard the whisper of footsteps. A shadow appeared in the doorway. He didn't bother swivelling the chair to face her. 'Here, I said.'

His voice was stern. Ominously so. On the monitor was an airline company's site: flights to Thailand.

She did as he asked and came to a halt alongside him. Despite being seated, his head was almost level with hers. 'What have I said about visiting these sites? I've told you not to. You know that, yet still you do it.'

She said nothing. Her aura of calm annoyed him. Words could never puncture it. His hand lifted, his fingers grasped her wrist, and she was jerked closer to the screen. 'Browsing history. I check everything. You can't hide anything from me. When will you get that into your thick head?'

He glanced at her face, saw her impassive expression and tried to crush the bones of her wrist. 'Hmm?'

The corners of her mouth finally tightened. A small movement, but enough to give him a victory of sorts. He threw her hand away from him. 'Now get out.'

He turned his attention back to the screen, and a moment later a floorboard in the hallway creaked. She was gone.

Craig Evans minimised the browser's window. Now a report from the head engineer at a manufacturing plant he owned over in Ireland filled the screen. Tax was more favourable in Ireland – but the production line had developed a fault. Something to do with the laser cutter.

He ran a hand over his face. A vein in his temple throbbed as he tried to calculate the best way to resolve the issue. He could pay for a consultant from a Dublin-based firm he'd used before. But even if identifying the glitch only took a day, the fee would be extortionate.

He tapped a finger up and down on his mouse. Bloody Pakpao. She'd robbed him of the ability to concentrate. It was nine years ago that he'd found her. The trip over to Thailand had been a fortieth birthday present to himself. Just him and a local guide, hiking in the vast forests of the country's mountainous north. Two full weeks watching birdlife: blue-winged pittas, rufous-necked hornbills, Gould's frogmouths.

Back in civilisation, he'd strayed into a bar on the Jet Yod Road in Chang Rai. Pakpao hadn't been one of the naked dancers up on stage; she lacked the beauty and figure for that. Hips that were too wide, legs too stout, nose too flat. But as she moved around the bar collecting glasses and wiping down tables, he'd noticed something in her. Stoicism? The brain-jarring din of music didn't seem to affect her. Nor the jostling groups of male tourists who had obviously taken a lot more than alcohol, judging by the way they staggered and giggled and blew out their cheeks. Observing her, he had admired the serene way she just got on with her job.

He checked the time: almost eight in the evening. Tomorrow was Saturday. The consultancy firm would charge a weekend call-out fee if he resorted to ringing them. Bloody shitty Taiwanese equipment. He should have made the extra investment and got the German machine.

She was in the kitchen quietly preparing breakfast when he entered it the next morning. Seven years ago he moved her into a spare room. One on the other side of the house. After they'd become husband and wife, he'd tried all the expected stuff. But he'd never really been bothered about it before, so why he thought marriage would provoke a taste for it, he couldn't imagine. He'd made a few attempts during their first couple of years together, her lying beneath him, body rocking slightly as he'd thrust back and forth. Her face had never changed. Eventually, he'd gone back to relieving himself in the shower. It was easier that way. Less messy, too. After he'd made that decision, it was pointless sharing a bed.

She poured him a coffee. Strong and flavoured with cinnamon and cardamom – the way they made it in the hill village she originally came from. He hadn't been sure about the taste at first. Now he couldn't start the day without it.

'Good morning,' she announced with a smile, placing the cup before him. 'Are you have porridge or the toast?'

He'd given up on correcting her English around the same time as they'd stopped sharing a bedroom. 'Porridge.'

His copy of the *Telegraph* was on the table, where it should be. As he unfolded it, he noticed the little vase in the middle of the table. It held fresh daffodils. 'Tomorrow, I may have to fly over to the plant near Dublin.'

She remained still.

'I'll try and sort it out from here, but I don't imagine I'll have much luck.' He waved at the flowers and when he spoke, his voice had softened. 'This is all very nice, but you're not going back there. You know that, don't you?'

He studied her back as she dug oats from a Tupperware container. 'Pakpao? Look at me.'

She replaced the scoop and when she turned round, her face was like a mask.

'Your sister should never have written,' he said. 'It's her fault that you're now sad.'

Her lips hardly moved as she replied. 'My mother sick. That why I'm sad.'

'How about we go to Chester Zoo on Sunday? Take your mind off things, hmm? I'll resolve the problem at the plant and we'll visit the zoo.'

The first time he'd taken her there, it was so that he could spend time in the aviary. Among the parrots were some of the finest Indigo Macaws in the world. He'd found her later in the tropical section, standing motionless below giant leaves as impossibly large butterflies glided over her head. He'd worked out, eventually, that the cloying atmosphere, loamy smell and pulsing colours reminded her of home.

'My mother sick.'

He flexed the paper so sharply the pages made a snapping sound. 'That may well be. And she might be better by now. Who knows?' His eyes traversed the text. 'You left that life behind when you came here. That is what we agreed, did we not?'

She looked to the side.

'Did we not?'

'I wish to see her.'

'Do you know how much a flight would be? Booking at short notice like this?' He lifted his eyes to the ceiling. 'Astronomical.'

'"Astromical"?'

'A lot. A bloody lot. More than you can imagine, that's for sure. So you're not going back, and that's an end to it. No more, do you understand?'

She bowed her head to show acquiescence.

'Good.' He raised the paper to remove her from his view.

The young men were in their usual place on the benches at the far end of the precinct. Boarded-up shops meant this had become their space, an area where they slouched and spat, and sold tiny plastic bags to teenagers and, occasionally, adults.

For Pakpao, the walk into town took close to an hour. The house where she lived was out in the countryside. To the side of the property was a large barn. Craig kept his aeroplane in there. It was small. Only two seats. Very similar to the ones that sometimes appeared back home. Those would clear the crests of the surrounding hills and swoop down as hissing clouds erupted from below their wings, vapour settling over the poppy fields her people grew. Sometimes the planes sprayed their cornfields, too. It was extra punishment, the village elders explained, for cultivating the forbidden crop.

When she'd been sent from the forested land to earn money in the bars of Chang Rai, she'd watched the *farangs* buying black opium paste. The young Westerners purchased other stuff, too. Clumps of mushrooms that grew in the hills; the type that painted pictures in your mind. Pills and powders that had a similar effect. She was puzzled by their carefree, indulgent existence. Was it how everyone lived in the countries they came from?

In the precinct, a young man wearing a black woollen cap became suddenly aware that a short figure had been standing silently beside him. 'Whoa!' His surprise was swiftly replaced by confusion. 'Where the fuck did she appear from?'

His mates twisted their heads, took one look at her and resumed staring at their screens.

He leaned away, his glance dropping to her feet then working slowly upward. She had trainers on, but they were an unfamiliar make, probably bought in Aldi or something. Dark socks and a grey skirt that came to below her knees. Over that, a sensible coat. Navy blue. Even though she was tiny, she seemed solid. Sturdy. The straps of a rucksack curled from view beneath her armpits. Her jet-black hair was scraped off her face into a bun. She was, he guessed, around thirty. Her face was kind.

'You lost?' he asked.

'No.'

'So…' He half lifted a hand.

'I buy some acid,' she whispered.

He started to smile, eyes cutting to the others as they looked round. 'For real?' He got to his feet and checked about. No one else was near. 'What was that you said?'

'Acid?'

Placing his hands on his knees, he flexed them so his face was level with hers. 'You what?'

'You sell drugs here. I buy acid.'

One of his mates doubled over laughing and parroted her accent. 'I buy acid. I buy acid. She wants to go on a trip!'

He was unsure what to do, now. All the others were still cracking up. They'd probably arranged the whole thing. It was all a piss-take.

'Get to fuck,' he said and sat back down, reaching uncertainly for his phone.

She inched closer. 'How much is acid?'

He turned to them while jabbing a thumb at her. 'You got her to do this? You fucking did, didn't you?'

Their mouths were open, fresh guffaws pouring out.

'Aceeed!' Another laughed. 'Aceeed! Fuck's sake, that's funny.'

He sensed the mocking was close to turning on him. 'Suck my dick, Ting-tong.' When she didn't move, he sat up straighter, making his face stern. 'Do one. Fuck off.'

Pakpao hesitated, looking into the young man's angry eyes, before stepping back and continuing towards the main shopping area.

When she was outside Asda she extracted her list. Craig didn't let her carry cash. Instead, she had a card. She didn't know exactly how it worked. They took it, gave it back and let her walk out, rucksack full. Each receipt had to be handed to Craig for checking on the computer when she returned.

She had, over the years, squirrelled away the occasional stray coin. They were all now in her coat pocket. Eight pounds, forty-five pence. She'd hoped it would be enough for some acid, if the young man had been prepared to sell.

On impulse, she continued along the pedestrian street. A road at the end led to a small playground. She skirted round the seesaws, swings and a group of mothers whose flow of conversation didn't alter with her passing. On the far side of the play area was another gate and a green footpath sign beyond it. This led her across a field to a steeply wooded slope.

Once among the trees, she stopped, tilted her head back and breathed deeply. Bird song arrowed down from the gently shifting canopy above. She heard the scratch of claws and quickly spotted the head and shoulders of a squirrel as it peeped round a nearby trunk. The animal ducked out of sight and, seconds later, reappeared on a high-up branch.

Something long-buried began to unfurl: the sense of where she used to live. Now she walked with measured, confident steps. Her progress up through the trees was swift. Muscles in her legs that hadn't been engaged in years started to awake.

She entered a section of woodland where the trees thinned. Signs of coppicing lay around: neat stacks of wood, fresh growth of bracken and saplings. Here, she slowed and began to search the ground. She was looking for thin, spindly stalks capped by delicate grey-blue discs. The type of mushroom her people sometimes ate when they wanted time to bend and their sense of self to dissolve. The type of mushroom the *farangs* were happy to pay absurd amounts of money for. Back home, the mushrooms thrived in dark, moist soil that was partly shaded from the powerful sun. Here the earth was sandier, grittier; she instinctively knew her search would be futile. Eventually, she sat down on the base of a felled tree.

To her side she could see the woodland stretching away, but only for a short distance before a line of streetlights formed an abrupt border. The drone of traffic carried on the breeze. She thought of where she grew up: endlessly rippling hills, their greens fading to blues then purplish-greys. She thought about sitting motionless at the base of mighty *takian* trees, waiting to watch gibbons sail silently through their distant branches. She tried to recall the scent from the cassia's bright pink blossoms. In the sky way above was a solitary plane, and she wondered whether her mother was dying and if she'd ever see her again.

When she left the supermarket the rucksack weighed heavy on her back. Ponderously, she made her way back along the precinct. But, as she reached the corner that led to the benches, she heard voices shouting.

'Police!'

'Stay where you are!'

'Do not move, you little bastard. Smithy, grab him!'

Pounding footsteps grew louder and a second later the young man with the woollen cap tore round the corner.

'Your lucky day,' he said.

He flung a plastic bag in her direction as he sprinted past. It skidded to a halt by her foot. He reached the next intersection and had just disappeared from sight when three adult men appeared in pursuit. Each wore a black baseball cap with the word 'Police' across the front.

Oblivious to her, the first two ran straight past before starting to slow. The third officer looked left, right and left again before spotting her. 'Where did he go?'

She nodded at the corner he'd fled round. Without another word, the three of them resumed the chase. She lifted her foot off the plastic bag and picked it up. Inside were several smaller bags. The sight of them brought back memories of the crowded clubs on the Jet Yod Road. Some held pinches of white powder. Some held little clumps of tightly packed green buds. Some held clusters of diamond-shaped pellets, each stamped with a little space rocket logo. Those were the ones she wanted. She slipped the bag into her pocket.

'Pakpao!'

She unhitched the rucksack then followed the call to his study.

His back was to her as he spoke. 'What have you been doing?'

'Shop.'

'Shop doesn't take all afternoon.' He clicked the mouse and the screen's glow altered. He studied it for a second. 'The credit card transaction in Asda was at forty-eight minutes past four. You set off for town before one. Where've you been?'

'I walking in wood.'

'Why?'

'Why?'

'Yes, why you walking in wood?'

'It nice.'

'Right. A delivery of logs arrives tomorrow afternoon, so all that rubbish in the far shed needs to be cleared.'

'I do now?'

'Yes. Start now – do what you can until it gets dark. And I will have to fly to Ireland in the morning.'

At breakfast, he didn't linger. As soon as he'd finished his coffee, he headed out the back door, briefcase in hand. Washing up, she watched him open the barn that housed his plane. The land he owned extended for a few hundred metres to a low fence. Beyond that, cows grazed. The animals vaguely resembled the water buffalo back home. But the animals before her stood idle for hour after hour. Often, only their jaws moved. They were flabby, and even walking to the farmer's gate on the far side seemed a challenge for them. She couldn't imagine them being able to drag a plough across a water-logged paddy field or haul a cart up a steep mountain path.

A throaty roar started up and the white plane rolled out from the barn's gloomy interior, its propeller blurring the air in front of the cockpit. She could see his head and shoulders, grey earphones clamped to his head as he spoke into a mouthpiece. The plane taxied round to the end of the makeshift runway, paused a moment, then accelerated across the closely cropped grass. The cows watched with dumbfounded faces as it lifted into the air, scaling some invisible slope into the sky. Before it was a speck, their heads had gone back down, lips brushing the grass as if murmuring to it in confusion.

The police car arrived at dusk. She opened the door to them and waited for one to speak. The male officer nodded awkwardly then immediately turned to his female colleague.

'Mrs Evans? Mrs Pakpao Evans?' she asked gently.

'Yes.'

'May we come in?'

She led them through to the kitchen and asked if they wanted tea. Or perhaps coffee? She lifted the cafetière from beside the sink.

'We're fine, thanks,' the female officer replied. 'Mrs Evans, your husband activated a flight plan first thing this morning with the aerodrome at Chester. Do you understand?'

'Yes,' she replied, still cradling the cafetière. 'He fly Ireland – for his business.'

'I see. Mrs Evans, perhaps you'd like to sit? We have some very sad news.'

'I stand.'

'OK, well…' She cleared her throat. 'Your husband didn't land at the aerodrome outside Dublin, as he'd planned. Recordings show that his flight path altered some thirty miles off the British coast. His route became erratic, before he turned in a southerly direction, away from the Irish coast and out into the Atlantic. I'm afraid Air Traffic Control then lost contact. Search and Rescue can find no trace of any wreckage, Mrs Evans. It appears he crashed somewhere out at sea. I'm so very sorry.'

Pakpao remained silent, her gaze directed at her feet.

From the corner of her eye she saw the officers exchange an uneasy glance.

'Mrs Evans?' The female officer said in a quiet voice. 'Do you understand what I just said?'

She looked up. 'He is dead.'

'It … it would appear so. Are you OK?'

The officer searched for a clue in the tiny woman's face, but her expression was unreadable.

The male officer spoke up now. 'Is there anyone we can call to come round? Perhaps a family memb…' He seemed to realise his mistake and came to a stop.

Pakpao breathed in slowly then replaced the cafetière on the draining board. Earlier, she'd washed what remained of the coffee that she'd laced with eight tabs of acid down the sink. She thought of her husband gulping it down. 'I would like to see my mother.'

'Your mother?' the female officer quickly replied, sounding relieved. 'OK. We can give you a lift; is she somewhere close?'

Pakpao took her purse off a nearby shelf and removed the credit card from inside. 'Can you show me to do this on computer? To see my mother, I must fly.'

Accounting for Murder

Christine Poulson

Item # 1

'Say it with Cake'
Speciality Cakes for all Occasions
1 Market Square, Silverbridge
Prop. Magdalene Dyer

Iced Victoria sponge with inscription:
'To my darling wife Laura on our 20th'
To be collected by Mr Jolyon Sleep 6 pm 25 June.
£25 to be paid

Item # 2

The George and Vulture
2–6 Market Square, Silverbridge

Visa:	xxxx xxxx xxxx 0307
Sale:	2 x 1 gin and tonic
	1 bottle Chardonnay
Amount:	£28.16
19:24	25/6/2012

Item # 3

Blooming Lovely
17 Market Square
Framley

27 June 2012

12 red roses to be delivered to Miss Magdalene Dyer at 1 Market Square, Silverbridge

Message: 'Enjoyed our drink. Lunch tomorrow? J'

£30
Paid in cash

Item # 4

Veronica's Secret: Bras, Lingerie and Nightwear

Veronicassecret.com

Welcome to your account, Magdalene:

Shopping Basket

Plunge push-up bra	£89
Waist cincher	£78
V-string panty	£62
Total:	£229

Item # 5

The Dragon of Wantly

Gastro pub,

Barchester

Lamb shank	£16.50
Salmon en croute	£14.50
Eton Mess	£6.00
Local Cheeses and biscuits	£6.00
½ Bottle of Pouilly-Fumé	£11.00
½ Bottle of Merlot	£12.00
2 x espresso	£4.00
Subtotal:	£70.00
Service at 15%	£10.50
Total:	£80.50

Date: 28/06/2012   Time: 14:16

Item # 6

The Beeches Motel,

Boxall Hill

27 June 2012

For 1 double room,

Received from Mr Smith:

£70 paid in cash

Date: 28/06/2012   Time: 17:02

Item # 7

CARPHONE WAREHOUSE

Annesgrove

Pay As You Go Nokia 225 x 2

£29.99 paid in cash

Date: 29/06/2012   Time: 15:26

Item # 8

CROWN SPA HOTEL

THE ESPLANADE

TORQUAY

11 JULY 2012

FOR 1 SUITE, £201

ROOM SERVICE:

BOLLINGER SPECIAL CUVÉE: £65.00
SMOKED SALMON SANDWICHES: £12.95

RECEIVED FROM MR SMITH: £278.95
PAID IN CASH

Item # 9

Hello, Jolyon, we thought you would like to know that we have dispatched your item(s). Your order is on its way and can no longer be changed.

Your estimated delivery date is: 13 July – 14 July.

Your order was sent to:
Magdalene Dyer
Flat 1b,
Cosby Lodge,
33 Courcy Road,
Silverbridge

Delivery Information: Jean Patou Joy Eau de Parfum Spray 75 ml: £110

Item # 10

The Riverside Hotel
London W1

Romance Package: £550 (inclusive of VAT) based upon two people sharing, including:
One night's sumptuous accommodation in an Edwardian inspired guest room;
Flowers, fresh fruit and a bottle of Champagne in your room on arrival;
Rose petals on turndown;
English breakfast.

Item # 11

Mssrs. Harter and Benjamin

Old Bond Street

London

19 July 2012

White Gold Watch: 18ct white gold and diamonds

- 0.18ct of round, brilliant-cut diamonds

- White mother of pearl dial

- Alligator strap with pin buckle

In 18ct white gold

£9,950

To be engraved: 'M mon amour J'

Item # 12

London St Pancras Int'l to Paris Gare Du Nord

Eurostar

Departs 09:17 on Tues, 07 Aug

Arrives 12:47 on Tues, 07 Aug

Business Premier

2 x adults (£245.00)

£490.00

Paris Gare Du Nord to London St Pancras Int'l

Eurostar

Departs 16:13 on Wed, 08 Aug

Arrives 17:39 on Wed, 08 Aug

Business Premier

2 x adults (£245.00)

£490.00

Total:

£980.00

Item # 13

Le Bristol Paris

112 rue du Faubourg Saint Honoré | 8th Arr., 75008 Paris, France

8 August 2012

Suite de luxe: €990
Dom Perignon Rosé: €109
Total: €1099

Item #14

James Scuttle Motor Company Ltd
Established 1977
27–39 West Street
Exeter

17 August
Vehicle Sales Invoice:

Mr Jolyon Sleep
Ullathorne House
Barchester

Vehicle	Porsche 911 Cabriolet
Colour	Red
New/Used	New
Invoice total:	£80,169 incl. VAT
Deliver to:	

Magdalene Dyer
Flat 1b
Cosby Lodge,
33 Courcy Road,
Silverbridge

Item # 15

www.credit-edelweiss.com/uk/en/private-banking.html

Discover how we can help you. Based in Zurich we
have the expertise and experience to deal with all
your banking needs.

Get in touch to arrange a meeting, speak to an
Account Manager or request a login to access our
Investment Research through My Credit Edelweiss.

Please note: the minimum investment for clients of
Credit Edelweiss is £1 million.
Numbered accounts available.

Item # 16

Littlebitofeden.com
Idyllic Ocean View Home. Sales Price: US$599,000

Ready for a new lifestyle? Welcome to Paradise!
This 2 bedroom, 2 bathroom house has easy
access to the beachside town of Santa Teresa, a
luxurious pool measuring over 550 sq. ft., large,
open living spaces, and a manicured lawn.
Built-in A/C makes sure even the hottest Costa
Rican days are cool and comfortable. It's a bargain
you really won't want to miss!
Good connections from local airport to San José
International Airport.

Item # 17

Barsetshire Bank
Crabtree Parva,
Barsetshire

29 August 2012

Dear Mr and Mrs Sleep,

We are writing to inform you that your joint current account is overdrawn by £213.86. This deficit cannot be made good from your other accounts, which we have closed as per your instructions. We would be grateful if you would remedy this situation at your earliest convenience.

Yours sincerely,

Matthew Todd, Branch Manager

Item # 18

Harry's Hardware
Scarington
Barsetshire

For All Your DIY Needs!
We're Here To Help!

Thick bleach 5 litre
Qty: 2: £16.58
Polythene Sheeting Black 4m x 25m 500g
Qty: 1 Roll: £25
Black gaffer tape 50mm by 50m
Qty: 1 Roll: £2.30
Total: £43.88
Date: 30/8/2012   Time: 09.34

Item # 19

White Goods Warehouse
Greshamsbury Retail Park
Barsetshire
30/8/2012

Chest Freezer, capacity: 250 litres
Energy rating: A+
Width: 111 cm
Suitable for outbuildings
One-year manufacturer's warranty

£229 paid in cash

Date: 30:8:2012   Time: 14:21

Item # 20

Self-Storage Units
8 Greshamsbury Industrial Estate
Greshamsbury

30/8/2012

One standard storage unit

£25 per week:
3 months paid in advance in cash: £300

Item #21

James Finney,
16 Knowle Road
Plumstead Epsicopi
Barsetshire
Private Investigations Undertaken
Absolute Discretion Guaranteed

26 September 2012

Re: Tracing their daughter, Mrs Laura James-Sleep,
of Ullathorne House, Barchester

Last contact, 28 August 2012

Initial payment of £500 received from Mr and Mrs
James.

Item #22

Silverbridge Police Station
Custody Suite

3. 10. 2012

Received from Mr Jolyon Sleep:

- Wallet containing £160 in cash, one American
  Express card, one Visa card, one Mastercard, one
  Barsetshire Bank credit card
- Loose change to the sum of £3.86
- One Rolex watch
- One bunch of keys

Item #23

Gumption, Gazebee and Gazebee   Mr Jolyon Sleep
Solicitors   Ullathorne House,
6 Cathedral Close,   Barchester
Barchester

Our ref: FEG. PP.017566.1

4 October 2012

Dear Mr Sleep

We acknowledge receipt of your payment of £5000
as a retainer for our services. As I explained on the
telephone, we intend to employ Geoffrey Bonstock
(QC) of Borleys & Bonstock, Barristers at Law, Gray's
Inn on your behalf and will arrange a meeting at the
earliest opportunity. My assistant will send you a formal
engagement letter which will cover various issues
including further payment of fees, which we require to
be paid on a monthly basis.

Kind regards,

Yours sincerely,

Fiona E. Gazebee

Item # 24

HM Prison Wormwood Scrubs
Du Cane Rd, Shepherd's Bush London

30. 4. 2013

Receipt for clothes belonging to prisoner no. 1938394.

One suit (Gieves & Hawkes)
One white cotton shirt
One tie
One pair underpants
One pair lace-up shoes (Church's)

Item # 25

Gumption, Gazebee and Gazebee	Borleys & Bonstock
Solicitors	Barristers at Law
6 Cathedral Close,	Gray's Inn Square
Barchester	Gray's Inn
	London

30 April 2013

Dear Geoffrey,

Just to inform you that a bank transfer of £25,000 to Borleys and Bonstock has been effected, being the balance outstanding in the case of Regina V. Sleep.

I've very much enjoyed working with you again. My best regards to Mildred.

Ever yours,

Fiona

PS. You win some, you lose some. I didn't think the sentence was unduly harsh, did you?

Item # 26

THE GAZETTE
OFFICIAL PUBLIC RECORD

Bankruptcy Orders

Sleep, John Jolyon

Ullathorne House, BARCHESTER

John Jolyon Sleep, a self-employed accountant, residing
at and carrying on business at Ullathorne House,
Barchester, lately residing at H M Wormwood Shrubs
Prison, Du Cane Rd, Shepherd's Bush London, London

In the County Court at Barchester

No 76 of 1015

Date of Filing Petition: 9 May 2013

Bankruptcy order date: 10 May 2013

Time of Bankruptcy Order: 10:40

Whether Debtor's or Creditor's Petition – Debtor's

A Prichart, 3 Paradise Walk, Barchester

Capacity of office holder(s): Receiver and Manager

24 May 2013

Item # 27

Businesses for sale in Silverbridge

Popular patisserie and bakery located in Silverbridge,
Barsetshire · Town centre location · Healthy turnover and
profits · Excellent local reputation · Fantastic change of lifestyle
opportunity · Good mix of complementary businesses nearby ·
Annual turnover £45,000

Seller relocating, favourable price for fast sale.

Offers in the region of £60,000

Item # 28

www.ebay.co.uk

PORSCHE 911 CABRIOLET RED, ONE CAREFUL LADY OWNER

GREAT SPEC
£63,990

WHITE GOLD WATCH 18CT WHITE GOLD AND DIAMONDS, ALMOST NEW
£8,999

Item # 29

LUXURY TRAVEL
FIRST CLASS ALL THE WAY
WHEN ONLY THE BEST IS GOOD ENOUGH!

25.6.2013

Itinerary for

Miss Magdalene Dyer

Flight

SAT 22 JUNE   HEATHROW TO ZURICH   DEP 10.00; ARR 12.40.
BUSINESS CLASS £255

TUES 25 JUNE   ZURICH TO SAN JOSE   DEP 07.30; ARR 15.50.
BUSINESS CLASS £6,446

Please note
NO RETURN FLIGHTS REQUESTED

Travel Is Dangerous

Ed James

DS Scott Cullen dumped his tray on the table and shrugged off his leather jacket. Slouching into his seat, he tore the lid off his coffee. The Leith Walk Station canteen was a wall of white noise, enough to take cover behind. Somewhere to hide from managing a team making a mess of case preparation. Hide from his boss. Perhaps they'd all be better off if he just stayed here and played some game on his phone, maybe something to practise his anger management. He yawned then took a sip of coffee. Let the brown sauce on his fried egg roll congeal.

Bugger it. He started up *Angry Birds*.

'Morning, Sundance.' DS Brian Bain plonked down his tray opposite, the plate overflowing with a wet fry-up. Bacon, sausages, haggis, tatty scone, heaps of fried bread and hash browns, all swimming in a sea of baked beans. His breakfast looked as tired as he did. The dirty-grey stubble on his head matched the sallow skin and the fuzzy beige goatee he'd been sporting for the last few months. 'Hard to get a decent breakfast in this shite town, I fuckin' swear.'

Cullen's shoulders slumped as Bain sat, wishing the inevitable heart attack would strike the man now. He took a glug of his coffee. 'Let me guess: the choice is nowhere near as good as in Glasgow, home of sectarian violence and divine fry-ups?'

'God's own fuckin' city, Sundance.' Bain bit the end off a sausage. 'Your fault I ended up back here, anyway. Those stripes you got were mine to start with.'

'And I keep hearing about it.'

'As well you should. You disrupted the natural order of things,

Sundance.' Bain scooped a mound of beans into his mouth and chewed, somehow keeping the sludge in without once closing his lips.

'There you are.' DI Colin Methven crouched at the end of the table like a sports coach who had just tracked down two boys skipping PE. The guy was fizzing with energy. Or righteous indignation. Always hard to tell with him. His giant eyebrows bobbed up as he got a look at Bain's plate. 'Glasgow MIT have passed us a case. Body found out east this morning; looks like murder. Need you to head through and get started. I'll follow through this afternoon.'

'Nae luck, Sundance.'

'I meant both of you, Brian.' Methven stole a hash brown as he stood up. 'Be like old times, eh?'

'Don't get fresh air like this in Edinburgh, Sundance.' Bain sucked in the stale cigarette smoke on the breeze like it was perfume.

Cullen still couldn't get over working with him again. Anyone but Bain. Bloody Methven. He followed Bain over to a dark-brick lane behind a row of payday lenders, bookies and barbers. They were deep in Glasgow's banjo country.

Two bins stood against the side wall, a pair of officers rummaging around in one of them; a bright light glaring into the dull morning. Low clouds and cold winds, but it hadn't rained. Yet.

A gorilla in a suit grunted at them, presumably to stop them entering the crime scene. Looked like he lacked the opposable thumbs to work the pen and clipboard.

'Gaffer!' One of the suited figures jogged over, tearing at his mask. DC Damian McCrea, an old colleague of Bain's. Bald head and a good three stone over regulation weight. Out of breath, of course.

'Damo!' Bain grabbed him in a bearhug. Started singing 'The Boys Are Back in Town', but McCrea broke free halfway through the chorus and did a double-take at Cullen. 'Christ, you brought the village idiot?'

'And you're more than enough for a whole city, Damian.' Cullen gave him a tense grin, trying but failing to hide his rage. 'Are you bin raking?'

'For my sins.' McCrea thumbed behind him. 'The body's in the other one.'

'I want to call it a dumpster, Sundance, but...' Bain reached for a set of ladders and started clambering up. 'It's just a big fuckin' bin, right?'

McCrea was back rooting around in its neighbour, tossing evidence bags on the brick paving, chain of evidence clearly not troubling him.

Bain reached the top and peered inside. 'Fuck me.' Less swagger in his step as he shimmied down. 'Here, Sundance, you take a peek.'

Cullen shot up the ladder. Almost lost his egg roll from the bleach stink wafting out the top. A middle-aged man lay on his side in the foetal position, naked except for a pink nappy. Some clear liquid spread halfway up the torso, giving the pale skin a sheen.

'Hoy!' Down the lane, a masked figure waved a fist at Cullen. A woman and a very, very angry one at that. 'Get down, you hooligan!' The nasal rasp of a local, distinct even through the crime-scene mask.

Cullen took his time getting down.

When he reached the bottom, she was shouting at Bain, who merely nodded. 'Absolutely shocking who they let into crime scenes these days, darlin'.'

'DS Scott Cullen.' He flashed his warrant card. 'DI Methven sent us from Edinburgh.'

'Oh.' She tore off her mask. 'Dr Rachel Flockhart.' Ruby-red lipstick and pale-white skin, a curl of ginger hair poking out of her cap. 'I'm the pathologist.'

Bain pulled down his own mask. 'Pleasure to meet you, darlin'.'

'Do you mind not calling me that?' Flockhart put her mask back in place. 'Now, I've got a body to inspect.'

'So I found that bloke, eh?' Steven Wright was leaning against a wall, his South African accent slicing through the city drone. Topless, showing off a dragon tattoo that crawled over his muscular torso. He shifted his attention to Bain. 'Hey, you fancy not checking me out, mate?'

'You fancy putting on a top?'

'Never wear one, eh?' Wright folded his arms, making a show of flexing his biceps. 'Be a crime to hide these babe magnets. Not that you'd know.'

Cullen held up a hand to stop Bain. 'You working today?'

'Tuesday's brown-bin day, mate. All the fucking garden waste, eh?' Wright nodded over at the crime scene. 'Thursday's for the dumpsters.'

Bain sniffed. 'That what they're called, aye?' He flicked an eyebrow at Cullen.

Cullen just turned a page in his notebook. 'So, if today's brown-bin day, why were you looking in dumpsters?'

'I check them just in case some fucker's put a tin of fucking paint in. Happens all the fucking time, mate.' His expression darkened, he even seemed to shiver. 'Anyway, I found the fella in there this morning. Fucking weirdest thing I ever saw, mate, and I saw some shit in Jo'burg, you know?'

Cullen didn't know. Didn't want to know.

Wright patted his shoulder. 'You mind if I get on, mate? These brown bins won't clear themselves, eh?'

'Tell you, Sundance, I've fuckin' seen everything now.' Bain shook his head as they walked back to the crime scene. 'A sexy binman. In my day, they were all big, fat hoofers with drink problems.'

A charcoal Range Rover blocked in Cullen's car, the engine idling, the window rolled down. Methven, looking like he was kerb crawling. Dr Flockhart was leaning against the door, shaking out her long red hair.

Methven waved over at them. 'You getting anywhere, gentlemen?'

'Aye, give us a minute, Col, eh?' Bain rested against the bonnet. 'Thought you were coming this afternoon?'

'Called in a few favours. Rachel's running the post mortem now.'

As if on cue, a pair of pathology workers pushed a gurney carrying a body bag up to the bin.

Bain smiled at Dr Flockhart, stroking his goatee. 'You find anything that might help us, darlin'?'

She stepped away from Methven's window, eyes narrowing at Bain. 'The victim died last night. Livor mortis suggests he's been in situ for a good ten hours. I've not been up close and personal yet, but it appears his throat's been slit. And not by a professional.' She dragged a pale finger across her own, as if they needed any reminding. 'The nappy was most likely on when he died. I had a … a little prod. It's heavily soiled.'

Cullen frowned back at the bin as the two pathologists humped the body out. He tried to reconstruct the chain of events. Couldn't get anywhere.

'It's likely your killer's a pervert.' Flockhart's turn to frown as Bain burst out laughing. Didn't seem to be the reaction she was looking for. 'Either way, that liquid he's in? Bleach. You're not getting any forensics off the body.'

That elusive chain of events slipped even further out of reach.

Flockhart got in Methven's Chelsea tractor.

'I'll be in touch.' Methven gunned the engine and tore off with screeching tyres.

Bain flashed the Vs at the disappearing SUV. 'Prick.'

Cullen couldn't help but laugh. 'Not many things I agree with you about.' Didn't stop him wishing Methven clocked the insult.

'Hoy!' DC Damian McCrea was charging towards them, grinning as manically as he was panting. 'What did you think? Pretty sick, right?'

Bain looked like he was going to be. 'Aye.'

'Someone's been date-raping men and women for months, trussing them up in nappies. First murder, mind.'

'Any idea who the victim is, Damo?'

McCrea waved an evidence bag in Bain's face. 'Found this in the other bin.'

Cullen snatched it off him. A wallet, with a driver's licence.

Paul Skinner lived in a Victorian villa, a storey-and-a-half of beige stone with a row of pot plants in the front garden, a cream bay window poking out from behind.

'Nice pad, Sundance.' Bain strolled up the front path, whistling, hands in his pockets like he was taking a stroll around the annual flower show, rather than visiting a murder victim's home. 'You want to have a wee practice at giving a death message?'

'Assuming the victim wasn't single, are you? Very professional.'

'If you'd looked close enough, you'd have seen that the guy had a ring on. His wife will need comforting.' Bain stopped outside the door. 'You up to it, Sundance?'

Cullen just thumped on the door and waited, resenting his failure to have noticed that obvious clue. The crime scene must've stunned him more than he wanted Bain to know. He'd never hear the end of it if he found out…

'You ignoring me?'

'Let's just get this over with, aye?'

The door opened. A thin man in his forties peered out through thick glasses. 'Lads, not this malarkey again.' His accent was half Glasgow, half Dublin. 'I've no time to talk about the Lord Jesus in the middle of the day.' He pulled the door back.

Bain kicked his foot in the way, blocking it, and thrust his warrant card in his face. 'We're police, sir, not Jehovah's Witnesses. Looking to speak to someone about a Paul Skinner.'

'He's my husband.' Red eyes flicked between them. 'My name's Gavin. Gavin Crossan.'

'Right.' A frown danced across Bain's forehead. 'Have you seen him today?'

Crossan clasped his hands together and dipped his head, like he was praying. 'Not since yesterday. He … didn't come home. Why do you ask?'

'That a common occurrence?'

Crossan frowned at Cullen. 'What's he done?'

'Mr Crossan, I'm afraid your husband has … passed away.'

📌

'Thank you.' Crossan took the cup from Cullen like it contained his husband's ashes.

Cullen poured out tea, then another one for Bain and slid it across the table. Looked like the crockery was from the Queen. So ornate it was hideous, and yet the front room was tastefully done, all beiges and browns.

'We were out at a party last night,' Crossan went on. 'It was good craic like, until…' He took a sip, then looked at each of them in turn. 'This is really hard for me.'

Bain was scowling. 'Just get—'

'It's OK, sir.' Cullen blew on his tea. 'Take your time. Start with the last time you saw him.'

Crossan took a deep breath. 'We were both there. At this party, yeah?' He let out the breath. 'And we went home with … with different men.'

Bain spluttered out tea. 'You were at an orgy?'

'It's not a crime. Everyone consented.'

'Just sayin', pal, you need to be careful.'

'We're both on PrEP. And besides, HIV isn't what it used to be when I came out. It's not a death sentence anymore.'

Bain put his cup down with a snarl, as if he could catch AIDS from drinking tea.

Cullen leaned forwards in his chair. 'Who did he go home with?'

'I don't know. I came back here.' Crossan dabbed at his eyes. 'I don't know where Paul went.'

'Can you at least tell us where the party was?'

📌

Cullen got out of his car and leaned against its side, waiting for Bain to finish his call. Another Victorian villa, but this one was in Bearsden, a twee suburb on the other side of the city – Glasgow's answer to Edinburgh's Morningside. Disco lights pumped out of an upstairs bedroom in time to The Killers. Bet the neighbours loved this house.

Bain's car door slammed. 'The victim's a fuckin' poof, Sundance. Can you believe it?'

Cullen set off towards the house. 'Was that Methven?'

'Who else?' Bain pocketed his phone and started across the road. 'He's a bummer, as well, isn't he?'

'Jesus, would it hurt your macho soul to quit with the homophobia? You sound like Roy Chubby Brown.'

Bain gave him a fierce look. Then it softened. 'Fuckin' love that guy. Absolute legend.'

Way, way beyond saving. Cullen stormed up the path to the house. Upstairs, The Killers segued into Erasure. He doubted anyone could hear him knock on the door. Thirty seconds later, nobody had. 'Stay there.' He left Bain at the door and peered in through the front window.

Two men lay on an L-shaped Chesterfield, both wearing dressing gowns, feet resting on a duck-egg blue coffee table. Both had dark rings around their eyes.

Cullen knocked the glass and waved.

One of them started like he'd been shot. Then got to his feet and left the room. The front door had opened by the time Cullen made it there. Erasure had stopped playing, but the lights still flashed.

The man stepped out onto the steps, barefoot. A thick garden of chest hair poked out of his dressing gown. Cullen clocked the wedding ring this time.

'Can I help?' Working-class Glasgow accent.

Bain held out his warrant card. Looked like he was going the full Judge Dredd. 'Need a word, sir.'

'If it's about the noise, I can—'

'It's about Paul Skinner.'

'Dave Farrelly.' He held out his hand. Bain didn't shake it, just looked at it like he was afraid it had touched more penises than hands since it'd last been washed. 'I know Paul. What's he done?'

'Gavin Crossan said they were at a party here last night.' Bain peered inside the house. 'Is that poppers I can smell?'

Farrelly ignored him. 'Gav and I go back a while. What's up?'

'Paul's dead.'

Farrelly threw his hands in the air, then clutched his chest. 'Oh, Christ.'

'So were you—'

Cullen stepped forward, trying to get in Bain's way before he could commit a hate crime. 'We understand he went home with a man. You know who?'

'Come in, come in.' Before Cullen could protest, Farrelly had slipped inside the house, his feet slapping across the stripped-wood flooring.

Cullen followed him into the front room. Loud, rasping snores greeted them from the sofa.

Farrelly nudged the man lying there. 'Paul went home with a friend of Marcus's.' He nudged him again.

The man blinked awake. Looked like a hairy potato stuffed into a silk gown. A matching platinum ring, though. Took a second to get his bearings, then he jolted upright and a part of him flopped out from under his dressing gown. 'What's up?' He frowned at the two cops and calmly tucked himself back in. 'Oh, Christ.' Held out a hand. 'Marcus Pretorius.' Sounded like he was from New Zealand. Scratch that. With a name like that, he was another South African.

Farrelly took a seat next to him. 'Marcus, who did Paul go home with last night?'

'It wasn't his husband, I know that ... What's his name?' Pretorius clicked his fingers a few times. 'That Jo'burg scumbag, what's his bloody name? The one with the dragon tattoo and all those lovely muscles.'

Cullen pulled up in the Recycling Centre car park and wedged his car between an old Audi and a VW camper van festooned with stickers from around the world. Quick check for any South African ones. None. Right, onwards. Like everything in Glasgow – the massive IKEA just over the roundabout, for instance – the site was three times the size of its Edinburgh equivalent.

A bin lorry hurtled past, two binmen hanging off the back, gloved hands clutching on tight. Looked like extreme sports types, baseball caps on backwards. It pulled into a depot, the rest of its activities hidden.

Cullen clocked a guy who looked like a foreman standing by a metallic-grey box, its roof corner turned up like a hipster's haircut. The man's acid-yellow safety jacket screamed like a flash of sunshine.

Then Cullen's phone went. Bain. 'Right, Sundance, I'm at this boy's address. Heading in now. You got anything?'

'Give me a minute.'

'What's keeping you? You've had half a fuckin' hour. Keep me updated.'

Click.

Cullen looked at his dead phone. What a pointless call. As pointless as Bain.

The supervisor was wandering over, pulling his gloves off. 'Can't park there, mate.'

Cullen showed his warrant card. 'Need a word with Steven Wright.'

'Aye, good luck with that.' He thrust out a hand so mucky he might as well not have bothered with the gloves. 'Jim Parrott. I'm his supervisor. Good worker. Shame about that topless shite, but what can you do?'

'Need to speak to him about the body he found this morning. He around?'

'What, you think he did it?'

Cullen looked at him, a question stinging the tip of his tongue: *What do you think? He went home with the victim.*

Deep breath. Instead of sharing his thoughts, he smiled. 'Just a few follow-up questions.'

'Aye, well, like I said, good luck. He pissed off home about an hour ago. Said he couldn't cope with the stress. First time he's found a body.'

'Happen often?'

'Once every couple of years.' Parrott tugged one of his work gloves back on. 'Found three myself. Tramps are the worst.'

'Thanks.' Cullen set off back towards his car. When he was out of earshot, he called Bain. It rang. Then it kept ringing and ringing and ringing. 'Shite.' He started running.

Cullen thumped on the door again and stepped back.

Wright lived in a council flat in Craigton, a beige box of misery. As if to make things worse, it was downwind of the crematorium, which for once wasn't burning, so instead the area stank of dog shit and fumes from a nearby factory.

No answer. He tried again, same result.

He checked his phone. Still nothing from Bain. He called him again. The faintest sound whispered out of the downstairs window: *The boys are back in town…*

Shite.

Cullen launched himself at the door, shoulder first. Ploughed it down, slid across shiny laminate, scrambled back to his feet. The flat was baking. He glanced around, saw a thermostat on the wall. Thirty degrees. Shot another glance down the hall. The two doors off it were open. Bain's ringtone chimed from the one on the left.

Cullen stormed in and stopped.

A bedroom, the walls covered in pictures of musclebound men and women.

Bain lay on the bed, eyes rolling round in his head, naked except for a nappy. 'Sundance, I fuckin' love you!'

What the hell?

CLATTER.

Came from the other room.

Cullen darted back out into the hall, then into a living room, a tiny kitchen in the corner. The window was open, dirty yellow blinds flapping in the breeze.

Cullen hurtled towards the window and clambered out into a yard.

Wright was crouched on top of a brick wall at the far end, looking like he was about to drop down the other side. He glanced back the way. 'Fuck!' And he was gone.

Cullen bombed across the cracked concrete and jumped at the wall, grabbing the top with stinging palms. Felt like his arms were going to tear. He pulled harder, cleared the top and came to a swaying stand on the narrow brickwork. Catching his breath, he scanned round for Wright.

No sign of him.

Shite.

Just a yard at the back of a factory, machines hissing away inside, a row of bins, some parked forklifts and a gang of workmen standing around, eating from Greggs bags.

Where the hell was he?

Shite, shite, shite.

Cullen lowered himself into a crouch and dropped off the wall, landing with a thud. He powered on towards the workies, warrant card already out. 'Police! Have you seen a man come this way?'

Just got shaking heads.

Shite.

Cullen scanned around. *Where would he go?*

Aha.

He stopped by the row of bins. 'I know you're in there.'

Nothing.

'I'll just search these, one by one.' He kicked the first.

A cough came from the far end.

Cullen went over and shook it. 'Get out, now.'

'Fuck off!'

Cullen wheeled the bin out and tipped it over.

Steven Wright tumbled out in a cloud of sawdust. 'I want a fucking lawyer!'

Bain lay in his hospital bed, the sheet pulled up to his neck. 'Fuck me, Sundance, feels like someone's skull-fucked me with a nail gun.'

'Rohypnol.' The doctor tossed a tub of pills at him. 'The effects have just about worn off. Keep taking one every hour, on the hour.'

'So, I can get out of here?'

'There'll be no lasting damage, so yes.' The doctor smiled at Cullen. 'Your friend here has to supervise you, though.'

'Babysit him, more like.'

'Quite.' The doctor opened the curtains and left them to it.

'You mind turning round, Sundance?' Bain twirled his fingers. 'Need to get dressed.'

Cullen complied, getting a good view of the rest of the ward through a crack in the curtains. 'Need to change your nappy?'

'See if anyone hears about this, you're fuckin' dead. OK?'

'You're asking me to keep it out of my report?'

'Sundance … don't make me beg.'

'What happened?'

'What do you think?' Bain was huffing and puffing behind him. Probably trying to remember how to tie his shoelaces. 'I went in, asked the boy a few questions. Next thing I know, you're standing over me and the room's spinning.'

'You remember telling me you loved me?'

'Fuck off, Sundance.'

'You did.'

'Fuck. Off.'

'So, did you drink a cup of his tea, or what?'

Bain coughed. 'Might've done.'

'You're an idiot.'

'You caught him, right?'

'He's in your old nick, waiting for his lawyer.'

Bain huffed behind Cullen. 'Anyway, you think Wright is a lust murderer?'

'Explain?'

'Trusses his victims in nappies. Makes them easier to dispose of.'

'You think he lusted after you?'

'Sundance, I fucking swear—'

The curtain swooshed open. Methven stood there, scowling. 'Jesus, Brian, put it away.'

Cullen turned round.

Bain was putting his shirt on, his distended belly hanging over his trousers. 'Afternoon, Col. How's tricks?'

Methven shook his head, shutting his eyes like he was trying to expel the image from his head. 'Christ, Brian, what have you been up to?'

'Nothin'.' Bain shot a glare at Cullen. 'And if anyone says any different, I'll fuckin' kill them.'

Cullen waited until Bain was bending over to tie his shoelaces before he leaned in close. 'I found him roofied and wearing a nappy.'

Methven wagged a finger at Cullen. 'Those in glass houses, Sergeant.'

'Sorry, sir.'

'Anyway,' Methven frowned at Bain, as he stood up tall, 'the PM's finished and Rachel's checking something out for me. In the meantime, I just got a call. Mr Wright's ready and waiting for his interview.'

Cullen got up from his seat to move away from DC McCrea. He stank of rubbish, almost as bad as Steven Wright did. He paced around the interview room instead then leaned against the wall. 'Why were you running, Mr Wright?'

'I said "no comment", mate.'

'OK. Sure it wasn't because you'd drugged and trussed up my colleague in your bedroom?'

His lawyer looked up from his silvery tablet computer. 'My client has reminded you of his wish to remain silent. I believe you are duty-bound to respect that, hmm?'

Cullen switched his attention from the lawyer to Wright, waiting for him to look up. 'What were you going to do to my colleague? Rape him like you did Paul Skinner?'

McCrea leaned round and whispered, 'We don't—'

Cullen's glare shut him up.

'You not listening, eh? No comment, mate.'

'Well, the circumstantial evidence is quite compelling. You drugged him and dressed him in a nappy. You were going to rape him, weren't you?'

'No comment.'

'DC McCrea told me about a few similar crimes. Men and women date-raped and dressed in nappies.'

Wright hammered the table. 'Fuck off!'

Getting somewhere now.

'Feels like it's the same person, maybe they're escalating. Got tired of emptying people's bins, so you started raping them, did you? Then you got a bit bored with that, too, and went on to binning them off once and for all. Discovered a taste for killing. That about right?'

'It wasn't me, mate!'

A knock at the door. It cracked open. Methven's monster eyebrows came into view, along with his finger, beckoning Cullen out.

'Interview paused at 15:23.' Cullen left the room and pulled the door shut behind him. 'Sir?'

Methven propped himself against the wall. 'How do you think it's going, Sergeant?'

Bain was next to Methven, silently fuming, fists clenched.

'You've been watching it, so you'll know how badly. Just about started getting a reaction, sir, but he's not the sort to just spill his guts or take all the credit without a bit of goading.'

'Well,' Methven sighed and jangled the keys in his pockets. 'I just received a call from Dr Flockhart. Rachel's finished tying up the loose ends. She's confirmed that the knife wound was inflicted post mortem.'

Cullen frowned at Bain, then back at Methven. 'What?'

'The actual cause of death was a heart attack.'

'You're serious?'

Methven nodded. 'I had her discuss her findings with Jimmy Deeley in Edinburgh. While he's obviously not seen the body, he agrees with the logic, so I'm keen to see what our boy in there has got to say about that. Chop, chop, no time to lose, yes?' He slipped off back towards the Obs Suite.

Bain stepped forward. 'Sundance, can you keep a fuckin' lid on it, eh? Not everyone wants to hear about my … about what happened.'

'Don't get your nappy in a twist.'

Bain lurched forwards. 'Fuckin' told you!'

Cullen grabbed his wrists tight. 'It's part of the case, OK? Get over it.'

Cullen let go and went back into the interview room. He restarted the recorder. 'Interview recommenced at 15:29.' He took his seat and waited until Wright looked up at him. 'So, turns out the cause of death for Mr Skinner wasn't the knife wound.'

'What?'

'That happened post mortem. Turns out he died of a heart attack.'

Wright stared at his lawyer for a few seconds, then at Cullen. 'No comment.'

'Sure about that?' Cullen left him a few seconds. 'Because, as it stands, you're going to be charged with a load of rapes. Five, is it, Damian?'

McCrea cleared his throat. 'Five, plus this one. And another attempted at lunchtime there. Let's call it seven.'

'And we're obviously going to charge you with the murder of Paul Skinner.'

'But it wasn't me!'

'Heard it all before.' Cullen sat back in his chair. 'Tell me, who was it, then?'

'I can't…'

'What happened?'

'No comment.'

Back there again. Just when we were getting somewhere.

'Mr Wright, like DC McCrea said, you'll be prosecuted for the rapes. By my calculations, that'll be probably ten years inside.' Cullen flashed a grin at Wright as he glanced up. 'I know, it's hardly anything for what you've done. But when you add in this murder, that's a life sentence. And given that there's a clear escalation from rape to murder, I suspect the judge'll make it two, just to send out a message to other filthy reprobates like you. So, you're not getting out. Ever. Unless…'

'Unless what?'

'Look, if it wasn't you, now's the time to tell us who actually killed him, OK?'

'No fucking comment, mate.'

Cullen let out a sigh. *He's not going down without a fight.* 'Let me get this straight, then. You were at a sex party. After all the fun and games, you went home with Paul Skinner. Next thing we know, he's in a bin, soaked in bleach and dressed in a nappy.'

'It's a fucking dumpster, mate.'

'Whatever. *You* put him there. Dressed him in a nappy. Slashed his throat after he had a heart attack. Was it the fear? You drugged him, dressed him as a baby and, what? His heart just stopped?'

'It wasn't me, man! Someone was fucking this guy and he had a fucking heart attack!'

'Who else did you go home with?'

'I didn't fucking go home with fucking anyone!' The lawyer gripped his wrist, but Wright shook him off. 'Now I'm getting blamed for this murder?'

'You're saying he died at the party?'

'Fucking heart attack, mate. Right there.' Wright let out a deep breath, like he'd been holding in the truth along with all the air. 'He died, and one of the guys said we needed to cover it up, pretend like he was fucking murdered, eh? Told *me* to do it.'

'And you just went along with it?'

'Didn't have a choice, man.'

'Because they knew about you raping people?'

'They cut his throat, man!' Wright stared at the desk. 'Fucking hell! Tried to make it look like he was murdered. We dumped his body, made it look like someone had just left him there.'

'And that somebody would be the person who's been raping all these men and women?'

'Told me that, if I found the body, I'd look innocent, right?' Wright let his head slump forwards. 'Those fucking prawns, man, they fucking grassed me up, eh? Fucking told you that I took him home.' He slammed his fist onto the table. Looked like it hurt, too. 'Fuck those guys. I mean, I'm just a fucking binman. You'll not fucking believe them over me, eh?'

Cullen sat back and folded his arms. 'No comment.'

'After that guy's husband went home, he started fucking him, man. Aggressively. Pinned him down. Started strangling him. Wouldn't stop. All of them just watched, man. Wouldn't stop until … until he fucking died, man.'

Cullen held his gaze. Wouldn't look away. 'So, who is he?'

Wright snarled. 'Guy I know from South Africa. Marcus Pretorius.'

Cullen checked through the front window of Dave Farrelly's house. Empty. He spoke into his Airwave radio: 'Clear at the front. Serial Bravo?'

'Clear at back.'

'Alpha?'

'Inside, Sarge.' McCrea, out of breath as ever. 'It's clear. Looks like they've gone.'

'Shite.' Cullen glanced at Methven. Looked like he was going to blow a fuse any second now. 'Anything on them?'

'Hang on, Sarge.'

Cullen gripped the Airwave tight. Felt like it might crack.

'Aye, found something. He's left a plane boarding pass on the printer. Flights for Farrelly and Pretorius.'

Cullen ran through the departures lounge at the airport, clutching his Airwave to his mouth: 'Have you got hold of them yet?'

'Negative.'

Cullen picked up his pace, tearing across the carpet floor behind Methven. The departures board read, 'Gate 10 >>> Closing'.

He sprinted past Gate 8, then bumped through the queue at Gate 9, winding out onto the walkway, and taking a large suitcase like a hurdle in a steeplechase.

Gate 10 looked ominously empty, just the ground staff speaking into handsets, yawning into fists.

Cullen skidded to a halt next to the desk. 'I need … to get … that flight…'

'Sir, the plane is taxiing. It's too late.'

'Pretorius and Farrelly.' Cullen sucked in breath. 'They're wanted for murder.'

She frowned at a screen. 'I'm sorry, but—'

The door behind her rattled open. Two burly security guards pushed Pretorius and Farrelly out, each with an arm wrapped tightly around a suspect's neck. 'All yours, gents.'

Cullen stood against the back wall of the Obs Suite, his legs aching with lactic acid. Not run like that in ages.

Methven and Bain were chatting in front of him.

On the screen, McCrea and another local were interviewing Farrelly.

Methven put the interview on mute. 'Well, gentlemen, it looks like we've managed to persuade Mr Farrelly to turn in his partner. That's enough evidence to support a conviction, I'd warrant. Mr Pretorius will be going away for a long time.'

'Cheers, Col.' Bain cracked his knuckles. 'All in a day's work for me.'

Cullen glowered at him. 'You wear a nappy every day?'

'Fuck off, Sundance.'

Methven laughed, shaking his head. 'You two should work together more often.'

Take the Money and Run?

Gordon Brown

The fishing boats trail each other, heading towards the harbour. Prows high, sterns low, bellies full of fish. The sun, past its zenith, has seared the land, boiled the sea – in old money the temperature is tickling ninety degrees. I'm a walking lake of sweat and suntan lotion as I stroll along the breakwater, watching the first of the line of fishing boats as it eases down on the throttle to enter the harbour; men moving on board with measured effort, used to the world of warmth, stirring slowly, preparing to off their cargo.

The boat slides past a row of berthed pleasure craft, sheltering from the Mediterranean, the wash creating a chain reaction that resembles dominoes toppling as each vessel, in turn, bobs on the wake.

A man, high on the mast of a small yacht, clings on as waves bump into his boat's hull – swinging his perch – the movement far more violent than he is comfortable with. He sees the other fishing boats queuing up to enter the harbour and decides that the deck of his boat is a more sensible place to sit out the shining fleet's arrival. He slides down the mast.

A young man and woman, strolling hand in hand, are walking towards me. Their hands fall apart. I hear them talk in a mix of Spanish and Valencian as they watch the fishing boats arrive. I can't speak either language but I have an ear for some of the key words. Around here people interchange the two languages as easily as the ambidextrous switch hands. The couple glance at me as we pass.

I look ahead. A small lighthouse, green, fading to mint in the sun, sits at the end of the breakwater. Fifteen feet high, its sister, red bleached to pink, is standing proud on the opposite side of the harbour entrance. The two structures guardians of the haven.

I climb the stairs to the plinth on which the green lighthouse rests. I walk round it and the bay opens up in front of me. I take in the vista, scanning from right to left. The harbour dissolves into the buildings of the port, which, in turn give way to a pebble beach dotted with temporary bars, bars that will be dismantled at the end of the season and packed away to wait on another year. The rocky shore, stretching in an arc, is lined with properties looking to the sea, no discernible pattern or reason to their form or design. As the beach ends, the Arenal rises, an area of bars, restaurants and dwellings that huddle around a small, sandy beach. The bay curves to a conclusion with more villas and flats, before cliffs rise up to bookend the cliffs behind me.

Behind the port, up on the hill, sits the old town, the *pueblo,* a maze of traditional Spain basking in the sun. My accommodation lies in there. Behind the old town, a mighty beast sleeps. The Montgó. Nearly two-and-a-half thousand feet high, it lords it over the valley. Pushed up by tectonic plates seventy million years ago, it resembles, from one side, an elephant. Its vast trunk falling towards the town. A cave its eye. The top of its head often sitting in cloud. A few days ago, I'd stood up there, a four-hour climb behind me, realising, not for the first time, that the fitness of my youth had been drained away by good living and the elapsing years.

I swing myself onto the concrete wall that surrounds the small lighthouse, dangling my legs over the giant concrete blocks that protect the breakwater from the sea. Below me a couple of men are drinking beer, fishing poles embedded in the blocks, chewing the cud about something or other.

I lean back on my arms, face up to the sun, eyes closed, soaking in the rays, knowing my time here is coming to an end.

A few hours later I'm sitting outside a bar in the old town, sipping at a beer. Something I can ill afford. My bank balance is in a critical state. At home, in the UK, my parents' house waits for me. The unescapable consequence of being skint. A book lies unopened on the table next to me, my sunglasses perched on top. The bar is busy with early-evening locals and visitors gearing up for a Friday night. As with everything around here there's no freneticism to this. Just a quiet sense of satisfaction that life is good.

The café sits at the top of a square the size of a couple of decent tennis courts. One side is open to the cobbled road that rumbles through the centre of town. A sister bar sits at the bottom of the square. The post office, *correos*, hides in the shade on the final side, the local men hanging around next to it, sitting on dark benches while putting everyone else's world to rights. Trees provide the square with sun cover and cool the eye. People stroll through the thick, liquid air.

I've grown attached to this bar. I'll miss it. I've even thought about asking for a job. But with no Spanish, I'd struggle.

I have a notion to open up my own place. A notion without the means.

Around me, getting high on caffeine or cool on alcohol, I hear the babble of French, German, Dutch, Russian, English. The young couple who I saw on the breakwater earlier are sitting in the same bar, still flipping languages. She smiles at me before returning to the conversation with her partner. I pick up my novel.

Ten minutes later the table next to me, just vacated by an older man and his friend, is taken by a man wearing a Panama hat. He orders a *café con leche* from the waitress. I catch the waitress's eye. '*Una cerveza más.*' It's about as far as my Spanish, and money, goes. I focus my eyes back on the book, trying to lose myself.

'Excuse me.' The man with the Panama hat is talking to the waitress. His face is tanned but free of wrinkles. The dominating feature is his nose, a hooked, twisted appendage that would sit well on one of Macbeth's witches. His accent is hard to place. I'm from Scotland and I'm not thinking he's from the UK.

The waitress approaches him. '*Sí.*'

'Is the market on tomorrow?'

'*Sí,*' she replies.

The waitress places my beer on the table. '*Gracias,*' I say.

'*De nada,*' she replies.

The Panama man adjusts his hat, tipping it forwards on his head. I saw him do that as he sat down. It's probably a nervous habit. He leans on an elbow, tipping his hat again. He pulls his chair back. I avoid eye contact. I'm not keen on company. I've been flying solo since I arrived here and don't want to break the pattern.

He adjusts his hat once more.

I tackle my beer, not wanting to contemplate what lies in the future.

The waitress brings the Panama man's coffee. I sip my beer slowly, conscious that he is looking in my direction. I can feel his eyes. I turn and discover that he's looking at something else. Over my shoulder, down the hill. He sees me looking and lifts his coffee as he looks away.

A few minutes later he rises, leaving money on the table.

I sit for an hour, stretching the beer so far that I fear I'll be thrown out for vagrancy. But that won't happen here. People are too chilled, and the café has tables to spare.

The Panama man appears again, this time from the street opposite, he looks down the road, down the hill again, and, after a moment, heads back the way he came. Ten minutes later he reappears, still looking down the hill. It's as if he's waiting for someone and knows that they will be coming from that direction. Before my hour is up he's appeared and disappeared four more times.

I pay the bill and leave.

The next morning I wake late. Thursday: the market will have taken over the old town – stalls stretching from the square where I sat last night, down through Plaza de la Constitución, a sizeable slab of concrete with underground parking, before dropping to another square. Name your wares and you can purchase them from the Thursday market. Leather goods, clothes, kitchenware, ornaments, hats, vegetables, fruit, meat, dildos. A few of the stalls are tourist traps, but most are geared up for savvy locals. I usually go for a stroll. Soaking up the vibe. Window shopping with no windows. A coffee the reward for my exploration – sitting, people-watching, a loadstone of curiosity burning in me.

It's closing in on noon before I get to the market. Prime time. The usual mix of home and away punters. My favourite café sits at the bottom corner of Plaza de la Constitución. I have my book with me. I'll not read it. The world around me is more interesting. The sun is already scorching my head.

I rise after an hour and I'm halfway down the thoroughfare that links the two parts of the market when I hear an alarm. It's coming from the main street.

I'm twenty yards from the intersection with the main street when a man rushes into view. Head down, he starts up the hill. He's carrying a large black holdall. He's heading straight for me. I sidestep left. He goes right. We collide. He drops the bag. His hooked nose inches from my face. Recognition zips across the Panama man's eyes. A young woman, pushing a pram, tries to squeeze through, jamming the bag against the wall.

Two police officers hurl around the corner. The Panama man gets up. He reaches for the bag but the lady's pram is in the way.

One of the police officers shouts out. The Panama man looks back, eyes wild. He glances at the bag and runs.

I turn to see where he's going. I see his back for a second more before he vanishes into the crowd. The police officers run out onto the road, dodging the pedestrians. Their focus is on the Panama man. They sprint past me, ignoring the bag. The lady with the pram moves on. I yank the bag towards me with my foot.

A *señora mayor*, pushing a fully laden trolley, taps my shoulder. '*Perdón.*' She points to the bag. It's blocking the pavement. I look to the street corner, waiting for more police to appear. Two men are standing there, looking at me. Both are dressed in black t-shirts and black jeans. One with short, bleach-blonde hair, the other sporting dreadlocks. The old lady repeats herself as the two men continue to stare at me. When she speaks a third time I reach down and move the bag to one side. She tuts and walks by.

The two men are still watching me.

I stand, my feet inches from the bag, a river of humanity surging around me.

The sound of the alarm cuts through everything. The two men in black are statues on the corner.

I glance at the bag, wondering what's in it.

The buildings on either side of the street provide shelter from the sun. A cool breeze, rushing from the mountain, breathes across the baking concrete. No one but the two men in black seem interested in me. I push the bag with my foot, crushing it back against the wall. There had to be a reason the Panama man was running with it. Running *from* the police.

I consider taking the bag back to the corner of the street. See what's going down. Check out the alarm – it has to be related. But the men on the corner still have me fixed in their gaze.

I look back to see if the police or the Panama man have reappeared. Nothing.

The alarm dies and the men in black vanish.

I bend down, trying to watch the corner, behind me, and the bag, all at the same time. The bag's zips are closed at the top, but a tiny gap, where they fail to meet, is filled with a familiar colour. I stand up. Look around. I know euros when I see them. Money. The bag has money in it.

I push the side of the bag with my foot again. It's full.

Full of money?

My mother's voice invades the moment. A phone conversation from the other night: '*So, son, have you done wasting your time out there? There's no more cash from our end. It's time to come home. Time to get a job.*'

I'm forty-three and, after a messy divorce, dependent on my mother and father for cash. This trip: a holiday they paid for; a holiday I have extended. Missing my flight home. Claiming I was ill. Laid up. A whining plea for more money met, but with reluctance. That money has leaked away.

I can visualise the door to my childhood bedroom. My mum having made up my bed. She'll have placed my teddy bear, Crank, on the pillow for me, ready for my home-coming.

I finger the bag's handle, pulling it up, feeling the weight.

Heavy.

The people around me are oblivious to the bag, to my thoughts. There's still no sign of anyone else. The men in black have not returned.

How much could a bag like this hold?

I turn away from the street corner, facing up the hill, back the way I came. Bag in hand.

One step. I realise that I just need to take one step. A step to something very different.

Just walk away.

Who saw the bag being dropped? The lady with the pram wasn't interested, neither was the *señora mayo*r with the trolley – they both just wanted to get past. The police were focused on the Panama man – not the bag.

Only the men in black showed any interest, and they've gone.

I take the step.

📌

I return to my flat, positive that I've been followed. I slump onto the worn sofa. Armed police are about to storm in and take me down.

Only that's not what happens. I hear the neighbours argue. I hear a dog whine. A car grinds gears. My A/C hums. If the armed response unit are around, they're chilling, taking their siesta.

I place the bag on the coffee table. It's a new bag, the mark where the price sticker has been removed still visible. I want to open it. I *need* to open it. I think CSI and dig around the kitchen for some form of gloves. The best I can come up with is cling film. I wrap my hands in the stuff. It takes four attempts before I create something that allows me to move my fingers.

I unzip the bag with my fingertips. I stare in. The brief glimpse in the street didn't lie. Cash – a lot of cash. The bag is brimfull with banded wedges of bank notes. I lift one out, flick through it. All tens. The band says one thousand. I count out the bundles. Two hundred and ten. I lay them on the table in neat rows. Two hundred and ten thousand euros.

Fly under Spanish immigration radar and there's enough there for a good few years of luxury.

Only not here. Not this apartment. Not this town. The thought flashes through my mind: *How hard will it be to track me down?* Someone will remember me. Later, when the police release a statement. Someone will have seen me walk away, bag in hand. The men in black?

I wonder where the money is from. The Panama man was clearly scouting somewhere last night. There are banks on the main street. This much money could only mean a bank, and banks have heavyweight CCTV. He'll be wanted. Already arrested? *Where's the money?* Me in the frame.

I stare at the cash.

I so *want* the cash.

My bedroom back home takes centre stage in my head once more. The door will still be marked off with my various heights as a kid. Mum has had the room painted numerous times but didn't cover up those pencil lines, which date back to 1976. I see myself sitting in the room, wondering what I'll do next. Having to beg for cash from my parents, until I land some shit-end job. My new flight, two days in the future, is the full stop on my life.

The bag is my way out.

It takes me ten minutes to pack.

When I'm finished, I reach for my mobile to check bus times on the internet. Then I put it away. You can be tracked online. If I surf the ALSA bus company's website I'll give away how I got out of town.

I can feel the panic in my chest. My heart running away with itself. My head buzzing. The need to move is driving everything else. What am I doing? A thief. Me?

I'm dragging the money bag and my case across the room when there's a knock on the apartment door.

I mothball breathing.

Another knock.

'Mr Denny, are you in?'

It's Cara Donaldson, the owner of the flat.

'Mr Denny,' she shouts through the door. 'I saw you come in. I was parked outside.'

I slide both bags into the bedroom.

I open the door. 'Hi.'

'Can I come in.' It's not a question. It's a warning.

I block her entrance. 'What for?'

The rebuke registers on her face. Cara is an ex-pat with a dozen properties spread across the Jávea area. She wears her hair short, her shorts short and her top short. She's also short with her temper. 'Because it's my house,' is her justification.

'I'm about to take a nap.' A weak excuse to exclude her.

She pushes in. 'I only need a minute. You're leaving the day after tomorrow. A lot of my cleaners are down sick. Flu. I want to see how much work is needed in case I have to do it myself.'

Normally I'd rile at the intrusion but all I can think about is the money. She opens the bedroom door and spots the bags. 'Are you leaving early?'

'No. I just like to be packed and ready to go,' I explain.

She spends a little too long looking at the bags before moving on. 'I'll have a quick look round,' she says, still eyeing my bags, 'and then I'll be gone.'

I notice that the zip on the money bag is open. Just a touch. Enough. In my haste, I forgot to close it. Notes can be seen. I'm sure Cara must have spotted them. As she checks out the living room I zip the bag closed.

Cara dives into – and then emerges from – the bathroom with an, 'OK. Looks fine.'

She's not looking at me as she talks. The money bag the object of her attention.

She gives it one more look, turns and leaves. No thank-you or goodbye. She just leaves.

I shut the door behind her.

If she saw the cash she'll put two and two together. News of the theft must be out by now.

I decide to give her ten minutes to get clear – then I'm out of here.

I pull the bags to the door and slide down the wall to wait.

It occurs to me that I could still hand the cash back. Hope there's a reward up for grabs. I stroke the bag and think about my childhood bedroom, and the thought of returning the cash fades.

Footsteps echo up the stairwell.

They stop.

Silence.

I can hear breathing on the other side of the door.

My heart hits overdrive.

I stand up, money bag nestled on my hip, and work my eye to the peephole.

The two men in black are standing outside. Blondie on the left, Dreadlock on the right.

There's a knock. I ignore it. Another knock. I stand back.

The wood around the lock splinters with a bang. The door ricochets off the bottom of the wall. Peeling paint showers from the ceiling. The two men dive into my world. No words. No demands. Blondie spots the bag. He grabs it.

Grabs my money.

I have the handle wrapped around my elbow. I pull back. Blondie throws a punch. It misses. I roll under him with the money bag in tow. Hitting the floor, I kick out, catching Dreadlock on the shin. He screams. Blondie tries to jump on me, but the hall is so small he can't get past his accomplice.

I'm up and moving a fraction of a second ahead of them. Throwing myself at the door. Months without exercise overcome by the sheer volume of adrenaline coursing through my veins. My shoulder bounces off the door frame, as I misjudge the exit. The bruise will be the size of a melon.

I hit the stairs, clear twelve steps in two leaps and fly out of the main entrance, bolting onto the road, unable to put the brakes on.

A car's horn blasts in my ear. Tyres scream and my hand pushes down on the car's bonnet as it stops.

Behind me Blondie and Dreadlock spew from the building.

I swing away from the swearing driver, run down the hill that my apartment sits on and dive into an alley. A man is smoking next to an open door. I can hear and smell cooking from the kitchen inside. When cash was less tight I ate in the restaurant the kitchen serves.

The man takes one last drag and flicks the cigarette butt onto the ground. He disappears inside, but the door doesn't fully close. I slide my fingers around its edge and prise it open a body's width. Inside it's dark. I slip in, pulling the door closed behind me. The latch is broken. It wants to swing free. I hold it shut. Seconds later I hear running feet. Door in one hand, bag in the other, I wait.

Nothing happens.

An eternity passes as I stand there.

Then the door to the kitchen opens.

The smoking man looks puzzled. '*¿Qué estás haciendo?*'

I don't need Spanish to know he's asking what I'm doing here. I shrug, trying to buy a few more seconds.

'*¿Por favor, vete?*' he says.

I don't move.

'*Deja o llamaré a la policía.*'

I recognise '*policía*'. I raise one hand. '*Lo siento.*' I'm sorry.

I push out through the door. At the far end of the alley the two men in black are standing. It's as well for me that they have remained a pair – that they didn't choose to cover both ends of the alley. They see me and I'm back to running.

Cutting back up the hill I enter the old town. A warren of small streets. I start a mystery tour designed to lose Blondie and Dreadlock.

Twice they spot me, twice I manage to lose them.

After twenty minutes of hide-and-seek I jog out of town, into the surrounding orange groves. Sweat is flowing down me in streams. I'm more fluid than solid.

For the next two hours I wander through the countryside. A couple of times I see them, and I'm forced to double back – but they don't spot me.

The sun drops behind Montgó, the mountain casting a shadow over its domain.

The mosquitoes begin to feast on me.

My clothes are back at the flat. Returning seems out of the question. Cara might have returned by now and found the flat abandoned. Maybe raised the alarm?

I pat my pocket. At least I have my passport. I swing the money bag onto my shoulder, listening to the night. A house sits across the road from me. A few lights indicate someone's home. Bats zip around, chowing down on the insects. I can see the light from the Arenal. People will be relaxing, chatting, drinking, having fun. I think of the fun I could have with the cash in the bag.

I aim for the lights and, as I exit the dark of the country, sliding onto a road bordered with concrete high rises, I consider my options, while keeping an eye out for the men in black.

I could fly home. Hole up somewhere until my flight is due, or, better still, buy an earlier flight. It's not as if I'm broke.

'*Sir, is this your bag?*'

Hard to explain two hundred grand to a security guard at the airport. Even harder the day of a bank robbery. Impossible if I'm a wanted man. Cara knows who I am. She saw the cash.

Mail the money home?

Possible.

'*What value is your package?*'

How often do UPS or FedEx fuck up?

Train?

I've always fancied a long rail journey.

Lots of CCTV on trains and at stations, though.

I reach the main road that slices through the back of the Arenal. The bars and restaurants are busy. I'm about to cross when I catch sight of Blondie. I recoil.

I retrace my steps and work my way along the back roads.

OK, so going home might present some issues. My name's known here. Cara has all my home details. Europol has long arms. Blondie and Dreadlock might come after me. But staying here is a worse idea.

I could look to buy a bar in some distant part of Spain. How much would one cost? Fifty thousand? Nice and quiet. Pass a few years. Maybe a lot more years.

The idea has deep-down and dirty merit.

'*Son, where are you? When are you coming home? What are you doing with yourself?*'

Two hundred K is not life-changing.

I need to go home first. To think.

The taxi rank sits near the beach. It takes me half an hour to walk what should take five minutes. My head is on a spring, flying side to side, looking for my pursuers. My neck is sore by the time I arrive at the rank. A police car cruises into view. I step into the shadows of a doorway until it passes.

Four taxis sit in a row, green lights above each indicating they're for hire.

I jump into the back of the first one.

'Denia,' I say.

It's the next town up the coast. Far enough away to give me time to think but close enough to get back if I need to.

The driver nods. I slide down the seat. Keeping my head low.

The driver is listening to Total FM, a local English station, not the usual Spanish. Spandau Ballet are singing about gold.

The driver's mobile rings. He hits the hands-free. 'Hi Jenny.'

'When are you finishing tonight?'

'I'm off to Denia then I'm calling it quits. See you back home in an hour or so.'

'Great. Love you.'

'Love you too.' He hangs up.

As we start to climb the hill out of Jávea I have a thought. *Back home.*

I tap the driver's chair. 'Where are you from?'

He turns the radio down. 'Manchester, but I've been out here for twenty years.'

'Do you get back to Manchester often?'

He half turns to look at me. He's a little older than I am. Bald, well tanned, I can see a stomach that has enough fat to touch the bottom of the steering wheel. 'Not as much as I'd like to,' he says. 'It's not cheap. I've got family back home but I haven't been back for a while.'

'You're the first English taxi driver I've met out here.'

He laughs. 'There's a few. We need to earn a crust somehow. Things are tough.'

I let my thought run around my head a little more. *Back home.*

'What's your name?' I ask.

'Colin.'

'Look, Colin. Tell me this. How much would it cost for you to drive me to the UK?'

He laughs again. 'A lot.'

'What's a lot?'

He thinks about this. 'Are you serious?'

'Yip.'

'Eh. I'd say two thousand euros.'

'OK.'

'Really?' Surprise is hard in the word.

'Half up front,' I offer.

'No way.'

'Yes way. I'm serious.'

'When?'

'Tonight.'

He pulls the car to the side of the road. He leans round, sizing me up. 'Are you *really* serious.'

I am. It's costly but it'll get me home. 'So, your answer?'

'Why take a taxi?'

'Does it matter?'

'Two thousand euros...' he repeats.

'Half up front,' I remind him.

His eyes screw up, the green glow of the dashboard giving him an evil look. 'Two thousand euros?'

I nod.

He taps the handbrake. Thinking.

I wait.

He switches the radio off. 'Heard that there was some nonsense in the old town today.'

I say nothing.

'Bank robbery,' he says.

I keep shtum.

'Lot of money. So I hear. Would you know anything about it?'

I pull myself closer using the headrest. 'How much?'

He must know I'm a bucket load of trouble but he leans round once more and says, 'Fifteen thousand.'

Inside I gasp.

He jumps in before I can reply. 'That includes getting back to the UK without bothering the border guards.'

I pretend to give it some thought. But I know that this isn't the time for negotiation. This is a time for decision-making. If he's willing to dodge customs and overlook where the cash came from then he's not new to this. I reply, 'OK.'

He adds, 'And I have one condition.'

My heart sinks. 'Which is?'

'I need to ask my wife.'

Relief. 'Right.'

'And if she's OK with it, she comes.'

I can't help but laugh. 'Sure. Just as long as you're quick about it.'

He turns round.

He rubs his temple.

He looks at me one last time.

He rubs the expanse of his gut.

He drops a breath.

He reaches for the phone.

My one thought as he dials: *Where the hell is this all going?*

No Way Back

J.M. Hewitt

Sweat blinded the boy and adrenaline pulsed through him. He looked down at his thin shirt, sure he could see the material moving, flapping slightly. It wasn't the warm breeze; it was the beating of his heart.

Balling his slight hand into a fist he thumped once on his chest.

Be still, now, he instructed. *Be a man.*

When his breathing had slowed he looked back up, squinting lazily at the horizon. He perched with a large, flat rock at his back, the misty-topped mountains of the Appalachian chain making him appear even smaller than he was.

He glanced behind him, allowed a small smile to twitch at his lips. So he'd had to travel 3,703 miles away from his father to prove that he was his son. That he could be his son. That he could be just as good as his father's *other* son. His father didn't know that he'd come here, nor did his mother. And that showed cunning, street-smarts, ingenuity and integrity.

It wasn't a training camp, either. The weapons handed out here were not filled with blanks, or paint or harmless laser tags. This was as real as it gets.

And he hadn't gone to the obvious places that he'd come across in his research, like Afghanistan, Iraq or Somalia. No, he had done his groundwork thoroughly, and travelling to a country that wasn't on a major security watch showed subtlety, stealth and savvy. Doing it on his own showed strength of character and skill.

Kiki was eleven years old but his father often told him – when he deemed it necessary to speak to him – that he looked like he was eight. His father didn't make it sound like a compliment, not like when his father told his mother she looked no older than thirty. Kiki thought like a grown-up, but had the body of a child. Desperately he wanted to be a man.

His father never looked at him, never saw his potential or his worth. Kiki wrote stories, fanciful tales that he was so very proud of. His mother cooed over them, stroked Kiki's jet-black hair and told him that his stories were wonderful, that *he* was wonderful. He used to shrug his mother off, head to his father and show him these works of fiction, but eventually stopped when it became obvious that flights of fancy were not what his father wanted from him. His father would shrug him off, the same way Kiki did his mother. A chain of whimsical love, spurned.

Kiki had become accustomed to sitting in the shadows, moving ghost-like around the home. From the dark corners he would watch his father interact with his brother. His brother was older, stronger, more handsome, more athletic. His brother was everything that his father wanted. In time it clicked: Dad wanted a different kind of son, not one who sat with a book in his hands, but one with a football, a rugby ball or a weapon. Kiki wasn't cut out for sports, so this fight was his best chance to prove himself to the men, his fellow soldiers here, who moved stealthily in the shadow of Mount Mitchell. Finally, he might be called a soldier too. But more importantly, he might be called a son.

A shiver went through Kiki's body as he stroked the rocket launcher with his small hand. He didn't know how the soldiers here had got their hands on it; they claimed it was a leftover weapon from the last war – their entire arsenal was made up of remnants from past battles. Kiki thought, though, that they were bought on the black market. He didn't fall for those tall tales, which in his mind showed foresight, intelligence and knowledge. As he had perused the weaponry he knew that they expected him to claim a small handgun, or maybe one of the Walther hunting knives. But Kiki had spotted the rocket launcher and immediately claimed it.

It was called a Quassam 4 and it was as big as he was. He knew he couldn't carry it on his shoulder like some of the bigger boys could, but it came with a wheeled A-frame, and it was determination more than physical strength that got it out of the crudely constructed warehouse to Kiki's base at the bottom of Mount Mitchell.

And now it was for real. Team-talk and training were done. It was time to bring out the big guns.

Kiki giggled, covering his mouth with a small brown hand at the thought.

All there was to do now was wait.

Before long a deep rumbling came from somewhere over the horizon. Kiki pushed himself up off the flat rock and got into position behind the Quassam 4. Knees flexed, eye to the optical sight, he wiped his wet palm down his shirt before placing his forefinger lightly on the trigger.

The Spitfire approached and he loosened his grip; it wasn't an enemy plane, but one of his own. He paused, watched the big metal bird with a half-smile. He thought about waving, but chastised himself immediately. Boys waved at planes; men and soldiers and sons didn't. So he just watched, still in position, still waiting for the enemy. And then – *clatter-clatter!* The plane pirouetted suddenly, down the other side of Mount Mitchell in a cloud of smoke, rust red.

Kiki heard himself shriek, aware that it sounded high-pitched and girlie; it was too late to change it to a roar. Kiki pushed the gun with all his might, toppling it to the ground.

Confusion jostled with self-flagellation. Wouldn't his father love this? The silly boy shot down their own plane. *But I didn't fire! Did I?* Kiki got down on his hands and knees and checked; the safety catch was still on, the ammunition still visible in the loading chamber.

He heard a laugh then, a deep, rumbling chuckle as his teammate, Braun, a big, burly eighteen-year-old, and the one who was of the impression that boys belonged with their mothers, stalked over the crest, so large that to Kiki's eyes he actually blocked out the sun.

'What are you doing?' Braun asked, still laughing.

'I … I don't know what happened…' Kiki moved his eyes from the gun to the smoking wreckage of the plane in the distance. 'I didn't do it!'

Braun laughed on, doubled over now, pointing a finger at the younger boy. And Kiki caught on, seeing the glint of triumph in the bigger boy's eyes.

Kiki gasped, felt his skinny legs begin to shake beneath him. 'You shot the plane down!'

And it made sense, Braun shot his man down because Kiki was that much of a threat. Or Braun was that much of a psychopath. Braun would do anything to prove that he was the bigger man, but shooting a plane down, their own, not an enemy plane, was the work of a monster.

Kiki's body reacted before he even got his brain in gear. How many times in his life had he been laughed at and ridiculed by people bigger than him? Not just his father or his brother, but those at school, those who played football and wrestled in the corridors, and drank beer and foul-tasting spirits before they were even in their teens. It was them that he saw in his mind's eye; the way they acted when they saw him sitting in the sunshine on a bench with his book; it was his brother, walking past him, smacking the book out of Kiki's hands when Kiki was so engrossed in his novel he hadn't even heard his brother's heavy footfall. And it was his father in front of him now, and Kiki could *see* him, rolling his eyes, huffing out a barely concealed sigh of impatience, throwing Kiki a disappointed look at finding him scribbling yet another fable.

Fairy tales, his father called them. Fairy tales from a fairy.

Remembering that particular incident and his father's description of him was all that Kiki needed for the red mist in his mind to explode into a nuclear mushroom cloud.

Righting the rocket launcher, he darted behind it, looked through the optical sight and saw Braun looming large in front of him. Kiki flicked the safety and squeezed the trigger properly; firmly this time and with meaning. At the roar of the gun Kiki let go and clapped his hands over his ears. He just had time to see the ragged red fulmination as Braun's chest opened and he was lifted up, over and away, landing heavily yards away in the flattened scrubland.

Now who was the soldier?

Now his father would see him.

Now his father would take notice of him.

✦

Up in the big manor house Graham was in his element. First he served his guests his best wine, one bought on his most recent visit to Italy. He wanted his guests to see what he had, materialistically, before he showed them his masterpiece. He wanted his guests, these officials from the museum, to understand that he knew the worth of everything, so they wouldn't try to dupe him. So first he led them around his home, making sure they saw the original 'Whistler's Mother' painting, and the authentic Cora Sun-Drop Diamond on display in his library, set off nicely by the four walls that were lined with first editions. He didn't read the first editions; he wasn't much of a reader at all. For him, the exterior was important, much more so than the content.

'And your family, do they appreciate all of these...?' the slightly snooty museum curator asked.

Graham faltered, felt the usual disappointment swim over him at her question. *Did his family appreciate it?* Hmm, well, his wife continually bemoaned the fact that he wouldn't let her hire a cleaner, due to his fear that the priceless artefacts that adorned their home might be damaged. His youngest son had no regard for the antiques and valuables, preferring to stay out of the house and make up meaningless prose to act out in the vast gardens of the property. His oldest son was his only hope; if truth be told, he was Graham's own Hope Diamond. There was a connection between Graham and his eldest child, a meeting of the minds that didn't exist between him and his wife or his youngest boy. In Graham's professional world, he got whatever he wanted and discarded what he didn't. He applied the same principle to his home life too, which meant he rarely had any interaction with his youngest son. It made no difference; his youngest boy didn't need anyone, as long as he had his goddamn books and bloody one-man plays.

'Shall we move on to the *pièce de résistance*, then?' Graham held his hand out, allowing his visitors to move down the stairs in front of him. 'Now, the piece I'm about to show you, and that I want to go on display in the Imperial War Museum, is in full working—'

They halted in the lobby at the sound of the explosion, quizzically glanced at each other, hands shooting out to clutch the highly polished banister as the house rocked on its very foundations. Graham replayed it in his mind, the whole house had bloody moved!

'W-what *was* that?' The curator's eyes were wild as she flicked her head from side to side and up to the ceiling before staring down at the floor, probably expecting it to open up and reveal a large chasm. 'Was it an earthquake?'

Leaving his guests in the lobby, Graham ran through the house, out of the rear doors that opened up to the manicured lawn and gardens beyond, and raced to the newly constructed barn. He pulled up short and felt his hands go to his head and tug at his hair as he surveyed the sight that greeted him.

'What are you DOING?' Graham roared.

His youngest son looked over the top of the rocket launcher, eyes flat and cold as his gaze settled on his father.

'I'm destroying the enemy, Dad.' Kiki smiled, but like his eyes, his expression was flat and cold.

Later, his boy, Kiki, would come to life long enough to babble sense-lessly to his mother – something he had made up about travelling to bloody America, of all places, somewhere on the Appalachian Trail; a fighting camp, nonsense about being a child soldier, something about an enemy plane that turned out not to be the enemy. Graham listened to this from behind the door, but when he shifted his weight the child heard and stopped talking. From that point on he wouldn't speak again. The boy had travelled too far, further than the Appalachian Trail that he thought he'd gone to. He had been on his own mystery tour, to a place far beyond the sky, past even the boundaries of space. Kiki had gone so far, there was no coming back.

There would be talk of conditions: mental, schizophrenic, emo-tional; 'emotionally stunted by his father's apparent distaste' was one label Graham heard. After that, he wouldn't listen again.

In any other situation Graham would have shrugged, thrown some money at the problem and turned his attention back to his eldest son. His worthy son.

But.

And time and time again, as the months, years and decades wore on, he would return to the moment that turned his heart into ice and his life into nothingness.

He surveyed the scene of devastation that was once the gardens of the property he was so proud of. Graham swallowed, sucked in by his son's glare, the fading sunlight bouncing shadows off the barn as Graham moved slowly towards his son and the rocket launcher. The question was on the tip of his tongue, but Graham was afraid to ask it. He knew the answer, because the rising smoke from over the laurel hedge and the strong, metallic scent of blood told him, quite clearly.

Too clearly.

Still he asked, and even as he spoke the words, he knew they would likely be the last words that he would ever utter to his youngest son.

'Where's your brother, son?' asked Graham as he approached. 'Where's Braun?'

Mystery Tour

Judith Cutler

'*EVENT CANCELLED!*'

The Books Bizarre had done very well for a small independent book-shop in a small Midlands town. Very well indeed. The bow-fronted window carried a huge display of the visiting author's books; the space was dominated by the newly published one the event was meant to promote, but there was also a pleasing selection from her backlist. And the proprietor – the displeasure and disappointment on his face clear for all to see – was snatching every last one out of sight so viciously I feared for their bindings.

His displeasure and disappointment were matched by mine.

They were my newly published books and it was my publicity event: what on earth was going on?

At last, in response to my frantic knocking, Mr Spear unlocked the front door. 'Can't you read?' he growled. 'Tonight's off. Kaput. Finished before it began. All those cakes her fans baked. All that wine I bought. And the bloody woman turns up half an hour before the event's due to kick off and says she can't do it. Not so much as a sorry. That's the last of her books I'll touch.'

'Who turned up?'

'The author. The audience were just starting to trickle in.'

'Are you still expecting more?'

Mr Spear looked at me as if I was crazy, but checked his watch never-theless. 'There should be another fifteen – maybe twenty. She's popular with my customers. Why do you ask?'

'Because I'm the author and I definitely did not cancel. But I'd dearly like to know who did.'

He picked up one of my books and scrutinised the author photo.

Then he peered at me. 'This looks like you. It was taken a few years back, maybe, but then you all do that, try to pass yourselves off as twenty years younger, don't you? It's the same on dating sites,' he added, bitter with experience, no doubt. 'But the woman that came – she looked just like this. Glasses, that's the only difference.' He jabbed the photo. Nonetheless he removed the handwritten sign from the window, making prissy little gestures to remove the sticky tape from his fingers. 'Come in and sort yourself out, then,' he said grudgingly. 'I'd better make a few phone calls and see if we can get folk back.'

I smiled my thanks and took off my coat.

Trips like this are part of a writer's life cycle: you think; you write the book; you edit it; you watch it go through the whole publication process; to promote it, you tour willing bookshops and grateful, ailing libraries – I had four to visit in the next five days. But this cancellation was the first time anything so strange had happened to me.

'I know you checked in, madam,' said the handsome Polish reception-ist, as, back at the King's Head Hotel, I asked for my key. I was still fizzing with adrenaline after a delightful evening with almost all the readers Mr Spears had organised. 'But you checked out almost imme-diately, didn't you? So we gave someone else your room. Sorry.'

Perhaps it was his accent that prevented the last word from sounding sincere.

'But my case is still in the room.' Did I sound angry or upset?

He shook his head implacably. 'You took your case with you.'

'I didn't. I left it there. Safe and secure in your keeping.'

'But I saw you. With my own eyes.' He fiddled with the computer; as far as he was concerned the matter was over.

It wasn't.

'How did this person gain access to my room? You keep all the keys behind you.' I pointed.

His eyes showed a gratifying flicker of anxiety. 'Did you have any-thing precious in the case?'

'The manuscript of my latest novel, for one thing.'

He pointed at the notice clearly visible over his other shoulder; it declared that all valuables had to be deposited for safe-keeping with the receptionist.

'Surely that refers to jewellery and money. This was half a ream of paper. Hardly the sort of thing anyone would want to steal.'

His immaculate if accented English cracked. 'I call manager.'

'Good – or I will call the police.'

To be fair, the hotel's interior CCTV footage of the woman carrying my suitcase did show someone remarkably like me, but younger and sporting glasses, as Mr Spears had said. Where my middle-aged double chin would have been, a scarf was elegantly but strategically tied. Her hair was covered with the sort of a woolly hat with a huge pompom one needed youthful chutzpah to carry off. Whereas I wore a quilted jacket complete with fur-lined hood, she sported a body warmer over a striped top.

I asked for, but was denied, a still from the footage. Actually, I also asked for another room for the night, but it seemed they had none spare. When, seeing my mounting anger, they phoned round all the neighbouring hotels, B&Bs and even grotty pubs, the answer was the same: no room at the inn.

At least I wasn't pregnant and I had a car, not a plodding donkey.

Except I hadn't got a car anymore. The passenger door hung off its hinges; the windscreen was smashed. A small suitcase smouldered beside it until someone found a fire extinguisher.

The security cameras that should have recorded every movement had been vandalised. Police? This time of night there weren't any local officers to tackle the situation. Eventually a rapid-response car arrived, despatched from the nearest city. But the two weary officers could make no obvious sense of the evening's events. They promised forensic support, whatever that might mean. In the warmth of the hotel, they reran the CCTV footage I'd already seen, pleading with me to recall some long-lost daughter whom I'd offended. Eventually, however, their conclusion was much the same as mine: someone really didn't like me, did they?

It seemed a lot more people didn't like me when I arrived at my agent's office the following day – my agent in particular. 'How dare you cancel all these talks and visits without consulting me – or at least letting me know. Plymouth; Exeter; Portsmouth…' Marion snarled a litany of libraries and bookshops I'd let down. 'It's so unprofessional.'

'It isn't quite like that,' I said, once I could get a word in. 'It seems someone is out to destroy my reputation and my property. Maybe even my life, Marion,' I added, since that was what the cheerier officer had pointed out. Despite my phlegmatic exterior, my voice wobbled. 'Meanwhile, before I explain, let's undo the damage that this person's inflicted – let's get in touch with everyone who's complained to you, and reassure any other people you think might be after my skin.'

'You should take down your Twitter account. And your Facebook page. No, don't look first. You won't like what you see.' She looked at me more closely. 'Are you ill, or something? You look as if you slept in your clothes.' She smoothed her immaculate jacket.

'I did. In a station café. My car was vandalised, you see. And I couldn't phone because my battery was flat and my charger, with the rest of the things in my case, went up in flames. Including the manuscript I promised you. However,' I said, digging in my bag, 'they didn't get this. You know I believe in belt and braces. Well, it's here on my memory stick. We can print it out now. I don't want my publishers to think I'm going to let them down, too.'

'They already do. Your editor was screaming down the phone to me just before you arrived. I'll download the file and send it straight off.'

I watched, my knuckles white as they gripped her desk: 'What if whoever it is has managed to corrupt not just my life but also my computer?' No. All looked well.

Marion smiled. 'This is good. I just want to keep on reading,' she said. 'But I'll save that pleasure for later.'

'Indulge me,' I said. 'Print it. Then save it under a different name. Just in case someone tries to hack your computer.'

She shook her head. 'How would they know I'm your agent?'

'I dedicated my last book to you, remember? And I bet, even as we speak, whoever this woman is will be hacking my computer, too. Please just do as I ask,' I begged. 'Now!'

She rolled her eyes, but she did set the printer going, and I watched with satisfaction as the words poured out. Yes! Everything down to the last colon was there.

Turning to her with a relieved smile I added, 'Now, just to please me, update your firewall. The moment you've forwarded it to the publisher. You never know…'

Marion sent me off to shop for a phone charger and new clothes before taking me out to lunch. Plus make-up, of course, and some hairspray – I looked as if I really had been tearing my hair out. She also forced an extra-strong cocktail down my throat as we waited for our table. There was something else she had to tell me, wasn't there?

'As you predicted, my website and yours have both been hacked,' she said the moment we sat down. 'My geek's working on mine even as we speak. You need to alert yours too. Here, use my phone.'

I did as I was told.

'Now,' she said, 'tell me whom you've offended. Because they're having a field day with their revenge. I've got back to all the libraries; the publicity people at your publisher's are already working on the bookshops scheduled for the rest of your tour. But you should see what their Twitter's picking up, too. Or rather, you shouldn't.'

'Maybe if I did,' I said, valiant on gin and a lot of other things, 'I could work out who's doing it.'

'You should leave that to the police,' Marion declared, confiscating my wine glass and giving me a tumbler of water.

'But I write crime,' I objected. 'Shouldn't that give me an insight or two?'

Her look sobered me up. 'Maybe criminals read your books: that's where they've got *their* insight or two.'

'Only into the politics of medieval Italy. In any case, you don't do something like this just because you object to someone's books, surely. This feels much more personal.'

'Someone you've snubbed on LinkedIn or Facebook? Someone annoyed by one of your tweets?'

'That would make someone tetchy, even turn them into a troll, but it wouldn't drive them to such a wide-ranging campaign, surely. Even now I don't know what's happened at home; I came straight here from the Midlands. The train fare cost me almost as much as last year's royalties.'

'You've not been home?! Why ever not?'

'Because I'm scared of what I shall find when I get there. And because I wanted to make sure you got the manuscript. I wanted,' I said in a smaller voice, 'some help.'

Our starter arrived. Absentmindedly Marion returned my glass and poured us both wine. An Australian red: ABV 14.5 per cent.

'All right: go through all the people you might have annoyed in the flesh.'

'I've been doing nothing else since it happened. When I'm doing author gigs, I meet a lot of people. I always try to speak to everyone afterwards, even if – especially if – they don't seem to have approved of everything I say.'

'Don't you sometimes teach writers' groups?'

'Not very often. And you've no idea how nice I am about what they write.'

When I got home, I said the same to the officer from our local force who came to interview me at the request of West Mercia Police. It turned out she'd read some of my books, though she was more interested in fellow writers I had met. As a dewy-eyed fan of them, not me, in fact. But then, medieval Italy isn't everyone's taste, as my royalties proved year after year. Which is why I'd changed tack completely with the new novel. This featured a sassy contemporary protagonist – a sharp-talking, quick-thinking, fearless version of the young woman I'd have liked to have been.

'Were you writing about anyone in particular?' asked DC Bracewell.

'I wasn't writing about anyone. I was writing fiction.'

'So no one you know might have thought it was about them?'

'How could they? The book's only just arrived at the publisher's!'

'Let's get back to your ideas: have you ever stolen one from anyone else?'

In a parody of trying to remember I ostentatiously scratched my head. 'Off the ideas tree in someone else's back garden?' She didn't laugh. 'OK, I'll come clean: I have a couple of times. Last time I read *The Prince* by Machiavelli. And when I was researching in the library of the Duomo in Florence. Just because my pursuer alleges the ideas aren't my own doesn't make that the truth, you know.'

'Think hard: have you ever, ever, seriously annoyed anyone?'

At first I shook my head. Then I recalled that I had. 'I was once the judge for a short-story competition, and declined to give the first prize to a story I'd read somewhere else. But that was twenty years ago, surely when the woman who looked like me would have been only a child. I can't recall the competition, let alone the person who'd tackled me and whom I'd accused – yes – of plagiarism.'

'What did you tell this person?'

'"I loved your story. And I loved it even more when I read Georgette Heyer's version." And actually, now I come to think of it, I was a tutor on a residential writing course once. I told the students they could send me their work when they'd finished it so I could comment on it. One woman's manuscript got lost in the post. It was very embarrassing. I asked her to send it again, registered post, this time. The problem was she hadn't got a copy. Can you believe it? Despite everything I said about making sure you always had back-ups. That should have been that, but she did get very aerated – as if it was somehow my fault, even though, when I'd seen the original, I had nothing but praise for her work.'

'Ah! What was her name? What did she look like?'

I spread my hands. 'I'm coming to the age where I find it hard to recall my own name, Ms Bracewell. As for what she looked like – young, healthy.'

'The course she was on?'

'I've taught so many…'

But she wasn't going to let it go. 'Could that have been the start of all this?'

I shrugged. 'I've lived uneventfully since.'

She got up to look at all the books on my shelves. 'You've been very prolific. Have you always been a writer?'

'I used to work in a library when I lived in London.' Imperial College, as it happened. One of the world's leading academic institutions. I'd have loved to tell her all about my time there – including working with great scientists from all over the world.

'Oh. A librarian.' She was practically yawning with boredom; it was all too clear that she saw me as a dull stereotype, too busy reading about life to live it. She could barely raise her pen to jot down the answer to her next question. 'Anything else?'

'For a time I worked for the government.'

'A civil servant. Hmm.' That confirmed it: what a grey person I was. She was looking at her watch, clearly ready to go. 'We'll keep you updated if there are any developments,' she said. 'If only the hotel or the shop had had adequate CCTV coverage…' She went off sucking her teeth at the failure of other people to do the police's job for them.

They didn't contact me again. I decided to let the matter rest.

The problem died down as quickly as it had started. My life fell back into its productive pattern of writing and talking about my books to the public. I remained watchful, however, especially as my publication date approached. My agent told me that one of my fellow writers had had the weird experience of seeing her Amazon page loaded with books apparently written by her but in fact nothing but gobbledegook. I should brace myself for a similar attack.

But nothing happened until after my new novel had been published and widely reviewed – a rarity for me. The critics were universally admiring, praising my original plot and clean fresh prose. It was tipped for an award.

Then the deluge began. Imagine the public humiliation of being accused of plagiarism – by a hitherto unknown writer whose work so far had only been self-published on Kindle. Kate Stone. Fortunately the traditional media were wary of printing her allegations, but as the Twittersphere got going, gradually even the *Guardian* started reporting on the furore.

'Legal action: that's the only option,' Marion declared emphatically. 'Stone says you took the novel word for word from a manuscript she sent you. She's rewritten it, and here it is on Kindle – and it is remarkably like yours, I have to say. Almost identical.'

My palms were sweating. 'Do you think … no, that's crazy.'

'Think what?'

'Could she possibly be the woman who caused all that trouble last winter? We know someone vandalised my car and burned my case. What if she removed the manuscript from my case before she set it on fire?'

Marion looked puzzled.

'Think about it. I came straight down after the trouble in the Midlands and handed you the memory stick. You printed it off. You sent a copy straight through to the publisher. If she's hacked it after that, then she's very clever indeed. When did her novel appear on Kindle, by the way?'

'No idea. But I can certainly find out.'

The answer took a few days, but it was what I suspected: it was published less than a week after the incident.

'I think you should tell the police,' Marion said. 'This is becoming more serious by the moment. Not only has this woman made libellous and slanderous allegations, she might have impersonated you and committed arson. That's a terrible crime!'

I had had enough fuss and palaver, though. I shook my head gently but firmly. 'Some people want something so desperately they actually believe they've already done it. Maybe she really, truly believes that this is her work and that I've stolen it. What if she went to court? What would we get? Perjury? It wouldn't be fair to her. No, I genuinely feel sorry for Kate Stone. I just want to shut her up, that's all.'

She stared at me with narrowed eyes. 'You really mean that, don't you?'

'I remember what it was like to be so desperate to be published I'd have done almost anything. Poor Kate.'

'I wonder if a lawyer's letter would fix everything. I'll talk to my solicitors, and we should get your publisher's team involved too. Then, with luck, everything should go back to normal. Have I shown you your sales figures, by the way...?'

So the public heard no more of Kate Stone, and a lot more of me. Despite the amazing success of my venture into contemporary crime, I returned to the Middle Ages, where I felt altogether safer. Part of me was sad I would have no more use for the work I'd researched in Imperial College's library, or the years I'd spent working for MI6. How many spies had I taken down in that time; how many false allegations had I successfully made? How many cars had I attacked with tiny explosive charges so that the damage looked like the work of mindless vandals? How many fires had I set from afar? It was a shame all that computer and other technological know-how, all my cleverness hiding in plain sight would wither after one brief late flowering. The trouble was that, in those days, I'd taught myself to be entirely amoral. Now I found the recent pangs of conscience quite uncomfortable.

And, of course, there were some things you simply can't get away with twice.

Wife on Tour

Julia Crouch

They finally got onto the 0800 EasyFly Gatwick to Frankfurt at the back of Boarding Queue Two.

'I can't believe they still don't allocate,' Larry said as they surveyed the crowded cabin. A couple of vacant single seats lurked in the back rows.

'We should have paid for Nifty Boarding,' Ruth said.

'Waste of money. In any case, you would have got us here too late to make any use of it.'

Was it really her fault that Google Maps had led them into icy gridlock on the M23?

'For fuck's sake get a fucking move on,' Larry muttered under his breath at an old man who, in his battle to cram his heavy bag into the overhead locker, was completely blocking the aisle.

'Excuse me, my dear.' Larry turned to a flight attendant standing in the exit row next to him. 'I'm Larry Speakman.' He tilted his Panama hat, took her hand and reached it to his lips. 'Performing for the opening of the Christmas Market. I've booked a ticket for this fine lady,' he stroked his violin case. 'And it's most important that we sit next to each other.'

The flight attendant fluttered stiff bars of mascara and almost curtseyed. 'I'll see what I can do for you, Mr Speakman.' She sashayed along the aisle. After a brief exchange with a lone young man, who gloomily rose and moved, she ushered Larry to two adjacent empty seats.

'Thank you so much, my dear,' Larry said, as, without a backward glance to his wife, he squeezed into the window seat and strapped his violin in next to him, slipping both Ruth's and his travel documents into his breast pocket. He always carried their papers, ever since an incident thirty years earlier when, distracted by a feverish toddler, Ruth had left her passport on a nappy-changing table at Orly.

Ruth was directed to a seat by the toilet, next to an overspilling obese woman who smelled of stale sausage.

She elbowed herself some space, fastened her safety belt and closed her eyes to perform the putting-yourself-to-sleep trick she had learned to cure her fear of flying.

One … two…

She rarely accompanied Larry on tour. She was only doing so this time because he had sprained his back playing squash and needed someone to help him with the bags.

Three … four…

She would have preferred to go somewhere warm. He had gone to Dubai two weeks earlier, to play at some oil magnate's son's bar mitzvah. His back had been fine then.

Five … six…

But Frankfurt, in early December, with a grumpy Larry: the prospect hardly lifted the spirits. She consoled herself with the thought of the Christmas market. She would have four or so hours alone while he rested before his performance. She planned to buy presents for the grandchildren.

Seven … eight…

She tried to imagine herself in a snowy, *Glühwein*-scented glow, surrounded by cheery, red-faced Germans offering her delicious tidbits.

Nine…

But she kept being sidetracked by the thought of damp, cold gloves and freezing toes. A familiar sick chill brewed in her solar plexus.

Ten…

'Drinks? Snacks?'

Ruth opened one eye to be greeted by the flight attendant's glowing face.

'G & T, please,' Ruth said. 'Slimline.'

'How are you paying?'

'Euros,' she said with a shiver of pleasure.

She reached into her bag for the fat wodge of notes she had picked up the day before. Larry didn't like taking money with them on a gig, insisting that they wait for his currency *per diems*. But because of the Christmas shopping plan, she had performed this act of secret insurrection. She liked cash. It left no paper trail he could pick up, no evidence of wanton extravagance.

The fat neighbour snored and shifted. Ruth sipped her G & T as she watched the flight attendant bending over Larry to serve him, rubbing her patent court shoe against the back of her stockinged leg. His pink, well-cared-for fingers fluttered over her backside as he regaled her with some amusing tale.

Larry could be quite charming with other women.

'This way,' he snapped, charging ahead through the brightly lit marble halls of Frankfurt airport, holding only his instrument. Ruth followed a little behind, blinking and bowed down by his carry-on holdall and her own large handbag.

Christmassy violin music piped through the corridors. Ruth recognised it as the work of a Korean soloist – a fifteen-year-old girl Larry considered to be his number-one rival.

'Why you had to put a bag in the hold, I don't know,' he said. 'Slows everything down.'

'My cosmetics…' she began. She had once lost a brand-new pot of Clarins moisturiser to an overzealous jobsworth at Heathrow.

'For fuck's sake. Poor dear Annaliese will be waiting for us in arrivals,' he said as they stood in line to show their passports. Annaliese was his thirty-five-year-old, Valkyrie-proportioned, German promoter. 'And my back's killing me.'

'*Danke, mein Liebling*,' he said to the dark beauty at passport control, in an altogether different voice.

'Why don't you rest in there?' Ruth pointed to a lounge at the side of the baggage reclaim hall. Inside, space-age Perspex egg chairs dangled from the ceiling on silver cables. 'And I'll get my suitcase.'

'Give me my holdall, then.'

As she left him hanging in a chair, cradling his violin, looking like a spoiled child, she realised that he had forgotten to reclaim her passport. It was still in her hand.

She zipped it carefully in the inside pocket of her bag, next to the envelope of cash.

As she stood by the carousel, watching the suitcases waltz past in time to the carolling violin, she noted how, with Larry encased in that glass lounge like some malevolent dinosaur embryo, she felt, well, free; unobserved, uncriticised.

Her jaunty red suitcase danced along the carousel towards her. She dived forward and plucked it away, taking some of its motion into her bones, and the thought brewing inside her turned the chill in her chest to fire. Checking one more time that her passport and cash were safe inside her handbag, she took her scarlet Samsonite Partner and tangoed it swiftly towards the 'Nothing To Declare' channel.

'Hello there, again,' she said to her fat plane neighbour, who was waddling just in front of her. She used the bulk of the woman to hide from Annaliese, who was standing statuesquely in arrivals with a holly-decorated sign reading 'Larry Speakman, Maestro'.

Cash in hand, Ruth headed straight for the British Airways counter. She didn't want to risk being at the back of the number two boarding queue again.

'I'd like a one-way ticket, leaving as soon as possible,' she said to the comfortably plain-looking woman behind the counter. 'Somewhere warm, please. Oh, and business class.'

The piped Korean violinist performed a magnificent crescendo, and, for some reason – it could have been coincidence; it could have been something in the ether – the airport lights flickered.

The Naked Lady of Prague

Kate Ellis

I tried to call Magda as soon as I got off the plane. But when there was no answer I told myself that she was bound to be working, trudging round the city with a group of tourists until her feet ached.

When we'd met in London she'd told me all about her life: her history course at Charles University, her part-time job as a tourist guide, and her cramped and shabby apartment in the New Town. Even though we'd spent less than a week together, I felt I knew her as well as I knew myself. Her parents were dead and her sister lived in Australia, so we were both alone in the world. Twin souls. United by our desire to be together.

Soon I'd see her again, but in the meantime I would have to entertain myself in a strange city. And if I did the usual tourist things, I might even bump into her – doing a little detective work to give serendipity a helping hand. I knew her tours began at the Old Town Hall, in front of the astronomical clock, where she waited for her customers with her purple-and-white umbrella. Magda had called the place a tourist trap, but I was sure her cynicism was born of long familiarity and I yearned to see it. I yearned to see anywhere associated with her.

According to the guide book I'd bought at the airport, I should cross Charles Bridge and head for the Old Town Square. As I walked I kept trying Magda's number but there was no reply. I told myself that she probably switched her phone off while she was working. Or maybe I'd written the number down wrong. For the first time I felt a tiny prickle of unease. I had grabbed the chance of a cheap flight and travelled to Prague on impulse. What if Magda was away for some reason? What if I couldn't find her? In her haste to catch her flight home she'd forgotten to give me the address of her apartment.

The temperature was rising and the rucksack on my back felt as though it was filled with rocks. I made for the Old Town Square, following my map. Even if she wasn't there, one of the other tourist guides was sure to know where I could find her.

Tourists meandered across Charles Bridge, flowing as relentlessly as the river Vltava beneath. A jazz band played in the centre of the bridge; carefree melodies for sunshine; the music of smiles. But I felt far from carefree. It was hot and I hadn't eaten since first thing that morning. I didn't know where I was going to sleep that night and I had the beginnings of a headache. I needed a coffee.

I walked through the streets, map in hand, tourist style. But I wasn't the average tourist. I was a lover on a quest to find the object of my desire. A prematurely balding, slightly chubby Romeo seeking out his beautiful young Juliet.

When I reached the Old Town Square it was crammed with tourists, who'd gathered beneath the tower of the astronomical clock and now stared upwards, awaiting the hourly parade of mechanical figures and the trumpeter who heralded the arrival of each new hour from the top of the tower. I gave the masterpiece of the clockmaker's art a casual glance. My guidebook told me that one of the figures was a skeleton representing death and that the clock's maker had been blinded on its completion so that he couldn't create another for a rival city. I've often wondered why beauty and cruelty so often go together.

I searched the milling crowd for Magda and eventually I spotted a purple-and-white umbrella bobbing above the sea of heads on the other side of the street. My heart pounded as I pushed my way through with mumbled excuse-mes, but when I was a few yards away, I saw that the holder of the umbrella was a stranger. Her long hair was a similar shade of honey blonde to Magda's, but she was taller, with sharper features. I hesitated, but I knew that if I didn't speak to her I wouldn't learn where Magda was. And I was desperate to find her.

When I asked the girl with the umbrella if she knew Magda, she looked at me warily as though she suspected I was some pervert. I explained that Magda and I had met in London and that I'd come to Prague to see her. When I'd finished speaking I smiled hopefully. The girl didn't smile back.

'Magda isn't at work today,' she said after a few moments, in perfect, unaccented English.

'Do you know where she is?'

'No.'

A group of Americans who'd drifted up in the hope of a guided tour were listening in to our conversation with expectant looks on their faces. The girl turned away from me, switched on a smile and took the tickets they handed to her, telling them that the tour would start in ten minutes, directly after the spectacle of the clock.

I persisted. 'Do you know Magda's address?'

'No.'

I knew the sharp-faced girl was trying to get rid of me and I couldn't think of a way to convince her of my benign intentions. So I slunk away in the direction of the huge square.

Once I'd had something to eat and drink I'd continue my search.

Magda was starting to regret that she'd ever agreed to it. But she felt she had no choice.

Bedrich had been adamant that it was art, but this didn't make the prospect any more appealing. She was to meet him at his apartment in the Old Town. The lovely apartment that had once belonged to his late grandfather; all faded grandeur, shabby silk drapes and old paintings in elaborate gilded frames covering every wall. She told herself it would soon be over. And that it would be worth every humiliating moment.

'Would you like me to walk there with you?'

She looked round and saw Vaclav standing in the doorway, his large frame filling the space and blocking out the light from the window on the landing.

She shook her head. This was something she'd rather do alone.

She walked over to Vaclav and he took her hand, holding it against his stubbly cheek before kissing it. He'd looked out for her ever since she'd moved into the apartment below his. And now she was about to repay him.

It was time to leave. Magda picked up her small pink vanity case and Vaclav stood to one side to let her out.

As she left the apartment by the tall front door a group of men entering the bar on the other side of the road turned to look at her. She ignored them and marched past a gaggle of tourists who were making for the hotel next door, trailing wheeled suitcases behind them like obedient dogs. Soon she'd have to get used to the avaricious stares of men. She suddenly felt sick at the thought.

She was used to walking; when she was working as a guide she covered miles every day, answering the most irritating of questions with a smile fixed to her face. Now she made for the Old Town, where grand art nouveau façades gave way to tightly packed buildings and squares filled with café tables. There were more tourists here, along with the odd stag party – young men laughing and enjoying the local beer. One or two of them looked at her appreciatively, but she was careful not to make eye contact. She had an appointment to keep.

Now the initial excitement of arriving in Prague had worn off, I was starting to feel a little foolish. I'd come all this way on a whim and now I knew I probably had no way of finding her before nightfall. But there'd been nothing to keep me in London. Few friends and no family. Well, there was a family, but they were hardly the loving kind and I hadn't seen them in months. My studio flat was one damp room the size of a cupboard, and my job in a chain coffee shop was hardly challenging – not for someone with my qualifications. I'd felt I needed a change, an adventure. And what better adventure, I'd thought, than a quest to seek out the girl of my dreams?

Magda had come into the coffee shop a month before and we'd started talking. Or rather, I went up to her and started a conversation on the pretext of clearing her table. She told me she'd come to London to bring something over for a friend and that she was at a loose end. Then I plucked up courage and offered to show her the sights; I was amazed when she'd agreed. She told me she worked as a tourist guide in her native Prague to help fund her studies, and as we toured the city she joked that I should have her job, which was nice of her. She hadn't organised anywhere to stay so I took her back to my flat. I knew the place was in a state so I asked her to wait outside for a few moments while I rushed in to have a quick tidy round, but she said it didn't matter. Most of the girls I'd known over my thirty-six years had made me feel like an inadequate idiot. But Magda wasn't like that.

It wasn't until my third night of sleeping on the floor that she invited me back into my bed. I was terrified my inexperience would show, that I would seem gauche and clumsy to the beautiful creature with the glowing flesh and the golden hair. But she said nothing and I was grateful for her kindness. I'd never met a girl like Magda before, and when she left for home she said I should come to Prague one day and look her up. But she forgot to give me her address, so here I was, hungry and thirsty, and with nowhere to stay.

It was seven o'clock now and my stomach felt empty. I crossed the Old Town Square in search of an eating place that wasn't too expensive. I'd changed my money at the airport, undoubtedly getting the worst exchange rate possible, and now I stood in the shelter of a doorway counting it. It would last me a couple of days, provided I found Magda and didn't have the added expense of a hotel.

I wandered down a side street and reached another, smaller square lined with old cream stucco buildings with fancy façades. It was a pretty place, filled with restaurant tables shaded by awnings and giant umbrellas. I ambled round, reading menus, noting prices, and finally decided that a pasta dish was within my means. I sat down at a table for two and ordered cannelloni and a glass of beer, inwardly cringing when a group of burly, laughing young men poured into the square and sat down at a long table nearby. From their matching sports shirts I could tell they were from a rugby club. And from their accents as they called and joked with each other, I knew they were Welsh. As far from home as I was, only with plenty of company.

The newcomers' banter was amiable, if a little loud. As I tucked into my cannelloni I couldn't avoid listening in to their private jokes … and the information that someone called Sian was up for anything, as was a well-endowed female called Rhiannon. I tried to ignore them, as did the German couple on the table next to mine, who were ploughing stoically through a pair of large pizzas. I tried to contemplate my next move, knowing that it would probably involve finding a cheap hotel.

As I raised my glass of beer to my lips I sensed something was amiss but wasn't sure what. The rugby club had fallen strangely quiet, as though they had just been told of the death of a friend, and I noticed that the German couple had put down their cutlery and were staring straight ahead, open-mouthed. Suddenly the German man delved into his bag and took out a camera. Something was happening. I craned my neck to see what it was.

The scene had a surreal quality: the city of Kafka come to life. In my experience, naked women didn't usually walk confidently through a public square, stopping every now and then to pose and pout for a camera. Perhaps this was a dream. A pleasant one.

The rugby club watched wide-eyed, silenced by their own astonishment. The photographer – a tall, dark young man, the untrustworthy side of handsome – walked ahead of the apparition like a herald, turning every now and then to point his camera at her. It was a large camera, the type used by professionals, and I guessed that this was some kind of photo shoot. But the girl's nakedness, her vulnerability in that public place, shocked me, even though I'd never before thought of myself as a prude.

I'm ashamed to confess that I was watching the girl's body, like a farmer evaluating livestock. For a few long moments her face held no interest for me. It was the perfect breasts and the neat triangle of hair between her thighs that claimed my attention. Besides, her face was turned away from me, so she was just a lovely body without a soul.

Until she turned her head and my world fell apart.

Bedrich had gone to great pains to persuade her that it would be fine; that it was wrong to be ashamed of your body. Besides, he'd be there to make sure she came to no harm. And how hard could it be? she asked herself. It was only another performance. An act.

She'd left her clothes at his apartment in the Old Town. He'd given her a pink feather boa to drape around her neck, as if he imagined it would provide some protection. Instead it had felt ridiculous, so, after stepping out into the street to the stares of passers-by, she'd discarded it.

As she walked she could hear Bedrich cooing encouragement: 'Come on, baby.' 'Show me you want me.' 'That's right.' 'Beautiful.' The words made her feel dirty but she did what was expected of her and thought of the reward. More money than she could dream of earning in a year of herding tourists around the historic sights of Prague.

She tried hard not to make eye contact with her audience; the men who watched her, first with amazement and then with barely disguised lust. As she pranced and pouted at the lens she did her best to concentrate only on Bedrich and his camera.

After half an hour it was all over and she returned to his apartment to get dressed. Interested only in his camera and the results of his work, he hardly spoke to her on the journey back, which made it easier somehow.

Once she'd done what she had to do, she rushed back to her own apartment, tore off her clothes and made straight for the shower, standing beneath the cleansing flow of water with her eyes closed, trying not to remember how she'd felt out there. She knew Vaclav would be waiting in his flat above and was relieved when he didn't come down; she needed to be alone for a while.

The next morning, when she switched on the radio and heard that Bedrich Novak had been found dead, she felt numb.

Although it hurt to see her flaunt herself like that, I followed her. I wasn't so naïve that I imagined she was as sexually inexperienced as I was when we'd met – in fact I could tell she wasn't; but I hadn't expected anything like this. My mother, who I hadn't spoken to for a year, would have called her a depraved whore and said that I should have nothing to do with her. But I wasn't so sure. I hadn't liked the look of the man with the camera. He was a Svengali if ever I saw one – a manipulative controller of innocent women. The more I thought about it, the more certain I was that this hadn't been Magda's choice. And if that was the case, it was up to me to rescue her from a dreadful and demeaning situation. I would be her knight in shining armour. And she would be grateful.

I trailed her as she walked back with the man to the grand building in the Old Town; it looked like a small palace, with exclusive shops tucked away behind its ground-floor arcade. She walked slightly behind him, attracting stares as she went. I was angry that he didn't even have the decency to provide her with some kind of robe to cover her nakedness. I hated him for the way he ignored her as she walked behind him, her eyes lowered modestly. I was tempted to call out to her, but I sensed she wouldn't want me to witness her shame.

She disappeared inside the building through an old, studded double door at the side of a shop that sold expensive jewellery. This place didn't match the description she'd given of her flat so I guessed it must be his. I waited five minutes before strolling up to the door and giving it a push, trying to look casual, as if I had every right to be there. The door opened and I stepped inside a huge hallway with chequerboard tiles on the floor and an elegant wrought-iron staircase sweeping up to the levels above. I saw a row of neat oak mailboxes on the far wall and walked over to examine the names. There was just one that looked like a single male name – Bedrich Novak – but of course I couldn't be sure this was him and I didn't want to risk a misunderstanding in a foreign land, so I stood and waited, unsure what I was going to say if I saw her.

I didn't have long to wait. I heard a door open and then shut with a bang, and when I looked up I saw a movement on the first-floor landing. Somebody was hurrying down the grand staircase so I dodged out of the front door and concealed myself behind one of the arches outside. Then I saw her, fully dressed this time in jeans and a simple black t-shirt. She looked so lovely. But, as she barged through the tourists strolling in the evening warmth, I noted that her face was an impassive mask.

I walked a few yards behind her, careful to keep out of sight. From the corner of my eye I thought I sensed someone else was following too. But I could have been mistaken.

Trying to keep her in view was difficult as she dodged through the crowds, and when the Old Town gave way to the new, I had traffic and passing trams to contend with. At one point I lost her for five minutes or so, but then I spotted her again down a side street. She turned down another street and then disappeared into a building, once grand but now faded, with flaking stucco walls and graffiti beside the front door. The place fitted the description she'd given me of her apartment and I was satisfied that I'd found her address at last. I didn't feel inclined to burst in on her, though. After what I'd just seen I needed time to think.

The building opposite caught my attention: a beer hall with an elaborate clock protruding from its façade. It looked like a good place to grab a drink while I decided what to do next.

As I walked into the great arched entrance, I was aware of somebody behind me. But when I turned my head there was no one there.

The victim, Bedrich Novak, had been stabbed with a decorative dagger that had been hanging on the apartment wall: a single wound to the heart. The police were looking for a young woman who was seen emerging from the building with the victim the previous evening. She had been naked, and a witness had said that she was beautiful. But he obviously hadn't taken much notice of her face and the vague description he gave to the police would have fitted half the girls in the city. Novak's expensive camera was missing, and with it any potential pictures of the girl in question. The police were keeping an open mind, but as several valuable paintings had disappeared from the apartment, robbery seemed the likely motive.

Magda held her breath as she listened to the news on the radio, clinging to every word. Nobody knew her identity and she wanted to keep it that way. She had to carry on as normal.

The arrival of Timothy at her apartment at ten o'clock the previous night had come as a shock. Her spirits had plunged when she saw him standing there, grinning nervously and smelling of beer. But she knew she had to make the best of the situation as she didn't want to draw attention to herself. After the events of yesterday, more attention was exactly what she didn't need.

Besides, she couldn't help feeling a little sorry for Timothy. When she was in London he'd provided her with free accommodation, and she'd paid for it with the only thing she had to offer. However, it had soon become clear that he'd mistaken her willingness in bed for reciprocated feelings, and she'd been glad to get away. He'd outlived his usefulness the moment she'd boarded the plane home. Now he'd turned up again she wasn't quite sure what to do.

Even though she wanted to get rid of him as soon as possible, some reserve of kindness she'd forgotten she possessed meant that she didn't want to hurt him if she could avoid it. He had been talking about accompanying her on her guided tours, and she didn't see any harm in it. Let him have his short break in Prague. His presence might even be useful if she needed somebody to vouch for her if the police came calling. A man in love is easily persuaded into a white lie.

Magda heard the door open and looked up to see Vaclav hovering in the doorway. He looked unkempt, wearing a sleeveless vest that revealed tattooed snakes chasing unseen prey up his muscular arms. At six feet three he towered over her, making her feel like a delicate doll.

'Who is he?' he asked.

'His name's Timothy. I met him last time I was in London. He's in town for a couple of days, that's all.'

Vaclav was frowning as though he didn't believe her.

She gave him a smile and tilted her head to one side. 'Be an angel and buy me some cigarettes.' She reached for the purse that was lying on the table and took out a note.

He hesitated before taking it. 'Where did he sleep last night?'

'The sofa,' she lied. Sometimes lies were easier.

He nodded, satisfied, and as he left she sighed with relief.

As soon as I walked into Magda's living room after taking a shower I sensed she was worried. But when I asked her what was wrong she just smiled sadly and shook her head. I hadn't mentioned that I'd seen her doing that photo shoot thing the day before, because as soon as she'd invited me into the apartment we'd started to kiss, then, before I knew it, we were making love and the moment was somehow lost. But, still, I needed to know how she'd become involved and who the man was. Every time I thought of his smug, vulpine face I felt anger rise inside me like a wave of nausea.

I thought that my anger might affect my performance in bed, but if anything, it probably improved it. Magda had no complaints anyway.

I must say I didn't think much of her flat … or of the bloke who lived upstairs. She said his name was Vaclav; he looked the sort you don't argue with. I didn't like the way he looked at Magda but, if everything went to plan, I'd soon find a job in Prague and we'd find somewhere nicer to live. It was time to say goodbye to my old life and make a new start. And this time I wasn't going to let anything stop me.

I was going to watch Magda doing her tourist guide bit. As we left the flat I saw Vaclav watching from the top of the stairs. I didn't trust him one little bit.

Magda could see police cars outside Bedrich's apartment building. The area had been cordoned off with tape and her tourists were staring at it, full of curiosity. A large American man in a baseball cap asked her if she knew what was going on; she said there must have been a robbery. Prague in general was a safe city and such things were unusual – although it was always wise to beware of pickpockets on Charles Bridge, she heard herself saying, her mind racing. She saw Timothy watching her and she felt herself blushing. She wondered if he'd guessed her secret; but if he knew, surely he would have said something last night.

As she led the way out of the Old Town into the Jewish Quarter, Magda held her purple-and-white umbrella aloft to prevent her flock from straying. There were always dawdlers who didn't make the effort to keep up – she was used to that by now. But she wasn't used to the devoted presence of Timothy, watching her adoringly, hanging on her every word. She was starting to feel like a prisoner under his rapt gaze. But it wouldn't be for long, she told herself.

When she reached the next place of interest she stopped to let the stragglers catch up before she spoke.

'On your left is the Old-New Synagogue,' she began. 'Built around 1270, it is the oldest synagogue in Europe.' She glanced at Timothy and saw he was listening intently, like a child enjoying a favourite bedtime story. 'In the late sixteenth century Rabbi Low, a Jewish scholar who was said to possess magical powers, made a man out of clay and brought it to life. The creature was supposed to defend the community from attack but it turned on Rabbi Low, who was forced to disable it and hide it in the rafters of the Old-New Synagogue.' She paused for effect. 'The creature was called the Golem and, according to legend, its remains are still up there, in the attic of the Synagogue.'

The usual question followed. Has anybody been up there to have a look? Magda gave the same evasive reply she always did: it was a good story; and nobody likes to douse a good story with the icy water of fact.

They walked on through the Jewish Quarter and then across Charles Bridge to the other side of the river, where the tour would wind up at the castle. Timothy never left her side. Another day or so and he'd be gone. And she'd be free.

I enjoyed the tour and I thought Magda really brought the history of the city to life. I liked the bit about the Golem. To create a creature to guard you from attack seemed like every inventor's dream. But stories like that never end well, do they?

When the tour was over we walked back from the castle. She hardly said a word. In fact she'd been subdued ever since we saw the police cars parked outside that man's apartment. The punters couldn't tell, of course, because she did her job so professionally. But I felt I knew her so well. Soul mates, that's what we were. I'd never had a soul mate before, and it felt so brilliant to know I wasn't alone anymore and that she loved me. I didn't know what I'd do if I lost her, I really didn't.

When we got back to her flat she asked when I was going back to London, and when I said I wasn't going back she seemed surprised. I can't deny that I was disappointed; I'd expected her to fling her arms around me and tell me how glad she was that we'd always be together. Maybe she just needed time to come to terms with the fact that I'd always be here for her.

She was in the kitchen, chopping vegetables, and I went to help her. It's the little things you do together that are important, after all. Thanks to my beautiful Magda – my perfect girl – I was no longer the old Timothy, the man from the coffee bar with no dress sense who was so frightened of women that he didn't have a girlfriend until the age of thirty-six. She had created a new Timothy. And my life began here.

It was the woman in the apartment opposite Bedrich Novak's who gave the police their first lead. She had seen the girl prancing naked down the stairs the day before Bedrich's body was found. Bedrich had been snapping her with that fancy camera of his, and the little trollop had been giving him the come-on. The woman was the widow of a doctor, sixty-eight years old and a regular worshipper at the Church of Our Lady before Tyn. She didn't hold with naked women flaunting themselves for all to see in the streets of the Czech capital.

She'd seen the girl there before and she knew exactly what she was up to. She was after money, as they all were these days. Bedrich Novak was rich, and there were any number of valuable paintings in that apartment, collected by his late grandfather, who had been a very wealthy man. The source of the old man's wealth had always been shrouded in mystery, but she suspected some sharp practice in the war years. And as for the paintings, a lot of priceless art had gone missing during the Nazi occupation and not all of it had been returned to its rightful owners. But that was really none of her business.

The police knew that a number of pictures had gone from the apartment, leaving tell-tale pale rectangles on the floral wallpaper in the drawing room.

And when the woman told them that she'd seen the naked girl return later, fully clothed and carrying a suitcase, and that she knew she acted as a tourist guide because she'd seen her in the Old Town Square carrying a purple-and-white umbrella, they thanked her and continued their enquiries.

Vaclav had a buyer in London for the Renoir that Magda had taken from Bedrich Novak's apartment, and he'd packed it carefully in the hidden compartment of the case. It was small enough to be taken as hand luggage, as was the Rembrandt. It wouldn't be a problem.

Magda had done well. Vaclav knew she'd only spent the night with that pasty-faced Englishman to allay his suspicions. In fact, she had turned deception into an art form. She'd managed to fool that rich idiot, Bedrich, who fancied himself as some cool photographer, and once he was dead she'd taken the paintings as instructed and disposed of the camera in the Vltava. Shame about that, it was an expensive model. But some things couldn't be helped.

From the moment Magda had moved into the flat below, Vaclav had moulded her. He'd persuaded her that he loved her and that, if she followed his plans, one day they would be rich and live happily ever after. She had become his creature. She'd even killed for him.

She had turned out to be a natural killer and that pretty, innocent face with the wide blue eyes hid a ruthlessness that sometimes frightened him. She had dealt with every obstacle in his path cleanly and efficiently.

But now he'd heard the police were looking for her. The last thing he needed was trouble, so he'd taken steps to solve the problem. Everything would be fine. He was in control.

The body of student Magda Marekova was discovered in the attic of the building where she lived alone in a first-floor apartment. She is believed to be the woman police wanted to speak to in connection with the death of wealthy photographer Bedrich Novak.

The police now wish to interview the dead woman's upstairs neighbour, Vaclav Janak, an unemployed fine art graduate, in connection with her death. They also want to trace an unidentified Englishman who has recently been seen with her.

It is believed that her body was found in a large travelling trunk when her landlady noticed an unpleasant smell on the landing. The young woman had been strangled. And the landlady told our reporter that she was naked.

I would never have imagined that I was capable of killing anybody, but when I emerged from the bathroom and saw her clinging to Vaclav, kissing him with such passion, I felt betrayed.

As soon as he'd gone, I tackled her and I was shocked when she turned on me. She didn't want me, she said. I was a stupid, ugly nobody and she'd used me because I'd been convenient to her in London. If I imagined she'd felt anything for me, I was a fool. I stood there, stunned. She'd become a monster – a creature I hardly recognised. I reached out my hands to stop the flow of filthy words coming from the mouth I'd once kissed. I hardly remember the rest.

I panicked when I saw her lying there quite still on the kitchen floor, her bulging eyes staring up at me. But when Vaclav returned he stayed cool, saying everything would be fine if I did exactly as he said. I really hadn't expected him to be so sympathetic, but he said that he could tell I'd been provoked. He understood what had made me lose control and strangle her like that, and he didn't see why I should spend the rest of my life in jail for one moment of madness.

I was numb with shock at what I'd just done so I let Vaclav take charge. He took Magda's clothes off, saying she'd be harder to identify that way, and he put her body in a trunk in the attic. He said it might be years before anyone found her and I wasn't to worry.

Then he asked me to take a suitcase back to London with me and deliver it to a man he knew who'd give me a package in exchange. I'm meeting Vaclav tonight by the London Eye to hand the package over to him. When he phoned me a couple of hours ago he said he'll have another delivery job for me next week. He said we make a good team and that, if I play my cards right, he'll make me a rich man.

So my new life's begun and it turns out that Vaclav's a really decent bloke – a mate who understands me like nobody's ever done before. And I'm totally happy to go along with everything he says because, after what he's done for me, I feel I owe him. I really do.

Snowbird

Kate Rhodes

I quit my job and flew south with the snowbirds when summer ended, the plane from New York packed with retirees hungry for sunshine and sea air.

Key West's beauty dazzled me right from the start: bougainvillea dripping from every porch, crab boats jostling in the harbour, a tall lighthouse marking the continent's edge. Weeks passed before I noticed that the road along the quayside was thin as a wire, hovering metres above the ocean, waiting for the first high breaker to wash it away. Street names came from hurricanes that had ripped the coastline apart, the local topography informed by natural disasters. Compared to Manhattan's brownstones, the wooden cabins looked dangerously insubstantial, yet my old life of rain and responsibility already seemed like ancient history.

By the end of October I had moved into a villa on Louisa Street, just as a heatwave arrived. The building was impractically large for a bachelor, but its stucco columns and old-school elegance were a feast for the eyes. One afternoon I was lazing on my veranda listening to snakebirds hissing overhead, girls' laughter, followed by a scooter buzzing down Seaport Avenue. The air smelled of jasmine and humidity, hot enough to sear the back of my throat. When I opened my eyes again, a woman was standing in the neighbouring garden, slim back turned, watering an immaculate flowerbed. Her dark hair left the nape of her neck exposed; I waited for a glimpse of her face. My work as a plastic surgeon had trained me to analyse patients' features with forensic care before making my first incision, the habit too engrained to shift.

When she finally spun round, her face was heart-shaped and

delicate. She must have been in her fifties, but looked much younger. To the uninitiated eye, her surgery would have been invisible, just a slight elongation between temple and cheekbone. I thought she seemed familiar, but when she extended her hand across the fence her eyes were cat-like and sea green, giving no sign of recognition.

'You must be the new neighbour. I'm Nicole Jackson.'

'Jeff Brubaker, delighted to meet you. Your garden's stunning, Nicole.'

'I wish it was mine; I'm just renting for the winter,' she replied, smiling.

A pale shadow drifted across one of her upstairs windows. 'Are your family with you?'

'I'm alone, which suits me fine – I get plenty of reading time.'

Nicole's voice had a whispering quality, soft and bell-like. She explained that she was widowed; she had flown down from Maine to escape the cold. 'Do you know the Keys well, Jeff?'

'Not really, I've just moved here. I should buy myself a guidebook and go exploring.'

She gave a thoughtful nod. 'I've vacationed here for years. Would you like a tour some time?'

'That would be wonderful. When are you free?'

'Tomorrow, around noon?'

My system was buzzing when I stepped back indoors. It had been a long time since a woman had affected me beyond the aesthetic level. I had dated plenty of pretty career girls over the years, but none had tempted me enough to sacrifice my freedom. I studied myself in the hall mirror; genetic good fortune had granted me a strong jaw and a full head of hair, with only a few streaks of grey. I felt certain the attraction between us had been mutual.

When I visited Nicole's house the next afternoon no one answered the bell. The screen door hung open, so I stepped inside and called her name. She appeared on the stairs in a chic summer dress, her smile lighting up her face.

'Come on in, Jeff. The door's never locked.'

'Never?'

'People here are too laidback to steal.' Her laughter was gentle, not mocking.

We took a rickshaw to the island's cemetery that afternoon, searching the Garden of Remembrance for writers and movie stars. The dead lay in marble vaults, toes pointing towards Cuba, jasmine twining between the gravestones. Afterwards we ate gumbo prawns and key lime pie in a Cajun restaurant off Flagler Street, hemmed in by pastel-coloured houses with balconies yielding to rust. The island's beauty and Nicole's charm made the clock spin backwards, leaving me young and nervous again; she had a way of fixing me with those feline eyes that made it impossible to lie.

'Ever been married, Jeff?'

'Work got in the way. Maybe I was a little obsessive.'

I was too daunted to kiss her when we got home, but her hand touched my shoulder as we said goodbye.

We fell into a pattern of meeting daily after that. I was determined to fill my house with beautiful objects, Nicole helping me find glassware, paintings and bespoke furniture from local antique markets. We took boat trips together, shared late suppers. My eyes skimmed other women's faces but never lingered. Once or twice I'd catch sight of an ex-patient, their names escaping me. The thousands of procedures I'd carried out had blurred into one; few patients had ever been dissatisfied, apart from the ones who expected their youth to be restored, perfectly intact. A businessman had taken out a lawsuit earlier that year, but it had been easier to quit before my fiftieth birthday than bankrupt myself defending my name.

'You look thoughtful, Jeff,' Nicole said. 'Dwelling on the past?'

'Not at all. The present's far more appealing.'

'Take me dancing. That should lift your spirits.'

'If there's a place with decent music.'

We ended up in a bar on Mallory Square, the band playing Tijuana jazz, her cheek on my shoulder, the intimacy between us far more intoxicating than the cocktails we drank.

Our walk home was slow and leisurely. I'd almost gathered enough courage to say how I felt, when Nicole suddenly pointed ahead, her eyes startled.

'Something's wrong, Jeff.'

Lights burned in every window of my house, the front door gaping. I made Nicole wait on the lawn before checking inside. The place was empty, but paint had been smeared across the furniture, graffiti faces leering from the walls, glass sculptures shattered. The damage upstairs was even worse, my bedroom filled with the sharp reek of red wine, which had been poured over my bed. My visitors must have planned to desecrate, not to steal; they had found my built-in safe, but the lock was intact.

Nicole's face was a shocked white mask when she finally surveyed the damage. 'This is terrible, Jeff. Let me call 911.'

Two police officers walked me through the building. The intruders had entered via the garden, then jimmied a downstairs window. One of the lieutenants was so fresh-faced and awkward, he looked like he'd just graduated from high school.

'We'll file the report tonight, sir, so you can make a claim.'

Their guarded expressions indicated that they already knew the vandals would never be found. Through the window I saw a neighbour shaking his head blankly at the cops, explaining that he'd seen nothing. Nicole's hand on my arm felt cool, despite the tropical warmth.

'Sleep at mine tonight, Jeff, please. Use my guest room.'

'Thanks, but I'll stay here. This thing can't beat me.'

Her offer held no appeal for the simple reason that I wanted to be in her bed, not her spare room. After she'd gone I set about cleaning the place, even though it was past midnight. The attack made no sense. Why would someone destroy my possessions, then leave empty-handed?

By lunchtime the next day my calmness was returning. Nicole's house was empty, so I searched for her in our favourite haunts. Duval Street heaved with lobster-skinned tourists in Hawaiian shirts and Bermuda shorts. Then, out of nowhere, a woman's voice whispered in my ear:

'No one to blame but yourself.'

When I spun round the street was too thick with pedestrians to identify who had spoken. The air felt sticky and too thick to breathe. Holidaymakers elbowed past, shoulders jostling me from the sidewalk.

I went straight to the police station, but the young lieutenant shook his head. 'We've interviewed everyone in the locality, Mr Brubaker. No one was seen entering your building. Burglars probably tried the safe then trashed the place and got out fast. I'll send a patrol officer round tonight, but you should take extra security measures, in case they come back. Some housebreakers like to try again.'

I thanked him for his advice through gritted teeth. The police department might consider the matter unimportant, but the wanton destruction that occurred at my home seemed too intimate for a random attack. I stopped at a bar on Higgs Beach, even though the sea's beauty no longer seduced me, its garish turquoise searing my retinas. I allowed myself a glass of wine and fifteen minutes of self-pity before deciding to track down the culprit myself. Key West was less than a mile long. Surely I could locate a single criminal?

I scribbled a list of suspects in my notebook, including the maintenance staff at my villa. Any one of them might be nursing a grudge against snowbirds like me, who were rich enough to live in luxury without working. It only took a little gentle persuasion for the employment agency to reveal that my helpers lived on Stock Island.

Affluence ended as soon as my car crossed the bridge, fields of trailers sprawling down to the beach. José, my gardener, sat on a folding chair beside his small cabin. His wife brought us coffee and we made halting conversation in pidgin Spanish. José's welcome was so friendly, I couldn't bring myself to interrogate him about the break-in. My cleaning lady's greeting was more muted, but she answered my questions politely enough. Only the pool man was openly hostile. He replied in a low growl when I asked if he had seen anyone hanging around my property.

His girlfriend bustled out onto the porch. 'The police already came by,' she snapped. 'Where do you get off, making accusations?'

I climbed back into my car before the situation could escalate. By the time I returned to Louisa Street, I had spoken to each of my acquaintances on Key West but found no proof whatsoever. Maybe the attack had been random after all, that afternoon's whispered threat intended for someone else.

It was seven-thirty when Nicole reappeared. She looked as lovely as ever, in a silk dress that accentuated her slimness, but her smile was tentative.

'My mother's ill, Jeff. I have to fly home tomorrow.'

'But you'll come back?'

'There's no one else to care for her. Shall we have one last dinner?'

'Sorry, I'm meeting an old friend.'

She floated a kiss across my cheek. 'Come and see me soon, won't you?'

I attempted a smile. Maine was two thousand miles away, much too far for a casual visit. In the hallway afterwards my shoulders slumped against the wall. My possessions were beyond repair, and Nicole's departure would remove another piece of beauty from my landscape. An odd pain swelled behind my breastbone. I covered it with my hand, trying to rub it away.

Nicole's departure hardened my determination to find my intruder. He might be foolish enough to pay me a second visit and try his luck with my safe again. This time I intended to give him the fright of his life. The handgun I normally hid in the glove compartment of my car was a cold weight in my pocket. I would use it to scare him senseless if he came calling, then turn him over to the police.

I left the house an hour later, jacket slung over my arm. If the intruder was watching, he would believe the house unoccupied. However, I circled at the end of the street, re-entering via the yard. Keeping the place in darkness, I settled on the living-room sofa.

Footsteps woke me just after ten. I crouched behind the door, gun trained on the middle of the room. A tang of paraffin hit the back of my throat, and two figures appeared in the half-dark, whispering to each other. When I hit the light switch Nicole was upending a kerosene can onto the floor, another woman cowering behind her.

When I finally managed to speak my voice was groggy with shock. 'I don't understand.'

'Put the gun down, Jeff. I can't speak with it pointed straight at me.'

I gave a shaky laugh then put the revolver on the coffee table. Nicole perched on the sofa, her companion's head bowed.

'This is my daughter Helen,' she said quietly.

The woman beside her slowly lifted her face and the picture came into focus. The family resemblance was what had made Nicole seem familiar to me when I first met her. Her daughter had reacted badly to surgery; her facial nerves were damaged, and my corrective procedures had failed. I had been lucky that the medical examiner recorded a verdict of clinical error, not negligence.

'She's been a recluse ever since,' Nicole said.

'Why did you follow me here?'

'To hurt you, of course.' Her voice was brittle with anger.

Suddenly Helen's maimed face leered close to mine, her mouth grossly misshapen, one eye skewed much too wide. There was an explosion as a bullet flashed past, shattering the window, then a fierce pain as my gun clattered to the floor. I managed to grab it, blood splashing from my cheek as I leaned down to seize the weapon. My gaze fell on the girl's broken features again as she yelled my name, cursing, before Nicole dragged her away.

The future repositioned itself when the door finally clicked shut behind them. The house was ruined now, and so was the island. I would return to New York, sacrificing the comfort of winter sunshine. After stumbling to the bathroom I studied my wounded cheek with concern; the livid gash would require a skin graft. My hands shook so badly it took a long time to apply tape and surgical dressing. When I finally stepped back into the living room there was a flicker of orange, before the heat registered. The sight in front of me was hard to comprehend. The floor was on fire, paint bubbling from the walls and ceiling. Thoughts jittered through my mind as flames licked at my shoes. They must have thrown a lit match through the window, the room already an inferno, leaving me no exit route.

The smoke overpowered me in seconds. There was no way to quell the flames, breath choking from my lungs. I had fooled myself all along: the snowbird is a non-existent species. Strip away the wings, feathers and dreams, and all you have left is a human being, too pale and spineless to sense danger, even when it's right in front of his eyes.

The Repentance Wood

Martin Edwards

'Would you do me a favour?' a soft voice asked. A female voice, quite young, the accent faintly American.

Jeremy was lost in thought, still trying to master his disappointment over Elaine's departure, just at a time when everything had seemed to be going so well.

Glancing over his shoulder, he said, with casual gallantry, 'Of course; if I can.'

The woman was young and slender, with short, fluffy blonde hair and gamine features. She handed him her smartphone. 'Could you take a photo of me, please?'

'Gladly.'

Her pink top was skimpy, her white shorts very short. He was tempted to offer a compliment on her looks, but checked himself just in time. She was young enough to be his daughter, and her looks had an innocence, a delicacy, that made it seem almost indecent for a man of his age to flirt with her, however harmlessly.

Taking a couple of dainty steps backwards, she posed with her spine against the safety rail, squinting to keep the harsh sunlight out of her eyes. Behind her, on the other side of the broad creek, the towers of Dubai shimmered, a modern mirage of steel and glass.

He took one shot, and considered the result. She was a pretty kid, but he hadn't done her justice.

'Let me take another one for luck.'

The second photo was a marginal improvement. She'd relaxed a little, and her smile seemed more natural.

He thrust the smartphone into her small hand. 'See what you think. I'm no David Bailey.'

She glanced at the pictures, and flashed him a quick smile. Her teeth were very white, her skin lightly tanned. 'Thanks so much.'

He felt tempted to linger and start a conversation. But it would be a mistake. Someone her age had probably never even heard of David Bailey. Giving an affable nod, he continued along the curving path that led between the lawn and the hotel pool and entered the air-conditioned lobby, which offered sanctuary from the sweltering heat.

At that moment, a lift door opened and Elaine Klein stepped out. Her sundress had been designed with a younger woman in mind, but she had the poise to carry it off. A diaphanous silk scarf disguised the wrinkles around her neck. Her wristwatch was a diamond Rolex, her Globe-Trotter suitcase the colour of her favourite champagne.

'I came to say goodbye,' he said as she approached.

She extended her hand, the gold wrist bangles tinkling. 'It was so nice knowing you, Jeremy.'

Nothing in her tone suggested any change of mind. For forty-eight hours, they'd come together, strangers in a strange land who met in a bar and ended up in bed together. Now their brief encounter was over. She was returning to her apartment in Manhattan, and he was staying in Dubai. She'd told him she didn't plan to keep in touch, though she'd always be glad that they'd spent time together. At first he'd had her eating out of his hand. Why had she changed her tune so abruptly? Irrationally, he felt as if he'd been used. He was seized by a sudden urge to catch hold of her and make a scene, but they were in a public place, with guests and porters milling around. He had to let her go.

'Safe travels.'

A uniformed flunkey carried her luggage out to the waiting taxi, and Elaine followed without a second glance.

He decided to drown his sorrows with a drink under the shade of the poolside bar. The temperature had risen above ninety, and dismay had drained him of energy. He wasn't in the mood for sight-seeing. Far less to attend any of the sessions in the conference centre.

He was drinking a piña colada when the young woman he'd

photographed strolled up to the bar. She'd been swimming; a towel was slung over her thin shoulder and her hair was damp. She sat down a couple of bar stools away and ordered a lemonade.

'Another beautiful day,' he said.

'It's scorching already. How do people bear the endless sun?' she said.

'I don't mind a bit of rain myself. Then again, I grew up in Seattle, so I'm used to it. Where are you from?'

'Lancaster, originally. The north-west of England. But I've lived in Sussex for years. A quiet cottage tucked away on the Downs, miles from anywhere.'

'Sounds idyllic.'

'It's very peaceful. I always prefer a house that's off the beaten track. The one downside is that commuting into the office in London is a nightmare; there's no quick route. But I don't go in every day, thank goodness. One of the benefits of being my own boss is that I can pick and choose my hours.'

'You're on vacation?'

'Yes and no. A publishing conference is taking place, you may have seen the banners by the indoor waterfall. It's my reason for being here, at least officially.'

A faint smile. 'And unofficially?'

'I've never been to the Emirates. I suppose I was curious about the place. So it's a bit of a junket, really.' He put a finger to his lips. 'Don't snitch to the taxman, will you?'

'My lips are sealed,' she said. 'So you're a publisher?'

'Sort of. It's a small company, almost a hobby, really.'

'Sounds great. Maybe I ought to read one of your books.'

'I'm afraid my business is very specialised. Get ready to stifle a yawn.' He returned her smile. 'We produce fine limited editions of copyright-free non-fiction books on medical and scientific topics.'

'Maybe I'll stick to my trashy thrillers.'

He took another sip of piña colada. 'You're on holiday?'

'For a week, yes. A spur-of-the-moment decision. The weather at home was even lousier than usual, and I'd nothing better to do. So I thought, why not?'

'You're here on your own?'

She gave him a direct look, and for a moment she no longer resembled a fragile teenager. 'In case you're wondering if I should still be at school or college or something, I ought to say I'm twenty-six in May, believe it or not.'

'Sorry, I didn't mean to be rude.' Women didn't often fluster Jeremy, but most of those he knew were his own age or older. 'Independent travelling; I'm a great believer in it myself.'

She turned her attention to her lemonade and the photos on her smartphone.

Still brooding about Elaine, he gazed out across the water towards the shiny pinnacles of downtown Dubai. As he finished his cocktail, the bartender came over, and Jeremy found himself asking the young woman if she'd care for another lemonade.

'OK, thanks.' She flashed a shy smile. 'I hope I didn't sound tetchy. It's a fault of mine, my mother always used to say so.'

'Well, parents can be hard work themselves, can't they? Mine were sticklers, much as I loved them.'

'They're dead?'

He nodded. 'Quite a long time ago. Remember next time yours fuss too much – it's only because they care for you.'

She shrugged. 'It'll never happen, I'm afraid. My mother and father were both killed the winter before last. Car crash.'

'Oh, I'm so sorry. Must have been a terrible blow to you and your family.'

'I don't really have a family,' she said. 'I'm footloose and fancy-free. No sisters, no brothers, no nothing, really. That's why I was able to come out here at a moment's notice. I suppose I'm impulsive. Just like Mom used to say.'

He smiled. 'Impulsive enough to accept an invitation to dinner from a complete stranger?'

'Sure.' She drained her glass. 'What time?'

Her name was Georgia. As they browsed the menu in the Skysplorer Revolving Restaurant, they exchanged memories of places they'd visited around the world. She'd been born in England, so they had something in common. Her parents had emigrated to Canada before her first birthday, and had moved around North America over the years as her father built up a software business.

'Sold his stake three months before he died, poor man,' Georgia said. 'He and Mom had decided they wanted to live a bit. So he fulfilled a lifetime's ambition and bought a Ferrari. That's the car he wrapped around a tree when he skidded on a patch of ice.'

Jeremy said all the right things, and before long Georgia's questions elicited from him the fact that his wife had died at much the same time as her parents.

'A week after her fortieth birthday,' he said. 'No age at all, really.'

'I'm sorry,' Georgia said. 'Cancer?'

'Heart attack.'

'Tell me about her.'

Pushing a slice of lobster around his plate, he said, 'You don't want to listen to a maudlin old widower harp on about his late wife.'

'You don't seem old to me,' she said. 'But I think you're sad. When I asked you to take my photo, that's what struck me. You seemed unhappy.'

He gave a rueful smile. While Elaine's decision to bring their brief fling to an end had disheartened him, he didn't want Georgia to gain the impression that he was a loser. He'd never thought of himself like that. For a minute or two he concentrated on his food. The lobster was wonderful, just like the ever-changing views of the twenty-first-century city rising out of the desert. Almost worth the extortionate price, he reflected.

'Sorry,' Georgia said suddenly. 'I didn't mean to be intrusive. I can tell that you value your privacy.'

'Please, there's no need to apologise. It's just that Val and I were together for seven years. It's taken ages for me to come to terms with what happened.'

'Seven years is a long time,' she said. 'To lose someone like that out of the blue…'

'Val's father was a publisher,' Jeremy said. 'We met shortly after his death. She was still grieving, I was drifting from job to job. I had a not-very-good degree in science from a not-very-good university. As a boy, I wanted to be a doctor, but I wasn't studious enough. Val helped me buckle down and set up in publishing. We were partners in the business as well as in life.'

'You had no children?'

He shook his head. 'Val was quite a maternal type, but we just never got round to it. I'm sure she'd have made a marvellous mother. She had a younger brother she used to fuss over endlessly before we were married. He was a neurotic rich kid, really, but she was always too tender-hearted for her own good. Saw the best in everyone.'

Georgia put down her knife and fork, and stared out through the vast glass windows at the city lights forty floors below them. The restaurant kept moving, almost imperceptibly, and a laser show played over the waterfront. Finally the gaudy colours danced out of sight, giving way to a panorama of light under the night sky and the darkness in the distance beyond the city limits.

'Amazing, isn't it?' he said, almost to himself. 'Think of all the money they've spent.'

'And think of how things used to be,' she murmured.

'I don't care to look back,' he said. 'The Emiratis have the right idea. They always look to the future.'

Georgia took another sip of Chablis Grand Cru, and he topped up their glasses. Without knowing why, he felt uncomfortable. He probably shouldn't have harped on about Valerie, but the girl had asked, hadn't she? Her short, low-cut black dress clung to her boyish figure and revealed plenty of flesh. His taste usually ran to mature curves, but for the first time in their brief acquaintance, he was conscious of a stirring of physical excitement.

'I mustn't keep droning about myself,' he said. 'Tell me about you.'

'Not much to tell. You probably think I'm a spoiled brat. A trust-fund kid, just floating through life without a purpose.'

'I'm sure you have countless admirers.'

'Not really.' She sighed. 'You could say I've not had much luck with

men. I did have one proper boyfriend, but he suffered a serious breakdown. It wasn't my fault, but … People need to be strong. What counts
in life is knowing what you want and being determined to go out and
get it.'

'I couldn't agree more.' Their eyes met across the table, and Jeremy
realised that he did know what he wanted.

When he felt Georgia stir beside him the next morning, Jeremy's limbs
and muscles were aching in a thoroughly satisfactory way. Her hair was
tousled and she looked more like a teenager than ever. He dropped a
light kiss on her cheek, but when she tried to drag him back under the
duvet he raised a hand in protest.

'Whoa! I don't have your stamina.'

She laughed, a musical sound. 'I don't believe you, not after last
night. That was amazing.'

'Really?'

'Trust me.'

The sun was already blazing as, over an *al fresco* breakfast, they
mapped out a plan to cram the day with sight-seeing. Georgia said she
wanted to experience as much of the Emirates as possible, and when
she asked if Jeremy needed to put in an appearance at the conference,
he shook his head.

'It was only ever an excuse,' he said. 'At heart, I'm a shameless tourist.
Having heard so much about this part of the world, I wanted to see if
it lived up to the hype.'

Her eyes shone. 'And does it?'

He reached across the table and squeezed her hand. 'I'll say.'

She offered to organise their day out; it only took her five minutes with
an app on her smartphone to make all the arrangements. He offered
to pay for everything but she wouldn't hear of it. Last night's meal had

cost him a fortune, she said, and in any case, she could afford it. It didn't seem right to argue. To insist on footing the bill would make him seem old-fashioned as well as old.

She hired the services of a softly spoken Indian driver called Sunil for the rest of the holiday. The first stop on their itinerary was the Burj Khalifa, where the lift sped them to the viewing deck at the top. Next came a visit to the shiny new opera house, designed to resemble a traditional *dhow*. They snacked in the Dubai Mall and investigated the sea creatures in the aquarium, before sailing along the Dubai Canal in the afternoon. As Georgia took pictures of the flamingos on the bank Jeremy put his arm around her waist, the first time he'd really touched her since they'd climbed out of bed.

'You're captivating,' he said.

'You're not in such bad shape yourself,' she replied. 'For an old guy.'

The age difference had become a joke between them. He'd managed to relax and forget all about Elaine. Anyway, Georgia was much better company. Last night, she'd confided that she was bored with men her own age. Did she see him as a father figure? Her compliments about his virility were so ardent that he didn't really care. Thank God he'd kept going to the gym, even though the subscription cost a fortune.

It was too hot to walk anywhere during the day, but after Sunil dropped them off in the evening they wandered hand-in-hand through the spice and perfume souks, breathing in the exotic fragrances. The headiness of the rich aromas made him wonder, just for a moment, if he was dreaming. But there was nothing imaginary about the way she dug her fingernails into his arm before dragging him off to the gold souk. When she lingered in front of one of the shops, he said he wanted to buy her something, a souvenir of a marvellous day.

'You're sweet,' she said, 'but I'm the girl who has everything, remember. Keep your wallet in your pocket.'

'But…'

'OK, you can buy me dinner again. Deal?'

'Deal.'

Her parents had been a money-no-object couple, and Georgia had grown up wanting for nothing. Except, he speculated, what she wanted

most – love. She wasn't exactly clingy, but even the most adoring middle-aged women of his acquaintance hadn't hung quite so much on his
every word.

They caught an *abra* and crossed the creek to take a look at the Basta-
kia Quarter before finding a place to have dinner by the waterside that
was, to his relief, much cheaper than the revolving restaurant.

'History fascinates me,' she said, gazing out towards the *abra* station.

'They don't have too much of it in the Emirates,' Jeremy said. 'I
admire their ambition. The largest this, the tallest that. A canal built in
record time, the biggest shopping mall on the planet. It's not just about
vanity projects or making a statement to the rest of the world. They're
planning for life when the oil runs out.'

'You don't think all this new architecture is a bit soulless?'

'Things change,' he said. 'It's natural. Life keeps moving forwards;
you can't live in the old days. Besides, what was here in the old days,
before the oil? A few tents and the occasional palm tree?'

She pursed her lips. 'But there's history here too.'

'Not as much as in Lancaster,' he laughed. 'Not to worry. There's
nowhere else I'd rather be than here in blingy Dubai, with you.'

The next day, Sunil drove them to Sharjah, though Jeremy wasn't quite
clear where Dubai ended and Sharjah began. They braved the heat for
a short stroll along the promenade, before taking an air-conditioned
break to look around an exhibition of Islamic art. After exploring the
fort of Al Hisn, they emerged into the open again, pausing by a wooden
post that rose up in the middle of the courtyard.

Georgia studied an explanatory plaque. 'I told you there is history
in the Emirates.'

'Go on, then.' Jeremy didn't mind humouring her.

'They call this the Repentance Wood,' she said. 'Before the oil, pearl
fishing was the main source of wealth in these parts. The punishment
for misbehaving divers was to be tied to their ship's mast. One day, a
blind man was cooking fish in a house made of palm fronds and he set

his home alight. The wind spread the flames as far as the creek, and they destroyed a pearling ship at anchor. The mast was salvaged and placed here, in front of the old fort. Criminals were tied to it so people could see the consequences of flouting the law.'

'It's a sort of history, I suppose,' Jeremy said. 'But the fort was rebuilt a few years ago, and the post is a replica. That's exactly my point. This place isn't about yesterday, it's about tomorrow.'

Georgia shrugged but didn't argue. He liked that about her. She might be young but she was prepared to listen and learn. That night in bed, he began to teach her about compliance. She was very different from Valerie, but both of them had a submissive streak, and that pleased him.

'Our last full day together,' he said as the waiter poured their coffee at breakfast next morning. Today the sun was forecast to be fiercer than ever.

She looked at him. 'Is it?'

'Well…' he speared a chunk of melon with his fork, '…you're going back to Canada tomorrow, and I'm on a flight to Heathrow.'

'Flights can be rearranged.'

He hesitated, not quite sure if he could believe his luck. 'Are you saying you'd like to come to England with me?'

'Would you like that?'

'I'd love it,' he said fervently.

She smiled. 'Of course, you have a company to run.'

'I'll let you into a secret,' he said. 'We've never made a profit since the business started up. Our books are lovingly produced, they're beautiful to have and to hold, but frankly, there's not much demand for them. If I'm honest, the business leaches money. Any true, hard-nosed entrepreneur would have closed the firm down years ago. Or alternatively, gone bankrupt.'

Her eyes shone. 'But it gives you pleasure. It's a vocation.'

'Precisely. You've already gathered that I love being in charge.'

She had this gift of empathy, he told himself. It came through in every conversation. It was as if she understood him intimately.

She hesitated. 'I could help.'

'You're interested in publishing?'

'You could show me the ropes. And I could put some money in, if things are really that tight.'

'I couldn't possibly let you…'

'Why not? Didn't your wife give you a helping hand? Surely she was willing to invest. You said she came from a wealthy family.'

'It wasn't quite the same,' he said. 'Valerie and I were married.'

She gazed into his eyes, and he realised that for once in his life he found himself blushing like a schoolboy.

Sunil took them out as far as Abu Dhabi, where they visited the Sheikh Zayed Mosque and the Emirates Palace. On the way back, Georgia told Jeremy she'd planned a special treat for their last night in Dubai: a traditional Arabian feast in the desert.

'You don't mind, do you?' she asked anxiously. 'I know you don't like to be bossed around.'

In the art gallery, he'd let slip that Valerie had accused him of being a bit of a control freak. This didn't seem to bother Georgia, but he didn't want her to think he was a bully. Someone of her age and background was bound to be independently minded. It would take time for her to grow accustomed to his ways. Though last night she'd once again proved to be a very apt pupil.

At the hotel, they had a couple of cocktails in the bar before separating to pack in readiness for the flight the next morning. Despite the short notice, Georgia had managed to find a seat in first class. Money talked, he thought; it spoke a special and rather wonderful language all its own.

At six-thirty, he found her waiting for him in the lobby. Tonight she was wearing a white dress, simply cut and yet, he felt sure, the work of some leading designer. He felt a proprietorial thrill as she took his arm.

He liked women to look feminine and didn't care for it when they wore trousers. Georgia seemed to be of the same mind. He liked that.

The sun was setting, but as they stepped out through the automatic sliding doors and onto the pavement beside the taxi rank, a blast of heat hit them.

'Tomorrow is supposed to be the hottest May day since records began,' Georgia said.

'Pity we'll miss it.'

She smiled at him, and tugged at his hand.

The traffic out of the city was always heavy, but once the skyscrapers were behind them, Sunil put his foot down, and the Lexus LX raced through the sandy wilderness.

'Where are we going?' he asked.

'The Arabs call the area Rub al Khali. Miles from what you'd call civilisation. I didn't want to sign up for one of those large-scale feasts they put on for tourists. Our last evening together in the Emirates has to be unforgettable.'

'It will be,' he muttered.

The cocktails were having an effect, she rested her head against his shoulder and they dozed. When she shook him awake it was pitch black outside the car and he had no idea how long he'd been asleep. Screwing up his eyes, he saw torches illuminating a small tent.

'We've arrived.' She was barely able to keep the excitement out of her voice as she fumbled with her seatbelt.

'Where is this?'

'Rub al Khali. Come on.'

She led him into the tent. It was still very warm. Two beautifully decorated satin cushions lay on the ground for them to sit on. As they made themselves comfortable they were joined by a tall man wearing a long beard and traditional Arab dress. He carried a tray with two cups full to the brim.

With a bow, he said softly, 'A welcoming drink.'

'*Gahwa* for you and *karak chai* for me,' Georgia murmured. She drank tea but not coffee, whereas Jeremy was a caffeine addict. Raising the cup of tea to her lips, she inhaled the fragrance before tasting. 'Mmmm, gorgeous.'

Jeremy took a gulp of coffee. 'This will wake me up after my snooze.'

'*Shukran lak*,' Georgia said by way of thanks. The man bowed again, and left the tent.

For a minute or two neither of them spoke. The air was hot and dry inside the tent, and Jeremy couldn't stop yawning. Once he'd drained his cup, he said, 'You've organised a wonderful menu, I'll bet.'

'I try to think of everything.' She smiled. 'I wanted to ask about the publishing business. I gather a cash injection is required. How much, would you say?'

He blinked. 'Oh, I don't know. Say…'

'Yes, Jeremy?'

He groped for words. 'Well, perhaps … four hundred thousand.'

'Isn't that quite a lot of money for a company that only publishes half a dozen books a year?'

He brushed this aside with a wave of his hand. 'Production costs are high, cash flow's not what I'd wish. Anyway, we turn out more than six books. Lots more.'

'Not according to your website,' she said. 'It's not terribly informative. In fact, it doesn't seem to have been updated since last summer.'

He strove for jocularity. 'You've been checking up on me?' His little laugh seemed false and nervous in the deadly quiet of the desert night.

'As a matter of fact I have. Your creditors are becoming impatient all over again. You kept your head above water with the money you inherited from Valerie, but now things seem to be going from bad to worse.'

'What … what makes you…?'

She leaned towards him. 'How are you feeling?'

He mopped his brow. 'Not too good, actually.'

She clapped her hands and the man in Arab dress stepped back into the tent. He must have been waiting just outside.

'What's going on?' Jeremy asked faintly.

'I didn't introduce you, did I?' Georgia said. 'Darling, you'd better take off the beard. It doesn't really suit you.'

The man peeled away the beard, revealing a clean-shaven jaw. He glared down at Jeremy.

'Jeremy, this is Darren Critchley.'

Jeremy tried to say something but wasn't able to form the words. *Critchley?*

'Yes, that's right. He's my partner. And also the neurotic brother of the woman you abused for years prior to murdering her.'

When Jeremy came round he was aware of tight cords cutting into the flesh of his wrist and ankles. He was tied up and couldn't move. Blinking, he saw the moon and stars. There was no sign of the tent, or of Sunil's land cruiser. He seemed to be in a hollow in between sand dunes. On the horizon he thought he could see the outline of mountains in the moonlight, but it was impossible to be sure.

Slowly he took in what had happened. That bitch and her lover had drugged him. When he was groggy and unable to defend himself, they'd bound him to a thick wooden post. The post, about six feet high, had been driven firmly into the dusty ground.

His throat was parched, and several minutes passed before he managed to shout her name.

'*Georgia!*'

He kept shouting but his voice was weak, and nothing happened until eventually he became aware of two shapes detaching themselves from the shadows. A torch beam blinded him.

'So you've woken up?' Georgia hissed. 'Took you long enough.'

'Where am I?' His voice sounded scratchy, like an old and infirm man's.

'I told you: Rub al Khali. It's a vast desert of sand, covering a huge area. I didn't mention before, it's also known as the Empty Quarter. Look around when the sun rises and you'll see why.'

'You betrayed me.'

'As you betrayed my sister.' Opening his eyes a fraction, Jeremy saw that Critchley had discarded the Arab dress. 'All she was looking for was tenderness and affection. The sort of woman you specialise in preying on: rich and vulnerable. Elaine Klein fitted the bill too, but we made sure she got wise to you.'

'Just as well,' Georgia said. 'When you and she got together, I was afraid it might be harder to insinuate myself into your life than I'd expected.'

'You planned … everything?'

'Like you planned Valerie's destruction,' Critchley said. 'Our father was a tyrant, and she thought you offered a chance of escape. You seduced her, and when you had her under your thumb, you persuaded that poor, infatuated woman to hand over a king's ransom to keep you in the lap of luxury. You isolated her from her friends and family. She and I were always very close, but she never even got in touch when I had my breakdown. You forbade her to contact me. All you wanted was to control her and every aspect of her life.'

'Even that wasn't enough,' Georgia said. 'You got bored with her and were desperate to get your hands on her capital. The easy solution was to kill her. So you used your expertise to poison her and pass it off as death by natural causes.'

'No…'

'Yes,' she said. 'There's a template for murder in one of the books you published eighteen months ago. *Perfect Poisons*, remember? The coroner was satisfied about the supposed heart attack, but we reckon you killed her with digitalis.'

'You'll never prove…'

'And we'll never need to,' she said. 'At long last we have you where we want you.'

'What are you going to do?' It was barely a whisper.

'In five minutes Sunil will drive us away,' she said. 'Tomorrow the temperature will peak at one hundred. This place is far more remote than the lonely country house where you made Valerie's life a living hell. Not a soul, not even the hardiest nomad, will pass by. If the sun doesn't do its work first, the jackals and hyenas will enjoy themselves. The scorpions, too.'

'You can't,' he muttered. 'I'll give you whatever you want.'

'We want justice.'

'But … have mercy.'

'What mercy did you show Valerie?' Georgia asked. 'You took her life, and, indirectly, came close to taking David's.'

'You can't … You won't get away with it.'

'David and I booked into the hotel as a married couple. Didn't you notice how careful I was not to invite you to my room? In his company, I was a well-upholstered redhead. Her wig is quite striking, and so is all the padding in her bra. If anyone tries to trace your movements and studies the hotel CCTV, they won't make the connection between a busty older woman with flaming hair and your skinny blonde girl-friend. They might suspect the girlfriend of having tipped off some local bandits, who then stole your wallet and abandoned you to die here, but they'll never find her. Because Georgia from Seattle doesn't exist.'

'Sunil…'

'His real name is Sachin, and he's David's closest friend,' she said. 'They met at school when they were eleven years old. Sachin was very fond of Valerie, too. If you'd ever listened to her, you'd remember his name.'

Jeremy swallowed. 'So you're not a trust-fund kid…'

'I'm not an orphan either, or even a Canadian. David paid for every-thing; Sachin and I worked out the plan. David's always blamed himself for not saving his sister from you. Once we're back in Britain, he'll finally be able to start over.'

'And you'll have your hands on his half of the inheritance,' Jeremy muttered.

She smiled. 'You should have listened to what I said in Dubai. You're the one obsessed with money.'

'And what do you care about?'

'David,' she said simply. 'And I care about history, too. That's why I told you the story of the Repentance Wood. So that, before the end comes, you'd understand why the past matters. Perhaps even feel some empathy. If only for those malefactors of old. The men left to repent their sins at leisure as they slowly burned to death under the unforgiving sun.'

A Mouthful of Restaurant

Martine Bailey

Naturally, I prepared my own reference of character in order to become manservant to young Lord Tilston. '*Gould is the best of men to serve a gentleman on a foreign tour,*' I wrote in my best copperplate. '*He will ensure his master dines well and carries a most serviceable box of remedies.*' Yes, every word of it was true – save the signature, of course.

Tilly, as I came to address him in the privacy of my mind, was then seventeen years old, sprawling before me in a suit of blue satin, the red pustules flaming on his lily-white face. His father, the duke, had granted him a year to visit Europe and I … well, I had a hankering to be gone from England and dine at another's expense. Young Tilly quizzed me in his strangulated drawl: he could stomach none of that continental trash, those frogs' legs and garlicked gizzards. I must feed him only plain substantials. And was it true I carried a discreet box of medicines?

His elder brother, the earl, sauntered in to inspect me. I am a stout man of thirty with something of the cherub to my rosy lips and sympathetic smile, and in a sober suit of clothes I pass pretty well for a gentleman. The earl leered at his younger brother and wished him a fine year's travelling with such an amiable fellow at his side. And so I gained the promise of twenty guineas for the year and the perquisite of dining with young Tilly when he had no better company.

We rattled off down the turnpikes, and I directed the coachman to the best inns for eatables: the fig tarts of Lancashire, fine Cheshire cheeses, pork pies of Melton Mowbray and London beefsteaks. But across the English Channel we suffered at French hands, facing a barrage of bone-crunching songbirds, or on Papist days, naught but stinking fish or mashed eggs. Seeing my young lord sulk, I loaded my pistol and destroyed a family of coneys to create my edible tableau, 'Rabbits Surprised'. Our dinners improved at Chantilly: the perch was exquisite and the chicken came dressed in yellow mushrooms, butter and cream. I developed a taste for truffled duck and Burgundy wine. Tilly was not a lad to bore himself with checking an inn's account.

In Paris my master found new companions: rouged trollops with patched bosoms and hooped backsides. Many a morning I tripped over his prone body on the drawing-room carpet. Like a nursemaid, I ordered him to vomit in the pot, piss in the privy, and attend upon me to cure his pox.

My tools are clysters, syringes, and a razor-sharp scarifier to open a vein. Tilly's blue blood was as scarlet as any pressed *canard* as it congealed in my basin. My tiny dose glass was also much in use. To treat my master's clap, each night I gave him one ounce of brandy combined with Morphia's Elixir. And it was then, while he lay tranced by the poppy, that I took a prowl around his chamber. Only fifty-four guineas remained in his travelling trunk. I bridled. I was in no position to be stranded penniless in a foreign land.

That year of 1773 the talk of Paris was a divine eating establishment that served *Le Goût Moderne*.

'I hear rumours of a hellish fine place to dine, sir,' I said, as I dressed my lord's greasy hair with clay rollers. To handle his person was not a pleasant task. Crusty red scabadoes plagued his scalp, yet still he spent his nights cunny-hunting. And so I added, 'All the prettiest *mademoiselles* parade there.'

The coachman drove us through the crowds; the revellers' faces tinted green by the new-strung oil lamps. Down the Rue Saint-Honoré we found an impressive door beneath a sign proclaiming '*Restaurants Divins*'.

'What is this place?' young Tilly grumbled, eyeing a salon populated by rouge-faced men and bone-thin women lounging at small tables. A moment later we were seated in a chandelier-lit corner staring at cards listing fancy French dishes.

'Damn you, Gould. Is this one of those foppish health-food places?' He pressed his fingers to his pimply brow, suspiciously eying the other diners.

'I believe it to be the first fashion of Paris, my lord,' I insisted, studying the *carte*. The prices were printed quite openly and I fretted to see that a full supper cost five whole *livres*. The appeal was that they served all those healthful dishes so much vaunted by Monsieur Rousseau: Savoy milk fresh from the cow's udder, and Alpine honey and fruits. It was the stuff from those novels of his that everyone pretends to read these days, but it intrigued me nonetheless.

They gave us quite a show. A handsome proprietress in a gown of spangled silk greeted us in English. 'I comprehend you have most sensitive souls, *messieurs*,' she cooed, as if she were our intimate of many years. 'I prescribe for you a nourishing health supper to rebuild your physiognomies.'

'Balderdash,' my lord snorted, and called the waiter for another baluster of brandy. I took a long look around me, at the gilded ormolu clock, the heavy silver candlesticks and cutlery. I was making calculations upon the figure of five *livres* collected from each diner. It was a devilishly forward-looking business.

Our supper arrived and my master's face turned sour.

'Damn me! I never saw food so monstrously small. And overdressed.'

To him, the *potage de santé* was nothing but a plate of laundry water. As for me, if I forgot that my master was being fleeced abominably, the breast of pigeon was the best I ever tasted. As for the jasmine ice cream, the coldness numbed my tongue for a moment, and then a meadow of flowers blossomed on my palate.

After washing down yet more brandy, my master turned spiteful. 'You, Gould, have a sly manner. I do not care for it.' His watery eyes narrowed. 'I engaged you to free me of all this flim-flam. Look at it!' He waved his arm unsteadily. 'I need an Englishman's dinner: beef, pudding, a pint of wine.' He banged his knife and fork, making the table rattle. The other diners nudged elbows and giggled at the drunken English *rosbif*.

'And as for that medical box of tricks, what the devil use is that? Every day I grow weaker and more queasy. You are a junketeer, sir! I am done with you. Pack your goods and be off. You are no longer wanted.'

So, the puerile ninny planned to dismiss me? I had to restrain myself from knocking the boy's empty head from his shoulders. 'I would pay for supper myself,' I said in a tone of ice, 'only you, sir, have not yet had the courtesy to pay my fee.'

'Pay you?' he snorted. 'Your belly has been paid tenfold at my expense. I should rather say that you owe me a fortune!'

I thrust back my chair and sprang away from the sight of him. I blundered through the first door I noticed and into the kitchen. The heat stunned me: rows of spitted meats revolved on racks before blazing fires. A number of man-cooks worked in the fog of steam, and even in my rage I saw there truly was a genius to the system of that place.

I backed away from the kitchen into a scullery and there I first sighted Cécile. She stood crouched over a chafing dish, a ripe kitchen rat of unknowable age, encased in a food-spattered apron. She raised two sloe-black eyes to me, entirely nonchalant. Then, with the reverence of a nun before a crucifix, she reached for a teaspoon and tasted her concoction. Carefully her wide mouth chewed and tested the flavour, her face transported to a culinary paradise.

'*Quintessence*,' she whispered, her languishing eyes meeting mine again, with all the force of a coach and six slamming into my soul. She presented the spoon to my own mouth and I parted my lips.

I tasted unctuous meat juice, rich with the pungent flavours of the earth. I also tasted her own *essence*. My brainbox emptied of grammar-school French. I bowed, I announced my name. I reached to kiss her hand, which was as hot and slippery as a roasted eel. She pulled away and laughed, showing pointed, childlike teeth. Then, pointing to the timepiece hanging on a hook, she said with a lizard flick of her eyes, '*À minuit?*'

I considered a moment.

'Indeed,' I said. 'I shall return at midnight.'

Then, begging a small portion of bouillon, I returned to my master.

Back in the salon Tilly was fretting to leave for the carnal frolics of the Luxembourg Gardens. I set the bouillon down before him: a tiny cup to which I had added a few of my own soporific drops.

'Here, sir,' I said meekly. 'Forgive me. This is gratis, their health speciality. I have summoned the coachman. Pray try it while you wait.'

He downed it in a twinkling and then watched me with disdain as I devoured a dish of enchanting *biscuits du Palais Royal.* Soon his eyelids drooped, his chin sank to his breast and he grew insensible. I caught him in my arms as he crashed across the table and then hailed a waiter to carry him outside. Within the quarter-hour he was loaded in the carriage and on his way home to a solitary bed.

At midnight I returned to enjoy Cécile's liberty. We got no further than the outhouse in the yard. I wanted her as hot as I'd first found her, still smelling of animal blood, her skin moist with sweat and gravy. I tasted sugar on her teeth and sank my fingers deep into melted-butter slipperiness. Even before I plunged into her circle of bliss my mind was resolved. Here was a creature I could devour each night afresh. She murmured my name and I vowed to her in my foxed French that I would send for her, and do it soon.

It is a shame my young master cannot see his former man's glory. The poor fellow was soon afterwards discovered by the *concierge* of that Paris apartment, stiff and silent in his chamber. Vomit had destroyed his gold-laced suit and blocked his windpipe. Naturally, I did everything in my command to assist the authorities. It was pronounced that my young charge had committed self-murder, no doubt overcome by the shame of the venereal buboes that uglified his person. The poor blockhead had mixed too great a quantity of Morphia's Elixir with his nightly brandy. As for me, I was entirely exonerated, and to avoid mis-understanding, produced two witnesses who swore to seeing me that day in distant Lyon.

Tonight Cécile and I celebrate our first year as proprietors of the Hotel Sybilla, just beside Rome's Colosseum. In the dining room Cécile is even now displaying her *pièce montée,* a sugar-paste Palace of Pandemo-nium dressed with miniature figures of fiends and she-devils. Yet always at the heart of our success is that doll's sized cup of *quintessence.* The French call the bouillon a *restaurant,* for it restores the body's vigour. A *restaurant* is also what they call those glamorous dining rooms of Paris now. By the time I sent Cécile money to follow me, all the innkeepers were clamouring to open one. The new rules of dining are these: at each table a person or family may sit alone; yet they are not alone – they are on display for all the public to observe. And the bill of fare must be listed on a paper – a *carte* or *menu* – and each guest may choose dishes according to their whim. And the bill is not shared, like at the harum-scarum table of an inn: one pays only for what one eats according to the bill of charges.

I congratulate myself. I understood from the first how these restau-rants were palaces of perception. To dine thus transforms the curious into the epicurean – for a few hours at least. Fashion, that ethereal will o' the wisp, is captured, priced and, miraculously, ingested by the body. And consequently my fortunes are also restored to robust health.

Ah, here she comes, my own Cécile. See, she appears quite the lady now in gold brocade, her fingerless gloves masking years of scarring at the cook's altar of fire.

'Monsieur Gould,' she whispers, that husky croak of hers whisking up my blood. She offers me a letter on a silver tray.

'The Earl of Tilston will be honoured to attend tonight's assembly,'

I announce after reading it. Naturally, my invitation to Tilly's elder brother had not revealed my own identity. The men I pay at the custom house tell me his business here is of an investigative nature. He has been asking the whereabouts of an English manservant once engaged by his poor brother Tilly.

'Cécile. Do you suppose you can tempt the earl with a taste of our special *quintessence*?'

She smiles at me; her carmine lips glistening, those little pointed teeth revealed.

'The pot simmers. A reduction of beef, bones, and…'

'…a secret addition?'

Her jet-black eyes flash with laughter.

Yes, my medicine box was also carried here from Paris, stocked with powders of mercury, lead, emetics, soporifics. I am forever grateful to that other former master who endowed it to my care, a physician who commanded large fees before he … Well, that is another tale. I rifle in its wooden compartments and find my dram glass.

'I am wondering,' Cécile asks, and her lips stay parted, breathless, 'if the earl might succeed in finding … Tilly?'

Polishing the glass before the candelabra, I consider how I always serve my masters according to their merits.

'If so, he will have reached his journey's end,' I announce, inspecting the flask of Morphia against the candle flame, its contents as tarry as molasses.

'The merest mouthful of *restaurant*,' I say, inserting the glass dropper in the flask, 'and he too will cross the river of oblivion and be restored to his brother's company for eternity.'

Cruising for a Killing

Maxim Jakubowski

In Nuku Hiva, in the Marquesas Islands of French Polynesia, the local population normally stands at around 2,660 people (plus hundreds of sharks in the neighbouring waters that you are requested not to feed, at any rate voluntarily). Once a week or so, however, a cruise boat swells this number by several hundred souls, who disembark at the jetty from the tender boats to the sound of a local *haka* and the beating of tribal drums, tasks that keep one per cent of the island's inhabitants in work, dressed for the occasion in traditional attire they no doubt hate with a vengeance.

Since the boat had left Acapulco, we'd been at sea for nine days, so the prospect of solid land had us queuing like lemmings on the stairs leading down to deck three, where we could embark on the smaller crafts that would take us ashore, the cruise boat being anchored some five hundred yards away from the island, which, unlike our previous ports of call, lacked mooring facilities large enough to accommodate it.

I'd travelled on the *M/V Magellan* once before, as a guest lecturer giving, in my capacity as a crime writer, talks on Agatha Christie, Miss Marple, Hercule Poirot, Chandler, Philip Marlowe, Sherlock Holmes and Inspector Morse. A nice, easy gig, even if on that occasion the audience had mostly consisted of retirees and geriatrics ticking off their bucket list by cruising the Amazon. Two elderly passengers had, in fact, died on that cruise – of natural causes. I was told by someone on the medical team this was not uncommon and that the boat's facilities had enough suitable space to fit up to half a dozen dead bodies in between ports. It was a feature of the giant cruise ships the large companies who owned them declined to advertise in their glossy brochures designed to attract the older generation and their grey pounds (or dollars or euros).

On that previous cruise I'd become familiar with the vessel's systems. On embarkation, every passenger was handed a personal cruise card, the size of a credit card, which he or she would use for all purchases and bar bills, which would then be charged to their accounts. This card also functioned as an ID of sorts and was scanned every time the passenger went ashore and again when they returned on board, thus informing the ship's main computer if anyone had been left behind. It seemed pretty foolproof and well thought out, until I discovered by accident that there was a serious loophole in the system.

So as not to have to carry the card in my shorts pockets all the time, when I didn't need it I had made a habit of storing it inside the top drawer of the desk in my cabin, only to find one morning that it had disappeared. I assumed that I had lost it somewhere the previous day, when I'd used it to go ashore. Maybe it had fallen out of my pocket as I came back from my excursion into Recife, laden as I was with both my rucksack and a shopping bag of various souvenirs. I made my way to the reception desk to have it cancelled and to prevent any other passenger using it to charge drinks to my account. The Ukrainian blonde staffing the desk was all smiles, cancelled the card with immediate effect and, after checking her screen and confirming that no extraneous charges had been posted to my account, printed out a new one for me, no further questions asked.

My worries put to rest, I was placing the new card inside the desk drawer, when I noticed that the old, presumed-missing card, was in fact still there; it had simply slipped into a corner and jammed itself flat against the partition of the drawer, invisible to the naked eye from all but a certain angle. I breathed a sigh of relief but decided not to advise the reception desk, for fear of appearing something of a myopic imbecile. The old, cancelled cruise card would make a good bookmark, I reckoned, and a sober reminder to be more careful in future.

Crime writers being what they are, however, this situation soon gave me the germ of an idea. A couple of evenings later, noticing Daria, the Ukrainian receptionist, off duty around one the bars, I fell into conversation with her and we spent a pleasant couple of hours in discussion, during which time I asked her a handful of questions about the way the boat and its systems worked, mentally storing away the information.

'So, your missing cruise card, it did not reappear?' she asked.

'No,' I lied.

'Is OK then,' she continued. 'But no one can use it to make you pay for drinks you not have,' she laughed.

'It was so easy to cancel,' I replied, sipping from my tall glass of Prosecco.

Daria was drinking vodka. 'We have good security system,' she added. 'All I do is cancel the way the card charges; all rest I leave unchanged.'

A bell rang in my head and, on the occasion of our next shore visit, in Rio, I tested the system by using my original cruise card when I disembarked. I half expected the white-uniformed cadet at the exit desk by the gangway who was scanning the passengers' IDs to stop me and point out my card was no longer valid. He didn't. Returning from the city a few hours later, I deliberately used the new card to recheck my theory, and, again, it passed muster, confirming that the personal details electronically inscribed into both the invalid and the valid cruise cards did not clash and were identical.

Maybe one day I'd be able to use this fact in a story, I thought.

And soon I would, but not in the way I'd previously expected.

I'd met Ophelia at a book signing. We authors don't have groupies the way rock musicians are rumoured to. I suppose there's nothing glamorous about typing at a keyboard in silence for hours on end and emerging, blurry-eyed, into the world every year or so with a new volume, and, if we're lucky, whoring it as best we can in sparsely populated public libraries and at far-flung literary conferences, and enjoying the attentions of at least a couple of reviewers who have ventured beyond the press release and actually read the book. At the end of this particular signing, however, I was confronted by a reasonably pretty young woman, with long dark hair, who had read a few of my previous novels and wanted to know when I would be writing again about Dominick and Summer, my amateur, feisty and ever-quarrelling society sleuths. She was annoyed that I had seemingly killed Dominick off with a heart attack at the outset of what I hoped would be the final book featuring the characters. I'd been sick and tired of them and would happily have despatched both Dominick and Summer, preferably having them torn to pieces by rampaging zombies or annihilated in a worldwide pandemic, had my literary agent and editor not counselled otherwise, suggesting I allow some ambiguity to their finale. Was Dominick really dead, Ophelia asked, or was it all a ruse to be explained in a future instalment, no doubt in a bid to mystify their nemesis, Jackson Vine? I was actually beginning to think I had maybe been a bit rash in my decision, as the new book I was promoting – a stand-alone with a brand new investigator (who also happened to be a killer) – had so far sold only half the number my books usually did, and the crowd at this particular signing had been sparse and uncommunicative. Even Ophelia hadn't actually bought the book at the store but had brought her copy along, no doubt acquired online at a discount that meant I would only be getting a reduced royalty on the sale.

I tried, nevertheless, to defend my reasons for what she considered to be Dominick's murder, but she stood her ground, arguing I did not have the right to get rid of a much-loved (by her) character. She was getting on my nerves, but then again she was rather pretty, in the English rose sort of way that often touched me inside, so I began flirting with her, for lack of anything else to do right then.

'Actually, you know, there's a lot of me in Dominick,' I revealed with a sly smile.

'I thought there must be; gut feeling, I guess,' Ophelia said. 'That makes me angry, too, you see.'

'Really?'

'Whenever I'm reading about him, I'll often turn to the dust jacket and see your photo and think he must look a bit like you…' she said.

Dominick only drank Coca-Cola, while I preferred wine. He always dressed with a strong sense of fashion, which allowed me to pad the narrative with the names of labels and superfluous descriptions of clothes (although Summer gave me even more licence on that front), while I always wore black Farah trousers and loafers. Dominic was extremely rich while I was nothing of the sort. But Ophelia was quite welcome to think of me that way.

The bookshop assistant picked up the small pile of a dozen or so books I had signed without being asked in order to ensure they remained for some time in the store and were not returned to the publisher's warehouse – a trick of the trade you get taught with your very first book. The shop was growing quiet, a few late-evening punters browsing unenthusiastically or seeking shelter from the thin drizzle of a London autumn evening. I looked up at Ophelia. Her eyes locked with mine. How had I signed the book for her, I tried to recall? Had it been a standard indifferent dedication, or had I been more effusive?

'Well, that's me done,' I said, as I rose from the chair and stepped away from the table. 'Care for a drink? We can chat a bit more…'

'I'd love that,' Ophelia said.

Affairs are often like flash floods. They begin with a rush of lust, a torrent of words, that you momentarily believe will drown everything in sight and in mind, only for them to fade under the pressure of time and life until all that is left is the steam rising from the street gutters, the shadow of what once was – an X-ray of perceived love. Or maybe I was just too demanding and misanthropic, or simply too selfish to compromise.

At first I found Ophelia amusing, affectionate, sexy, cheeky and devoted. But then, one slow inch at a time, her idiosyncratic traits began to irritate, annoy and irk me, and I began to wish we had never met. I have no wish to go all porno here and relate the exquisite, intimate details of our lengthy tryst – I'm not that sort of writer. Neither do I have any intention of going into all the psychological ramifications involving the two of us, or why, at the end of the day, I came to the unhappy conclusion that we were totally unsuitable for each other.

Suffice to say she'd come down from Scarborough via a minor redbrick university, where she'd, of course, read media studies. She had no extant family, few friends – maybe those she'd once had had seen through her early and avoided her presence – and, damn it, she was possessive. By sleeping with me she felt she owned a part of me, wanting to know all about the book ideas I had, hoping to influence me and to become my muse so to speak, seeking some form of minor glory from our carnal relationship, when all I sought was the carnal and no more, and flinched at the idea of anything serious. I was too much of a loner and basically selfish for that.

I was about to call an end to what we had, for what it was worth, but something inside me intuited that Ophelia was not the sort of girl who would take an enforced break-up well. There was a dark side to her, the potential for destruction. Self-destruction, maybe, or, in the worst possible scenario, my own. Would she become a stalker? An avenger? Whichever it was, I knew she would not react well.

Faced with these possibilities, I dithered. I continued sleeping with her, saw her weekly but resisted any suggestion she move in with me. She was in the final months of writing her thesis (on the male gaze in indie movies), and lived on a small inheritance from her parents, who'd died some five years earlier in a car accident in Lanzarote.

One night, we were in bed, sheets humid with the sweat of our exertions, the silence now weighing heavily on both of us, the sounds reaching us through the half-open window from the road fading as the traffic whittled down to a crawl.

'What are you thinking about?' she asked.

A typical Ophelia question. I was thinking of nothing, blissfully oblivious to the whole world, still coming down from my orgasm, calmly floating in that ineffable region between pleasure and oblivion.

'Nothing.'

'Surely, you must be thinking of something. You're a creative sort of guy. I can't believe you can just switch off.'

'I can. It's a way of recharging my batteries, I suppose. What about you?'

'What? What am I thinking?'

'Yes.'

'Well, you know our birthdays are coming up?'

We'd discovered at an early point in our relationship that our birthdays were just a few days apart, even though I was a clear ten years older.

'So they are…'

'We should do something. Together. Go away, say, not letting any of our acquaintances know. A magical mystery journey somewhere.'

'Hmm…'

'Wouldn't it be a great idea?'

We'd once gone to Brighton for a few days and, on another occasion, Ophelia had accompanied me to a festival in Bristol, where she had annoyed me intensely by never leaving my side, seemingly attempting to bask in the glory of telling the world she was fucking an actual published writer. She also had ambitions to write, but so far was all talk and no typing.

I nodded. I was no longer thinking of nothing. An idea had taken root. Knowing Ophelia would never go quietly, I had hit on a scenario that might prove foolproof.

A few days later, thoughts ordered, my plan mentally moved from a fragmented jigsaw to reality.

'Have you ever been on a cruise?' I asked Ophelia.

'Wow … for our birthdays, do you mean?'

'Yes.'

'That would be just amazing.'

'As you know, I'm struggling a little, with the deadline looming for the next book, and I was thinking about what Larry Block once told me. He often goes on cruises to get away from it all and concentrate on writing. He says he finds it incredibly productive.'

He'd actually written that it was 'like being on a writer's retreat but without the distraction of all the other writers'. In this case Ophelia would be the main distraction but her presence there would have both pros and cons.

'Where to, then?'

'French Polynesia and New Zealand.'

'Amazing.' It was an expression she overused and that often set me on edge.

'Tahiti, Bora Bora, both the New Zealand islands. We'd fly out to Acapulco to board the boat and fly back from Wellington at the end.'

'Amazing,' Ophelia said again and I winced. 'Do you think that in New Zealand we could visit the *Lord of the Rings* set? It's supposed to be fantastic.'

'I don't see why not.'

The sail into Tahiti proved a massive disappointment. I had memories of Paul Gauguin, topless natives, palm trees, Robert Louis Stevenson and all sorts of exotic vistas, but for over an hour and a half we had navigated our way through a landscape of container docks, larger than any I'd ever seen, which, weather apart, could have been part of any old Northern European bleak immensity of derelict industrial areas, straight from a 1950s espionage thriller. Fortunately, Papeete itself was an improvement, if a touch tawdry. We visited the municipal market, where I bought Ophelia a necklace of black keisho pearls, the price of which I haggled down and felt quietly triumphant about, only to later see the same piece on another stall at an even cheaper price. But she looked nice wearing it, even more so when we made love for the last time in our cabin, by the light of a moon flickering like a will-o'-the-wisp in the Marquesas Islands night.

I'd done my research and had planned the deed for our next stop – the smaller island of Nuku Hiva, which we would have to reach by tender as the dock was not big enough for a large cruise vessel.

I'd made it a habit to carry both our cruise cards in my shirt pocket. Ophelia didn't mind this, as all our drinks and other expenses on the boat were charged to my account. The officer in charge swiped both cards as we stepped onto the smaller vessel that would take us ashore. In my shorts pocket I also had a third cruise card – in my name – which I had obtained the previous day at the reception desk by reporting that I had mislaid my original one. After we disembarked from the tender, I found a pretext for Ophelia to carry her own cruise card with her for once – 'accidentally' dropping it on the ground as we purchased a couple of soft drinks from a quayside vendor. What I actually gave her though, was, by sleight of hand, my spare one. Her card remained safely in my pocket.

I had already suggested that we didn't book onto the official excursion, so instead we made our own way around the small island. I'd previously Googled all there was to know about Nuku Hiva – research is always a writer's best friend – so I knew I had two options at my disposal.

Having made it a fair way across the island, we reached a small cove where, according to my information, the sharks congregated. There was no warning sign about their presence, the spot being so secluded, few locals, let alone visiting tourists, ever came this far. Sadly, there was only one around; it was visible in the distance but seemed totally uninterested in our presence, racing through the waters far out, ignoring us.

He looked rather large though; Ophelia squirmed when she noticed him. And right there and then, I realised that I was not a violent man and wouldn't be able to begin struggling with Ophelia in a bid to throw her in the water. And anyway, for all I knew, she might be a good swimmer, able to escape quickly. And there was no way I was about to summon up the strength to hold her under as the shark approached. Plan one was therefore a washout.

Which left the crater of the dead volcano.

It was a hell of a climb and we were both sweating like hogs by the time we reached the top of the path leading to it. Ophelia complained non-stop about the heat, her tiredness and the mosquitoes that appeared to have a definite appetite for Boots Insect Repellent. However, I managed to convince her to complete the trek, telling her that the views and the photos she would be able to take would truly be phenomenal – or in her words, amazing.

Finally we emerged from the twisting, narrow path.

We were literally in the clouds. Beneath us, the canopy of trees was like a second ocean, rivalling the one in the distance with its infinite variations of green and brown. The air was still – a thick, pregnant silence. The black dust leading to the crater crunched under our feet, topping the jagged edge that separated us from the void.

I went first and peered over. It felt as if the slope wound down for miles into a foggy darkness. For a brief moment it was like going aeons back in time to a day when creation was still in its infancy, forming, shifting, alive. I drew in a breath. A few steps behind me, Ophelia was taking photos of the jungle we'd left behind on her digital camera, sweeping it around as she took selfies and then made a panoramic video of the mighty landscapes surrounding us.

'It's unbelievable,' she exclaimed.

'It is. Well worth the effort, eh?'

I suggested she move to the ledge and I take a photo of her with the crater in the background. She hesitated for a brief moment, but then agreed, putting a brave face on her rising vertigo.

She stood, a fixed smile on her face, looking back at me.

'I'm sorry,' I said, and, dropping the camera to the ground I rushed towards her. She looked surprised at first, then questioning; then fear spread across her pale features as I made rough contact with her shoulders and pushed her backwards.

It lasted barely a second, but for what felt like an eternity she swayed on the spot, realising what was happening, then lost her balance and finally toppled over, her body making its fast, inexorable descent down the slopes of the crater. She remained silent all the way, until her white cotton shirt faded from view and I caught my breath again.

There were a lot of different things I could have said; I could have attempted to explain why I was doing this, why it made me unhappy but that I had no choice. That I had genuinely loved her, but … but … but…

But real life is not like a story. Time passes faster, and you are nowhere as articulate as you can be on the printed page or the computer screen.

I picked up the small camera I had dropped, pulled out the memory card, broke it clumsily into a few pieces and threw both the camera and its remains down the wide crater, in Ophelia's trail.

I did hope she hadn't suffered long.

I hurriedly returned to the quay and caught the final tender back to the boat, making it just in time, as the climb up the volcano had taken so much longer than I had hoped or expected.

Stepping onto the deck of the ship, I gave my cruise card for the crew member to swipe, then shouted out that I forgotten my baseball cap on the bench of the tender and ran back down the gangway to retrieve it. It was late in the day and the crew were too busy processing the returning crowd of passengers to take note of the fact that I had my cruise card scanned a second time. Ophelia's absence from the boat would create no alarm.

Job done.

I was now free.

I would play the same trick upon leaving the boat at the end of the cruise, before being driven to the airport. According to all the computer records, Ophelia would duly have departed the *Magellan* on arrival in Wellington, just as she had returned to the vessel in Nuku Hiva.

Trust a crime writer to commit a perfect crime. Would I get away with it? Only time would tell, I reckoned, and that might be another story altogether.

Three on a Trail

Michael Stanley

They hadn't spoken for quite a while. The climb up from the seashore to the crest of the cliffs had been tough, and now they were resting, looking out to sea.

'I remember this,' Gillian said suddenly. 'I *do* remember it. The way that cliff curves into the bay. Like a hand grasping it.'

'Was there anyone with you?'

Too eager, Tom thought. *I should just let her talk.*

She frowned and shook her head. 'I remember I wanted … something … and I said to Claire…' She paused, then grabbed his shoulder, her plain face suddenly lively. 'So she *was* with me!'

'That's good. Good.' So a day into the hike, the two girls had still been together. Claire had been here, had probably rested right here, watching the sea. Tom's heart ached.

Gillian was concentrating, the frown back again. 'I don't remember anything else. I remember that curve of the cliffs. And that it's still quite far to where we camped.'

Tom nodded. The Tsitsikamma Trail was five days of tough hiking, and this was only their first day. They'd better get moving.

'Thanks for bringing me with you,' Gillian said as he helped her into her backpack. 'All those people asking me questions, interrogating me. It was horrible. And the more they pushed, the less my mind would focus, and the harder it was to remember anything. But out here it's different. I sort of get snatches. Like that bay.'

Tom settled his own pack on his shoulders. 'Don't force it. Just wait for something to trigger a memory. Then tell me about it when you feel like it.'

They were making their way along the top of the cliff now, at least fifty metres above the sea. Sometimes the path had stunning views of the coast. Other times it wound through the indigenous forest, where monkey ropes hung from the white stinkwoods and yellowwoods that crowded in on them.

'Oh, look!' Gillian pointed as they emerged over the sea again. Beyond the breakers, a school of dolphins was arching through the swells. Tom was struck by how gorgeous the hike was, how much he would have enjoyed it with Claire. She'd asked him to come, but he couldn't get away. So it was only Claire and Gillian who'd gone.

And only Gillian who had returned from it.

You were only allowed to camp at a few marked places along the route, and it was dusk by the time they found their site. It hadn't rained for weeks – the drought across southern Africa was hitting the Tsitsikamma too – and Tom easily found dry wood. He settled to making a fire and dealing with the steaks and freeze-dried vegetables, while Gillian put up the small two-man tent. She said it was easier to do on her own. They had a litre pack of red wine with them, and when the tent was done and Gillian joined him by the fire, they sipped it from plastic mugs.

'Why did you let me come, in the end?' she asked.

'You really wanted to. And you said maybe you could help.'

'I thought you'd want to do it alone. To be here just with Claire…'

Tom took several moments to answer while the fire spat and smoked. 'I spoke to Dr Harcourt. She said it was OK.'

In fact, the psychologist hadn't been keen at all. She'd said she had no idea how Gillian would react to retracing the trail from which she'd previously emerged babbling, a week after she and Claire should have returned. She'd staggered towards a group of searchers, with no memory of what had happened. The National Parks people and the police had searched for weeks and found no trace of Claire. So even though the psychologist had advised against it, Tom had let Gillian come with him; awakening her memory seemed his only hope of discovering anything.

'I *have* to know what happened, Gill. She could still be alive.'

'I need to know as much as you do. She was your sister, but she was my very, very best friend. And I left her out here somewhere.' Gillian lowered her head and silent tears started down her cheeks.

'I'm sorry.' Tom reached out but didn't touch her. He poked the fire. 'Hey, how do you want your steak?'

'Rare.'

'Just as well. I think the fire's dying. Maybe the wood wasn't as dry as I thought.' He faked a laugh, but she didn't respond.

They were both hungry and wolfed down the steaks, which were on the raw side of rare. Gillian played with her reconstituted vegetables and potatoes, and handed her plate to Tom at once when he asked if he could finish what she didn't want. As they drank their wine, they kept their conversation to politics and religion – safe topics, Tom thought wryly – until they were both ready to turn in. It had been a tough day, and Tom fell asleep almost at once, the first time that had happened since the news about Claire had reached him.

He woke in the middle of the night to Gillian talking in her sleep. At first, he couldn't make out the words, but she seemed to be arguing with someone. Suddenly she said 'Claire' in a husky voice. Then 'let me go' in a different voice. Claire's? Then she rolled over, her breathing became regular and sleep reclaimed her.

Tom lay awake. For the hundredth time he thought about the possibilities. An accident? Had Claire fallen from the cliffs, been swept out to sea? But what reason was there for Gillian's amnesia? She loved Claire – more like a sister than simply a friend – but surely an accident wouldn't have produced this bitter trauma? Why did she cry out 'let me go' in her sleep?

Tom twisted in his sleeping bag, trying not to disturb her. Someone else must have been there. Someone who'd done something so horrible that Gillian couldn't tolerate the memory. He thought of the *sangomas* who wanted body parts from young women for their black-magic potions. Had Gillian somehow escaped, but Claire…? He didn't want to think about it. Instead he thought about the razor-sharp hunting knife he'd brought with him. He knew how to use it. He wanted to.

The next day there was heavy cloud, and the humidity was oppressive. Tom guessed a thunderstorm was brewing. He lit their camping stove and put the water pot on to boil while he dug in the packs for their ponchos. If there was a storm, all they could do about it was keep as much water off them as possible.

Gillian emerged from the path leading to the long drop nearby.

'Looks like the drought is about to break – on us.'

Tom smiled. 'You sound cheerful this morning.'

She nodded and accepted a mug of hot tea.

Once they'd had their tea and energy bars they set off. They were heading back to the sea, down a steep, rocky path that took them to the mouth of a river that had carved an impassable gorge through the hills ahead of them. Tom was grateful the rain held off – the rocks were rounded and loose, and smoothed by aeons of being tossed in the sea. They would be dangerous wet.

They rested at the bottom before they forded the river.

'Claire was scared,' Gillian said suddenly. 'She had a phobia. But you know that. She was always terrified of drowning.'

Was that what happened? Tom asked himself. Did she drown? Was that where her fear came from? Did she have a premonition that somehow the sea would claim her?

'So you recall being here with her?'

Gillian nodded. 'We'd better go. I think the tide's coming in. That's what she was scared of.'

'Gillian – nothing happened? Nothing happened here?'

She shook her head, her face closed.

They waded across easily, but then the storm hit, leaving them stranded on the beach. The downpour was torrential, while lightning flashed over the hills above them. They had no option but to wait it out – the path climbed up the cliffs again; impossible to negotiate in the drumming rain. They huddled together under their ponchos, but with no cover they were soon wet through and chilled by the wind.

The storm didn't last long. After there was just the sound of the drops cascading off the broad-leafed shrubs and trees above them. The sun came out, and the temperature started to rise rapidly.

'Let's go swimming!' Gillian laughed. 'We're so wet anyway. Why not?'

Without waiting for a reply, she stripped down to her underwear and ran for the breakers. Tom shrugged, pulled off his sopping shirt and jeans and followed. Nice figure, he thought. Probably has plenty of guys after her. Funny, I've never thought about her that way. She was always with Claire, almost part of the family. Maybe after all this … But he couldn't think about it.

Afterwards they sat on the rocks until they were more or less dry. Then they pulled on their jeans and boots and started up the cliff path. Now the sun was hot, and they were happy not to be wearing their tops.

'You'll burn,' Tom said. But Gillian shook her head. 'The sun's too low.'

She was right, Tom thought, realising they'd be hard-pressed to make the next camp in daylight. He was leading and stepped up the pace, but Gillian had no trouble keeping up with him, right on his tail.

It was dark by the time they found the next campsite, and this time it took two of them to deal with the tent in the sputtering light of their gas stove.

'Is there any more of that steak?' Gillian asked. 'It was great.'

'Sorry. It's finished, and I can't make a fire anyway. Everything's wet. So it's freeze-dried *Texan* steak – whatever that is. There's wine left, though.'

They set about the preparations, and soon they had a meal.

'It tastes OK,' Gillian said. 'Spicy. But it's mushy. Somehow doesn't feel real. Funny – at home I really like vegetables and pasta and stuff, but out here I'm craving meat. The protein for energy, I suppose.'

Tom nodded and washed the last of his food down with wine. He wasn't full, and guiltily hoped that Gillian might leave some of hers. But this time he was disappointed.

When she'd finished, he said, 'You said something in your sleep last night. I was wondering about it.'

'What?'

'You said "Claire". And then "let me go". It sounded like an argument.'

'I did? I don't know. Unless…' She shook her head.

'Please, Gill, if you think of anything, tell me. It could be important.'

She frowned. 'For a moment there was something, but now it's gone again. I'm tired, Tom. Let's turn in.' She started collecting the dishes.

They climbed into their sleeping bags, but Tom decided to stay awake. He'd wait for Gillian to fall into a deep sleep, hoping she'd say something more. Tomorrow was their third day. So far, all he'd discovered was that Claire and Gillian had crossed the river together, and maybe one of them had said 'let me go'. Not much. He closed his eyes, pretending to sleep.

When he woke, the sun was already up and he was alone in the tent. He checked his watch: six-thirty. If Gillian had said anything, he'd slept through it. An opportunity missed. He pulled on a t-shirt and worked his way out of the tent.

'Morning, Tom.' Gillian was cooking up a yellowish concoction. 'Maybe I talk in my sleep, but you snore!'

'*Ja*, maybe.' He laughed.

'I'm making scrambled eggs – at least that's what it says on the packet. I'm hungry this morning. That stuff last night wasn't … real. Anyway, it's a change from energy bars, and it's still early.'

Tom headed for the long drop and by the time he was back the breakfast was ready.

This time there was plenty – Gillian had used two packets of dried egg – and it was good. The lumpy, rehydrated food actually tasted like scrambled eggs, and the consistency was not too far off either.

They were dry, fed, and the day looked promising as they set off.

This time the path went deeper into the forest – a tunnel through the thick vegetation. They'd been walking for about an hour when Gillian, who was leading, stopped so suddenly that Tom nearly bumped into her.

'We turned off here,' she said, looking to the right, away from the sea. 'Right here we went into the forest.' There was a narrow path snaking up the hill, maybe made by bushbuck or duikers. There was nothing to show where it went or that humans ever used it.

'You turned off here? Why? This doesn't go anywhere.'

'You can get back to the road from here.'

There were a few exit routes that could be taken back to the main coastal road if you needed to leave the trail to get help, or if you'd just had enough. There was one on this day's hike, but it should be clearly marked. Tom was sure this wasn't it.

'But why did you want to get off the trail?'

Gillian looked puzzled. 'We needed water and there's a spring up there. I think that was it.'

'But surely you brought plenty of water?'

'I don't know, Tom. But I'm sure we turned off here.'

Tom bent down to look at the path. 'No tracks at all.'

'After that rain yesterday? And it was weeks ago now.'

'OK. Let's see where it goes.'

Suddenly Gillian seemed reticent. 'We're going to follow that path?'

'If that's the way you went, we have to.'

'Are you sure? Maybe it's not such a good idea. We have to reach the next campsite by tonight.'

'We must. That's why we came.'

Once they got going, Gillian seemed to be quite sure of the way. The track followed a creek, which she crossed, back and forth, picking up the path when it disappeared into the rocks. They climbed steeply and for quite a way. The creek was flowing strongly after the storm, and small waterfalls emptied into clumps of sword ferns.

They came to a mass of rocks flung down the hillside. 'We have to go over these,' Gillian said. 'Careful. Some of them are loose.'

Once they'd clambered up, they paused to catch their breath.

Gillian turned to go on, but Tom asked, 'But how did you know where to go? There aren't any signs or paint splashes on the rocks.'

'Oh, she showed us.' Gillian started walking.

Tom grabbed her arm to stop her. 'Wait. *She?* You mean Claire?'

'No, not Claire. The other woman. She must've been here before.'

'Shit! What *other woman*, Gill?'

'Gill, Claire…' Gillian was frowning, as though counting to three was a problem for her. 'Just the two of us?'

Tom clenched his teeth. What on earth was going on?

'You're hurting me, Tom.'

He let go of her arm.

'Look, I can't answer your questions. I know this path leads up to a saddle in the hills, and the road is somewhere on the other side. But I don't know why we came, or who was with us, or even if anyone was with us. Maybe someone told us? Back on the main trail. That must be it.'

Tom said nothing, possibilities churning in his mind.

'Look, let's go back to the trail. Please, Tom. I'm getting hungry.'

He shook his head. 'No, we go on. We can stop here and eat.'

They dug out energy bars and other snacks, and drank from their water bottles. Neither of them said a word. When they were finished, Tom packed up.

'You OK?' he asked.

She shook her head. 'I'm still really hungry. I need…' She seemed to lose the thought and jumped up to go on. She started to lead the way again, but now she was much slower and sometimes had to search for the right route. Once she seemed lost and had to backtrack.

'I can't remember anything from here, Tom. I remember running through here, *down* the hill. And I was alone. I think I was alone. But I can't remember going up.'

'Maybe through here?' Tom pointed to a gap between the shrubs. You couldn't call it a path.

Gillian shook her head. 'No, that's not the way. We mustn't go that way. I think we should go down now, Tom. Really. I'm tired. I don't want to go further. We need to get to the campsite.'

'I'm going on.'

Tom started off, pushing between the bushes. He was sure they were close to the place where something traumatic had occurred. Perhaps if they reached it, Gillian would finally be forced to face what had happened. But he couldn't force her. If she wouldn't come, he'd have to go back. He couldn't leave her alone in the forest, not after what she'd been through there.

After a few minutes, he heard her behind him. Then she brushed past and started to lead again.

With the saddle of the hills in sight, they came to a dead end. In front of them was a mass of huge boulders, dumped at crazy angles on top of each other. On the left the boulders cascaded steeply down the way they'd come. On the right was sheer rock face. There seemed no way to go further, but Gillian stared at the boulders in front of them.

'I'm not going in there. I'm not. I'm going back. We shouldn't be here.' Tom saw that she was looking at a narrow crack between two massive boulders.

'Why did we come here, Gill? What's in there?'

She just shook her head. 'Nothing. There's nothing in there. I want to go back, Tom. There's nothing here. I'm not going in there. I'm not!' She sounded almost hysterical, but then suddenly she seemed to calm down and in a quite different tone of voice said, 'I'm very hungry, Tom.'

Tom took no notice. He'd caught sight of something between the rocks further down the slope. He clambered closer and found a backpack, its contents spilled out, rummaged through by something – perhaps a jackal or a Cape wildcat in search of food. The backpack was khaki with a maroon trim; Claire had owned one just like it. And it hadn't simply been left here; it had been discarded, tossed down the hill. So robbery hadn't been the motive, then. Whatever the reason had been, he was absolutely sure that this was the place where the women had been attacked.

Tom reached for the backpack, but then pulled back. He shouldn't touch anything. They would need to bring the police here. Instead he returned to Gillian. She stared at him, her face unreadable.

'Gill, it's Claire's backpack down there. I know it is.'

She said nothing. He turned to the crevice between the rocks.

'I have to see what's through there. It's all right – you can wait for me here. Then we'll go back. OK?'

She nodded slowly, her eyes fixed on him.

Once he was close to the rocks, he realised squeezing through the crack wasn't going to be that easy. He'd have to go in sideways and then twist left to get past the boulder behind. It was the first time he'd been unhappy about his wide shoulders. It was going to be tight. He took off his pack and left it with Gillian.

In the end, once he hit on just the right angle, he went through fairly easily. He found himself in a low shelter formed by a huge flattish boulder lying across the others. He had to bend over to avoid hitting his head, and there was an unpleasant musty smell he couldn't place. Maybe animals lived here. The far end was blocked by a pile of boulders, but light filtered between them.

As his eyes grew accustomed to the dimness, he made out the remains of a fire at the far end; the gaps in the rocks had obviously been used as a chimney. Next to the fire was a pile of wood and another backpack, this one still closed. And behind it was something else.

He knew at once what it was, what it had been.

Moments later he was looking down at what remained of Claire.

The hot, dry weather and the time that had passed had turned her corpse into a mummy, the skin blackened and pulled tight around her bones. As awful as this was, there was something still worse: gaping slashes where her breasts should have been.

So he was right about the *sangomas*, he thought. The two women were abducted and brought here. But how had Gillian managed to escape?

Part of Claire's right leg had been removed too. And then he saw that there were bones matching the missing ones lying next to the fire.

He felt the sudden urge to throw up. No, not here. Not with all that remained of his sister lying at his feet.

That was when he heard the voices. Gillian was talking to someone, loudly, scared. The other voice much deeper, husky.

Tom swallowed the bile in his throat as he rushed back to reach Gillian, cursing himself for leaving the knife in his pack. She'd warned him there was danger here, but he hadn't listened.

Now there was silence outside.

'Gillian!' he shouted as he forced himself through the crevice.

He ripped his shirt in his haste, scraping his skin. Then he was out, blinded for a second by the full sun, and momentarily relieved to see Gillian waiting for him, right in front of the crevice.

She was quite alone. When he saw her eyes and his hunting knife grasped in her hand, he knew how wrong he'd been about everything.

She spoke in the husky voice. 'I'm sorry, Tom. Gillian really liked you, but you shouldn't have come here. And I'm so hungry.'

Faster than Tom would've imagined possible, she plunged the knife deep into his throat.

It took a few minutes before Tom stopped moving. When it was over, she easily negotiated the crevice into the shelter. With a half-smile at what was left of Claire, she kicked away the loose bones and lit a fire.

The Riddle of the Humming Bee

Paul Charles

1

The journey up from Cork had taken too long – much too long; and the four-and-a-half-hour drive had been a hot and sticky one. Harry Hammond meant to make a note (he was always meaning to make notes) to instruct his agent never to book the Humming Bees on back-to-back Cork and Belfast gigs again. The road from Dublin up to Belfast was as good as you'd get anywhere in the UK, but the Cork to Dublin section hadn't improved since his father had started gigging with showbands in the sixties.

Needs must however, and Hammond could only dream about the success that had so far evaded the band; success that might have brought them luxuries, such as a better level of on-the-road comfort, of course; but better hotels, too; better equipment, better vehicles, better venues, a better crew and better audiences. Better everything in fact.

There was one thing that served as an effective antidepressant on the 250-mile journey, though: the power shower in the main artist's dressing room at the 149-year-old Ulster Hall in Bedford Street, Belfast. Since Newry, Hammond had travelled with his eyes closed, not necessarily in search of much-needed sleep, but rather day-dreaming about peeling off his clingy, sweat-drenched clothes and stepping into the best shower he had ever experienced.

When he reached the aforementioned dressing room, he resisted the temptation to dive straight into the shower, choosing instead to prolong the anticipation. He had his trusted life-long friend and roadie (a frog-eyed, five-foot-four-inches-small native of Belfast called Litz) deliver to his dressing room his two guitars, his suitcase, his laptop computer and his personal deli tray from the catering rider. Then he escorted Litz back to the dressing-room door, instructing him, as usual, to stand guard outside while he locked it from the inside. In the distance he could hear the roadies as they noisily wheeled the heavy flight cases of equipment up the steep ramps and onto the stage.

The shower still foremost in Hammond's mind he had two tasks to complete before surrendering to the water-powered massage. He checked his emails (that took at least thirty minutes) and then he helped himself to about half the deli tray (that took perhaps another dozen minutes). Then he rang Litz on his mobile and said he was just about to step into the shower but could he – no please or thank-you – wheel in the wardrobe flight case as he needed a fresh change of clothes after his shower. He also instructed Litz to remove the deli tray. He didn't seem to mind eating decaying animals, he just didn't like the smell of them. He advised Litz that he'd already unlocked the dressing room so he could accomplish his chores. Litz completed the said tasks in five minutes. Apparently, though, Hammond hadn't yet taken his greatly anticipated shower, because, a few minutes later, Litz heard the dressing-room door being locked again from the inside.

Now there would be no distractions. In one of Hammond's lyrics he'd written that anticipation was better than participation. However, for anticipation to exist there had to *be* participation. At long last it was time for him to partake of the bliss that was the Ulster Hall's power shower. Taking off his clothes at this stage felt like shedding a coat of dead, tired skin. He wondered if snakes felt such elation while shedding theirs.

He placed the freshly laundered towels by the shower door. He preferred to turn on the shower only when he was already standing naked in the shower tray. He just loved that initial blast of cold water, which would invigorate him before the water heated up to relax and recharge him.

It felt every bit as glorious as he'd hoped it would. He closed his eyes, raised his head in the direction of the showerhead and let the high-speed jets of hot water dampen and then shrink his trademark bottle-blonde crown of curls away from his brow.

He raised his hands to swish back his hair in an elaborate Tony

Curtis DA. The water felt denser than normal. Come to think of it, it smelled different too. It smelled – and he had a quick chuckle to himself about this – it smelled like blood. He wondered for a split second if in his excitement getting into the shower he'd cut or grazed himself somewhere. Instinctively he grabbed his privates. Simultaneously he opened his eyes as his fingers moved to search his scalp for any leaking abrasion. The moment his eyes registered the crimson density of the water, he went into shock, collapsed into the shower tray and, in doing so, inadvertently suffered a minor cut to his forehead.

In the meantime, the trusted Litz had been trying to enter his boss's dressing room with his traditional post-shower cup of herbal tea. Unable to gain entry, despite eleven incessant minutes knocking on the door, the resourceful Litz, aided and abetted by the Ulster Hall caretaker, William Mulholland, eventually gained access. When Litz was assured his boss was OK, he and Mulholland headed off to discover the source of the crimson Nile.

In the loft space above the artist's dressing room, they discovered Barry 'Joey' Simpson, the Humming Bees' lead guitarist, his body still warm, but face down in the five-hundred-gallon water tank.

Joey's days of running around the stage like someone possessed – while Hammond perfected his Jim Morrison static pose – had come to a very abrupt and very permanent end. Litz and Mulholland frantically tried to rescue Joey from the bloody water, only to find that he'd been garrotted by a guitar string. That same guitar string – a famous Ernie Ball 'B' string – was still embedded deeply in his neck.

Those were the facts as relayed to McCusker by Litz and Hammond.

2

McCusker sent DS Willie John Barr to question the remaining members of the band and crew, plus their associated girlfriends, wives and partners.

He didn't know a lot about pop music or musicians, but he had heard quite a few stories about the legendary excesses of the catering rider, so he thought he might like to sample some of the alleged delights.

Litz, as it so happened, was also feeling a little peckish, so a few minutes later, McCusker and the Humming Bees' chief roadie joined various other members of the crew down in the basement of the Ulster Hall, where the tour caterers had set up camp.

Considering what had just happened to one of the principals of their troop, McCusker felt they were all incredibly blasé. He figured they were either experiencing delayed shock or they were just acting the macho men they thought McCusker expected them to be.

'Well, at long last Joey's gone to play with Hendrix in heaven,' the only roadie not dressed in denim began. His (apparent) daily wardrobe was a fading grey-black romper suit. He wore his long brown hair parted in the middle and flowing down to mix with his moustache-less goatee beard. He was seated at the head of the table, acting as though he'd been holding court before McCusker and Litz had arrived.

'Aye Urry, just as long as Jimi doesn't expect Joey to tune his guitars,' replied the crew member sitting closest to McCusker; he was dressed head to toe in black, and had a 'Dougal' hairstyle.

They all fell about laughing at that one. Urry looked at McCusker, checking to see how their irreverence was going down with the detective. McCusker laughed casually even though he didn't get the joke.

Needing no further encouragement, Urry continued. 'Aye and as long as Jimi doesn't leave Joey alone with any of his women they'll get along fine.'

'Well, from what I've read about Jimi and what I know about Joey, they're both going to be pushed when it comes to standing each other a pint when they visit heaven's version of the Crown Bar,' Litz said, looking at McCusker, who was pretending to be preoccupied by his soup.

'Yeah,' Urry continued. 'In the Humming Bees, Joey got the glory and scored the birds and Harry Hammond got to count the money and sweat a lot.'

'Aye,' Litz sighed loudly, 'I've never known a man who sweated so much as Harry Hammond. As long as I've known him he's been in need of a shower. If he hadn't needed all those showers he'd be as big as Ed Sheeran by now.'

'Did they get on well?' McCusker asked, feeling he'd gone as long as he could without contributing to the conversation.

Litz, Urry and the two other crew members not so much laughed as offered their own version of a four-part, out-of-tune harmony of Frankie Howerd's tittering.

'Now then, Mac,' Urry started, pulling on his fingerless gloves, 'we should start to pack the gear away.'

'I shouldn't bother if I were you,' Litz interrupted as Mac searched in vain for his gloves, 'Harry is talking about going ahead with the gig, and the entire tour for that matter, as a … a … tribute to Joey.'

'You're fecking kidding?' Urry said, spitting out the words.

'No way,' Mac screeched.

'Typical,' the remaining crew member offered meekly.

By now they were all on their feet.

'You can definitely count me out,' Urry said.

'Aye, I'm with Urry,' Mac offered in what sounded like a habitual soundbite.

'OK, fair play to you. But before making any rash decisions, tell me this: how much wages are you owed?' Litz asked, looking from one to the other.

'Right lads,' Urry said, visibly changing gear, and moving away from the table, 'the rest of this equipment won't get set up by itself now, will it?'

In a matter of seconds they were all gone, leaving McCusker and Litz at the table by themselves.

'Whose band is this?' McCusker asked.

'It was originally formed by Joey and his brother Brian. In the beginning it was an Everly Brothers kind of act, with just the two of them. Joey's real name is Barry, and when they were growing up, they were allowed to rehearse in their parents' sitting room on condition they were very, very quiet,' Litz began and dropped to a whisper for the last few words. 'In fact they were so quiet their dad christened them the Humming Bees – you know B for Brian…'

'…and B for Barry,' McCusker added seamlessly.

'And it stuck,' Litz continued. 'Brian was an excellent songwriter but he had no stomach for the road, so Barry changed his name to Joey and recruited Harry, a mate of mine who lived close to Barry and myself. Harry learned all of Brian's vocal parts. They found another three musicians, kept the name and, before they knew it, they'd secured a record deal with EMI. The first album consisted entirely of Brian's songs; it received incredible reviews and the band had a reasonable first flush of success. Then, for the second record, Harry started to write some songs, at first with Joey, but then by himself.'

'How were his songs?'

'Agh you know,' Litz said with a shrug of his shoulders so effective that McCusker knew immediately. 'However, they still had one song of Brian's left from the first batch. It was one they'd always done live but for some reason it never made the first album. Anyway, they recorded it for the second album. It was called, "Skybird"…'

'I know "Skybird"…'

'Everybody knows "Skybird",' Litz chuckled, 'but they don't have to listen to it every bleedin' day of their lives, like the crew and I do. It was a big hit and made the second album a very respectable seller. And guess who had the majority of the publishing on that one? … Harry of course. Joey had a few co-writes, so he was making a few bob, but he was spending more than he was earning living the lifestyle … Let's just say he was rather fond of self-induced chemical imbalance. So much so that didn't he only go and shag Brian's girlfriend while under the influence? I don't think the brothers have spoken since.'

'So Joey ran out of money?'

'Well, not before Harry persuaded him to sell his share of the band and the publishing company they'd formed for the first album.'

'Causing resentment?'

'It wasn't as blatant as that,' Litz replied, 'I mean, not to those of us on the outside. Harry is a very cautious and considered man. He plans all his moves with great care and attention. He'd have made sure not to be seen to be taking advantage. On top of which, Joey had a hunger he was preoccupied by. He would boast about wanting to be the prettiest corpse in the graveyard. I had the feeling he always hoped that Ash or Snow Patrol would steal him away, so he could sell his soul and share their glory. But until then he seemed content to do Harry's bidding.'

Litz went quiet for a while clicking his tongue a few times.

'What? You remembered something else?' McCusker asked.

'Well, it could be something and it could be nothing, but I did get the impression there was someone sniffing around him over the last few months.'

'As in wanting to steal him?'

'Perhaps,' Litz replied blankly, 'he was just a wee bit more content than normal, so it was either another group wanting him or he was off chasing a new bit of skirt.'

'Is Harry married?' McCusker began, distracted as a pretty catering assistant replaced the empty soup bowls with plates of sausages and champ.

'No,' Litz replied quickly; then mumbled, 'he's very keen on Janet though.'

'Janet?'

'Ah yes, Janet Morrison,' Litz continued, his eyes lighting up again. 'We've both known her since we ran around together up on Cyprus Avenue as kids. She's not really serious about Harry. She always makes sure she has a mate around when she's with him. You know, safety in numbers and all of that?'

'Aye, I know what you mean. So you're still fond of her yourself then?'

Litz looked at McCusker with a mixture of hurt and respect in his eyes. 'She's definitely not interested in anyone involved in all this travelling around with this auld rock and roll carry-on. But, then again, I'm not going to want to be doing this for ever, now am I?'

3

DS W.J. Barr joined them at the dinner table, and Litz used this interruption to go and attend to some duty or other.

When he'd left the room, McCusker said, 'Right DS, what information did you manage to pick up for me?'

'Well, let's see,' DS Barr started, playing with his tie as he read from his notes. 'This was a short-notice booking and hadn't been selling too well. The promoter, a Peter Kane from City Concerts, said the band was already in decline and it was costing him dearly. He said he was paying them ten grand. The tickets were priced at £17.50 and he would need to have taken over twice the box office just to break even!'

'But, surely, if he couldn't at least cover his costs he shouldn't have agreed to do the show?'

'Well, I asked him about that and he said the agent blagged him that, with all the cruise ships now visiting the city, the band would benefit from tourists. On top of which if *he* hadn't done the concert, Wonderland, another promoter in the city, would have stepped in just to have a chance to work with the act.'

'So, he was happy to lose money to protect his relationship with an act he openly admits were on the wane?' McCusker asked.

'Yeah, pretty much.'

'How much could he have lost?'

'Well, that's another funny thing, up to an hour ago, the ticket sales were under five hundred, so he reckoned he was going to lose about ten grand. Then Joey was murdered and Harry decided he still wanted the show to go ahead, "as a tribute to Joey".' DS Barr raised his right eyebrow as he mentioned the word 'tribute'. 'Now it's all over Radio Ulster and the box-office phones are going crazy. The promoter predicts the show will be completely sold out before the doors open.'

'So, now, instead of losing ten thousand quid, he's going to *make* a few bob?' McCusker said, polishing off his jam roly-poly and custard.

'Yep, I reckon he'll turn a profit of about five grand,' the DS replied as he checked his notes.

'Which means, altogether, he's about fifteen thousand pounds better off?'

'But surely you're not suggesting it was worth killing someone for fifteen grand?'

'Oh, I've met people who'd consider it for a lot less than fifteen thousand lids,' McCusker said. 'On top of which, those fifteen big ones could have been considerably higher if you take into consideration the entire tour. Tell me this, W.J., did you learn anything else from the promoter?'

'Well, only that he felt Joey's brother, Brian, was the real talent behind the band. Did you know he wrote "Skybird"?'

'Yep, Litz filled me in on some of the band's history. Did the promoter feel there was any bad blood between the brothers?' McCusker said.

'Apparently not,' DS Barr replied. 'He thought Harry had cultivated a battle between Joey and Brian just for the press mileage, but, according to him, Brian no longer held any grudge against his brother. In fact he was truly concerned over the helpless state Joey was in.'

'Can we talk to Brian?'

'Not until tomorrow morning. He's in London.'

'Who told you that?'

'The promoter, he's now Brian's manager. He had him over in London recording his first solo album. He spoke to him on the phone and told Brian what had happened to Joey. Brian confirmed he'd be arriving at George Best City Airport tomorrow morning.'

'How long has he been there?'

'For the last three weeks.'

'Are you certain he's actually in London?'

'I thought you'd ask me that so I got the number of the recording studios from the directory and I rang him there.'

'Right, good man,' McCusker grunted, visibly pleased. 'At least that's one name we can strike from our suspect list.'

'And how many names would that leave us with, Inspector?'

'Oh, we'd have to consider just about everyone else in this travelling circus. Then you'd have to add families and friends, plus the promoter. Yeah, the promoter, with his financial exposure, must be in the frame somewhere. Plus there'll be other suspects we don't even know about yet.'

'Everyone except Harry Hammond of course…'

'You reckon?' McCusker asked, mostly with his eyebrows and a friendly smile.

'Well, he was locked in his dressing room with Litz outside the door on guard when Joey was garrotted,' Barr said.

McCusker didn't reply, appearing preoccupied.

'It'll take us forever to check the rest of them out,' DS Barr offered, uncharacteristically downbeat.

'Maybe W.J., but maybe not,' McCusker offered, wandering off in search of the caretaker, Andrew Mulholland.

4

Eventually, the promoter officially asked McCusker's permission for the concert to go ahead. By this stage it was six-forty and the doors were about to open. Joey Simpson's remains had been removed from the premises and the majority of the audience, (baby-sittered up, where appropriate) were already on their way to the Ulster Hall. Apart from which, McCusker was cute enough to know that there was a bit of history taking place in their midst. Musicians, crew and fans alike would discuss the riddle he was trying to solve for many, many years to come – possibly for longer than the band's name would survive. And anyway, McCusker had been well fed and was therefore disposed to be accommodating.

DS Barr, for good measure, discreetly placed constables at the entrance and exit points, on Bedford Street, and on Linden Hall Street, to the rear of the venue.

5

As McCusker sat beside the caretaker, Mulholland, up in the back row of the balcony, he couldn't help but be excited by the energy generated by 1,800 punters as they took their places in the auditorium. He was indeed experiencing first hand what Litz had described as the buzz of the audience. The detective could actually feel the collective energy of the people gathering around him with common cause – to celebrate the music of one of their favourite artists.

'This is nothing,' Mulholland said, noticing McCusker's reaction to the buzz. 'You should have been here on New Year's Eve in 1959 when the Royal Showband had almost five thousand people gathered in here. That was quare craic, I'll tell you. Aye, I remember seeing them walking down through the choir seats, which were packed with punters. The band members were mobbed before they were able to take their positions on stage. Another great night was March the fifth, 1971, when Led Zeppelin took to that there stage in front of you and performed "Stairway to Heaven" for the first time anywhere in the world. And then there was Rory Gallagher; oh boy, he was on fire every night he played here, either with Taste or with his own band when Taste split up. Rory loved this city, and this hall in particular. Aye, I'd watch him from up here and, be jinkers, I'll tell you something, there were some nights I was convinced he was going to physically rise up in front of those giant organ pipes at the back of the stage there.'

McCusker followed the caretaker's stare down to the stage, which was now packed with roadies, including Litz, Urry and Mac, all wandering about doing their last-minute checks and rechecks.

'Has there ever been…' the rest of McCusker's question became inaudible because the house lights went down and the roar of the audience went up as Harry Hammond, with the surviving members of the Humming Bees, sauntered onto the stage.

Harry Hammond, dressed all in black, wrapped himself around the centrally positioned microphone stand. The keyboard player started to play very solemn (synthesised) organ chords. This signature introduction to what was one of their hits was enough to send the fans into another tizz. Hammond wailed like a banshee, and a few lines later the band kicked in, at which point McCusker gave up all hope of deciphering the lyrics. He wasn't even sure why he tried; it wasn't as if he expected to find any clues therein.

Following the third of their stadium-style rock anthems, Hammond silenced the crowd with his first direct words to them of the evening:

'This one's for Joey!'

The drummer immediately counted the band in to a tune even McCusker recognised: 'Skybird', the Humming Bees' biggest hit.

The roof of the Ulster Hall was lifted off its proverbial rafters as the audience's singing easily drowned out even the band's amplified sound.

McCusker's attention was fixed on the stage and proceedings there. Hammond was, as Litz had predicted, 'sweating buckets'.

As the band reached the part where Joey's trademark searing guitar solo would normally come in to take the song up another notch or two, the arrangement broke down. Obviously the Humming Bees, in their Joeyless state, hadn't rehearsed anything to fill this gap.   .

But then an amazing thing happened. Just as the band's sound was about to disintegrate into a chaotic mess, the audience with one voice started to sing, as best they could, the notes of the missing solo. The keyboard player quickly cottoned on to what was happening and a few bars later he was leading the audience through the correct melody.

The spell was broken when the caretaker screamed in the detective's ear, 'If you want to attend to those chores you mentioned earlier, now would be a good time, because I've got a pile of stuff I'm going to need to do shortly before the concert comes to an end.'

Twenty minutes later, McCusker was back in his original seat. The concert seemed to have sagged quite a bit during his absence. He went into a bit of a trance and pretty soon started to think about Barry 'Joey' Simpson's demise.

If the reaction on the stage below was anything to go by, Simpson's bandmates seemed to be doing better than OK without him.

But, McCusker wondered, who could have murdered the unfortunate musician?

His brother perhaps? Maybe Brian Simpson had just bided his time and was now taking his revenge for losing out on the Humming Bees' publishing and royalties honeypot. That was before you even considered the ultimate betrayal by his brother and his former girlfriend as a possible motive. Perhaps Harry Hammond, who'd already legally taken ownership of the band and their income, still (emotionally) needed to be the main man on stage? But surely Harry had been locked – not to mention, guarded – in his own dressing room at the time of the murder?

Then there was the promoter on the verge of a financial bloodbath. Had he found a rather lethal way to reverse his fortunes? And then, considering all of this, was there a chance that the ever-trusted Litz, in his endeavours with street-smart Miss Morrison, had decided to eliminate the competition once and for all? Or could the aforementioned promoter, this time in his role as Brian Simpson's manager, have decided that he could help his budding artist's interests by derailing the Humming Bees? Could Brian also have been involved in this scenario? He did, however, appear to be conveniently away in London exactly at the time of the murder.

People with nice tidy alibis always attracted McCusker's attention.

He tuned back into the concert again as it neared the end. In truth, the Humming Bees hadn't managed to revisit the ecstatic heights they had achieved during the performance of 'Skybird'. The band was clearly aware of this, because they encored with the same song.

Fifteen minutes later, the hall had emptied and McCusker was still sitting alone in the balcony, watching the crew break down the equipment. He felt there were few things in life as sad and lonely as a post-gig empty venue. In the moments prior to the doors opening, when the auditorium was also empty, there was anticipation about the magic that was about to happen. The air would be so thick you could cut it with a knife. After the performance, however, the atmosphere was heavy with the regret that it was all over; the magic moments were gone forever.

All these thoughts brought McCusker neatly back to the Humming Bees' lyric: 'Anticipation is always better than participation'.

Since McCusker had visited Hammond's dressing room mid-set to have a good old look around, including spending thirty minutes on his computer, he was now thoroughly enjoying anticipating the events that were about to unfold in that same dressing room.

6

McCusker, accompanied by DS William John Barr, entered the star dressing room. They had to push their way past the liggers and well-wishers lucky enough to have secured coveted backstage passes. The death of Joey Simpson did not seem to have dampened the post-gig proceedings. This troubled McCusker greatly, but he'd also have to admit to being particularly taken by the number of great-looking women present, the majority of whom seemed to be wearing skin-tight jeans tucked into knee-high stiletto boots.

Never liking to be the centre of attention, McCusker whispered something in DS Barr's ear. The young DS showed none of his superior's reluctance for the spotlight.

'OK, OK, we're going to need this room cleared immediately,' he barked at the top of his voice. When it became clear that the thronging mass was intent on ignoring him, he stood up on a plush leather chair, stuck two fingers from each hand under his tongue and gave one of the loudest wolf-whistles McCusker had ever heard.

'OK. Everyone apart from band, crew and promoter, *out now*!' Barr ordered.

The two constables on guard at the door helped clear the room of the guest list, all of whom seemed to be working on the age-old principle that the only place worth being backstage was the place you weren't meant to be. Pretty soon, though, McCusker had his less public room. The only person missing was chief roadie, Litz.

McCusker went over to speak to Urry and Mac discreetly, and they immediately sauntered off, Urry walking away like John Wayne making his final triumphant exit at the end of a movie.

'OK, let's all make ourselves comfortable while Urry and Mac find Litz,' McCusker said.

Harry Hammond looked at his watch several times, not once clocking the time. The promoter, Peter Kane, kept staring at his mobile, checking and sending texts.

Hammond eventually asked the question that was on everyone's mind: 'Do you really think Litz murdered Joey?'

'I'd say not,' McCusker replied confidently.

'Yeah, that's what I thought,' Hammond said, forcing a smile. 'I mean, I know for a fact he was outside my dressing-room door all afternoon.'

Hammond's sweat rate still hadn't slowed back down to normal, so he used a non-stop supply of tissues to remove the irritating film of sticky, salty moisture from his brow and neck. He immediately discarded the soiled tissue into the ever-filling wastepaper bin by the side of the fridge. McCusker quickly put a single plastic glove on his right hand, removed the latest tissue and carefully placed it in an evidence bag, which he sealed, marking up the location, date and time on the label.

'Sorry; why did you do that?' Hammond said, half laughing.

'Just collecting evidence,' McCusker replied.

An embarrassingly long minute later Urry and Mac returned, nonchalantly wheeling a flight case between them. When they'd wheeled the flight case over to beside Hammond's wardrobe on wheels, Urry said, 'We couldn't find Litz anywhere, Inspector; he seems to have vanished. Very strange if you ask me. Is this the flight case you wanted?'

'That's the one,' McCusker replied.

The flight case was identical to the four-foot cube already in the room, except that one had been stencilled with 'Humming Bees, Belfast', then, in smaller letters underneath, 'H.H. Wardrobe'; whereas the other – the new arrival – had been stencilled 'Humming Bees, Belfast', then in smaller letters, 'Band. Dressing Room'.

'OK, we should start,' McCusker announced. 'Litz seems to have been unavoidably detained; perhaps he's with Janet Morrison.'

Hammond tried to appear as if this hadn't registered, making it even more obvious that it had.

'Mr Harold Hammond I'm arresting you for the murder of Mr Barry Simpson. I have to advise you that anything you say…'

The remainder of McCusker's caution was lost amid Hammond's moans, groans, protests and the noise of the members of the band and crew all trying to talk at the same time. Nonetheless, McCusker completed the caution by the book. Urry made a fist-first dash towards Hammond, only to be thwarted in his efforts in the final second by the ever-alert DS Barr.

'Oh, come on, Inspector,' Hammond spluttered. 'It couldn't possibly have been me. I was in here in my dressing room. The door was not only locked but also guarded by Litz. On top of which, Joey was my mate, my fellow band member – my song-writing partner. What motive could I possibly have for murdering him?'

When McCusker refused to reply, Hammond, looking like he'd been saving his trump card, added, 'What possible proof could you have?'

'Well Mr Hammond, in the middle of all that you would appear to be asking three good questions. One, what was your motive? Two, how did you commit the murder? And three, what's my proof that you did in fact commit said murder? So, if everyone would like to settle down again, I'll deal with your questions in that order.'

'I think that's a good idea, Inspector,' Hammond said. 'In the meantime Urry, ring for my lawyer. I feel a very expensive lawsuit coming on.'

'From the look in the detective's eyes, I have a funny feeling that even Perry Mason couldn't get you out of the shit this time,' Urry replied.

'Peter?' Hammond pleaded with his promoter, who avoided eye contact with the singer.

'Let's start with the motive,' McCusker announced in a louder voice. 'I'd a wee go on your laptop during your concert, Mr. Hammond.'

'That's private,' Hammond protested.

'Oh, don't worry,' McCusker offered dismissively. 'I didn't go into any of your personal files; we can have the experts do that later with the proper warrants. In the meantime I just wanted to Google a few topics. It really is incredible what you can find out there in cyberspace.

'Anyway, I Googled "Humming Bees", and you know what? There were over eight hundred thousand documents filed on the subject. Eventually I found a site, one of the fans' chat rooms, which had been enjoying quite a bit of activity of late. There I discovered that one of the original two Humming Bees – Joey's brother, Brian Simpson – is currently in a studio making his first album.'

'That's hardly headline news – Eddie McIlwaine had it in his column in the Saturday *Telegraph* at least two months ago,' Hammond snapped.

'Fair point, Mr Hammond, fair point,' McCusker continued, unfazed. 'But the other information I uncovered in the same chat room might not be such common knowledge; and that was that Brian was forming a band to tour in support of his album *and* that Joey had agreed to join them. Is that right, Mr Kane?'

'Yes,' the promoter replied. 'But not only that; what you should also be aware of is that the only reason Brian agreed to make an album was because Joey was going to put the band together and lead it for his brother.'

The crew looked troubled – obviously unaware of this news.

'Mr Hammond, from what I gather from the chat rooms,' McCusker continued flawlessly, 'the fans seem to agree that even if you could have survived Joey leaving the Humming Bees, you most definitely could not have survived him teaming up with his brother again. The possibility of such an eventuality had the Humming Bees' fans positively buzzing with excitement. There was absolutely no doubt where their allegiance lay.' McCusker stopped talking as though to allow that fact to sink in.

Hammond started to laugh, but it wasn't as nervous a laugh as McCusker had expected.

'Anyway,' McCusker resumed, 'next we get to your method of murder. You had your agent book you back in here for tonight's show. Everyone, including the fans with their poor support in terms of ticket sales, agreed it was much too soon for the Humming Bees to play a return concert here. That's what made me suspicious in the first place. Why would a cautious man such as yourself risk ruining such a buoyant market as Belfast for your band? There had to be something about this venue that was vital to the solution to our riddle. But what could it possibly be?'

'I'm not hanging around wasting any more time here,' Hammond snarled to no one in particular.

'Please don't forget, Mr Hammond,' McCusker announced, 'that you're no longer at liberty to leave; you're under arrest. But as you're obviously rather impatient, let's cut to the quick. Here's what happened. Once Litz was positioned at the door you set up everything for your shower. While you were pretending to spend thirty minutes on your laptop doing emails and, 'a dozen minutes' eating half the contents of your deli tray, you rang Joey. You probably tempted him with drugs and asked him to meet you in the roof space above your dressing room. Then you nipped out of the dressing-room window, dropped down to the fire-escape gantry and made your way into the roof space via the fire exit, which you'd obviously conveniently left open. Joey came up via the proper staircase. When he got there, in order to protect your livelihood you strangled him with a guitar string, leaving him face down in the water tank.'

'But you're forgetting that Litz was by my door all of this time,' Hammond said in an 'OK, I'll humour you' tone. 'I take your point about being able to drop out of the dressing-room window, but it would have been impossible to climb back up and in again. The window ledge is much too high above the gantry. So the only way I could have regained access to my dressing room was past Litz at the door.'

'Well at the very least that shows us you considered the possibility,' McCusker replied, realising for perhaps the first time in his life that he was conscious of trying to avoid laying on the Ulsterspeak. 'But let's discuss that point. You rang Litz from your mobile, didn't you?'

'Yeah, I needed him to bring in my wardrobe,' Hammond claimed.

'Could you please do me a favour, Mr Hammond, and ring Litz again for me now?'

Hammond gave a 'no bother' shrug and speed-dialled his chief roadie, burying the programmed phone inside the golden curls by his left ear.

A few seconds later they could all hear the muffled sound of a ringing tone.

McCusker walked over to the flight case Urry and Mac had wheeled into the dressing room. They could all now clearly hear the sound of a mobile ringing from within. He knocked on the top of the case three times, and slowly the ringing tone, which was the guitar introduction to Them's 'Here Comes the Night', grew louder and louder as the flight case gradually opened and Litz hopped out, stretching this way and that to relieve the cramp he'd incurred in the twenty or so minutes he'd been hiding inside the confines of the case.

DS W.J. Barr seemed most impressed by McCusker's revelation.

'Where were we, Mr Hammond?' McCusker asked, gaining everyone's attention once again. 'Oh yes. So, after you strangled Joey, you slipped down from the roof space and over to the backstage street access, where you knew your flight case was parked. You hid inside your own flight case, rang Litz on your mobile, pretending you were still inside your dressing room, and ordered him to deliver your flight case to your dressing room, so you could finalise preparations for your shower.

'When Litz delivered the flight case containing yourself into your dressing room, you waited a few moments to make sure he had left your dressing room. You hopped out of the flight case and locked the dressing-room door again from the inside. You then jumped into your shower to complete your farce of bumping your head, passing out, and being "discovered" by Litz and Mulholland with the perfect alibi.'

'Sounds more like a case for Inspector Colombo,' Hammond sneered. 'All a little too far-fetched, if you ask me. But tell me this, Inspector, where's your proof?'

'Ah well, that's where Google comes to the rescue. My problem, Mr, Hammond, is that I'm not really that up-to-date on the scientific side of police work. I confess that I find it impossible to keep up with all the developments in the DNA field, so while I had access to your computer, I ran another check.' McCusker paused as he walked over to the table on which he'd left the evidence bag with Hammond's perspiration-soaked tissues. The Portrush detective gingerly lifted the bag using his thumb and forefinger and held it aloft.

Barr involuntarily said, 'His DNA!'

'*Exactly*,' McCusker confirmed. 'I found two very interesting things when I Googled "Sweat DNA". In the million or so documents posted under the subject, I discovered that a human's perspiration does in fact contain their DNA. Now, having witnessed your performance on stage tonight, I've seen that you leak a lot. What I'm trying to say is that your sweat glands are habitually overactive. I would bet my entire fortune that at least a few of your beads of sweat found their way onto Joey's clothes when you were strangling him with a guitar string. Our team of experts are currently examining Joey's clothing and now we have your DNA sample for them to compare any findings against.'

'Surely if I strangled him with a guitar string my hands would have cuts on them,' Hammond said, offering them for inspection.

'May I?' McCusker asked, as he walked over to Hammond's wardrobe flight case.

Hammond looked confused but nodded his consent.

McCusker searched the inside of the stale-smelling flight case for a few minutes. He eventually found what he was looking for.

'Mac,' McCusker said, 'I believe you lost a pair of gloves earlier today.'

'Yes, I did.'

'Would these be them?' McCusker asked, trying not to sound like David Copperfield making a big reveal, as he passed the fingerless gloves over for inspection.

'Yes, these are definitely mine!'

Harry Hammond looked like he was a beaten man, then finally he admitted as much, muttering something about the anticipation of Joey's demise being much more enjoyable than his actual participation in it. At least that's what McCusker thought Hammond was saying as the musician was handcuffed and led away.

For his part, McCusker would have to admit that, in this particular case, his participation in the solving of the crime had been much more enjoyable than the anticipation of the investigation.

Writer's Block

Paul Gitsham

The woman I was destined to spend the rest of my life with refused to even acknowledge me when we first met. Seeing as I was pressing a gun against her forehead, screaming at her to fill the bag with money and not do anything stupid, this is hardly surprising.

I realise that I'm not painting myself in the most flattering light, so let me explain my side of the story. To do that, we need to rewind precisely twelve hours and twelve minutes to a time before my hitherto humdrum existence imploded and Jeannie entered my life.

It started at eleven p.m. in the dingy nightclub where my two best friends had conspired to dump me and my blind date. With a cheery wave they had departed, leaving me and the desperately single Kelli alone in the night. They meant well of course. Claire worried about me and I had to confess that being stuck in a dead-end job, single and becoming more so wasn't where I'd planned to be at twenty-nine and three-quarters.

My original plan had involved travelling the world with nothing more than some clean underwear and a stack of blank notebooks, in the hope that the freedom of the road and the inspiration to be found upon it would conspire to unlock the novel that I knew lay within me.

Unfortunately a crippling case of papyrophobia and my parents' concerns about how I'd keep contributing to my meagre pension pot finally convinced me to give up that fantasy and stick to a more prudent plan. A safer plan. A mind-numbing, excitement-free plan, which, while devoid of risk, also left my dreams unfulfilled and my hopes crushed.

Knowing my luck, I would probably drop dead the day before I was due to start drawing my pension anyway.

So, back to the date. After an hour and two drinks' worth of stilted small talk, shouted over music neither of us liked, I retired to the bathroom to think. Decision time. It was clear that, if I wanted to, I could take Kelli home right now. But as always my conscience had its own opinion. Even without Claire's admonishment to 'be kind, she's had a hard time' it was obvious that Kelli needed more than a commitment-free roll between the sheets. She needed someone special. Not me.

I decided to call it a night; it wasn't fair to keep stringing her along. We'd exchange numbers, make empty promises about ringing each other later in the week and go our separate ways. She'd probably be as relieved as me. God I hated blind dates.

Mind made up, I re-entered the pounding energy of the club.

The first thing I saw as I crossed the dance floor, looking pathetic and lost, was Kelli. Immediately, my courage deserted me. I couldn't do it. I had to hide. The gents was out – she'd probably come in – so in desperation I opened the door marked 'Staff Only' and ducked inside.

The three men wearing hoodies, seated around a battered table, looked up in surprise. The handguns on the table made me wish I'd taken my chances with Kelli.

Stepping back outside would be suicide: I'd seen them and they'd seen me.

'You must be Skinner. I didn't think you was coming.' The biggest of the three inclined his shaven head towards me.

'That's right,' I lied, instinctively.

He slid a gun across the table. 'Don't touch it without gloves.' He gestured to the other two, younger men. 'I was about to start explaining the job.'

And so there I found myself, in the back room of a nightclub, planning a jewellery heist and wondering exactly how this state of affairs fitted my life plan.

Eleven o'clock the following morning found me dressed in black in the back seat of a stolen Mondeo, the gun on my lap heavy, the balaclava hiding the perspiration pouring down my face.

Despite their initial misunderstanding regarding my identity, the gang was actually very professional and well organised. After a few hours terrified at being found out, I'd finally accepted that the real Skinner was unlikely to suddenly materialise and demand to know who the hell I was, and so found myself increasingly drawn into the situation.

Our leader, known only as Rex, ran a tight ship. We spent all night in the tiny backroom, undisturbed by revellers or bar staff. We'd kept our phones but surrendered the batteries. Trips to the bathroom were in pairs, and our only visitor was a pizza delivery at two a.m., paid for by a twenty shoved under the door, keep the change.

As Thursday night became Friday morning my hopes of escaping or calling the police slowly evaporated, and, despite my misgivings, I found myself more and more involved in the preparation of their crazy scheme.

Screeching to a halt we piled out of the car in a tight, practised formation. Our intelligence was spot on; 11:09 Friday morning and the shop was empty, the safe open and the two unarmed Securicor guards collecting the week's takings quickly overwhelmed. Even the dustbin lorries had finished clearing the street. The driver of the Securicor van would already be calling the police, but we had at least four minutes until they arrived.

Our duties were clear: Rex covered the manager as he shakily emptied display cabinets into a bin bag; Crow-bar trained his gun on the two guards cowering, hands tied, on the floor; T-bag stood guard, and I grabbed the sales assistant, Jeannie, and frogmarched her to the open safe, demanding she fill a bag and not do anything stupid.

Three minutes and we were done. As I reached to take the bulging bag a shot rang out. The manager slumped to the floor. Without pausing, Rex turned to one of the guards, placed his gun under the chin strap of the man's helmet and pulled the trigger again, before dispatching the man's colleague in the same manner.

Crow-bar opened his mouth in protest. This hadn't been part of the plan. Rex shot him between the eyes.

Planned or not, I knew what came next. Grabbing Jeannie's arm I shoved her in the direction of the back office. 'Run!' I hissed.

We'd barely made it through the doorway before another bullet punched a hole in the plasterboard. Racing through the staff area we crashed through the fire door into the yard outside. It took both of us to block the exit with an overflowing wheelie bin from the restaurant next door.

'Do you have a car?'

She nodded and we sprinted to her Mini, parked in an adjacent street. Under my direction, she steered us towards the river, finally parking out of sight, under the road bridge at the mouth of the estuary. Beside us, swollen brown waters raced out to sea.

'You saved my life. Why?' Her voice was surprisingly steady.

Weariness swept over me, and, before I knew it, I found myself telling her all about the terrible situation I'd found myself in and how it was all one big mistake.

'What will you do?'

I shrugged; I was an accessory to murder now, not just some fool who'd stumbled into a robbery.

'I guess I'll wrap the gun in these clothes and chuck it in the river. It'll be halfway out to sea in ten minutes. Then I'll just walk away and hope for the best. Nobody alive has seen my face, except for Rex, and I doubt he'll say anything."

She shook her head. 'They'll never stop looking for you.' She paused. 'I have a better idea. Hand yourself in. Come clean. You saved my life, I'll vouch for you. Give me the gun to show everyone you're sincere. You'll be a hero.'

I weighed up the options. What choice did I really have? A life on the run, always looking over my shoulder, scared that either the police or Rex would one day find me? Or the chance to get my old life, such as it was, back.

And maybe she was right. Maybe I would be a hero. If not to the world, then at least to her. Up close I couldn't help noticing that she was rather pretty. I glanced down at her left hand: no rings.

I handed over the gun.

Turning it around, she pressed it against my temple. 'You stupid bastard. Rex and I have had this planned for months. Two million quid, dead easy. Then you come bumbling in.'

I felt numb as she ordered me out of the car, pausing only to stuff the black bag in a litterbin, before making me climb up onto the railings. Below me the waters surged. There was a huge boom, an almighty kick in the back and I was falling...

So why am I here, three weeks later, pen in hand, notebook on knee, watching the sun go down over the Indian Ocean? And what about spending the rest of my life with Jeannie? Well as far as she's concerned I did. My life ended on that pier, my body washed out to sea.

And I very nearly was dead too. The multicoloured bruise in the centre of my back reminds me that not even Kevlar is perfect at close range. Fortunately, the cold water revived me and I hauled myself out of the river about half a mile downstream.

According to the news, Jeannie was abandoned unharmed by her kidnapper – whose description bore no resemblance to me – who then made off with the money.

I can only imagine her fury when she returned to the bin and found it had been emptied. The following day I texted my friends that I was quitting my job to become a writer and flew out of Heathrow with a one-way ticket and enough spending money to keep me in clean underwear and notebooks for as long as it took.

As for that novel ... well what do you think so far?

Lady Luck

Peter Lovesey

You would never have guessed the adviser in the job centre was Lady Luck. True, there was something otherworldly about her, like one of the strange stone heads on Easter Island, which stare fixedly at the horizon, except her gaze was on the clock. In front of her was the form Danny had been told to complete. She must have read it because she told him he'd been unemployed for far too long.

After several untroubled weeks of signing on, Danny had been ordered to attend a work search review. He didn't need one. Unemployed by choice, he was living a contented life in a council flat in Twickenham on state handouts and burglary.

He tried his winning smile, but there was no meeting of minds. At this stage in their relationship Lady Luck's charm eluded him.

She said a new supermarket had just opened on the edge of town and was looking for night stockers.

At first Danny thought she'd said 'night stalkers'. He was tempted to give that a try. It would fit in nicely with the housebreaking.

When she explained that it involved stacking shelves for eight hours starting at ten p.m., Danny turned white. He didn't fancy that at all. He needed to keep his nights clear.

She told him there was no physical reason why he couldn't do the work and he'd better go for the interview at three p.m. sharp or face a cut in his jobseeker's allowance and questions about his flat.

Lady Luck meant what she said.

Later the same day Danny went to meet the recruitment manager. The supermarket was only ten minutes from the flat. With every step he racked his brain for a get-out, some allergy or phobia that would allow him to fail the interview. A deep-rooted fear of shelving? A habit of dropping things? Too obvious.

He could say he was affected by the moon. That might worry them. 'I can't help myself. I have an uncontrollable urge to howl and run about on all fours. It's harmless – I think.'

But he didn't need any of these excuses. The moment he stepped through the supermarket door a remarkable thing happened. A young woman dressed like a cheerleader in the shortest of bright-red skirts, silver tights and a glittery top, and carrying a string of balloons, came from nowhere and linked her bare arm with his.

If there was such a person as Lady Luck, Danny thought, this ought to be how she looked. But deep down he knew he was here thanks to the stone-faced woman in the job centre.

A trumpet fanfare sounded from the public address system, followed by an announcement: 'Ladies and gentlemen, to celebrate the opening of our brand-new Twickenham store we are presenting an amazing free gift each day this week to one of our customers, who is randomly chosen as they step through the door. We decided that today's winner would be the first customer to come in after three o'clock and he – lucky man – receives a week's free holiday in the wonderful city of Marrakesh, all expenses paid.'

His new friend said, 'You'd better hold the balloons. I'm supposed to tie them to your trolley, but you didn't bring one in.'

Danny decided it was best not to explain why. He'd forget about the night-stocking interview. Holding the balloons high, he allowed his glamorous escort to lead him past the long row of checkouts to the far end of the store, where some people with champagne glasses were waiting to greet him. An important-looking man in a bow tie and suit shook his hand and gave him an envelope. Cameras flashed and there was another public announcement about his lucky win.

Within the week he was in Morocco.

Except for a couple of stag-party trips to Benidorm, he'd not been abroad, so this was an adventure. Finding his hotel bus was the first test. As soon as he got past immigration he was bombarded by locals offering taxi rides. With a sense of purpose he made a beeline across the terminal to the shuttle bus area.

The bombarding was to become the staple feature of his week in the city. If it wasn't for taxis it was for Berber rugs, leather goods, spices and offers to show him belly dancing and snake charming. He quickly learned how to say no with a firmness that would get you a punch in the eye in Twickenham.

The Marrakesh experience was all a bit much at first – the crowded streets, the noise, smells and strange sights – but as the week progressed he started to get the hang of it. Part of his prize was a pocketful of *dirhams* – the local currency – and he learned to haggle in the heaving souks and find places to eat and to escape from all the noise and relax with mint tea and sweetmeats.

As a professional burglar he took a particular interest in the architecture. Not the Koutoubia minaret – which you could glimpse from almost any part of the city – but the private dwellings of rich Moroccans. These were mostly villas, pink or ochre, nicely spaced in their own grounds in the Nakheel district just off the tourist beat. The streets were wider than motorways, and almost deserted. Danny did see one Rolls-Royce glide by with a silver horseshoe tied to the front. These people believed in their good luck. They couldn't get enough of it.

The most appealing thing about the millionaire homes was their construction. True, the exteriors appeared like fortresses – featureless, unforgiving stone walls. But they had one thing in common that would appeal to any burglar: flat roofs.

Even better, they were limited to a couple of storeys because of some local decree that the only tall buildings in the city were minarets. Get up there and you'd be laughing. You'd be spoiled for choice. The villas were evidently planned around enclosed courtyards where the good life was enjoyed in private.

Security? The owners didn't seem to bother. There wasn't an alarm to be seen, or CCTV.

One residence in particular was an open invitation. It wasn't the largest, but it had a well-kept exterior surrounded by shrubs and trees, which don't come cheap in the desert. Among them was a handsome palm that overhung the roof in a graceful curve.

Danny went back to the hotel and thought long and hard about that palm and how it might be used. He'd seen film of barefoot boys shinning up palm trees with the aid of rope tied loosely around their ankles. They made it look easy.

He weighed up the options.

Lady Luck had got him to Marrakesh but it was up to him to make the experience pay. This night would be his last in the city. Tomorrow he'd be back in Twickenham, living on the social and the small rewards he got from burglary. These Moroccans were so rich they wouldn't notice if anything was taken. Why not make the most of his luck and collect some souvenirs? He'd happily settle for small stuff, such as banknotes, jewellery and designer watches.

Soon after midnight he set off for Nakheel equipped with a torch and a strip of towelling – the belt of the complimentary bathrobe from his hotel room.

Climbing the tree was harder than he expected because he had to learn the knack of getting purchase against the trunk while bracing his legs with his bare feet held in place by the flannel belt and pulling with the arms.

Eventually he scrambled onto the roof, rubbing his aching biceps. Luckily he'd made no sound. If there was a guard dog here, it was asleep – or smart enough to know it couldn't reach him.

He crept to the edge and peered over. A heady scent wafted up to him – orange blossom mingled with stale cigars and cannabis. As he'd guessed, the moonlit courtyard was a rich man's hideaway. Statues, a pool, sunshades and loungers strewn with empty bottles and intimate items of clothing. But no people. They would be out to the world.

All the windows of the villa were within this enclosed area and some were open. Danny had no difficulty descending from the roof to a ledge and from there, inside.

His torch beam showed him some kind of dining room with a large oval table low to the floor and surrounded by cushions. In the centre on a tray was a gleaming silver tea set of the sort he'd seen in the souks:

tall, ornate pots and small cups without handles – too large to steal. He couldn't take items as big as that and he'd never know where to fence them in this alien city. He wanted smaller stuff.

Move on, he told himself. Find the private rooms. The good thing about this stone-built house was that there were no creaking floorboards.

At the far end of a passage was an open door. Danny purred. He'd found some sort of boudoir with multicoloured drapes from the ceiling and huge silk cushions. First he checked that no one was in the bed. Then he started opening the drawers in an exquisitely carved sandal-wood unit that stretched right across one wall.

Inside was sexy underwear, fine to the touch – enough for an entire harem. Thongs, bras, basques, camisoles and skimpy nightdresses in profusion.

High quality make-up and perfume lined open shelves under hinged mirrors.

There ought to be jewellery, but where was it? A safe?

Maybe hidden inside the wardrobe. Danny jerked open a door and almost suffered a cardiac arrest.

A pair of beautiful brown eyes was staring at him from between the hanging clothes.

'Oh, shit,' he said.

His luck had run out.

He had no idea whether she understood, but he started talking, as much to gain control over his own shattered nerves as hers. 'I won't hurt you. It's not you I'm after. I just dropped in, like. Thought the place was empty. Really, ma'am, I'm not going to touch you. I don't do violence.'

The woman was crouching at the bottom of the vast wardrobe. As far as Danny could tell, she was dressed in a t-shirt and jeans, definitely a Moroccan woman, but in Western clothes. She, too, was alarmed. She'd started hyperventilating.

'I'm backing off,' Danny said, making a calming gesture and taking a step back. 'You can come out if you like.'

She wasn't willing to do that, but she seemed to respond because her breathing slowed a little.

'OK, I'm out of here,' Danny said.

She spoke – and in English. 'Who are you?'

As if it made a difference.

'Just a visitor,' Danny said. 'I'm a tourist.' Then he added, deciding some honesty might be no bad thing, 'Everyone calls me Danny.'

'These rooms are kept locked,' she said. 'How did you get in?'

'Over the roof and through a window. Are you alone then – like a prisoner in here?'

'It is the way my husband decides.'

Husband? A warning bell sounded in Danny's head. 'Is he about?'

'He won't come in now,' she said.

'Aren't you allowed out?'

'Please. I don't wish to speak of this.' As if to discourage more questions, she pulled one of the hanging garments partially over her face. As she did so Danny noticed a bruise on her forearm.

'Does he hit you?'

She was silent.

'That shouldn't be allowed. That's out of order.' The reason she had been hiding in the wardrobe was now obvious. She was hiding from her brutal husband. 'Listen, you don't have to suffer this. You could escape.'

She shook her head, but her eyes showed the suggestion had some appeal.

'I'm serious,' Danny said – and he was. He felt genuine sympathy for this abused woman. For the moment, her situation mattered more than the burglary. 'Listen, this is your lucky day. I can climb out of a window and unlock the door from the other side.'

'It's no use,' she said. 'I have nowhere to go.'

He took his room key from his pocket. 'Hotel Splendide in rue de la Liberté. It's not far. Do you know it?'

She nodded. 'Do you really mean this?'

'Hundred per cent.'

She took the key and emerged from the wardrobe. She was larger than Danny had expected. Probably doesn't get much exercise, he thought, walled up here. Not that her size mattered, but her eyes and voice had made him picture someone frail.

'I can help you through the window and down to the ground,' Danny offered, not without wondering whether it was physically possible. 'Is the main gate locked?'

'Yes, but from the inside,' she said. 'I can open it if I get down.'

'Let's go for it. You'd better put a few things in a bag. Do you have money?'

She shook her head.

'Doesn't matter. I have some back in the room. I'll join you later.' He still hoped to find something of value here.

She stuffed some clothes into a backpack and Danny dropped it from the open window. 'You next. It's not far down.'

'I can't jump.'

He still had the bathrobe belt. 'Can you hang on to this? I'll lower you down.'

'Are you sure?'

He said yes, but it was easily said. Achieving it would be another challenge. She couldn't lift her leg up to the window ledge.

'Do you mind?' Danny said. He put his hand under her thigh and helped.

By slow stages and with a stomach-wrenching, arm-straining effort from Danny, the descent was completed. If there was a gallantry award for helping ladies in distress he would have earned it, no question.

'On your way now,' he gasped.

She needed no second bidding.

After recovering his breath, he got back to the main purpose of his visit. More of the villa awaited his inspection. Was Lady Luck still plotting his destiny from her control room at Twickenham job centre?

He left the boudoir, pushed open another door and got his answer.

This was a sitting room of some kind, with cushions of many colours. Face up on the floor was a dead man with a dagger in his chest. There was no question that he was dead and his murder hadn't happened long before, because the blood that had seeped from the wound was still wet. In his right hand was a phone.

Danny had never been slow to size up a situation. The man was the jailer-husband, fatally stabbed by the woman before Danny arrived. She had bruised her arm in the struggle. She had hidden in the wardrobe and escaped thanks to the help Danny had given her.

From outside came the heart-stopping wail of a police siren. The victim must have called them on his phone before expiring.

As Danny's lawyer explained after the trial, 'It could have been a whole lot worse. The cops really believed you were the killer. You were well advised to stick to your story, and as you didn't actually steal anything you aren't technically a thief. Three years for trespass and helping a murderer escape is a light sentence. You're a lucky man.'

Back in Twickenham someone allowed herself a slight smile.

A Postcard from Iceland

Ragnar Jónasson

Hi Mum,

I'm sorry that it has taken me so long to write to you.

I have really enjoyed the stay in Iceland, but it's been very cold, like you told me. No one goes to Iceland in January, you said. But you know me, I'm adventurous. The snow is so mesmerising, the darkness is so overwhelming, and I've fallen in love with the sea.

No one goes to Iceland alone, you also said.

I needed to go, though, after the break-up. To try to figure out where my life was heading, where I want to go from here.

And it's been an adventure! I've done quite a bit of skiing and hiking, and I've experienced the elements; it's been cold – colder than hell – and it's been windy, but it's also beautiful, Mum.

I wish you could see it, the endless wilderness of ice and snow. I haven't ventured out on the glaciers – the locals tell me it's not safe.

I want to stay safe. You told me to, and believe me, Mum, I've tried. I've followed every piece of advice to the letter … or almost.

And I've made some new friends, but to be honest they advised me against going up on the mountain here in the north. I did it anyway.

You know how I've always needed to challenge myself, and it was going great. Really great. Such beauty, Mum. The silence, the isolation, I've never been so alone, but I've also never been happier. It's amazing, I've been able to do a lot of thinking. A lot of soul searching.

But now I have to admit I feel a bit scared. You've always told me that there is no reason to be afraid, and I'm sure I'm imagining things. It's just, you know, being alone in this small cabin, in the darkness (writing this by candlelight!) can get the imagination going. (Well, 'cabin' is a rather nice word for such a ramshackle building). It's really, really cold, so I'm glad I'm suitably dressed for the weather, that's one thing I did make sure to do.

But I could swear I heard strange noises out there, Mum.

I'm pretty far up north, close to the sea, actually. Close to the Arctic Circle.

This one guy I met on my way here, in the village nearby, did warn me. He said that there was always a chance of them appearing. He said it didn't happen often, maybe every five years or so. I thought he was joking at first, but he looked serious. However, I did like my odds: every five years, you know. So I just went on, regardless. It was a hike I really wanted to do.

But the noises are there, not too far away. Maybe I'm just imagining things, the wind can probably sound like a growl.

One thing he mentioned, this guy, was slightly unnerving, though. He said that when they did make their way inland they were always hungry. *Very hungry.*

Mum, I hear it again, right now. I'm pretty sure there is something out there.

It's getting closer.

I wish the cabin were a bit more sturdy, but I think I'm pretty safe here.

I'll just keep quiet.

You know I love you, Mum.

I'm sure I'll be safe here.

There is no reason to be afr

A Clever Evil

Sarah Rayne

You don't expect evil to walk in through your office door in the middle
of the afternoon, but if it does, you assume you'll recognise it for what
it is.

I didn't, though. Not until it was too late.

It was the early-evening shift at the news desk – the shift everyone
tried to avoid, because it always seemed to last longer than any of the
others. News *desk* is a bit of a misnomer, because there isn't actually a
desk in here anymore. Once there were several: smart, modern structures of steel and vinyl and wood, each one bearing those three initials
that are familiar and instantly recognisable across most of the – well, I
won't say across most of the Western world; I'll just say they're letters
that are very widely known.

By now, though, all we've got left are a couple of trestle tables – which
collapse when you least expect it, precipitating you and whatever you
happen to be working on at the time onto the floor – together with several
lopsided chairs. As for modern technology, we've managed to hang on
to the foreign editor's laptop, which we share on a rota, although, since
it was the foreign editor who drew up the rota, he gets the longest turn.

It does mean we can bash out news stories, although, as the wifi
connection is wildly erratic, there's never any guarantee when we'll be
able to send them. Sometimes by the time they reach their destination the news can be twenty-four hours old. Those nineteenth-century
war reporters wouldn't have had that problem, of course. I'm talking
about those stylish gentlemen who camped elegantly on a high ridge
to report on the Charge of the Light Brigade, and those earlier ones
who sipped chilled wine and scoffed caviar and smoked salmon while

the Duke of Wellington routed Napoleon. They wouldn't have had to bother about wifi or failing batteries. They'd simply have scribbled their stories, added suitable flourishes about death and glory, stressed the victories, skimmed over the defeats then handed the missives to a passing aide. After that they'd have returned to their wine and to cheering on the cavalry and shouting encouraging things like, 'Onward into the valley of death, boys', at judicious intervals. I expect it might have been a tad dangerous for them at times, but whatever else they might have had to endure, it wouldn't be the uneasy boredom of early evenings in a war-torn city like this one.

Sometimes during those long evenings, I even wonder if the world has dropped into a black hole without anyone noticing it. Or whether Earth's rotation is slowing down and we haven't managed to keep up with it. I once said that to the interpreter who is part of the news team, to which he replied that he didn't give a tinker's toss if the world was slowing down or going backwards or whether it was performing somersaults across the universe, because it wasn't likely to make any difference to the people in this devastated city, or stop the relentless shelling. And since we would all probably be blown to smithereens by the next round of air strikes, how about breaking out the remaining bottle of whisky. (Alcohol's forbidden out here, of course, but there are caches of it if you know where to look.)

I made a mild protest about it not being a good idea to drink on an empty stomach, and the interpreter said that could be damned, we were all doing everything on empty stomachs by this time, because the promise of another food consignment being on its way was starting to look as hollow as a blown egg.

We venture out when we think it's safe, to gather news about what's happening. We interview local people as well – that's supposing we can find anyone who's prepared to talk. It makes for a good human-interest story when they will, though.

When a report comes in of an actual disturbance, we grab bulletproof vests and dash off, brandishing cameras and recorders. I say 'dash' but it's more a kind of half-skulking, half-prowling. You tiptoe through the rubble, constantly looking over your shoulder for snipers. There's a line of poetry – I forget who wrote it – about a man tiptoeing down a lonesome road in fear and dread… 'And having once turned round, walks on, and turns no more his head – because he knows a frightful fiend doth close behind him tread.' Something like that.

I quoted that once when the interpreter and I were making our cautious way through the streets. He said, somewhat caustically, that he wouldn't know how people behaved on lonesome roads; he thought we were more like escapees from a French farce, trying not to be caught in the wrong bedroom. Of the two he would prefer the wrong bedroom, he said, because at least you'd have got your leg over. He has no romance in his soul, that interpreter. That was one of the many times when I wondered what I was doing out here, trying to report what's happening, trying to establish who's gaining the upper hand, trying to work out which of the spies can be trusted. All the time dodging shells and snipers. All the time eking out the food.

I was on my own at the start of one of those uneasy, unending evenings when the stranger turned up. And that was when the evil came in, although I didn't realise it at the time. Or did I?

I'd been staring out of a window, trying to dredge up sufficient energy to go out and find one or two people to interview, wondering if the interpreter could be found and whether he was likely to be sober.

It was only when the shadow fell across the door that I looked up and saw the stranger standing there. He smiled hesitantly, as if he was unsure whether to come in. Then he said, very politely, 'Good evening, sir,' and stepped inside. And despite his demeanour, just for a few seconds I had the strongest feeling that a menace had come in with him. Almost as if he might be dragging it behind him like an invisible cloak, or something out of Dante or Victor Hugo – those leaden cloaks that weigh down the souls of liars after death. And then I thought: Hell's teeth, I'm sitting here in the midst of a ravaged city and the next time I go outside I'm likely to be blown up or shot into tattered fragments, and I'm quoting Dante's *Inferno* for God's sake!

I asked how I could help.

'I think I might have something unusual to report,' he said. He spoke English, but with an accent that I couldn't pin down. He was dark-haired and dark-eyed and he had one of those smooth, olive complexions. He could have been anything from Arabian to Spanish. 'And,' he said, 'I've come to see you because I think it might be interesting – something you'd want to follow up.'

When I was learning my trade in provincial newspapers we used to get people coming in all the time saying they had things that would be interesting and unusual. Nine times out of ten they weren't interesting at all, of course. But there was always the tenth time...

So I said we were used to odd things. 'But you should know right away that we don't pay for stories.'

'Of course not. I wasn't expecting ... Could I sit down? I've been standing out there in the square, trying to summon the courage to come in.'

I pulled out a lopsided chair, but even after he sat down he seemed not to know how to continue.

To help him along, I said, 'How about if we start with your name and address.'

He supplied these willingly enough. I thought the address was somewhere on the edge of the city. One of the once-spacious apartments. Always supposing it was a genuine address he was supplying and a real name.

He had, it seemed, been walking home a couple of days earlier when a cripple – a youngish man – limped out of a building and into his path.

'That wasn't unduly alarming,' he said. 'All he wanted was for me to deliver a letter to an address on the other side of the city. He couldn't walk as far as that, he said. Well, that was obvious to anyone, because he was badly lame. And since all the public transport stopped running...'

We exchanged wry looks of understanding regarding public transport.

'So I agreed to take the letter. It seemed a harmless request, and we're all in this appalling situation together. You'd want to help a poor crippled soul, wouldn't you?'

I said you would indeed.

'It was only later that I realised I couldn't keep my promise,' he said. 'I work at the food centre, you see. Quite long hours.'

He paused and looked at me, and I said encouragingly, 'I know the food centre. They had soup yesterday.' This was such a rare event it was worth a mention, although I didn't add that most people eating the soup – in fact most people eating the majority of the centre's meals – deemed it advisable not to enquire too closely into the precise ingredients of the dishes. If anyone ever writes the history of this particular segment of this war, they may paint dark word-pictures of men eating the rats before the rats ate them. They won't know how close to the truth that is.

'I was on the rota for duty all day,' he said. 'And I don't like to let them down.'

'What did you do?'

'I gave the letter to a friend – another of the helpers at the centre. He's very trustworthy, and he promised to deliver the letter that same afternoon.'

'And did he?'

'I don't know. He set off to deliver it, but no one's heard from him since.'

'That's not unusual,' I said. 'People are vanishing all the time. Have you been to wherever he lives?'

'Yes, of course. No sign of him. No answer to knocking or calling through the windows.'

I made a note of the disappeared man's name and address so we could check it for ourselves. 'What about the destination for the actual letter? Can you remember the address?'

'Only that it was somewhere in the Old City.'

The Old City. With the words, the images came unbidden. Bombed buildings jutting up like decaying teeth, some of them still smoking from the blast that had destroyed them, others drying and decaying where they stood. Incredibly, families still lived in those husks.

'I'm sorry I can't remember exactly where it was,' said the man.

'Fair enough. But why come to us about this?'

'There doesn't seem anywhere else to report things any longer. At least, nowhere you can fully trust. And I thought – well, you people are used to investigating things, to finding out the truth. That's right, isn't it? And a single person vanishing so quietly in the midst of all this…'

I said, thoughtfully, 'Blowing up a hundred people and the street with them is almost routine now. But the silent disappearance of one law-abiding citizen – an aid worker – there's something different about that.'

'That's what I thought,' he said eagerly. 'You don't know what might be going on, do you?'

It sounded as if he was visualising the uncovering of a malevolent spy ring of complicated nationality and intricate loyalty – even of being hailed as the brave and conscientious citizen who led to its being cracked. Nor was it so outrageous an idea. The letter could have contained information. Or payment for information received. For a wild moment I had similar visions on my own account. Even if you work in a bombed-out shell that was once a recording studio and you only have a fifth share in a laptop, it doesn't mean you don't occasionally dream of journalist of the year awards. Even Pulitzers.

However, I said, temperately, 'Can you leave it with me for a couple of days?'

'Yes, but what will you do? Will you try to find the crippled man? I'd try to do it, only I've promised to be at the centre.'

Tracing the crippled man was the obvious initial course of action. 'Whereabouts did you see him?' I said.

He pointed out the location on the big map we had pinned to one wall – although the contours of the actual places no longer bore much resemblance to the printed streets and squares.

'I know where that is,' I said. 'What time of day was it? People usually have a routine.'

'I know,' he said, and we shared the unspoken thought that most people's routines were tied to when it was considered safe to scuttle along to somewhere like the food centre, or to dodge between the shadowy old buildings. It provides a semblance of security to think you're dodging the snipers and the bombs. It's a false security, of course, because the snipers and the bombers are playing the same game – but whatever gets you through.

'It was just around sunset,' he said.

Of course it would be sunset. That halfway time when the day is handing over to the night, uneasy to relinquish its spurious hold, but unable to resist the encroaching darkness.

'I'd be really grateful if you'd try to find out a bit more,' he said, sounding relieved. 'You could let me know at the food centre what you find out. Would you do that? I'd like to know. There's so much clever evil in this city, isn't there?' He paused, and stood for a moment, outlined in the open door, and the impression of something menacing brushed against my mind again. His voice – his whole manner – seemed subtly to change. 'And when it's not clever, it's a hungry evil, isn't it?' he said softly, and went out.

Those last words stayed with me as I went along to the Old City an hour later.

A hungry evil sounded like the title of a slash-and-gore horror film, or a paperback with a lurid jacket and promises in the strapline of macabre cavortings.

But a clever evil … that was a term that had class. It could almost be Shakespeare. The best quotes usually were from Shakespeare, if they weren't from the Bible. Whatever they were, those three words struck a resonance in my mind – I felt I recognised them. Probably, of course, I knew them because it was the name of a computer game or a rock group.

Sunset in this city – probably in any city in the world – is a strange time. An Irish journalist once told me that in Ireland it used to be called the purple hour. The mists steal in from the mountains, he said, like violet cobwebs. The Irish always like to spin a good story.

Here sunset is a mixture of rust and a dry-looking terracotta. If you happen to be of a fanciful turn of mind you'd say it's as if all the blood that's been spilled in this war has leached into the air, tainting it for ever.

Actually, of course, it's simply the dust from the old buildings, scorched and tanned by the centuries of sun. There are even traces of the really old city here and there – fragments of Greek and Byzantine influences. When you walk through certain parts you feel as if you're glimpsing that legendary rose-red city, 'half as old as time'.

But rose-red cities notwithstanding, on that evening I felt as if I was walking through a blood-tinged tunnel. It was quiet, but it was a listening quiet. Several times I whipped round, convinced I was being watched, and twice I looked up to the jagged tops of the buildings, thinking I had seen the glint of a rifle. Nothing moved though.

I was starting to think it had been a bad idea to come out here on my own. It was vanity, of course; if this turned out to be a wild goose chase, I didn't want the rest of the team to know about it. I'd never have lived it down.

This was the area where the stranger had been accosted by the cripple. It might once have been quite a prosperous district – with merchants and suchlike. No one was around now though. But even as that thought formed, as if answering a cue, I heard footsteps.

At first I thought they were echoes of my own steps, but then I realised they weren't quite matching up. They were uneven, dragging. The footsteps you'd get from someone who was trying not to be seen. Or from someone who couldn't walk very well.

Like a crippled man.

I turned round and saw him. Thin, slightly hunched over, not a hunchback exactly, but as if there might be a deformity of the spine. And one leg – the left – dragged, giving him a lurching, lopsided gait.

He was younger than I had expected and there was a surprising look of agility – even of strength – about him. But if he made any kind of attack, surely I could overpower him. Or I could run away. This last thought was not one that did me any credit, but there are times when you have to be realistic.

I slowed my pace and allowed him to catch up with me.

He drew level and regarded me, his head on one side. Then he said, 'English?'

'Yes.'

'You have the look.' He considered me for a moment longer, then he said, 'And you have the look of a man good and trustworthy.'

'I hope so.'

'Then I shall ask a kindness.'

Here it comes, I thought. And so it did. 'I have a letter,' he said. 'Very important – for a cousin living here.' He pointed to the address on the envelope. It was written in English – I couldn't decide if that was strange or not. 'It's my cousin's house,' he said. 'You know the place?'

'I think so. The general area, certainly.' I frowned, and then, with the feeling that I might be reading from a script prepared for me by someone, I said, 'That's quite a long way from here.'

He pounced eagerly on the words. 'I cannot walk so far, you see. Could you take pity on a lame man and deliver it for me? It is urgent – there are details about care for my cousin's young children. So it should be taken to him this very evening. There will be a reward.'

'A reward?'

'My cousin will reward you.' His eyes held mine.

A sensible man would have refused the request outright. A sensible and a kind man would have said something about taking the letter to the cousin later – and then returning very speedily to the newsroom to enlist back-up. Only a fool would have said, 'All right,' and put out his hand to take the letter.

I said, 'All right.' And put out my hand to take the letter.

As I walked to the address on the letter I was doing my best to think myself into the part of the intrepid lone investigator. It wasn't because I was apprehensive – well, not really – but the donning of a mental disguise felt like the donning of armour, or at least a bullet-proof vest. I tried out a kind of Philip Marlowe character first – hard-bitten newspaperman who kept a bottle of Chivas Regal in the collar drawer. But by the time I had reached the next intersection, I had discarded Marlowe in favour of George Smiley – until I remembered that Le Carré had described Smiley as having the 'cunning of Satan and the conscience

of a virgin', and while satanic cunning was all very well, I wasn't sure
about the other part. So I switched from Smiley to James Bond, which
meant I could pretend there would be a dry martini and a slumbrous-
eyed lady waiting at journey's end.

Journey's end.

Here it was. The place written on the envelope. It looked as if it was
a warehouse, and it was surrounded by similar buildings, all of them
huddled together, as if they might be propping each other up. They all
looked deserted and had that eyeless appearance of most derelict buildings. But appearances can be deceptive, and for all I knew they might
have housed anything from the latest consignment of Kalashnikovs to
nests of agents from any one of half a dozen countries. Still, people
were living in all kinds of unusual places now, and a warehouse might
provide quite spacious accommodation for several innocent families,
dispossessed of their homes.

Shadows were spreading thickly across the ground, which was turned
to a mosaic of crimson and gold by the sinking sun, so that it was like
walking across one of those Persian carpets from the old legends.

The warehouse had those massive double doors that unfold to admit
large vehicles. They were closed now, though, and if there had been anything resembling a letterbox I would just have posted the letter through
it and beaten it out of there like a bat escaping hell. But there was no
letterbox. What there was, was a small, inset door, with a tiny grille at
the top. I knocked as loudly as I could, but there was no response, so I
stood on tiptoe and peered through the grille. There wasn't anything to
see – just a dark void, with anonymous shapes.

The disguise-fantasy had taken a new turn now, probably a result
of walking across that *Arabian Nights* swathe of sunset patterns on the
ground. I was no longer James Bond or a whisky-drinking investigator; I was the hero of some gothic horror fairy tale, faced with a locked
chamber. Still, this was hardly the *Arabian Nights'* copper castle with its
forbidden and fateful golden door. It was a battered old warehouse, not
the forbidding turret that the gallant and foolhardy knight must enter
by hook or by crook, by picklock or jemmy … Nor was it Bluebeard's
castle with its sinister inner chamber, which turned out to contain not

priceless treasure or the elixir of life, but the mutilated, clotted bodies of his brides hanging from butchers' hooks…

With this last image, something so bizarre and so macabre stirred in the depths of my mind that I immediately pushed it away. But it stayed with me, like sun dazzle printed on the retina, so vivid that I wondered if I might even be hallucinating – from the heat, the lack of food, the interpreter's whisky… Because it's all very well to don a smidgeon of courage by pretending you're James Bond, but when it comes to visualising Perrault's murderous villain, salting away bartered brides and piling up mangled bodies in the seventh chamber…

Almost without realising it, I reached for the handle of the inset door. It would be locked, of course, and I should have to see if I could slide the letter under the door and trust to luck that it reached its recipient.

But the door was not locked. It swung inwards with a faint creak that might have been a cracked, whispering voice, saying, 'Come inside, you are expected…'

Still, all I had to do was step inside, deposit the letter somewhere where it could not be missed, and beat it back to the newsroom.

After the sultry radiance of the setting sun, the interior of the warehouse was so dark that it was confusing, and I stood in the doorway waiting for my vision to adjust. I had the impression again of massive shapes grouped everywhere, some of them swaying slightly, as if the slight ingress of air from my entrance had disturbed them. There was something wrong about them – they were in the wrong place and I could not work out why.

But there was one thing that was not confusing and that was the smell. It came at me like something solid, and I gasped then flinched.

The darkness was not quite so thick now, and I could see that the shapes seemed wrong because they were suspended a couple of feet above the ground … They were hanging from massive iron hooks driven into the rafters overhead … Pallid shapes, but streaked with dark, livid red … mottled … Here and there globules of yellow fat clung to their surfaces…

A dreadful comprehension started to unfold and my stomach lifted with nausea.

Because if you've ever smelled meat that's recently been slaughtered – if you've ever walked into a butcher's shop when they're re-stocking the freezers – if you've ever entered an abattoir…

Incredibly, in this bomb-torn, shelled-out city, where the inhabitants were living on scraps and charity, this warehouse was filled with the unmistakable scents of raw meat – not all of it fresh.

Behind me the door which I had left open was slammed shut, and there was the sound of a key turning. I spun round, but it was already too late. A man stood there, barring the way. He wore an overall, darkly stained, and in one hand he held a long knife. In the other was a saw.

He said, 'You have brought me a letter, I think?'

A letter … 'Yes.' My voice seemed to be coming from a long way away.

'If you read it, you will understand.'

The single sheet of paper slid from the envelope easily enough.

On it were written the words, 'This is the only one I could send you today.'

The Prodigy

Shawn Reilly Simmons

Gary always knew he would go places. Mother had told him so for as long as he could remember.

'Eat your oatmeal before it gets cold,' she'd tell him every morning at breakfast. 'You need your strength for practice.'

'Practice,' Father grumbled from behind the newspaper. 'Boys his age should be practising ball, not messing around in a room by himself.' He pulled the paper taut, his meaty fists straining the edges.

Mother would swat the towel over her shoulder and go back to the sink, clanging the dishes a little too hard against the porcelain as she washed them.

Gary is going places now, no doubt about that. He shrinks closer to the window and hugs his violin case to his chest as the large man comes down the centre aisle of the bus, glancing from left to right at the available seats. He lowers himself into the spot next to Gary, who keeps his eyes on the glass as the bus pulls out of the depot and lurches onto the dark highway.

Gary's favourite place at Kalamazoo Middle School had always been the music room, tucked away at the end of the second floor apart from the other classes. The walls were lined with construction paper cut-outs of clef symbols and music notes, taped over a five-lined staff in a repeating ascending scale. The music room was his favourite because it was either the quietest place at school, or it vibrated with music from his violin.

Gary spent fifth period every day in the music room by himself, practising his scales. The rest of his class was at gym, but Mother had told the principal that Gary couldn't risk injuring his fingers, or hands or anything else roughhousing with the other children. Gary sat outside the principal's office on a hard plastic chair, swinging his legs in perfect 3/4 time, quietly humming Bach's *Minuet No. 2*. The principal's secretary glanced at the door when Mother's voice grew louder, then slid her eyes towards Gary, tapping the cap of her fountain pen against her bottom lip. Gary pretended not to see her.

After school Gary would stand in the middle of his bedroom, practising his lessons in a spotlight of sun until the shadows moved to the edge of the carpet. Then the garage door would rumble up and Father would be home from work again.

Gary liked it when all of the calluses on his fingers were uniform, thick and hard like little yellow tortoise shells. But his favourite was when he bled after practising. He'd suck on his fingers until the bleeding stopped, then bandage the tips before heading downstairs to dinner.

When Gary fumbled his fork and it clanged loudly against his plate, Father would sit stonily quiet and stare at Gary's bandages as he shovelled mashed potatoes and peas into his mouth.

One night Gary was awakened by a thumping sound and his parents' raised voices coming from the bedroom next to his.

'You've turned him that way,' Father shouted.

'You don't understand,' Mother wailed. 'He's a prodigy!'

Gary lay still in his bed as he listened to Father's heavy footsteps go down the stairs.

'Where's Father?' Gary asked the next morning at breakfast. Father's chair was empty, the bundled newspaper lying damp in the driveway.

Mother put his oatmeal down in front of him and smiled weakly as he gazed into her puffy red eyes. She placed a cool hand on his cheek then went back to the sink, washing the dishes carefully, rinsing each plate and cup under the tap, turning each one over several times in her hands before gently propping it in the drying rack.

'Mother, what's a prodigy?' Gary asked. He watched Mother's shoulders fall, then shake with sobs. Gary ate his oatmeal before it could get cold.

When Gary received his invitation to audition for a seat at the Nottinger Institute of Music in Chicago, Mother cried again, but those tears were filtered through a red gash of a smile. Her mouth moved but no words came out as she read the letter. Dark streams of mascara cut through the white powder on her face then pooled under her puffy chin. Mother had gotten a job at the make-up counter at the mall in downtown Kalamazoo.

Mother bought Gary a bus ticket for the three-hour trip to Chicago. They didn't have a car and Mother had never learned to drive. She depended on rides from friends or walked four blocks over to catch the city bus to her job at the mall. The morning Gary left home, she'd sprung for a taxi, a bright-yellow one that waited for them at the end of the driveway.

At the bus depot, Mother held Gary's face in her hands, her palms warm against his cheeks, and kissed his forehead. She told her boss at the department store she'd work through her lunch break if he'd allow her to take a personal call from her son when he arrived in Chicago. Gary fingered the change in his pocket and promised he would call the minute he arrived.

Gary hadn't bothered to tell Father about auditioning for music school in Chicago. He'd only seen him once since he'd left that morning several years before. It was one late-spring day in Gary's junior year. Father was standing in front of Kalamazoo High School, waiting for him to come out after dismissal. When Gary saw Father standing there, he stuttered to a stop on the sidewalk, then thought about hiding his violin case behind his long, thin legs.

Father bought him a scoop of chocolate ice cream. They sat on a bench in Bronson Park and stared at the fountain in front of them.

'I'm remarried, you know,' Father said.

Gary looked at him cautiously.

'We have a son, just born. Christopher's his name.' Father's tone was matter-of-fact, conversational. 'We're leaving Kalamazoo,' he said. 'A fresh start for the family. I got a good job lined up in Indianapolis. I came to say goodbye.'

Father clasped Gary awkwardly on his bony shoulder. The cool chocolate taste in Gary's mouth turned to copper. His shoulder sagged under the weight of Father's hand.

'I have this,' Father said, as an afterthought. He pulled a Swiss Army knife from his pocket and handed it to Gary. 'It was my dad's. During the war. Thought you might want it.'

Father continued to mumble words but Gary just stared at the scratched red tool and his callused fingertips, not hearing him. At some point Father must have left. Gary watched the sun set behind the falling water of the fountain.

When the bus to Chicago pulled into the station, Gary stepped onto the asphalt, clutching his violin case in one hand and his mother's frayed tweed satchel in the other. He passed by a bank of payphones and stopped to study a faded map of downtown Chicago encased in thick, scratched plastic. He took two trains to Nottinger then stood for a moment across the street to admire the school's redbrick walls and sturdy white columns.

'Gary Graham Smith,' the woman in the admissions office muttered. 'Your mother has left several messages for you.' She leafed through a few folders on her desk. 'Yes, here you are. You're in Building C, Room 219.'

Gary took the packet and set of keys she handed him. The folder was embossed with the school's seal. He ran a finger over the shiny upraised letters as he said, 'May I use your phone to call her back? I'm out of change.'

The secretary sighed and handed him the receiver from her desk phone, dialling the number he gave her. Gary slipped his hand into the pocket of his trousers as he spoke into the receiver, gripping the coins tightly in his fist.

As he grew older, Gary practised less in the afternoons in his room at home. As his arms and legs grew longer, his fingers did too, and they seemed to know where to go on the neck of the violin without him having to think about it. He found himself increasingly bored with practising scales, or playing concertos he knew he'd performed perfectly dozens of times before. Gary spent more and more time lying in bed, tracing his eyes over the drawings of female characters in his comic books. He memorised the curve of a breast, the fullness of a thigh, painted lips curled into a sneer. Gary thought about the times he'd seen Mother through the crack in the door while she got dressed, squeezing her soft body into her girdle, grunting and cursing under her breath.

He felt no shame afterwards, only temporary relief from the tension.

Building C was in the back of the main conservatory, the farthest student dormitory on campus. He passed by Buildings A and B, which were reserved for upperclassmen who had earned their seat for another year at Nottinger. Desks at the school were competitive, only the best student musicians got a chance to try out. And only the best of the best were granted desks and a scholarship, which included room and board.

Room 219 was halfway down on the right side of the narrow hall. Gary could hear muffled conversations and laughter, and a mingling of notes from different instruments seeping from behind the brown wooden doors he passed.

He turned the key the woman from the office gave him and the door swung open. The first time Gary laid eyes on Travis he was sitting on the window ledge carved into the cinder-block wall, exhaling a stream of smoke outside, a hand-rolled cigarette pinched in his fingers. A wispy girl with white-blonde hair lounged on the mattress at Travis's feet, her head propped on her thin arm.

'Shut the door,' the boy in the window hissed, waving Gary into the room and flicking the cigarette through the window.

Gary stood still and studied their faces, his violin case and satchel pulling down his shoulders. He debated going back to the office and demanding his own room.

The boy in the window hopped down and hurried to close the door.

Gary dropped his gaze, training his eyes on a cracked tile on the floor.

'I'm Travis. Looks like we're roommates.' He stuck out a hand for Gary to shake. Gary stared at it, then shuffled his violin case to his other hand, looping his fingers through the handle. He wiped his palm on his pants and shook Travis's hand.

'Gary Graham Smith.'

'This is Layla, second chair flautist.'

"Former second chair soon, hopefully,' Layla said dreamily. 'I plan on moving up after auditions.'

Gary remembered the first solo concert he ever gave at Kalamazoo Elementary. He stood on stage in front of the assembly, a warm spotlight trained on him from above. A music stand next to him held the sheet music for Tchaikovsky's *Sixth Symphony*, but Gary didn't need it. He'd memorised the piece, which he performed for his classmates and teachers, the student expressions ranging from mild interest to dejected boredom.

Mother stood and led the other adults in a round of applause when he finished, clapping wildly from her seat in the front row. Eventually everyone joined in as Gary stepped to the front of the stage and took a stiff bow.

Gary was invited to perform in the Honours Youth Orchestra, which offered spots to the best musicians from each of Kalamazoo's schools. The conductor appointed Gary first violin, second desk.

Gary sat behind Tiffany Hart, a gifted violinist and junior at Kalamazoo High, who was occupying first chair, first desk for her third year in a row. Gary stared at the back of her neck concert after concert, studying her starched white collar and dark-red tendrils of hair curling with sweat under her ponytail, which bobbed and swayed along with the music.

At the end of Gary's first season, the youth orchestra was invited to perform at the summer opener at Kalamazoo's concert hall to a sold out crowd. The conductor asked them to gather in the orchestra room before they made the trip downtown for one final run-through of Stravinsky's *The Rite of Spring*. Large jugs of lemonade and water sweated on the back table next to a tray of cookies, the conductor's gift to the students for their hard work, and for being invited to perform in front of Kalamazoo's elite, including the mayor.

Gary stood by the snack table and attempted to read Tiffany's lips as she talked with a couple of the clarinet players across the room. She glanced Gary's way and smiled, then walked over to him. Gary picked up a cup from the table and filled it with lemonade, then handed it to Tiffany.

'Thanks,' she said gratefully. 'Excited about tonight?'

Gary mumbled, 'Sure am,' and chewed on a cookie as he gazed into her blue-green eyes.

Tiffany selected a cookie for herself and downed the rest of her lemonade.

'Watch your pace during the second movement,' she said, placing a hand on his shoulder. Gary focused on the pressure of her slender fingers. 'You're getting better,' she continued. 'Keep it up and you'll get my chair when I graduate.'

The concert hall was standing room only by the time the orchestra took their seats. Gary stared at the back of Tiffany's neck and the darkening ring of sweat around her wilting shirt collar. As they began to play Gary followed her movements, matching the strokes of his bow to hers, keeping his eyes on her thin elbow. Tiffany's hair grew damp and her arm shimmered wetly, drops of sweat falling on the floor around her. Tiffany's elbow shuddered then became rigid as she dragged it across her violin one last time before she slid from her chair and collapsed onto the floor.

A jarring note escaped from her violin as Tiffany crumpled to the ground. The string section paused, followed in a ripple by the rest of the orchestra. Audible gasps came from the audience and, for one long moment, there was only silence in the overcrowded hall.

'She's having a seizure. Someone call an ambulance!' shouted the conductor.

He jumped from his podium and rushed to Tiffany's side. Her face was pale and her eyes half open and glazed as she visibly shook on the floor. The audience leaped to their feet and several men rushed to the stage, one of them shouting that he was a doctor.

Tiffany was carried away, mumbling incoherently, her clothes damp with sweat.

Gary slipped his hand into his pocket and fondled the now-empty pill capsules he'd swiped from Mother's medicine cabinet that morning. The bottle said take one daily for weight loss. Now he knew what taking ten of them together could do.

Tryouts at Nottinger were that morning. Gary was the first one in the conservatory, up before dawn practising his audition piece. He hadn't slept much, spending most of the night staring at the ceiling in the dark, listening to the fluttering snores from Travis's side of the room.

The studio door opened and a few other students filed in, Travis among them.

'I didn't even hear you leave this morning,' Travis said as Gary placed his violin in its case and released the tension on his bow.

Gary smiled at him and shrugged. 'Wanted an early start.'

'Good luck today,' Travis said, clapping Gary on the shoulder, his own case dangling in his fingers.

'You too,' Gary said, glancing at the hand on his shoulder.

Nottinger's head dean called the students into the studio one at a time. Gary closed his eyes and leaned against the wall in the hallway, waiting his turn. He and Travis were the last two to go, and the only violinists auditioning that morning. The students stood silently, straining to hear the others through the door.

Heading in last, Gary chose to play a piece he knew he'd perform flawlessly, Vivaldi's *Sinfonia in C Major*. He watched the faces of the instructors on the judging panel as he worked through. They sat completely still as they listened, studying his form, searching for any mistakes or missed notes. When Gary finished playing he knew it had been perfect. He nodded and bowed to the panel sharply, then left without a word.

Gary holds his violin case tighter to his chest and shrinks closer to the window and away from the man who has fallen asleep next to him on the bus. The man's heavy shoulder sags closer to Gary with each passing mile. Gary sighs and sets the case down on the floor between his feet, closing his knees around it and crossing his arms.

He looks down and notices a spot of blood on the cuff of his shirt. Darting a quick glance at his seat partner to confirm he is sleeping, Gary eases the cuff around to get a better look. The blood has dried and seeped through the threads of the fabric into the shape of Lake Michigan. Gary straightens out his cuff and pulls his jacket sleeve over the stain, then stares out of the window at black nothingness, his reflection gazing back at him from the glass. A floating green sign appears in the darkness on the side of the highway: '*Welcome to Indiana!*'

On the afternoon of auditions it was tradition at Nottinger for the applicants to hang out at the Burger Palace next to campus and await the decision of the dean. Gary sat in a booth across from Travis and Layla, who were shoulder to shoulder, their fingers laced together under the table.

'What did you play?' Travis asked.

'*Winter*,' Gary said. 'Vivaldi,' he added. He kept his eyes on the pop in front of him, the tall glass sweating a pool of condensation on the table.

'That's weird,' Travis said. 'I could have sworn I heard *Sinfonia*.'

Gary levelled his gaze with Travis's eyes. 'You stayed to listen to my audition?'

Travis laughed. 'Of course I did. It's only fair – you got to eavesdrop on me. And everyone before us.'

'I'm sure you did great,' Layla said, laying her head gently on Travis's shoulder.

'She's been here for a year already,' Travis said, tilting his head toward her. 'Waiting for me.'

Layla lifted her head and tapped him playfully on the arm. 'I spent all my time practising.'

'Me too,' Travis said. 'So I could join my high school sweetheart at Nottinger.'

'Excuse me,' Gary said, standing up and heading to the men's room. He winked at the pretty blonde waitress behind the counter as he passed.

When Gary stepped out of the men's room he saw that Travis and Layla were kissing. He approached them slowly from behind, catching glimpses of their pink tongues darting into each other's mouths.

Gary sat down heavily on his side of the booth and they broke apart. Layla's cheeks glowed pink. The blonde waitress appeared at their table and set a bowl of ice cream down in front of Gary.

'Good luck today,' she said, twisting the bottom of her apron in her fingers. 'I hope you did well.'

'Thank you,' Gary said. He watched her wander away and check on the other tables, glancing back at him after each one.

'She's got eyes for you, Gary,' Travis chuckled. He picked up a fry from his plate and chomped on it hungrily.

Gary looked down at the melting ice cream, two scoops of chocolate sliding into each other under a stream of hot fudge. His mouth tasted of copper.

The dean's decisions were posted at the end of the day, tacked to the wall in the main hallway outside the school's office. A crowd of students gathered around the postings, eager fingers sliding down the list of names, then over to see if they'd made the cut, and if they had, what orchestra position they had been appointed to. Gary watched as several made their way to the front, and observed their expressions of elation or dismay when they turned back around.

Gary stepped forward, his spine rigid beneath his jacket. He found his name and slid his finger over. Something gave in his chest when he read the word 'YES' under the 'ACCEPTED' column. He slid his finger further and read 'SECOND VIOLIN, SECOND CHAIR' and his heart thudded to a stop.

He heard Travis whoop from somewhere close by, then turned to see him in the middle of the hallway, hugging Layla as he swung her around in an arc. Gary's eyes darted back to the wall and he found Travis's name. He'd made it to first.

'We have to celebrate,' Travis said, back in their room at the dorm. He waved a flask of something that smelled like gasoline under Gary's nose. Gary smiled and waved it away. Travis shrugged and went back to sitting on his bed next to Layla, looping his arm loosely over her shoulders.

Gary faced them in his desk chair, legs crossed and arms folded. He watched Travis and Layla pass the flask back and forth until the sky darkened and the moon shone brightly through the window.

'I'm going out for some air,' Gary said.

'Good idea,' Travis said, his words slurred. He kissed Layla sloppily on the cheek.

She laughed too loudly and pushed him away.

Gary watched the Burger Palace waitress through the restaurant's windows from across the street, leaning against the edge of the neighbouring building, hidden in the shadows. When she gathered her things and came out the front door, Gary waited a moment, then crossed the street and followed her down the block. When she turned down a side street, Gary caught up with her.

'Walking home alone?' he hummed over her shoulder.

The waitress spun around, a look of panic on her face, and hugged her purse closer to her chest. She took a few backward steps away from him.

Gary stepped toward her and more light fell on his face.

The waitress relaxed her arms as she recognised him. 'You scared me to death,' she said.

'I thought it would be nice to see you again,' Gary said. He took another step closer to her.

The waitress smiled, a mix of relief and uncertainty. 'How did it go today?' she asked, clearing her throat.

'I'm in,' Gary said, smiling. 'First chair violin.'

'Wow, that's great,' the waitress said, relaxing further. She looped the strap of her purse over her shoulder and straightened her uniform blouse.

Gary took another quick step towards her and grabbed her by the back of the neck, pulling her forwards. He pushed his tongue into her mouth as she struggled against his grip. Gary looped his other arm around her waist and pulled her body close to his. Her body stiffened and she pounded on his shoulder with a clenched fist.

Gary paused a moment to look into her eyes then smashed his lips to hers again.

'No,' she mumbled into his mouth. The waitress raised her knee and stomped down hard on Gary's instep. Pain shot up his leg and he released her, staggering back against the wall of a boarded-up apartment building.

The waitress stumbled away, crying for help hoarsely as she fled.

Gary crouched down in the alley, his back against the wall and held his head in his hands. The taste of old coffee and waxy lipstick mixed with the copper in his mouth.

Gary met with the dean the next morning. He'd waited outside the office, staring at the names on the walls until they blurred in front of his eyes. The old man sighed when he saw Gary, then reluctantly ushered him in.

'Congratulations on your accomplishment,' the dean said after waving at one of the leather visitor chairs across from his desk. He stowed his overcoat and hat on a rack by the door, then sat, fingers laced on the desktop.

'I'd like to be moved to first,' Gary said. 'I'm better than second chair.'

'Decisions from dean and the admission committee are final, young man,' the dean said.

'I'd like you to reconsider,' Gary said, crossing his legs and leaning forwards. 'I'm a prodigy.'

The dean smiled sourly. 'You're surrounded by them, my boy. Do you know how many students didn't make it into a spot this year?'

'Fifty-three,' Gary said.

The dean paused and studied him a moment. 'That's right. So you must know, you're fortunate to be here, and on a scholarship, I might add.'

Gary's face remained neutral as he stayed silent.

'Son, take my advice. Be grateful for the opportunity you've earned, and work as hard as you can so when a spot comes open, you'll be first in line. That's the key to success in life.'

When Gary got back to his room, a necktie was hanging on the door. Gary used his key and turned the knob, catching a glimpse of naked flesh on Travis's bed before opening the door widely and stepping inside.

Layla pulled the blankets over her head and hid while Travis fumbled to find his shorts on the floor. Gary stood in the doorway watching him.

'Didn't you see the tie?' Travis laughed under his breath.

Gary went to his desk and sat down. He opened his music theory text book and started to read.

Gary dropped three notes during rehearsal that afternoon during a simple piece he'd played a number of times before. The conductor waved his arms manically in the air, bringing the music to a dribbling stop, then pointed his baton at Gary's forehead.

'Stand,' he demanded.

Gary stood, his violin dangling at his side.

'Play,' the conductor shouted.

Gary propped the violin under his chin and began again. The invisible notes he normally followed in his mind floated away from him as his fingers forgot the rhythm of the piece. He dropped his instrument to his side again and caught Travis's eye. Travis's expression urged him to continue.

'Out,' the conductor sighed, waving his baton at the door. 'Come back when you know it.'

Gary stood outside the door and listened to them play without him. He could hear Travis playing, he knew it had to be him, clear and true and bright.

'Tomorrow will be better,' Travis said in their room that night. He handed Gary his shiny flask and turned his back.

Gary smelled the liquor inside and winced. When Travis turned around again, Gary handed it back, pretending to have taken a sip.

'I know it will,' Gary said.

Travis tilted his head back and took a large gulp. He wiped his mouth with the back of his hand and said, 'Everyone at Nottinger is already really good. You have to be great to get ahead.'

Gary stood up from his desk and motioned for the flask in Travis's hand, slipping his other hand into his pocket. Travis walked over and handed it to him, clapping Gary loudly on the shoulder. Gary glanced at Travis's hand, then jabbed his Swiss Army knife into Travis's stomach.

Gary pulled out the knife and stabbed Travis five more times in quick succession, feeling the give of his flesh against the blade. Travis's expression morphed from drunken surprise to pain, and then to disbelief before he crumpled onto the linoleum floor.

Gary calmly washed his hands in the bathroom sink then gathered his things. Before slipping out into the hall and pulling the door closed, he took the small stack of notes from Travis's desk, slipped them into his pocket, and looped Travis's necktie around the doorknob.

When the bus pulls into the depot at three in the morning, there is a police car waiting, its blue-and-red lights lighting up the night sky. Gary watches from the window as two officers board the bus, looking back and forth between the photographs they each hold and the people in the seats. Gary watches their expressions as they scan the passengers, finally coming to a stop when they reach his row.

'Come on, wake up,' one of them says as they rouse the big man next to Gary.

The man snorts as he wakes, then tries to bolt from his seat when he sees the police.

They lead the man away in handcuffs, telling him he is under arrest for armed robbery. After the police car pulls away Gary steps down from the bus, heads past a bank of payphones and studies the map of downtown Indianapolis, tracing his callused fingers across the scratched plastic before disappearing into the night.

A Slight Change of Plan

Susi Holliday

They meet at Clapham Junction railway station at 7:45. Simon has travelled from the west. His pokey, overpriced flat is much closer to Hounslow, but he likes to pretend it's in Chiswick. Joseph has come from the east. Leytonstone. Even the name makes Simon shudder. There's probably nothing wrong with the place. Lots of people love living in the east. He grew up there after all. For Simon, though, it's just a bit too … *easterly*. Like Essex. Simon has never understood Essex. He couldn't wait to escape the place.

'Whose idea was this again? I was all set for that weekend in Brittany, you know. Cheese, wine, French sticks, French chicks … Can't say this is *quite* what I had in mind!' Joseph drops his rucksack onto the platform and extends a hand. He's grinning, and Simon notes that he's missing a couple of teeth. Not at the front, thank God, but noticeable all the same. Sloppy grooming, Simon thinks. There's no excuse for that. 'You and your missing bloody passport! Anyway, don't worry. Let's think of it as a mystery tour. It's good to see you, Simon,' Joseph continues. 'You're looking very fresh.'

Simon pumps his hand and returns the smile. 'You too, Joseph. To be honest, I *am* looking forward to this.'

Joseph crouches down and starts fumbling with something attached to the back of his bag, and Simon takes the time to have a good look at his old friend. He lied when he said he was looking well. Joseph has a bald spot on the back of his head, and the hair surrounding it is thinly spread.

Joseph stands up. 'Well, I popped into the local bookshop last night. Got us a walking map. I was thinking we could do a ten-mile circular.

There's a great pub halfway. Homemade pies and cask ales. Tell me you still drink ale, Simon. You've not switched to that fancy lager since you moved west, have you?'

'West is best, eh, Joseph? You know what they say. As for pies and ales – not really my thing these days.' He pauses to pat his finely honed six-pack. 'I'm more of a protein shake and sushi man, now. That Japanese lager is fantastic, by the way. You shouldn't be so snobbish about it.'

Joseph laughs and Simon notes the crinkles at the sides of his eyes. Simon hasn't had crinkles or wrinkles or as much as a blemish for years. Not since he started the Botox and the chemical peels. You have to look after yourself once you reach thirty, don't you?

'I'm sure you can squeeze in a pie for old time's sake … and you can try an IPA, if you can't stomach beer like a real man anymore.'

Simon wants to punch him. 'I'm sure I can make an exception for one day, Joseph. For old time's sake.' He grins, and hopes that Joseph is impressed by his perfect row of veneers. Bloody expensive, but worth every penny. He's lost count of the number of women who've passed comment on them. Whoever said that champagne and oysters were the way to woo a woman obviously hadn't experienced the benefits of LaserWhite Smile Clinics.

They board the train. It's barely pulled away from the station when Joseph opens his rucksack and takes out a flask.

'I brought an extra cup,' he says. He lays two plastic cups on the table and produces a packet of Hob Nobs. 'Lucky I still had all this hiking stuff, eh?'

Simon tries not to look aghast. He'd planned to buy a double-shot soy latte from the artisan coffee stand in the connections tunnel, but he'd run out of time. The last time he drank something from a flask he was in the Scouts. He can still remember the metallic taste of lukewarm, watery hot chocolate, puffs of undissolved powder floating around, exploding inside his mouth. He shudders. 'Thanks, Joseph. Very *dib-dib-dib* of you.'

Joseph says nothing, dips his biscuit into his tea and takes a bite. Smiles at Simon with teeth coated in chocolate. 'How's Marianne?'

It's all Simon can do not to grab the other man by the curled-up collar of his cheap polo shirt and throttle him blue. He swallows. Composes himself. 'We've split up, actually. A month ago. I suppose we just grew apart. No biggie. Besides … we're still young, aren't we, Joseph? Plenty more fish and all that. I've been having a ball, actually. Some top-notch little fillies out west.'

'Ah, that's a shame … I liked Marianne.'

I fucking know you did, you weaselly little bastard. 'Like I said, Joseph, old boy. No biggie. You should give her a call some time. I'm sure she'd appreciate the concern. She used to talk about you, you know…' He lets the sentence trail off. Watches as Joseph's cheeks turn pink before he turns to stare out of the window to check that the countryside is still there.

They arrive at their destination. One of those stations in the arse end of nowhere, where there's nothing but a platform and a gate into a potholed car park. Simon feels a brief flash of something. Fear? Guilt? It's not too late to turn back. Knock it on the head. Tell GI Joseph he's got a migraine coming on or something. Joseph hands him his rucksack then adjusts the straps on his own. His eyes are bright, his cheeks already flushed in anticipation.

Fuck it, Simon thinks. 'So, this hike … not too arduous, is it?' He suppresses a smirk as Joseph looks him up and down, taking in the designer outdoor gear he purchased especially for the trip.

'Nah … I'll break you in slowly, mate. Mostly flat. A few hills. Just one craggy bit near the end, but we can take a detour if you're not up for it? I've brought all the kit: ropes and belays and what have you. I'll let you decide.'

Simon smiles. He's trying his hardest to stay calm. Act polite. But the effort is actually making his stomach flip, the sharp tang of bile threatening. Joseph. Fucking *Joseph*. Of all the people Marianne could've confessed to having slept with. He wouldn't have cared if it was anyone else – he'd had more one-night-stands than she'd made him dinners, never mind hot ones. Ten years, though … and the fact that she'd slept with Joseph *right at the bloody beginning*. That night he'd gone out and not come back. She'd called Joseph, asking if he knew where Simon was … *I was worried*, she'd said … *I was scared*. Not too scared to jump into bed with GI-Fucking-Joseph. Of *all* people. 'Let's take the hard route, eh, tough guy? You can show me what you're made of…'

If Joseph senses Simon's undercurrent of boiling rage, he does nothing to suggest it. He spends most of the frankly *tedious* hike pointing out random pieces of undergrowth and commenting on the sounds of birds. The lunch in the pub is good, Simon concedes. At least his 'old friend' has a decent last meal.

Two hours after the steak-and-ale pies and the craft lager that tasted like something Simon had once vomited up, they reach the foot of the crag. Their walk through the valley has been pleasant enough. Nothing too strenuous, which suited Simon well. He's more than aware that he's treadmill-fit only; he's not a huge fan of major-league sweat.

He looks up at the path of ascent and tries hard to suppress a frown. They should've gone the easy way … they'd be at the top right now, and all Simon would have to do was push the bastard off. Now, because of his bravado, he was going to have to climb up the damn thing first. *Oh well*, Simon thinks. *At least I'll have earned my reward.* He wonders how it'll feel, being a murderer. He glances across at Joseph, who is humming away to himself, busy sliding ropes through harnesses and clipping on karabiners. Simon knows then how it'll feel … It'll feel fucking *fantastic*.

'Ready?' Joseph says.

Simon sees he's got a piece of meat stuck between his front teeth. It makes him feel sick. 'I can't wait,' he says. He grins so hard he almost splits the skin across his cheeks.

The climb's not as hard as he imagined it to be. In fact, he realises he's quite enjoying it. It's almost a shame to reach the top. He's sweating hard, feels cold rivulets coursing down between his shoulder blades. Joseph hands him a water bottle and he drinks greedily, letting the liquid run down his chin and into the neck of his t-shirt.

'Good?' Joseph says.

'Great … bloody great. Cheers mate. You know what? I never imagined you'd be the one to teach me something good – something I'd enjoy so much. It's a shame, actually … I actually feel a bit bad about this now…'

He drops the water bottle on the ground. Takes a step towards Joseph, then another. Joseph steps backwards, then falters, realising he's too close to the edge.

'Bad about what, Simon?' There's a slight tremor in Joseph's voice.

He knows. He must do.

'Well I can hardly let you live, now that I know what you've done. Or should I say *who* you've done. You little snake. Did you really think she wouldn't tell me? Did you really think you were *special*?'

Confusion flashes across Joseph's face. Then realisation. His eyes pop wide open in fear. 'No ... listen, you've got it all wrong, Simon. Mate ... come *on*...'

Simon takes another step closer. He rubs his hands on his trousers, wiping off the sheen of sweat that's spread across them like mildew.

Then it happens.

Simon takes one final step, but Joseph's fast. He darts out of the way, ducks under Simon's outstretched hands. There's a reason that people call him a snake and a weasel. He's small, he's slippery ... and he's away from the edge, while Simon is teetering on the brink of it, propelled by his own adrenaline. He windmills his arms, and for a brief moment he thinks he's going over ... until Joseph grabs the straps of his rucksack and drags him back to safety. Simon spins round. His face is burning. His heart is hammering so hard he's sure Joseph can hear it.

'So,' Joseph spits. 'You brought me up here to, what ... to kill me? For *Marianne*? It was one night. One night! After everything you've done to *her*? This is absurd. You can't have thought you'd get away with it?'

Simon has regained his composure. He's still shaking, but he feels his energy coming back. It's not over yet, not by a long chalk. 'Oh but I can, little Joseph,' he says. 'It. Was. An. Accident. That's all I'd need to say. It's slippery up here, loose stones. And no one even knows where we are, do they? It's not like you had anyone to tell...'

Joseph puffs out his chest. 'I don't think so, mate.' He takes a step towards Simon, and it's Simon's turn to feel confused.

'You what...?'

'You didn't really think you were going to do this, did you? Because

I brought *you* here. Remember – this hike was *my* idea. I joked earlier that I couldn't remember whose idea it was; well I can: It was mine. "Fancy coming along for a hike, sometime?" I said to you. You suggested the trip to France, but I knew I'd be able to change it at the last minute without you suspecting anything. You *do* remember that pub on the South Bank … the night I bumped into you and Marianne? What was it, five, six months ago? She'd covered up the bruises with make-up, but I saw right through her beige camouflage, just like I've always seen through you. You vain, odious bastard.'

Simon's mouth falls open.

'Just for the record, mate, it wasn't just the one time, it was *lots* of times – every time she felt the need to escape from you and your over-friendly fists.'

Simon feels like his head is about to explode. 'Who the hell do you think you're talking to, Joseph?'

Joseph doesn't bother to reply. He lunges forward and throws his whole weight behind the thrust.

Simon feels his arms windmilling again as he slips over the edge. This time, Joseph doesn't step forward to save him. Simon feels air whoosh behind him, then a jolt and a crack as he bounces against the side of the rock face. A sharp blade of fear slices through his chest. He looks down, and realises he is no longer falling. Something has stopped him. He spins and grips at the rock, his slippery hands struggling for purchase. He barely feels the stab of pain as a fingernail snaps off as he tries to wedge his hand into the smallest crevice, clinging on for his life.

'Well,' Joseph says, peering down at him over the edge. 'That was unexpected.'

Simon looks up in horror as Joseph reaches one of his snake-like arms behind him and removes a walking pole from where it has been strapped to the back of his rucksack.

'Any final words, Simon, *mate*? I'll be sure to pass them on to Marianne when she collects me from the train station. By the way, has anyone ever told you that your teeth look like they've been painted with Tippex?'

'Please … for Christ's sake, man! You can't leave me like this … I'm slipping … help me … I'm *begging* you … just take my hand, *please*…'

Joseph watches as a flurry of rocks tumble and bounce down the ravine, out of sight. 'I'd like to say I'm sorry, but I'm not going to lie. There've been too many lies. It's over now. It's the only way. You know it is.' He feels a lurch in his stomach. He could stop this. Grab hold of Simon, wrench him up over the lip of the jutting rock. But he won't. He's in control now. This is his story now.

A sickening realisation dawns in Simon's eyes. 'No … God, no … please, I'll do anything … You know I will…'

Liar, Joseph thinks. You're a fucking *liar*. It's the pleading that convinces him. He's right. He's always been right. 'It's too late. So long, my friend. Don't worry, I'm sure it'll be over quickly.'

He takes a deep breath. Crouches down. Keeping a hand on the largest of the rocks to steady himself, he leans over and pushes the tip of his walking pole into the loop of his Simon's rucksack. The loop that had caught, by freak and by chance, on a piton left embedded in the rock from someone else's ascent. One innocuous metal peg. If not for that, they wouldn't be here now. It'd all be over. None of this last-minute pathetic begging.

Joseph stares into Simon's eyes as he carefully lifts the walking pole like a giant crochet hook and slips the loop off the peg. There's a split second where nothing happens, like in a cartoon. Then he watches as Simon's hands slide away from their tenuous grip on the too-small ledge.

'No … no! What're you … you can't just … *aaaaarrrrggghhh*…'

His old friend's voice diminishes with the fall until there's no sound but the blood rushing around his skull. Bubbling and cascading like a river smashing against rocks.

He thinks of Marianne, waiting for him at the station, ready to start their new life together. The words she said to him on the phone that morning, when he'd been full of doubt, ready to call off the whole thing.

Just make sure it looks like an accident.

Bombay Brigadoon

Vaseem Khan

'They found the body inside a well, out in the Aarey Milk Colony.' Inspector Jamshed Bukhari glanced up at the stuttering ceiling fan as it ladled the glutinous air around his office, gently ruffling his thinning hair. 'Burned black. No idea how long it's been out there. ACP Shukla took one look at the First Investigation Report and decided it was some petty ruffian come to grief at the hands of the local underworld. Case closed.'

'But you're not convinced?'

Bukhari tapped his finger on the lunar-cratered surface of his ancient desk. 'Something's not sitting right, Chopra. You know what I mean, I'm sure.'

Inspector Ashwin Chopra (Ret'd) did know.

During his thirty years on the force he had come to believe that a policeman's intuition was a finely calibrated instrument, something good officers developed over time, an instinct meticulously honed and polished, kept in precise working order by the twin lubricants of conscience and duty. Since his forced retirement from the service the previous year – the result of a bout of unstable angina – that instinct had weighed heavily upon him. The result had been the Baby Ganesh Detective Agency, and a renewal of his commitment to the cause.

Now he increasingly found himself consulted on cases that the over-stretched Mumbai police service had neither the resources nor the will to tackle themselves.

Bukhari was an old friend, and an admirer of Chopra's spotless reputation. After three decades in the Indian police service – recently 'lauded' by a national paper as only the *third* most corrupt institution in the country – his companion's achievement was, in and of itself, worthy of accolade.

'Who found the body?' Chopra asked.

'Two schoolkids. They were looking for somewhere quiet to canoodle. Their statements are in the file.'

'Forensics?'

Bukhari gave a short bark of laughter. 'Last week Shukla told us not to switch the fans on until the thermometer hit thirty. You think he's going to waste money on forensics for a dead nobody?' He picked at his khaki shirt, saddlebags of sweat under his arms. 'There's been a turf war recently. Petty criminals turning up dead all over the place, like bad pennies. If Shukla's right then this one was dealt with in a particularly brutal fashion. I have a horrible feeling our friend was burned alive.'

'There's been no autopsy?'

'I've asked for one. The pathologist has promised me the results later today.'

'Won't Shukla hit the roof?'

'Possibly. But some things cannot be allowed to stand, can they, old friend?'

These words stayed with Chopra as he headed to the Sahar hospital.

In the rear of his modified Tata van, Ganesha, the baby elephant that his long-vanished uncle Bansi had sent him a year earlier, looked out into the impossibly crowded streets of Mumbai, a phantasmagoria of honking rickshaws, hooting trucks, buses, bicycles, handcarts, cows, goats, dogs and the occasional lumbering elephant.

Chopra still had no real idea why Bansi had sent him such a strange bequest.

In time he had accommodated the little elephant into his life – no easy task for a man who lived on the fifteenth floor of one of Mumbai's trademark towers. Ganesha now resided in a compound behind the restaurant Chopra had established after his retirement, a restaurant that also served as the headquarters for his fledgling detective agency.

Recently he had got into the habit of taking the elephant out on his rounds – Ganesha needed the exercise, and his keen senses had proven useful on more than one occasion.

In the hospital mortuary, Chopra found his old friend Homi Contractor elbows deep in a fresh corpse.

'Do I look different?' asked the pathologist, from behind his bottle-green surgical mask.

Chopra hesitated.

He knew that Homi, depressed after his recent fiftieth birthday, had embarked on an all-consuming programme of diet and exercise. It seemed strange that a man so successful, with a stable marriage and children he could be proud of, could fall victim to such late-blooming insecurity. Homi himself didn't understand it.

Yet Chopra also knew that, even in a city of twenty million, loneliness and disillusionment stalked the gilded towers of the rich as readily as the slums of the poor. In his late forties now, he too sometimes succumbed to an inexplicable feeling of melancholia.

'As good as Sachin batting on a hundred.'

This brought a smile to Homi's lips. They were both cricket lovers, and fans of Sachin Tendulkar, India's premier batsman.

Homi pulled the corpse out from the row of cold storage units.

Chopra regarded the blackened body, a few wisps of burned hair remaining on the melted scalp.

'He was—' Homi began.

'You're sure it's a he?'

Homi gave him a caustic look. 'He was immolated, old friend, not given a sex change.' He showed Chopra a photograph of the body as it had arrived in the mortuary. 'You see the pugilistic stance? It's a result of muscle contraction as the body burns. We found elevated levels of carboxyhaemoglobin in his blood and soot in the airways. Do you understand what that means?'

'That he was burned alive.'

'Yes,' said Homi, emphatically.

'How old?'

'Early to mid-thirties. Take a look at this.' Homi put an X-ray up on a lightbox. It showed the back of the victim's skull, fractured by a spider's web of cracks. 'Blunt force trauma. Heavy object. Definitely ante-mortem. Looks like someone tried to bash his head in, then burned him with an accelerant to cover up the crime.'

'How long has he been dead?'

'Best estimate, based on insect colonisation of the body: two to three weeks. There's a couple of other things, might help with an ID.' Homi put another X-ray onto the lightbox. 'First, he has a metal fixation plate in his right tibia. From what looks like a Y-type fracture of the right tibial plateau, a few years old. Second, he has a tattoo, just above the heart. I found it using infrared photography. Most of the body had third-degree burns, destroying the dermis, but this patch was relatively shielded, possibly because his arm was slumped over it when the initial burning took place.'

He handed Chopra an infrared photograph of the tattoo.

It showed Christ on the cross, the foot of the cross enfolded by a banner emblazoned with the words: '*Only God forgives*'.

'He was stripped naked before he was burned. My guess is because the killer wanted to make sure his skin was fully blackened. The clothes were never found.'

'Why? I mean, why would the killer do that?'

'Because this was no local ruffian. Our victim is not even Indian.'

'What does that mean?'

Homi hesitated. 'Based on an analysis of the skull – the mastoid process, the nasal aperture, the palate – it is my belief that this is the body of a Caucasian. A white man.'

Chopra felt the wind go out of him.

He considered the ramifications of a Western tourist murdered in Mumbai – in such a grotesque fashion. He felt the case coil itself around his throat like the tail of a snake.

The Aarey Milk Colony: a sprawling, four-thousand-acre expanse in the suburbs of the city, housing villages, lakes, gardens, Mumbai's Film City, and some sixteen thousand cattle spread across innumerable farms and smallholdings.

It was on one of these smallholdings that the body had been discovered, in an area of relative wilderness.

The plot, a collection of crumbling brick buildings and tin cowsheds, was fenced in with rusted chain-link. A faded sign on the gate said 'KEEP OUT. PROPERTY OF OMKARA LAND DEVELOPMENT PVT. LTD'. A ragged tear in the fence beside the gate negated the sign's edict.

The sun beat down mercilessly as Chopra scanned the area. Witch grass burned dry as tinder. An old wagon wheel propped against the nearest building, two spokes missing. A wooden outhouse, the wood warped by cycles of monsoon rain and relentless sun.

He walked into the outhouse.

Vines from a strangler fig behind the building had worked themselves through the roof, and hung down in snaky fronds. A scorpion scuttled away from his shoe.

The well was at the rear of the space, filled in to all but the top three feet. It was in this cavity that the body had been discovered by the two teenagers. It was, Chopra supposed, a comment on the city's chronic overpopulation that youngsters had to come out to this desolate wasteland to find privacy.

Who was he? How had he ended up here?

Outside, he circled the plot, looking for anything, any sign out of the ordinary.

Ganesha watched him, then began to do the same, snuffling at the ground with his trunk. An elephant's trunk was one of the most sensitive organs in the natural world.

Chopra's eye was caught by a flash of white. He bent down to a log pile stacked up against the outhouse; a piece of paper caught between two gnarled and desiccated trunks.

He plucked it out.

It was a single page from a pocket bible, charred around the edges. The bottom of the page was stamped 'St Francis Gospel Mission, Mumbai'.

He turned and saw Ganesha rooting around in a patch of darker soil by the edge of the plot, under the fence. The little elephant had found something.

Chopra walked to the patch of discoloured earth, fell to his knees, and began shovelling at the loose soil with his hands.

A foot down he found the charred ashes of clothing.

The St Francis Gospel Mission was a low, whitewashed building in the gentrified suburb of Malad East.

Inside Chopra met with the white-robed Brother Victor Mascarenhas, who examined the bible page that he had been handed with a frown. 'Yes, this is from one of our texts. It is troubling that you found it while investigating a murder.'

'Did you have a white man staying with you recently? About five-nine, dark-haired, early to mid-thirties. He would have vanished, probably without warning, some two to three weeks ago. He was last wearing blue jeans, possibly a white t-shirt.'

'Many people don't inform us that they are coming, or when they will leave. We are a house of God, open to all in need of shelter.' Mascarenhas hesitated. 'But there *was* a man who corresponds to your description. He stayed with us for a number of months, though he spent most of his time outside the premises. The name he gave us was John. I'm afraid that is all. We do not ask for identification. However, it is my belief that he was English. I have met many Englishmen and I can always recognise the accents.' Mascarenhas gave a faint smile. 'I asked him why he was here. I could see that he did not wish to discuss the matter, but once, in a moment of weakness perhaps, he joked that he was searching for a mirage, the ghost of a long-dead woman, and that he had a message to deliver to the past. It reminded me of an English film I had once seen: *Brigadoon*. Though the woman in that film wasn't exactly a ghost, I felt the same sense that John was chasing something not quite real.'

John – John Doe's – room had remained unoccupied since he had vanished. Mascarenhas explained that they had touched nothing, awaiting his return.

Chopra searched it quickly. There was little to find. A suitcase full of clothes – John Doe hadn't bothered to hang them up in the room's solitary steel cupboard. Some toiletries in a plastic bag. A pair of worn sandals.

Under the mattress of the steel-framed bed he discovered a folder.

Chopra sat on the bed and flicked through it. It was a scrapbook of sorts, tracing, haphazardly, the genealogy of an Indian woman named Nirmala Bhagayshree Wadhwa. Nirmala had been born in 1928, the only daughter of a royal Indian household, the Wadhwa dynasty of the Palsekar clan. The Palsekars, Chopra knew, had once served as military commanders to the Peshwas, the ancient rulers of the Maratha Empire.

Nirmala had married in late 1947, shortly after the upheaval of Partition, and had had a daughter in 1948. She had died just months after the birth.

The file tracked the daughter, born Kalpana Bhagayshree Shankar, up until the age of about fifteen – photocopies of old newspaper articles, official registry documents, land records – then the trail stopped cold.

The file was incomplete.

Why would John Doe be digging into the history of a long-dead Indian noblewoman?

'May I keep this file?' Chopra asked.

'If it helps you to identify this poor young man, then, by all means,' said Mascarenhas. 'In the meantime, I shall pray for his soul.'

The British High Commission in Mumbai was housed in an imposing glass skyscraper in the elite Bandra-Kurla complex in an affluent suburb of the city. Chopra called ahead and managed to wangle a fifteen-minute meeting with the high commissioner.

Inside the commissioner's office, he was greeted with hurried enthusiasm.

Robert Mallory was newly in post and was discovering that wading through the swamp of Anglo-Indian diplomacy was a trickier endeavour than he had expected. Chopra had become acquainted with the man during his recent investigation into the theft of the Koh-i-Noor diamond, brought to Mumbai as part of a special exhibition and subsequently stolen in a daring heist. By recovering the great diamond he had made a friend of the high commissioner, and, through him, earned the gratitude of the British government.

'What can I do for you, Chopra?'

Mallory was in a brisk pinstripe suit, pacing up and down as his personal assistant read out the agenda for his upcoming address to the Indian Christian Theosophical Society, an encounter he was dreading. He stopped mid-stride as he saw Ganesha trot into the office behind Chopra. Bending down he chucked Ganesha under the chin, the little elephant responding with a delighted tap of his trunk on Mallory's cheek. 'How are you, young man? Still hard at work in the detecting business?'

'Thank you for seeing me,' said Chopra. 'I wanted to speak to you personally before this matter becomes public news … Two days ago a body was found in the Aarey Milk Colony. The man had been dead for two weeks, maybe more. He had been attacked, violently, then burned alive. Initially, the police thought he was a local. But we now know that he was a white male, almost certainly English.'

Mallory straightened, exhaling slowly, his finger tapping at the side of his leg. 'Do you know why the previous incumbent of this office quit, Chopra? It was all that trouble over the Sussex woman raped in Delhi last Christmas. Turned out she was from a well-connected household – connected all the way to the House of Lords. But, in spite of my predecessor's best efforts at cajoling the Indian authorities, neither he, nor they, got near to finding the culprit. The stress almost killed him.'

'I remember,' said Chopra.

The fallout had led to acrimonious words between the British and Indian governments, a public spat that had left a lingering bitterness in both countries.

'What do you know so far?'

'Not much.' Chopra then quickly brought the commissioner up to speed.

'Let me guess. You want me to make some calls, see if I can find out who your John Doe is?'

'Yes,' said Chopra. 'That is precisely what I wish.'

The commissioner called back six hours later, as Chopra was sitting down to an uneasy dinner with his wife, Poppy. The day had drained him. The revelations of John Doe's death – the thought of a man burned alive, his last moments – stirred something inside him, killing his appetite. He had seen death in all its forms. Good deaths and bad deaths. But this was something else; a death that called from beyond the grave.

'Are you sitting down?' said Mallory.

Chopra stood up and went to his office, closing the door behind him, ignoring the expression of irritation on his wife's face.

'Tell me.'

'It was the combination of the tattoo and the steel plate,' said Mallory. 'I contacted some old friends in the security services, people who are used to finding other people … Your John Doe is a Jason Edward Latimer. Born in London, aged thirty-five, married … Here's where it gets sticky. Latimer is a career criminal. He's been in and out of prison since he was fifteen. Eleven months ago, he was released from a category B prison after serving three years of a six-year sentence for aggravated assault.'

Chopra was silent. The feeling of unease that had been with him all day seemed to sharpen to a point. 'What was he doing in India?'

'No one seems to know. Passport and airline records show that he entered the country precisely seven months and eleven days ago. Effectively, he's overstayed his visa. What he's been doing here in all that time is anyone's guess. His former parole officer told us that he had been involved in petty drug trafficking for many years. It's a good bet that he was in India looking for a new supplier. It might explain what happened to him. Perhaps he made enemies of the wrong people. A deal gone bad. I'm sure you know better than me the sort of thing I'm talking about.' Mallory sighed. 'Look, I know this is a terrible thing to say, but it's probably for the best that he's turned out to be a bad penny. I mean, compared to the alternative.'

Chopra felt a rush of anger at Mallory's palpable relief. He did not share the commissioner's sentiments. 'What about next of kin?'

'Already notified. His wife is on a plane. She'll be here in the morning.'

'I will pick her up from the airport.'

'You don't have to do that.'

'You are correct,' said Chopra. 'I don't *have* to. I wish to.'

Susan Latimer's flight arrived at what had once been Bombay International Airport, before the government's frenzied renaming spree, an attempt to excise the lingering echoes of the country's colonial past.

Chopra was an hour early.

His first surprise was to discover that Susan Latimer was pregnant.

She was a tall, elegant woman, dressed in jeans and a simple cotton blouse, strawberry blonde hair cut short to the nape of a long neck. An angular, but pleasant face, set with two brilliant blue eyes.

'Are you sure you won't go to the hotel first?' asked Chopra.

'I want to see his body.'

She spoke only once more. 'Why do you have an elephant in your van?'

Chopra hesitated, a slight flush rising to his cheeks. It was always this way when he was asked about Ganesha. What could he say without sounding insane? The elephant was not his partner. Ganesha didn't speak, or fly, or solve mysteries. But there was something about his young ward that defied explanation … And he could not deny that in these past months he had learned to appreciate the little calf's company. He had stopped dwelling on how fantastical it was for him to be wandering around the city with a baby elephant in tow. And, after all, this was India, where the impossible became merely the improbable.

'I … ahh … I look after him,' he said eventually. 'Though sometimes I feel it is the other way around,' he muttered, under his breath.

Ganesha looked on from the rear of the van with solemn eyes.

In the morgue Chopra observed her quietly as she gazed down at what was left of her husband, presumably the father of her child.

He thought that she would cry, but she did not.

'The British Embassy will fly him back to England once you give your consent,' he said.

'No. I want him to be cremated. I'll scatter his ashes in the river. Isn't that what you do here?'

'He is Hindu?' said Chopra, surprise lifting his eyebrows.

'No. He's a born-again Christian. But it's all the same in the end, isn't it? Stories for children.'

He drove her to her hotel.

In the lobby they sat down and he explained what he had learned in his short investigation. He floated the theory that Jason Latimer had come to India to source drugs.

'I don't believe it,' she said, vehemently. 'He wouldn't do that.'

'My understanding is that he spent many years in the drug trade. His last spell in prison was the result of an assault on a rival dealer in London.'

'Whatever else he was here for,' said Susan, firmly, 'the one thing he most certainly was *not* here for was drugs. I know because I was the prison counsellor that got him out of that life.' Her hands clasped each other in her lap, but her gaze was strong and steadfast. 'It's how we met, how we fell in love. He was a prisoner, a criminal with a record, but I saw him for what he was – a basically good man who had made some bad choices. A man seeking redemption. I helped him to find it. And then, at some point, God took over.' She sighed. 'I encouraged it at the time because I could see the effect his new-found faith had on him. He became a model prisoner, and that took years off his sentence. When he was paroled we moved in together.'

She took a photograph out from her handbag and handed it to Chopra.

Jason Latimer, a brown-haired, handsome man with dark, quick eyes and an easy smile.

'He made me laugh. You may not want to believe this, but he was one of the most honest men I had ever met. Beneath everything that was his life, he had a sense of morality, a conscience. It bothered him, what he was: a criminal; but he could never find his way out of the maze. I helped him do that.'

'Why did he come to India?'

'I don't know. He didn't tell me he was going. Just left a note.' She handed Chopra a slip of paper.

It read: *'I'm going to India. There's something I have to do. If I don't sort it, it won't let go of me. I'm sorry.'*

'You have no idea what he meant by this?'

'No.'

'Did he ever mention a prior connection to India?'

'None.'

'Why do you think he didn't discuss this with you?'

'I don't know. I guess he thought I would talk him out of it.'

'I discovered a file in the room that he was staying in,' said Chopra. 'Did he ever mention a woman named Nirmala Bhagayshree Wadhwa? She died in 1948.'

'No.' She hesitated. 'Look, he's never even been out here before. But his grandfather was stationed in India, a long time ago. He died recently.'

Chopra filed this away. 'Did he call you from India?'

'Yes. On and off. I begged him to come back, but he wouldn't listen.'

'He knew that you were pregnant?'

'Yes. He kept telling me he was almost done, that he was getting closer.'

'Closer to what?'

'I don't know.' Grief quivered her cheeks. 'I guess, in the end, it was closer to his death.'

Chopra left the woman in the hotel lobby.

Sitting in his van, he went back through the folder he had discovered in Latimer's room, examining each document anew. He found something that he had missed. A photocopying receipt, tucked into the spine of the folder, stamped with the name of the charging organisation: the University of Mumbai.

The drive to the university, which was located in the southern half of the city, took an hour along potholed roads and through gridlocked traffic. If the road to hell had been paved by the Mumbai Municipal Corporation, Chopra had often thought, sinners could have slept safe in the knowledge that they would not be arriving at their destination anytime soon.

In the university library he spoke to the librarians one by one, showing them the photograph of Jason Latimer. He found a young-ish woman who remembered him. An Englishman was a rare enough sight to be memorable. They had got talking. She recalled that he had mentioned he was working with a Professor Vikram Shroff in the Department of War Studies.

Professor Shroff was a military historian in his sixties, with a thick head of wavy grey hair, albatross eyebrows and an intense stare.

'Yes, of course I remember him. He asked me to help him access old military records – British army records in India. Specifically, the court martial of a British officer in 1947.'

Chopra felt his senses quicken. 'Who was the officer?'

'A Reginald James Willoughby. Aged twenty-six at the time; commanding lieutenant of the First Battalion, Somerset Light Infantry. The battalion was based in India throughout the war and helped oversee the transition of power during Partition, supervised by the Mumbai High Command. The First was the last British unit to leave the subcontinent, in fact, in late 1948.'

'Why was this Willoughby court martialled?'

'It was unusual, to say the least. A British officer tried under Section 354 of the Indian Penal Code: outraging the modesty of a woman.' The professor shifted in his seat. 'You have to remember that in those days the British rode roughshod over both our laws *and* our women. It was inconceivable to put a British officer on trial for such an offence.'

'But they did … I presume you managed to get the trial document for Jason?'

'The trial was conducted behind closed doors; the proceedings have been sealed for decades. But I have a contact in the military who was able to dig up the records.'

'Do you have copies?'

The professor fetched a manila folder from a battered steel filing cabinet.

Chopra scanned the documents while Shroff waited.

There was a photograph of Lieutenant Reginald Willoughby. He compared it to the one of Jason Latimer. The likeness was too distinct to be a coincidence. 'This man was Jason's grandfather.'

'Yes, I believe so. Though he never admitted it.'

'Who was the woman he was accused of…?' Chopra hesitated.

'Raping?' Shroff pursed his lips. 'Her name was Nirmala Bhagayshree Wadhwa. Nineteen-year-old daughter of a princely household. Her twin brothers both served in the Somerset Lights – officer level

f course – that's probably where they befriended Reg Willoughby. He
ecame a regular at their residence in Pune – it was close to the Mumbai
ase. They were keen polo players, and Willoughby was, by all accounts,
good horseman. I believe it was only because of the influence wielded
y the family that Willoughby was even tried.'

'Did he do it?'

'He was found guilty,' said Shroff. 'But *in absentia*. You see, just after
e was charged, Willoughby deserted. Fled the city. A deserter's record
as created for him, but no one knows what happened to him.'

What happened, thought Chopra, was that Reg Willoughby found
way to return to England, changed his name, and spent the rest of
is life living in the body of his false persona. Until his death, when,
urdened by the same conscience that was Jason Latimer's curse, he had
evealed his crime to his grandson. The decades of guilt must have bled
ito his soul. He could not die without absolution and so he had sent
is grandson to find it for him.

'Jason had compiled a file on Nirmala. He was tracking her family.
Do you know why?'

'He wanted to find her living descendants. It is my belief that he
vished to meet them.'

To carry his grandfather's deathbed confession, his apology, to those
ho now stood in Nirmala's place, thought Chopra.

'Did he find a name?'

Shroff nodded. 'I asked an acquaintance, a genealogy expert, to assist
im. She traced the family to the present day. Right here in Mumbai.'

'Give me the name.'

he bungalow rose up, ghostly white, against the Mumbai night, a
right moon picking out the red tiles of the roof, the *jharoka*-style
ecorative windows.

Chopra left Ganesha in the van and spoke to the security guard
rinking chai and smoking a roll-up outside the gate. He took out the
hoto of Latimer, showed it to him.

A call was made to the house and Chopra was taken to the front entrance.

A servant led him up a grand spiral staircase to a large, bookish room – a study.

A tall man rose from behind the solitary desk and dismissed the servant.

As the door closed, the man came around the desk to stand before Chopra.

He was a big man, six-four or five, thick through the shoulders, hefty midriff, with a square bush of dark hair, a burly moustache and hard-boiled eyes.

'You say you are investigating the death of an Englishman. What has that got to do with me?'

'You are Vikaas Khanna?'

'I am.'

Chopra took out the photograph of Latimer. 'Do you recognise this man?'

'No.' But the slight contraction of that hard stare spoke volumes.

'His name is Jason Latimer. He was murdered, burned alive. His body was found in a plot in the Aarey Milk Colony. The plot belongs to Omkara Land Development Pvt Ltd. I checked the company's details with the Ministry of Corporate Affairs. Omkara is owned by Sunrise Textiles Corporation – *your* company.'

'My company owns many plots.'

'At the time of his death Latimer was investigating the family of Nirmala Bhagayshree Wadhwa. Nirmala passed away in 1948. The circumstances of her death are shrouded in mystery, but there is a good chance that she committed suicide. She was survived by a daughter, Kalpana Shankar.' Chopra paused. 'Your mother.'

Khanna breathed deeply, but said nothing.

'Your mother married Vikrol Khanna, the textile king of Pune, in 1971. You were born in 1972, an only child. Your father passed away fifteen years ago. Since then you have looked after your mother. I would like to talk to her.'

'No!' Khanna stepped closer, something wild in his eyes.

'Your security guard remembers Jason Latimer arriving at your residence two weeks ago. He does not remember him leaving. One way or another the police must be involved. It is your choice what happens next.'

For a second Chopra thought the man would charge him. He stood there, like a bull, his hands writhing by his side.

And then something went out of him. He walked behind the desk, slumped into his chair, glassy-eyed. 'Yes, he came here. An Englishman full of his own moral righteousness, seeking absolution for an evil that took place all those years ago.'

'His grandfather raped your grandmother.'

'His grandfather violated us *all*.' Khanna's eyes flared. 'A month after the rape, my great-grandfather arranged for his daughter to be married to the son of a man he knew. This man – my grandfather – was told nothing of the rape. Eight months later my mother was born. A half-white baby with dark hair and dark eyes. It is fortunate, is it not, that the women of our family have always had fair skin?' He almost spat the words. 'My mother knows nothing of this. And, until two weeks ago, neither did I.' He lifted his gaze to meet Chopra's eyes. 'Yes, Latimer came here. In the space of half an hour he destroyed everything I have ever held dear. He tore down my past. He wanted to speak to my mother. He wanted to tell her everything, beg her forgiveness. He wouldn't accept that my mother's ignorance was the best thing for her. She does not need to know. She must never know. It would destroy her.'

'You killed a man to keep her from the truth.'

'I did what I had to. I did it to protect her and to protect my children. Do you understand what it would mean for us if this were to become public?'

'I understand,' said Chopra. 'But this does not change the fact that you burned a man alive to protect your secret.'

'I … I didn't realise that he was alive. Not until he started scream—' Khanna stopped, unable to continue, his great head bowed with guilt.

Chopra took out his phone, held it across the desk.

'Will you call the police, or shall I?'

Matricide and Ice Cream

William Burton McCormick

It was a burning 35°C in the Kiev train station when I bought the fir
two tubs of ice cream. A kiosk on the second level, sandwiched betwee
overstacked magazine stands and flowery souvenir shops, sold a rang
of Ukrainian frozen delights. With President Poroshenko's trade restri
tions choking off Russian imports, European products filled the ga
flooding Ukrainian shelves with goods in trendy Western packaging.
little digging in the freezer, however, and I found the tubs made of th
old-fashioned materials I needed: insulated cardboard packages litt
changed since Soviet days. I purchased *Витчизна* brand – 'Homelan
ice cream – in chocolate and banana-strawberry flavours and hurrie
back to the train and the compartment I shared with Mother.

Soon we were on our way, the unending passenger train chuggir
west over the Dnieper Upland on a fourteen-hour trip towards th
border town of Uzhhorod, where my fiancée and her expensive tast
lay waiting. The summer was the hottest in Ukrainian history. Passer
gers lay drenched in sweat, infants crying, the elderly cooling themselv
with cheap hand fans bought at the station. No one drank the nation
alcohols; only water would do at such nightmarish temperatures. Fe
moved, fewer still could think. It was Hell. It was opportunity.

At Lviv station, along the route, I found two more *Витчизна* ic
cream packets.

At Skole, in the first foothills of the Carpathians, I bought the fin
pair.

Six in total. I hoped it would be enough.

Returning from this last ice-cream purchase, I slid open the do
to our compartment, the cabin little more than an emaciated broor

closet: two small bunks climbing one wall with Mother resting in the lower, a solitary window, and a recess over the door, where we'd shoved our luggage, the whole bag collection looking like it might crash perilously down on us at the slightest bump or change in acceleration.

'Well, Milo,' wheezed Mother in her gravelly voice, 'what did you buy this time?'

'Some treats for us. And a present for Vika when we get to Uzhorod. Another four hours or so…'

'The money of mine you spend on that girl.'

'Mother, I'm a man. I'm thirty-eight. I don't—'

'You're thirty-eight, Milo, but you're far from being a man. At this rate, you'll never get there.'

'Thanks, Mom.'

'It's the truth.'

'Just because it's true, doesn't mean you need say it.'

Mother propped herself on one elbow, watching me as I set the ice-cream tubs in the bag with the others. I could feel her disgust from here.

'Does Vika realise that I'm cutting you off? I won't support two, Milo. Or three if you plan a family.'

'Mother, all Vika knows is that you are coming to the wedding and you're very excited about meeting your new daughter-in-law. These should be happy days for us all. Let's not argue.'

She held up a cigarette-yellowed index finger. 'Not a cent after the honeymoon, Milo. Not one—'

Her words were cut off as her wheezing breaths turned into a succession of coughs, her fleshy face contorting in pain…

'Mother?'

The coughing grew more aggressive, her skin turning purplish as she tried to get air.

The sight didn't completely displease me. Still, I pulled a bottle of Bon Aqua from among our things and poured the water into a plastic cup.

'Here, drink slowly, Mother…'

After several choking minutes sipping the water, the cough faded and her colour returned.

'Did you take your medicine?'

'Yes,' she said as if it were somehow my fault that she'd smoked three packs a day for fifty years. But then most things were 'my fault'.

'You know the physician at the hotel said you shouldn't travel today, Mother. It's too hot with your emphysema. And Doc Folger back in Rochester didn't even want you to go abroad this summer.'

'Well, what was I supposed to do? Miss your wedding? You'd never let me live that down.'

'I'm just telling you, Mom—'

'You're in no position to tell anyone anything, Milo.'

'Fair enough.' I sighed and gently took the cup from her. 'Have a rest, Mother.'

She lay back on the bunk and closed her eyes. I sat on the floor, as always, the dutiful son at her side, listening to the train pull away from the station.

My thoughts growing ever darker.

Once twenty minutes had passed and I was sure Mother was asleep, I took her large foot-wash tub, which she'd carted with her all the way from New York, and quietly exited the compartment.

The corridor outside was nearly empty, only a few children at the other end of the car looking out of the window at the rising terrain of the Carpathian foothills. I went in the opposite direction, to the public toilet, stepped inside, and filled the washtub to the brim with water. I felt its weightiness, the water shifting from side to side with the train's every shudder. A glance in the mirror and I discerned weight of a different character, one of consequence, of pending fate. *Mother or Vika*. Who gave me more pleasure? I couldn't live with both. And Mother might linger another twenty years...

A man has his rights.

With a remorseful sigh, I returned to my cabin. Mother slept on.

I set the washtub at the foot of her bunk. Next, I withdrew a pair of scissors from our luggage and an ice-cream packet from its plastic bag

I carefully cut out the large, semicircular dry-ice coolant bar from the packet's bottom and set it on the cabin table.

Mother stirred, coughed a bit. I waited her out.

When she was again restful, I removed five more dry-ice bars from their packaging and placed them with the first. Then I closed the window and, taking an old Cornell University t-shirt from my things, I rolled it up and set it along the bottom of the cabin door.

With the window shut and the door draught blocked, the room's already sweltering temperature quickly rose. Perspiration rolled over my brow and dripped off my nose as I worked, my shirt growing damp and stained.

With something between a prayer and a wish, I dropped the first dry-ice semicircle in the washtub, then the second, and watched the white clouds rise to fill the lower half of the cabin. By the third dry-ice bar, the tub's water had nearly evaporated, and I had to use every last litre bottle of Bon Aqua as I fed it bars four, five and six.

The mist thickened. I could barely see Mother on the bunk, but I could hear her coughs as her frail lungs tried to pull usable oxygen through the clouds. I climbed up to my own bunk, up with the free air that had been pushed higher by the heavy dry-ice clouds. There I waited and listened.

Her coughing grew hoarser, more violent. I thought of my boyhood. I thought of Vika, of sex and money.

I awaited freedom.

My gold-plated birthday watch, the one with the digital display, said the temperature in the sealed cabin was 111° Fahrenheit and rising. At 115°, Mother's gasps and explosive coughs reached their apex. I thought I heard her call my name. Or maybe it was only my conscience speaking…

By 122° Fahrenheit both Mother and conscience were silent.

I waited another ten minutes, then climbed down and checked the body.

No pulse. Eyes dilated. A perfect smothering.

Emancipation.

I'm not certain I truly thought in the next few minutes. I only reacted, mindlessly following the plan I'd imagined a thousand times before. I opened the window to air out the cabin, and when the clouds were dispersed, I lifted the t-shirt from the bottom of the door and stuffed it into the luggage.

Taking the washtub, and shutting the compartment door securely behind me, I followed the corridor again to the toilet, passing a young woman in a flower-print dress carrying a little dog. She smiled but said nothing. Inside the restroom, I emptied the remaining water into the toilet bowl and washed the tub clean of any film with paper towels. Then I flushed the towels and water down the vacuum of the train's drain and returned to my cabin.

That first foray into my new murderous reality exhausted me. Several contemplative minutes passed before I found any strength for further action. When I did, I dumped the ice-cream packets out the window casually, one by one over a half-hour. Let them be lost forever in the Ukrainian wilderness.

I scoured the cabin for anything I'd missed.

Empty water bottles? Not suspicious in this heat.

A pair of scissors? Nothing unusual. Still, I slipped them into a pocket of the luggage. Why answer questions about what I was cutting?

I looked through the plastic bag, discovered a receipt for ice cream and had just thrown both bag and receipt out the window when a knock came at the cabin door.

I shut the window, gave a last glance around the room, calmed my nerves then answered the door.

It was the young woman I'd passed in the corridor earlier, her dog down on a leash, a chocolate bar in her hand.

'Would you like a sweet?' she asked in accented English, a smile on her pleasant, twenty-something face.

'A sweet?'

'I saw that your ice cream had spoiled. So I thought you'd enjoy a chocolate bar.'

'My ice cream spoiled?' She'd seen me eject the last packet … seen it from her cabin window … or the dining car…

OK, OK, I was a litterbug. What of it?

I willed my pulse to slow, answered her in a whisper. 'Please excuse us. My mother is sleeping. Would you mind coming back later?'

'Oh. I'm sorry. Forgive—'

'No trouble. And take your pet…' I pointed down. Her dog – a toy beagle – had curled up on the floor at our feet.

The woman laughed loosely, her hand on my shoulder. 'He likes it here. Pocket beagles can sense kind-hearted people, you know.' She bent down and picked up the dog. 'Maybe he'll drag me back to you one day.'

'Another time,' I said firmly.

'Enjoy the chocolate.'

'Thank you. Good day.'

I slid the door shut. Locked it.

I released a long breath. Well done, Milo. The first conversation was over, though it had shredded my nerves. Again, I searched the room, checking for any final detail that had escaped me. All looked clear. I scooted the washtub below Mother's bunk, then with a bit of inspiration, pulled off her colourful stockings, shoved them into a bag overhead and sprinkled droplets of water over her feet from the remnants in my last Bon Aqua bottle.

Done.

With my preparations complete, I relaxed, ate the chocolate bar the stranger had left and dumped its wrapper out the window.

One had to be consistent.

At last, I pooled my courage for the penultimate moment. I reclosed the window, let the temperature rise again, then threw open the cabin door and shouted: 'Help! Help! Someone, please … my mother … she's not breathing!'

A buzz of Ukrainian voices filled the corridor, faces popping out of every cabin door.

I screamed again. 'Please! Somebody help us!'

Porter Panchenko came running up the corridor.

'It's my mother,' I cried, my voice cracking. 'She won't wake up.'

The hefty porter shoved his girth into the compartment and bent over my mother on the bunk. For several minutes, Panchenko examined her, muttering sad-sounding words in Ukrainian. At last he said in thick English, 'The heat has claimed another one.'

I thrust my face into my hands. 'It's my fault, my fault. She has allergies and emphysema. And I had the window shut…'

'Mr Capela, don't blame yourself. This happens all the time with older passengers. There are warnings in the stations for those over sixty not to travel on days over thirty centigrade.'

'I can confirm the heat was stifling, porter,' said a feminine voice. The stranger with the beagle appeared in the doorway. 'My dog collapsed when I visited this cabin not half an hour ago. I had to lift the poor little thing out, didn't I, Mr…'

'Capela. Milo Capela,' I said between sobs.

'Beagles are well-suited to high temperatures, Porter Panchenko. They're among the most heat-tolerant of all canines. To affect my dog in mere seconds, I'd guess the room was what, Milo? Forty degrees centigrade? The dog lapped up a quarter-litre of water as soon as I got back to my own cabin.'

My opinion of the woman changed drastically. Perhaps she was helpful after all.

The porter sighed. 'It's a tragedy all too common this time of year. I'm sorry for your loss, Mr Capela. There's nothing we can do until we reach the Mukacheve station, I'm afraid.' He offered me his hand then, unsure of American customs during a tragedy, sheepishly retracted it. 'Unfortunately, every cabin in the train is occupied. If you don't wish to travel with the deceased I can offer you only the porter's booth.'

'No one should be alone when losing a parent,' said the woman. 'He can stay in my cabin, if he wishes, Porter Panchenko. You'll remember my colleague missed the train and left an open spot.'

'Thank you, miss,' I said. 'I may take you up on that offer. But for the moment I wish to be by myself. This is so … so … shocking.'

'Of course. If you need me I'm in berth sixty-four, two doors down in this car.'

'Thank you.'

The woman placed a gentle hand on my forearm. 'She wouldn't want you to grieve, Mr Capela. Life is for the living. Your mother is waiting for you in a better place.'

'If I need you, I'll come.'

She disappeared from the doorway. Porter Panchenko reiterated his condolences, then told me he'd return shortly with some paperwork.

Soon, I was alone.

So far, so good…

I shut the cabin door. Took a Valium. Changed my shirt. I considered texting Vika, but it occurred to me that the beagle lady was quite attractive.

How sympathetic might she be to a man who'd suddenly lost his mother? European sexual morals, after all … I put on some cologne.

Leaving Mother to her fate, I set out for berth sixty-four. I found the door open. The woman sat inside, reading a Rankin novel, her dog curled up on the floor at her feet. She'd changed out of her dress into casual jeans and a form-fitting black t-shirt with 'Miss Quote' across the breast.

'Hello,' I said, rapping on the door frame. 'Is that invitation still open?'

She looked up from her reading and smiled. 'It is.'

Her cabin was larger than ours, with a full-sized twin bed on each wall. I sat across from her, the pocket beagle jumping up onto my lap.

'He likes you.'

'Yes,' I said, scratching the dog's head. 'Very friendly. How old is he?'

'I'm not exactly sure. Young I think…'

'And his name?'

'You wouldn't be able to pronounce it.'

I smiled. 'How long have you had him?'

'A week. I solved a murder on a tour bus in Kiev. This little fellow was a gift from the victim's family. I'm headed to Bratislava now. I don't know what I'm going to do with him at the EU border. I hope they'll let me take him through.'

'Solved a murder, you say?'

'Yes. And not my first, frankly. I'm a journalist. Trouble follows me everywhere.'

'A nice girl like you?'

'Not so nice. You don't know me.'

I felt my pulse rise in an unexpected way. 'Are you famous? Should I ask your name? Or is it something else I couldn't pronounce?'

'Santa Ezeriņa.'

'Santa Ezeriņa. Did I get the Ukrainian right?'

'It's not Ukrainian. I'm Latvian. Don't get your Eastern Europeans mixed up. Balts are not Slavs. You'll offend us if you do. Have you never been to Rīga?'

'No. Should I?'

'Everyone should go to Rīga at least once. You may never go home.'

'What brings you to Ukraine – besides murder?'

'Journalism, in theory. My colleague came on assignment and I tagged along. Of course, she met a boy, decided to take another train and left me all alone. Typical of Līva.' Santa crossed her legs and rubbed a knee as if it troubled her. 'It's my first time in western Ukraine, that's why I was looking out of the window at the beautiful Carpathian uplands when I saw you throw out all those ice-cream packets. I counted six…'

'Six, yes. But how did you know it was me?'

'The gold watch on the wrist of the discarding hand. I observed you wearing it in the car's corridor when you were carrying that tub to the dining car.'

'To the toilet actually. I'd just washed my mother's feet and wanted to pour the dirty water into the sink.'

'What was wrong with the ice cream?'

'Spoiled. I was saving the rest for later, but the first was so disgusting that I didn't even risk the other packets. Ejected them all, as you observed.'

'Ukrainian ice cream always spoils. But in Rīga … Oh, I'm sounding like a tour guide…'

Her voice trailed off and we sat for several moments listening to the chug of the train in the growing altitude. Finally she said: 'I'm sorry to bring up the tragedy of the evening, Milo, but given the rancid quality of the ice cream, have you considered that perhaps it was food poisoning that took your mother's life?'

'Mother didn't have any.'

'Maybe she had a taste while you were taking the foot tub to the toilet? Or simply had your back turned?'

'A taste wouldn't be enough to make her ill, much less kill her.'

'Forgive me. I was only looking out for you. As a journalist, the stories I've heard about what is found in food in this part of the world .. well, it would make your skin crawl. I did a story in Tallinn about what a woman discovered *still living* in her pecan yogurt. Ninety thousand euros she received in the settlement…'

'We have enough money, thank you, Miss Ezeriņa.'

'You and your mother?'

'Me and my fiancée in Uzhhorod, now.'

'I see.'

My attraction to this 'murder-solving' journalist had waned. I set the beagle on the cushion next to me and got to my feet. 'I should be going. There'll be a lot to do about Mother. I just wanted to thank you for the support with the porter. And the chocolate bar, of course.'

'You're welcome, Milo. You seem to be holding up well. I only wish I could do more.'

'Have a pleasant journey.'

I left berth sixty-four and headed back to my cabin. I discovered the door open and Porter Panchenko waiting inside, holding a folder full of papers.

'Mr Capela,' he said as I entered, 'we'll be arriving at Mukacheve in thirty-five minutes. I should tell you what will happen. At that station, the police will come on board, as will a medical official, a doctor named Zima. He'll do an examination of the body and you'll formally identify the deceased. A death certificate will be issued and the police will submit—'

'No autopsy?'

'Not unless you request one. Or the doctor or police feel there are unusual circumstances. In this heat, sad as I am to say it, we lose an elderly traveller twice a month. I'd be surprised if the examination and paperwork took fifteen minutes. I did the same for a Moldovan gentleman on Sunday. The procedure went so quickly we left the station on time. Not a second's delay. No less tragic, of course.'

'Of course. Tragic.'

He withdrew a document from his folder and held out a pen. 'I you'll sign here, sir, we'll provide for transportation of the remains t any Ukrainian city with an international airport. You can then fly hom to America with the body, if that is your intention.'

'What am I signing exactly?'

'That you won't sue our company, sir. That all involved accept tha this death was a result of natural causes with no party at fault.'

'Can we say "natural causes" before the doctor's evaluation, Porte Panchenko?'

'As I said, sir, two deaths a month…'

I took the pen and signed.

He seemed relieved. 'I'll have an English copy printed out for yo at the station, Mr Capela. The death certificate too. With the bilingua papers, you should have no difficultly leaving Ukraine or retrieving th remains in America. These are international documents accepted by a countries.'

'Thank you, Porter Panchenko.' I handed the pen and documen back to him.

'It's heartbreaking that these things happen, sir. I wish the procedur weren't quite so routine.' He bowed and went out of the door.

I laughed internally. A doctor's certificate in English saying 'death b natural causes' and clearance back to America. With no siblings, aunt or uncles to question anything.

The perfect murder.

I shut the cabin door. Texted Vika the single letter: 'V'

V for Vika. V for victory. V for vindication.

I'd never been so happy.

I was dreaming a strange dream – about Freud talking backwards – when a knocking on the cabin door awakened me. I slid off the top bunk, careful not to disturb Mother on the lower one, and stumbled groggily to the door.

The knocking repeated.

I slid open the panel. 'Yes, Porter Panchenko…'

It was Santa Ezeriņa. 'I'm sorry to bother you, Milo,' she said. 'But we might consider more seriously the food poisoning possibility. I no longer believe your mother's death was temperature-related. It simply wasn't as hot in this cabin as we thought.'

I patted my bed-head hair into place. 'Miss Ezeriņa, you're quite the fussbudget…'

'Hear my reasoning, Milo. You washed your mother's feet to cool them, yes? And afterwards, she put her stockings back on. If it was sweltering, I don't think she would do that. She'd want her feet to remain open to the air.'

'You are mistaken. Mother didn't put them back on. Look, they're off now.'

Her eyes didn't stray from mine. 'They were on when I visited your cabin while she slept, Milo. That was after you'd emptied the washtub. She wore rainbow stockings, unusual for an older woman. I remember them clearly. And I can see by your face that you do too.'

'No … no … they were lying on the bed by her, not worn. And it was boiling hot, Miss Ezeriņa. After all, your dog swooned.'

'There are many reasons why a toy beagle might swoon.'

'Such as?'

'Gas.'

'Gas?'

'These old, Soviet-era trains reek of diesel fumes. This could affect a little dog.'

'Please, enough.' My voice turned harsher. 'You've many wild theories, Miss Ezeriņa. Diesel fumes. Food poisoning. What imagination! You'll blame extraterrestrials next. Now, have some respect for a son in mourning and kindly leave me in peace.'

'Insist on an autopsy when the authorities come aboard, Milo. Have them check the stomach and lungs, blood and body tissues. I can help you communicate if you want. I speak fluent Russian and some Ukrainian.'

'I think I've "communicated" with you all I want, Miss Ezeriņa.' I began to shut the door.

She caught its edge. 'Milo, if there's any reason you'd fill a washtub other than to wash feet, you need to tell me now. It'll be better for all of us.'

I forced the door closed. Locked the bolt.

I paced the cabin, feeling the vibrations of the car beneath my feet. For the first time, I avoided looking at Mother.

What did Santa Ezeriņa know? Nothing. Just a sleazy reporter, grasping at straws for a story.

Still…

I called Vika. It went to voicemail. I redialled. Voicemail again. I left a message. Tried to relax, rest.

When at last my beloved called back, Vika's first words were: 'Did she suffer?'

'No.'

A pause. 'She should have suffered after all she's done to you.'

'Listen, sweetie. There's a change of plans. Is your Schengen visa still valid? … Good. Find us a flight tonight to the EU. Doesn't matter where. Budapest, Warsaw, Rome. We're eloping, getting out of Ukraine … No, the body too. You'll need to arrange it with the airline … Use Mother's credit-card number. Price isn't a factor anymore.'

A fresh knocking at the cabin door.

'Santa Ezeriņa!' I shouted. 'If that's you, go away … No, no, sweetie, I'm alone. Just a nosey girl … I assure you she's not even attractive … Please, sweetie, just get the tickets. I gotta go … Yeah, everything's all right. Love you too.' I ended the call.

The knocking repeated. Harder.

'Miss Ezeriņa,' I said through the door, 'if you're here to harass me further, I'll be alerting the porter.'

'This *is* the porter,' replied a masculine voice.

'Oh.' I unbolted the door and slid it open.

Outside stood Porter Panchenko, a fresh document in his hands, a slightly sour expression on his face.

'What is this?' I asked.

'Your "request for post mortem" form, sir. I can help you fill it out if— "

'A post mortem?' An autopsy? You said no autopsy!'

'The young woman in berth sixty-four asked for it on your behalf. She said you were confused by our procedures.'

'No! No! No!' I plucked the form from his hand, tore it up and threw it back at him, the pieces raining down and sticking to the sweat stains on his plump body. 'There's no confusion. And no autopsy. Do you understand my English?'

'Only trying to assist, sir,' he said, brushing the paper from his uniform, then stooping to pick up the litter.

'You can assist by letting me grieve in solitude. And fulfilling our agreement.'

'Yes, sir.' He turned abruptly and headed up the corridor, growling something in his mysterious language.

I stood in the doorway tempering my anger. When rage passed and reason resumed, I stepped into the corridor and slid the panel shut behind me. I had to nip this inquisitive reporter's interference in the bud before we arrived at the station and the doctor came aboard. Frankly I didn't trust I'd be able to stay reserved if she asked pestering questions in front of authorities.

I found her door open, Santa Ezeriņa sitting on her bunk, stroking her little pet. Ernest Blofeld came to mind.

'Come in, Milo.'

Her dog jumped down to greet me. I ignored it, remaining in the doorway. 'I wanted to let you know, Miss Ezeriņa – Santa – that I've taken your advice on the autopsy issue. No need for your kind assistance. I called America. The best pathologist in Manhattan will examine Mother on Tuesday afternoon when I arrive with the body.'

'You'll miss that appointment by twenty years or more, I'd say.'

'What? What do you mean?'

'You'll be in a Ukrainian prison unless the US government seeks your extradition, which is unlikely once the facts are known.'

'Are you accusing me of some crime, Miss Ezeriņa?'

'Only matricide. The autopsy, performed in this country, will show excessive carbon dioxide in your mother's lungs and blood. Not poisonous, but in enough volume to indicate inert gas asphyxiation in a confined space. Am I wrong?'

Sharp pains shot through my stomach and I had to lean hard against the door frame to keep from trembling. 'As I said, Santa, you've got quite a perverse imagination. Previously you thought it was food poisoning.'

'Food poisoning was a ruse to test your resistance to an autopsy. No imagination was needed, however, when I kneeled to pick up my dog on my first visit to your cabin and smelled the sour scent of dry-ice gas, i.e., carbon dioxide. I knew then. Sublimated carbon-dioxide gas is heavier than air, Milo; opening the window dispersed it in the cabin above, but let invisible traces linger at floor level. That is why the beagle grew lethargic.' She shrugged. 'It was a simple matter to deduce where it came from on a train: the mixing of the coolant from the discarded ice cream and water in a washtub that was never used on feet. In that tiny compartment, six bars were enough to smother your sick mother as surely as if you'd thrown a pillow across her face. You gambled on murder, and for now, you've won.'

'Well, this is a perfectly disgusting theory. You reporters will make up anything for a story. But you've no evidence to detain me or the body. Those ice-cream packets are lost in the wilderness. By the time you find them – if you find them – I'll be in another country, Mother long cremated.'

Santa lifted her iPhone from the cabin table. On the phone's screen was a waifish woman, casually dressed, with long, Michelle Phillips hair to her waist. She stood in hilly grasslands alongside a set of railroad tracks, a *Витчизна* strawberry-banana ice-cream tub in her hands. Santa swiped to the next image, a close-up of the packet, the opened and empty cavity meant for a dry-ice bar clearly visible.

I felt suddenly dizzy.

'Your mistake was throwing the packets out the window sequentially. By the fourth packet, I found it curious enough to use the GPS on my phone to record the locations. My colleague's train is an hour behind ours. When your mother was discovered dead, I sent the last three packets' coordinates to Līva, had her get off at the nearest spot. She's already found two. Your fingerprints will be on these and the coolant has clearly been removed,' said Santa. 'For what purpose, Milo?'

A kind of palsy seized me, my hands shaking with rage as I pointed at her screen. 'You and your friend are doctoring those yourselves ...

for your newspaper. It's your word versus mine … The police will never believe you…'

Santa sighed and flipped to the next image: a man stood in the same hillscape, the same ice-cream tub in his hands. 'This is Līva's beau, First Lieutenant Andrey Karpanko of the Dnieper Homicide Department. They met in Kiev when I solved the bus murder. They're inseparable now; they're even travelling this way in a private train compartment – "The Honeymoon Cabin".' She smiled sardonically. 'Līva always did have a thing for men in uniform. I think they'll have more influence with the police than you. And in Ukraine influence matters as much as evidence. Perhaps more.'

I stepped quickly into the cabin, the dog yipping at my shins.

Santa slipped the phone safely into her pocket. 'No, Milo. Līva and Andrey know everything and it's all in the cloud anyway.'

'What do you want? Money?'

'Justice,' she said bluntly. 'To murder the one who gave you life, Milo? I know seven languages yet have no words for what you've become. Maybe there is a tongue somewhere with something worse than "satanic". Or perhaps we'll coin a term just for you.'

I reached into my pocket, nearly stumbling as the train decelerated as it approached the station. 'I've fifty dollars here. And another two thousand in my mother's bag. You, Līva, Lieutenant Karpanko, can split it. It's yours. With more, much more, when I get the inheritance.'

'Do you have enough for them too?' She nodded towards the window.

The train pulled up to the Mukacheve platform. I dropped my money in horror. A dozen uniformed policemen stood waiting, some with dogs, others in body armour sporting automatic weapons. The flashing blue lights of police cars parked nearby gave the scene a deeply surreal glow.

'With the militant problems in Ukraine these days, they take no chances with reports of killings on public transport,' said Santa. 'We called ahead.'

She picked up the beagle and set it in her lap. 'I'd be careful in the way you move. The Ukrainian phrase "*Stiy, ya budu strilyatu*" means "Halt, I will shoot", Milo. Just so you know…'

The Spoils

William Ryan

Stacy Kropotkin sat behind her desk, her pale face mirrored in its polished surface. The desk was wide and empty of clutter, except for a small bronze statue of Minerva, Roman goddess of wisdom. The dealer Stacy had bought it from – for a lot of money – had told her it was a genuine antiquity. Stacy liked it. It was attractive. It signalled wisdom.

'This isn't easy for me,' Stacy said, with a pained smile.

Of course, the statue wasn't an antiquity. It was a fake. A bad fake. Which was probably not the statement Stacy wanted to make.

'Really?' I said.

Stacy was sad. Poor Stacy. I should have felt sorry for her. I didn't. Her pained smile flattened out. Perhaps now we could get past the bullshit.

'After all, we've worked together for a long time,' she said. 'We're friends. Neighbours.'

This was true. And because I knew her as well as I did, I also knew, with absolute certainty, that Stacy Kropotkin was savouring this moment.

Well, let her.

I waited. One minute. Two. I guessed Stacy was waiting for me to speak next. I didn't much want to but I had to pick up Sally from her basketball practice. I didn't want to be late for that on top of everything else that was going wrong with today. Anyhow, Stacy's sad-puppy face was making me nauseous.

'Shall we do this?' I said and wondered how long it would take her to mention her recent elevation to partner.

'You know The Firm has to make difficult decisions sometimes. Neither I nor any of the other partners take any pleasure from this.'

Not long.

She shook her head slowly, as if I was somehow to blame. As if it was my fault that I hadn't slept with Brad Schmidt at the Reno conference. Because if I'd done that then I could have been the one sitting behind the big desk instead of her. But I hadn't. And she had.

My mistake. I'd just have to live with it.

'Spit it out, Stacy. I've got to be somewhere.'

She looked surprised, then reached into the desk drawer where she'd had the file waiting. The HR files were always green. She placed it in front of her, tapped it twice, as though she were reluctant, then slid it across the table. She left it just out of my reach, so I had to lean forwards to pick it up. It was deliberate. She had probably measured the distance.

I opened the file. It contained a letter – addressed to me.

'You'll find we've been very generous,' Stacy said.

That, at least, was probably true.

After all, I knew enough about The Firm to put Stacy and the other partners in a federal penitentiary for a very long time.

'You knew it was coming,' Doug said. 'Once she made partner instead of you.'

Doug was right – but he could have dressed it up a little. I looked him over. His jowls and his gut. The way the extra weight had started to push in around the ice-blue eyes that had drawn me to him. Other women said he was still handsome, but I'd been looking at him for a long time and it was hard for me to tell for sure.

'It's the way it works. Winner takes all. It's partner or out. You know that.'

'I didn't lose, Doug. She won, yes. But I didn't lose.'

I'd lost, all right, but a girl was allowed a little grieving time. Twenty years I'd put into The Firm – only to get cut just as the goose was about to crap golden eggs. Twenty fucking years. Two less than I'd put into Doug; but he was different. I don't curse much but – seriously? Twenty fucking years? And all because Stacy gave Brad Schmidt head in a Reno poolside cabana?

'It's nothing personal, Amanda. It's business.'

But it wasn't *just* business. And it sure as hell *was* personal. When Stacy Kropotkin came back from Reno she'd called me the moment she landed and told me about that damn poolside cabana. Oh, she'd been crying and wailing and saying how she'd made a terrible mistake, and what would she do if Jack found out, and how she was a terrible wife, and how she'd been drinking. Every word had been bullshit, bullshit, bullshit. Because Stacy knew, and I knew, that she'd won. Right there. Right at that moment when Brad had dropped his towel and she'd dropped to her knees.

And she'd wanted me to be the first to know. From her.

And she wanted me to know why I'd lost as well – that when it came down to it, Brad Schmidt's dick decided who got the first partnership to come up in three fucking years.

To the victor the spoils.

'I'm already past it,' I said. 'I've moved on. It is what it is.'

'I know it's hard. But you've got to tough it out. About tomorrow? We could cancel but, you know…'

'It wouldn't look good?'

'I think we should go. It's not just about The Firm.'

This was the problem. Stacy and Jack were our *friends*. Our kids went to the same school. Their daughter was upstairs in our son's bedroom, at that very moment. Probably giving him head.

She took after Stacy.

Whether I liked it or not, I was going to see a whole lot of Stacy Kropotkin over the next while. It would be a couple of years, maybe more, before Stacy and Jack would move to the Lakeside mansion. All the other partners did. Just like it would be a couple of years, maybe more, before we'd have to 'downsize', or however we dressed it up.

Brad Schmidt's dick.

'It will be fun,' I said.

We were sitting on the porch, watching the empty street. Nothing ever happened in River Hills, and people paid a lot of money to keep it that way. The only movement was generated by a sprinkler on the lawn. It made jagged rainbows out of the last of the sun.

I should never have let Doug talk me into moving to the same gated community as the Kropotkins.

I should have remembered that, sooner or later, it would be winner takes all between Stacy and me.

We were dining at the country club, like we were most Saturdays. Jack and Doug had been drinking whiskey sours in the bar since four and were starting to slur their words. Stacy had a new necklace – a diamond the size of a cockroach. She thought she deserved it.

I had a migraine. The wine wasn't helping it much.

'I guess you'll be working pretty close with Brad from now on,' I said, allowing my gaze to stray towards Jack. He was talking to Doug about a baseball game they'd watched. They'd forgotten we were here.

'I don't think so,' Stacy said. 'I made a proposal to the partners last week and I've just heard back. I'll be running a special project. My own team. Brad wanted oversight but the other partners want it independent.'

I raised my glass in tribute. I knew better than to ask what kind of special project. The Firm was discreet – but we weren't off the radar. The Feds kept tabs on us. Just like we did on them. We didn't discuss shit in public that could get us jail time.

'Brad was becoming a problem,' she continued. 'It's better this way.'

His dick had served its purpose – he could have it back now. I raised my glass once again. She smiled and I couldn't help myself smiling back. She was good. Very good.

'What about you?' she said.

'I've seen a few recruitment people, made a few calls. And taken some as well. There are opportunities, but I'm in no rush. It's Matt's last year in high school and Sally will be sixteen in June. I haven't been there much the last few years. I could spend some time at home, I think.'

Doug and Jack were still talking but I could tell Doug was listening now. That interested me. We hadn't talked as a couple about my plans as yet. I'd been the main earner since he'd been let go by Klein & Lynch two years back. He still pulled in money from consultancy and whatnot, but I doubted it would be enough if I wasn't earning. I thought about that and wondered how much he made from the consulting. He'd been on edge since I'd told him about The Firm. I'd left the money side of things to him the last few years, since he'd been at home with time on his hands. He'd looked after the tax returns, insurance, investments and pensions. He had access to everything. But I was only aware of, at best, half the picture.

That would have to be rectified.

'I need a cigarette,' I said, pushing back my chair. 'Jack, you want to keep me company?'

We all went along with the story that I was the only smoker out of the four of us. It was easier that way.

Outside, as Jack dipped his head to bring his cigarette close my lighter, I found myself looking back into the restaurant. I saw my husband, his eyes smiling, reach his hand across the table to touch Stacy's. I thought at first that he was reassuring her about something. But no. He was congratulating her. On her victory. Over me.

And he liked her. He liked her a lot.

And the thing was, I'd known this for some time.

I just hadn't realised it.

We had a new neighbour that summer – Angela Romano. Not her real name. I liked her; Stacy didn't – for the same reason, I was pretty sure.

When you work for The Firm, you meet people like Angela. That was what The Firm did – help people like Angela do what they do. Or, in Angela's case, did.

I missed people like Angela. I missed the way they looked at every object, every situation, every person as an opportunity. How nothing is as important in a decision as the balance of risk and reward. Criminals are the purest of capitalists. At The Firm you learned early that morality is a hindrance to success – that money is just about the only pure measure of anything.

Brad Schmidt, before he started thinking with his dick, used to say this to us: 'A dollar is a dollar. It's a unit of currency – not a page from the fucking bible.'

He made a good point.

Anyhow, Angela was funny and charming, but her eyes were always moving, her brain was always working, and I knew, from the first moment I met her, that she was not a florist by choice. And I knew I saw a reaction when I told her I worked at The Firm. She tried to hide it but she knew who we were and that we didn't just do tax returns for small businesses.

I was careful around her at first. If she was here, in this community, running a florist business that clearly didn't make anything like enough money, then it was because somewhere, sometime, somehow she'd given the Feds what they wanted. And this was the Feds looking after her.

Maybe Stacy knew what Angela had done before she'd ended up in River Hills. It didn't matter. The fact was, if you ran Angela Romano's barcode through a checkout it would come up 'Mob'.

Which didn't bother me. We all do what we have to when it comes to putting food on the table. And working at The Firm didn't give me much moral high ground, even if I cared a damn. What was more, I liked her. She was easy company. I discovered I could be relaxed around her. There was no need to pretend to be anyone else but me. And after eighteen years of being a mom, that was a relief.

We became friends.

And because I liked Angela, when she asked me to propose her to the country club, I did. But, because Stacy *didn't* like Angela, she killed the application – and made sure Angela knew it.

Which I did not think was a good move on Stacy's part.

Anyhow, if we couldn't play golf out at the country club, we could do something else.

The first time I took Angela to Scott's range, she was surprised. I take shooting seriously. She understood this when I opened the trunk.

'Holy shit.'

The weapons were cased – but there were a few of them.

'You can use whatever you like. Except the Remington. It's been adapted for me.'

There were twelve weapons in total. Everything from a Hudson H9 up to an AR 15 assault rifle. And then there was the Remington MSR – my joy. It cost as much as a new BMW, but it was worth it. Angela ran a hand along the cases, very carefully. She respected guns, I could see.

'You can use these?'

I smiled at her. She had no fucking idea.

The thing I like about Scott's range is that it has everything – a two-hundred-yard distance range for longer guns, as well as shorter ranges for the pistols. He also has a tactical range that offers something more realistic. I always save that for last. But best of all was the outside range out back that only a select few of his shooters even know about. It's the longest in New England, so Scott says, and perfect for the MSR. Plus Scott allowed me to shoot .388 Lapua Magnum ammunition out there.

Which is nice of him.

I like to shoot the Remington MSR fresh. Scott came out of his office to watch me. He spotted for me as I adjusted for range and conditions. Then I fired six bullets in quick succession. I knew the grouping was tight.

Scott handed the binoculars to Angela.

'Holy shit.'
A playing card would have covered all six strikes.

Scott did three tours with the Green Berets in Afghanistan and, when he laid out the tactical range, he'd had a professional clientele in mind. Scott and Angela followed me as I moved through it. Bad guy: shoot. Civilian: don't shoot. Scott had changed it round since my last visit and he'd ramped up the reaction times.

I flowed.

Target – shot to chest, shot to head. Move. New target, same again. The gun was hot but my mind was cold.

Fuck golf.

When I was finished, it was silent – except for the sound of the last brass cartridge tumbling across the concrete floor.

I looked round at Scott, who smiled. You didn't see Scott smile often. I could almost hear his lips cracking with the unexpected strain. Angela was also smiling but there was a kind of calculation in the way she looked around at the flattened targets.

'Holy shit.'

I breathed in deeply, sucking the cordite into my lungs. I felt good. In control. I missed being in control.

Scott lifted up the final target I'd knocked down. A little girl with a balloon. I'd punctured the balloon with my last shot.

Scott chuckled. 'Showing off?'

'Maybe,' I said, and nodded to Angela.

I don't know why I nodded to her. Why I wanted her to know just how fucking good I was. Maybe I just knew. Sometimes fate puts two people together.

Angela was quiet on the drive back to River Hills. I guess we'd reached that stage where we didn't need to fill silences between us. It began to rain and the wipers squealed across the windscreen. My shoulders hurt, but in a good way. I smiled. Here I was, less than a week after leaving The Firm, and I was relaxed – happy to be in this moment. Maybe Stacy getting the job instead of me had been a good thing after all.

I smiled again. Maybe not though.

When Angela spoke, it was a practical question: 'What goes through your mind when you shoot?'

'Nothing. Shooting is a series of problems and challenges that you don't have to think about. You just do it. I like that.'

Out of the corner of my eye, I saw the slight nod she gave. She wasn't surprised by the answer. She'd expected it. I wondered where she was going with this.

'And what do you feel – when you shoot?'

'I feel nothing. Emotion would complicate something that needs to be simple.'

'You can do that? Shut down your emotions?'

'I can step back from them – when I need to. When decisions need to be made. When things need to be done. You know how it is.'

Another pause, while she considered this. 'The way you shoot is … well, it's exceptional. Beautiful even. But let me ask you this: if you were in a different situation, if the bad guys were real, if you or your family was under threat, if you had to make a decision – them or you – do you think you could do it? Press that trigger? Wouldn't emotion play a factor?'

'Most decisions are an attempt to shape the future. I wouldn't shoot someone unless I thought the consequences of not shooting them would be worse than if I did.'

'But, by that logic, if there were no consequences and some reward, then you'd blow someone away?'

I considered this. 'There are always consequences. Anyhow, this is a conversation about hypotheticals – you can't know what way you'll go until the choices are there.'

Angela said nothing more.

I thought it had been an interesting conversation.

When the kids were younger I had some software installed on the family computers by a young man called TJ Milbank; I wanted to make sure they were safe. I thought it best if Doug didn't know about my concerns – he'd only have worried and, now I was checking in on them, he didn't need to. And, anyway, the way the software worked, I was able to check up on him as well. And who really wants to know that every key stroke they make might be monitored?

As it happened, I hadn't monitored anything of Doug's – I hadn't felt I'd needed to. But now I was curious about the state of our joint finances. And now I entered Doug's world.

That he liked to watch porn wasn't exactly a surprise. There were some variations that I hadn't anticipated – clearly there had been more to the male bonding in his fraternity house than I'd been led to believe – but most of it was pretty straight.

The gambling was something I hadn't anticipated. At least, not in the amounts he had been risking. So far, the damage was minimal. He had been lucky. By which I mean, he should have lost more. A lot more.

What kind of asshole bets on basketball spreads when he doesn't even watch basketball? My husband, it would seem.

The consultancy work? There wasn't any. There was golf with Jack. And squash with Sam. But there wasn't much that paid money. And what there was of that was done badly.

Doug had been an investment banker with Klein & Lynch for twenty years and now I knew why they'd let him go.

The worst of it was that his incompetence extended to our investments.

I blamed myself. I had a husband who liked to roll the dice and didn't know when to quit. I had trusted him. I had been a fool.

I had some thinking to do. I drove to the beach and took off my shoes and walked in the sand. The water was cold and there was a strong breeze. I could feel the salt drying on my skin.

I had to make a decision. But before I did that, there were some things I needed to know.

I drove back home and accessed Doug's email. I found the messages he'd exchanged with Stacy. I read them. There were a lot. They were intimate. They spoke about the things they did to each other. I could handle that. If they were having an affair, they were going to be fucking each other. That was logical.

But they also spoke about me sometimes. It was clear that Stacy didn't much like me. It was clear that Doug went along with things. But Stacy instigated them.

I thought about Stacy. About her affair with Doug. About how she spoke about me and how she spoke about him in those emails. She was noncommittal with him. But she was not noncommittal when it came to me. It seemed to me that Stacy Kropotkin had most likely fucked my husband to get at me.

The following Saturday we met Jack and Stacy for dinner at the country club – same as always. I watched Stacy and Doug. And pretty soon I realised Jack was watching Stacy and Doug also. And, it turned out, me.

'When did you work it out?' he asked me when we went outside for a cigarette.

I didn't ask him what he was talking about. I could see the hurt. 'Not long ago. You?'

'I've known for a while.'

I lit a cigarette and passed it to him. Then lit one for myself. 'Are you going to do something about it?'

He considered the question, inhaling a lungful of nicotine as he did so. 'I haven't decided. You?'

'The same.'

We said nothing for a while. Jack blew perfect smoke rings that hung on that summer evening air like grey shadows.

'I'm sorry,' I said.

'Me too.'

'Doug though? Fucking Doug?' When Jack spoke it was in a low growl. 'I think her fucking him is more about you than Doug. She fucking hates you.'

I sighed.

'I'm sorry,' Jack said. 'That came out wrong.' He stubbed out his cigarette on a marble column, leaving a black smudge, and then dropped the butt onto the gravel.

Normally that would have annoyed me. But I didn't seem to care much that night.

Angela knew about Stacy and Doug. It turned out the reason Stacy didn't like Angela Romano is that she'd let Stacy know she knew. I didn't ask Angela why she hadn't told me. I wouldn't have either.

I went over our finances with a different eye, wondering if they'd stretch to cover two households. Not very well, it turned out. Not if we wanted to put the kids through college. We had stocks; we had two rental properties in Brooklyn but they weren't producing much return; we owned the house outright. In capital terms, we were solid. But income was a problem. And it would be another twenty years before Doug would be getting that fat Klein & Lynch pension.

A thought occurred to me. I looked at the pension terms. I looked at the life insurance policies we had. Then I looked at our expenses.

The thing was, if Doug died suddenly, things looked pretty good again.

I don't know why I looked. Matt was eighteen. He was a confident, attractive young man – he wasn't a boy anymore. I didn't need to worry about him.

But suddenly I knew something wasn't quite right.

It had been going on a while.

Stacy fucking Kropotkin.

I'd seen how Sally had become withdrawn recently and I'd thought it was just a growing-up thing. But when I found out about Stacy and Matt, I thought I'd check it out. I looked at Sally's social media accounts. Someone had been targeting her. Someone who knew a lot about me, and Sally, and Doug, and Matt.

I called up TJ, the guy who installed the software, and asked him to try and trace it.

He did.

I wondered what was the point of it all – Stacy picking apart my family.

I decided to ask her.

We met for a coffee on a Saturday morning. It was unusual for us to meet up, just the two of us, especially since I'd left The Firm.

I watched her as she walked through the room towards the corner table I'd taken. I didn't want us to be overheard. She smiled at me as she sat down. There was a challenge in that smile. And there was pleasure. She wanted me to know. That was the point of it all.

I was going to ask her why, but I didn't. I watched her drink her coffee and she watched me drink mine. We didn't say one fucking word. There wasn't anything to be said.

Eventually she stood up to leave. 'I'm glad we had this conversation,' she said.

I watched her walk away – how her shoulder blades moved under her tight cotton shirt. How vulnerable her pale neck was above the collar.

It was a tragedy. No one could understand how it happened. They were together in a cheap motel room on the other side of town. There was a fire. A gas explosion. They said death was instantaneous. They found Stacy on top of Doug. I believe the position is called 'reverse cowgirl'. The heat was so intense that their bodies fused together. We had to pay the undertaker to cut them apart. He said it was impossible to be certain which bit belonged to who.

So I buried most of Doug and some of Stacy. And Jack did something similar.

Jack and I were thrown together by the deaths. We'd always liked each other. One thing led to the next.

It was a small wedding.

Brad Schmidt came to visit me after a couple of months. He said they had a partnership opening and would I consider it? I looked at Brad and thought of him naked in the poolside cabana in Reno. He asked why I was laughing.

I apologised.

I didn't take the job.

Angela brought me the original fire report from the motel. She explained to me how the accelerant had worked, how the gas leak had been caused by a cut pipe. She explained how the inspector had been paid to overlook these small details.

I said nothing.

She placed the report on the coffee table between us. 'My gift to you. A sign of our friendship.'

I nodded. I knew enough not to say anything. She could be wearing a wire.

'Do you know what I did before?' she said.

I considered the question. I decided it was safe to answer with another. 'Before what?'

'Before I ended up in the programme and they set me up here in River Hills?'

Maybe she didn't need to wear a wire. I'd have TJ come and sweep the house for bugs.

'No.'

'I was a sort of an agent. For people like you.'

'Like me?'

'People with a certain skillset and a certain mental aptitude. You know what I'm talking about.'

I said nothing.

'The thing is,' Angela said, 'I hate fucking flowers. And you're bored. And you have that certain skillset and that mental aptitude.'

I thought about it. I looked around our comfortable lounge area – mostly beige, a lot of natural wood. Elegant. Classy. I guess I was bored, now that Angela brought it to my attention.

'I'm listening,' I said.

About the Authors

Martine Bailey writes about food and mystery and was credited by Fay Weldon as inventing a new genre, the 'culinary gothic'. Her debut in the genre was *An Appetite for Violets*, and while living in New Zealand she wrote *The Penny Heart* (retitled *A Taste for Nightshade* in the US). Martine is an award-winning amateur cook and now lives in Cheshire.

Gordon Brown lives in Scotland but splits his time between the UK and Spain. He's married with two children and has been writing since his teens. So far he has had five books published – his latest, *Darkest Thoughts*, being the first in the Craig McIntyre series. Gordon also helped found Bloody Scotland – Scotland's International Crime Writing Festival.

Paul Charles was born and raised in the Northern Irish countryside. He is the author of the Detective Inspector Christy Kennedy series, set in Camden Town, and the Inspector Starrett series, which is set in Donegal in Ireland. The short mystery in this collection features retired PSNI Detective McCusker from *Down on Cyprus Avenue*. Paul is currently working on a second McCusker novel.

Ann Cleeves began her crime-writing career with a series featuring George and Molly Palmer-Jones, and followed it with books about a cop from the North-East, Inspector Ramsay. More recently she has won international acclaim for two further series, featuring Vera Stanhope and Jimmy Perez, respectively, which have been successfully adapted for television as *Vera* and *Shetland*. *Raven Black* won the CWA Gold Dagger, and in 2017 Ann was awarded the CWA Diamond Dagger.

Julia Crouch has been a theatre director, playwright, drama teacher publicist, graphic/website designer and illustrator. It was while she wa doing an MA in sequential illustration that she realised what she really loved was writing. Her debut novel, *Cuckoo*, was followed by *Every Vow You Break*, *Tarnished*, *The Long Fall* and *Her Husband's Lover*.

Judith Cutler has produced no fewer than five series of crime novel and more than thirty books in all. Her first regular detective was Sophie Rivers, and since then she has featured Fran Harman, Josie Welford Tobias Campion and Lina Townend. She has also published stand alone novels, and is a former secretary of the CWA.

Carol Anne Davis is the author of seven novels and eight true-crime books, the latest of which is *Masking Evil: When Good Men and Women Turn Criminal*. She is currently one of the judges for the CWA's Gold Dagger for Non-Fiction, and when she's not reading or writing she love to dance. Unfortunately she's dyspraxic so can't tell her left from her right and has been in the beginner's flamenco class for the past five years

Martin Edwards has published eighteen novels, including the Lake District Mysteries. *The Golden Age of Murder* won the Edgar, Agatha H.R.F. Keating and Macavity awards. He has edited thirty-five crime anthologies and has won the CWA Short Story Dagger, the CWA Margery Allingham Prize and the Poirot award. He is president of the Detection Club and current chair of the CWA.

Kate Ellis worked in teaching, marketing and accountancy before finding success as a writer. The latest title in her series featuring Wesley Peterson is *The Mermaid's Scream*, while she has also published a series about another cop, Joe Plantagenet, and two historical crime novels including *A High Mortality of Doves*.

Paul Gitsham started his career as a biologist, before deciding to retrain and impart his love of science and sloppy lab skills to the next genera tion of enquiring minds as a school teacher. Paul lives in a flat with more books than shelf space, where he writes the DCI Warren Jones series of police procedurals and spends more time than he should on social media.

.M (Jeanette) Hewitt is a crime-fiction writer living on the Suffolk coast. She is the author of *Exclusion Zone, The Hunger Within* and *The Eight Year Lie*. Her short story 'Fingers' was published in *Twisted50*, a horror anthology, and she was the winner of the BritCrime Pitch Competition in 2015, a success that led to the publication of *Exclusion Zone*.

Susi Holliday grew up in Scotland and now lives in London. She was shortlisted for the CWA Margery Allingham Prize with her short story 'Home from Home'. She has published three crime novels set in the fictional Scottish town of Banktoun, and her latest novel is a Christmas-themed serial killer thriller, *The Deaths of December*.

Maxim Jakubowski is a crime, erotic, science-fiction and rock-music writer and critic. He is also a leading anthologist. Born in England to Russian-British and Polish parents, he was raised in France and ran the Murder One bookshop for many years. He is the current chair of judges for the CWA Debut John Creasey Dagger, and also serves as joint vice chair of the CWA. He is a frequent commentator on radio and television.

Ed James writes crime-fiction novels, predominantly the Scott Cullen series of police procedurals set in Edinburgh and the surrounding Lothians. He is currently developing two new series, set in London and Dundee, respectively. He also writes the Supernature series, featuring vampires and other folkloric creatures.

Ragnar Jónasson was born in Reykjavik, where he still lives, and is a lawyer. He teaches copyright law at Reykjavik University and has previously worked on radio and television, including as a TV news reporter for the Icelandic National Broadcasting Service. His novels include the Dark Iceland series.

Vaseem Khan is the author of the Baby Ganesh Detective Agency novels, a series of crime novels set in India. The books feature retired Mumbai police inspector Ashwin Chopra and his sidekick, a baby elephant named Ganesha. Vaseem says that elephants are third on his list of passions, first and second being great literature and cricket, not always in that order. He plays cricket all summer, attempting to bat as an opener, while fielding as little as possible.

Peter Lovesey's short stories have won a number of international awards, including the Veuve Clicquot Prize, the Ellery Queen Reader's Award and the CWA Short Story Dagger. When the Mystery Writers of America ran a competition to mark their fiftieth year, *The Pushover* was the winner. Peter is a recipient of the CWA Diamond Dagger (among many other honours) and also a former chair of the CWA.

Anna Mazzola writes historical crime fiction. She studied English at Pembroke College, Oxford, before becoming a criminal justice solicitor. Her debut novel was *The Unseeing*, and her second, about a collector of folklore on the Isle of Skye, will be published in spring 2018. She lives in Camberwell, London, with two small children, two cats and one husband.

William Burton McCormick's fiction appears regularly in American mystery magazines. A Nevada native, William earned his MA in novel writing from Manchester University, was elected a Hawthornden Fellow in Scotland and has lived in Russia, Ukraine and Latvia. His novel *Lenin's Harem* was the first fictional work added to the Latvian War Museum's library in Rīga.

Before **Christine Poulson** turned to crime, she was a respectable academic with a PhD in the history of art. Cambridge provided the setting for her first three novels, *Dead Letters, Stage Fright* and *Footfall*, which were followed by a stand-alone suspense novel, *Invisible*. The first in a new series, *Deep Water*, appeared in 2016. Her short stories have been short-listed for a Derringer and for the CWA Margery Allingham Prize.

Sarah Rayne is the author of a number of acclaimed psychological thrillers, and ghost-themed books. Much of the inspiration for her settings comes from the histories and atmospheres of old buildings, a fact that is strongly apparent in many of her books. She recently launched a new series, featuring the music historian and researcher Phineas Fox.

Kate Rhodes went to the University of Essex and completed a doctorate on the playwright Tennessee Williams. She has taught at universities in Britain and the United States, and now writes full time. Her first books were two collections of poetry, and her novels *Crossbones Yard* and *A Killing of Angels* are both set in London, her birthplace. She lives in Cambridge.

William Ryan is an Irish writer, living in London. He was called to the English Bar after university in Dublin, and then worked as a lawyer in the City. He now teaches crime writing at City University. His first novel, *The Holy Thief*, was shortlisted for four awards, including a CWA New Blood Dagger. His latest book is *The Constant Soldier*.

Shawn Reilly Simmons lives in Frederick, Maryland, and has worked as a bookstore manager, fiction editor, convention organiser and wine rep. Currently she serves on the Board of Malice Domestic, is a member of the Dames of Detection, and an editor and co-publisher at Level Best Books. Her Red Carpet Catering Mysteries feature Penelope Sutherland, an on-set movie caterer. She has also published several short crime stories, and co-edited crime anthologies.

Chris Simms graduated from Newcastle University then travelled round the world before moving to Manchester in 1994. Since then he has worked as a freelance copywriter for advertising agencies throughout the city. The idea for his first novel, *Outside the White Lines*, came to him one night when broken down on the hard shoulder of a motorway. More recently he has written a series featuring DC Iona King.

Cath Staincliffe is an award-winning novelist, radio playwright and creator of ITV's hit series *Blue Murder*. She was joint winner, with Margaret Murphy, of the CWA Short Story Dagger in 2012. She also writes the Scott & Bailey books, based on the popular ITV series. She lives with her family in Manchester.

Michael Stanley is the writing team of Michael Sears and Stanley Trollip. Both were born in South Africa and have worked in academia and business. Their first mystery, *A Carrion Death*, introduced Detective 'Kubu' Bengu of the Botswana Criminal Investigation Department, and was a finalist for five awards, including the CWA Debut Dagger. Their third book, *Death of the Mantis*, won the Barry Award and was a finalist for an Edgar Award.

C.L. Taylor was born in Worcester, studied psychology in Newcastle and has had a variety of jobs, including fruit picker, waitress, postwoman, receptionist, shipping co-ordinator, graphic designer and web developer. Her debut novel was *Heaven Can Wait* and in 2011 she won the RNA Elizabeth Goudge Trophy. More recently she has enjoyed success with psychological thrillers such as *The Missing* and *The Escape*.